M000119447

THE
LAST
SQUADRON

THE
LAST
SQUADRON

DAN JAYSON

Copyright © 2017 Dan Jayson

The moral right of the author has been asserted.

Apart from any fair dealing for the purposes of research or private study,
or criticism or review, as permitted under the Copyright, Designs and Patents
Act 1988, this publication may only be reproduced, stored or transmitted, in
any form or by any means, with the prior permission in writing of the
publishers, or in the case of reprographic reproduction in accordance with
the terms of licences issued by the Copyright Licensing Agency. Enquiries
concerning reproduction outside those terms should be sent to the publishers.

Matador
9 Priory Business Park,
Wistow Road, Kibworth Beauchamp,
Leicestershire. LE8 0RX
Tel: 0116 279 2299
Email: books@troubador.co.uk
Web: www.troubador.co.uk/matador
Twitter: @matadorbooks

ISBN 978 1788033 275

British Library Cataloguing in Publication Data.
A catalogue record for this book is available from the British Library.

Printed and bound by CPI Group (UK) Ltd, Croydon, CR0 4YY
Typeset in 11pt Minion Pro by Troubador Publishing Ltd, Leicester, UK

Matador is an imprint of Troubador Publishing Ltd

For my wife Baba and children

"*Don't rejoice in his defeat, you men.*
For though the world stood up and stopped the bastard,
The bitch that bore him is on heat again."
Bertolt Brecht

"*We love death. The US loves life. That is the difference between us two.*"
Osama bin Laden

"*A single blow must destroy the enemy... without regard of losses...*
a gigantic all-destroying blow."
Adolf Hitler

"*We have to face the fact that either all of us are going to die together or we are*
going to learn to live together and if we are to live together we have to talk."
Eleanor Roosevelt

CHAPTER 1

AIR DUEL

The best of plans is the one that is unknown.

A jolt of turbulence woke Captain Natasha Kavolsky. She turned over in the crew bunk and looked out through the aircraft's heavily scratched internal plastic window. Barber's *Adagio* was playing through her earphones. Outside, a series of faint yellow flashes illuminated a grey and white montage. Absently, she wondered whether the flashes were lightning or the aircraft's navigation strobes. She checked the time: she'd had two hours' rest; it was time to get back to the flight deck. She untangled her headphones, briefly trying to understand how they could get into such a mess without having strangled her.

Her aircraft, call sign ST-6, was an Allied Stratocruiser, a fourth generation, armoured, heavy-lift freighter. The 360-tonne payload comprised the 1st of the 9th Mountain Squadron, which was made up of ninety-seven combat troops, nine air crew, fifteen armoured fighting vehicles (AFVs) and enough weapons and ammunition to allow for an extensive tour of duty.

She turned off Barber and then clambered down the ladder that led from the flight crew rest compartment and opened the thin door into the passenger cabin. It had been prepped for logistics instead of combat insertion, the seating rearranged to allow comfort rather than rapid dismount. She had picked up the squadron and their cargo from a cold and barren sector of the north-eastern front, where fierce fighting had been raging. Her passengers now lay or sat slumped in a state of exhausted sleep or silent meditation. As she made her way along the starboard aisle she counted just half a dozen reading lights, two video screens and three columns of cigarette smoke. Cushions, blankets, empty cups, newspapers and other personal belongings

1

decorated the space. A colourful pennant that contrasted starkly with the grey military colours and fittings of the cabin hung from the ceiling proclaiming that the 1st of the 9th Mountain Squadron were *Going on holiday*.

She looked at one soldier who was fast asleep with a smile on his face. Whilst she contemplated what, if anything, he was dreaming about, a tap on her shoulder brought human contact.

"Coffee, ma'am?" asked her loadmaster.

She nodded and removed one of her earpieces, the other remaining in situ so she could hear any communications from her flight crew.

"Thanks; smells almost real," she replied, taking the coffee and quickly clutching a headrest as the aircraft bucked in another bubble of turbulence. She sipped gently to avoid the otherwise inevitable tongue scalding.

"We're just into Norwegian airspace and starting to turn south-east," the loadmaster said. "We should be over Frankfurt within the next three hours. The guys warned that we're in for some bad weather; but, as they say, every cloud has a silver lining – at least it'll degrade the image seekers on the Barracuda."

"It will," she replied, her mind rapidly recalling the technical specifications of the Brotherhood's new air-to-air missiles known by the allies as Barracuda. The aircraft rose then dropped abruptly in more turbulence, this time accompanied by a thud. No one except Natasha seemed to notice.

*

One hundred and fifty miles north-west of Natasha, a Brotherhood patrolling long endurance antiaircraft platform (PLEAP) that consisted of a missile battery suspended from an enormous helium balloon built from radar-absorbing materials rode the jet streams at 95,000 feet.

Target data was provided to it by a network of high orbit satellites known to the allies as FROG. Equipped with an array of powerful multiple spectrum cameras, the satellites scanned the skies searching for fast-moving black spots traversing the face of the earth, hence its name.

For a lone Stratocruiser the PLEAP selected two Barracuda missiles. One advised that it had a steering fin malfunction, so PLEAP selected another, and then downloaded the target data and an engagement plan.

PLEAP made one last check to see if there were any better targets that had presented themselves or potential threats to it that would occur if it launched. There were none, so PLEAP released the missiles, which freefell to 30,000 feet prior to igniting their solid-fuel rocket engines.

The Barracudas closed to within fifty miles of ST-6 on inertial guidance before one briefly initiated a single active radar sweep and cross-loaded the data to its partner using a short-range undetectable laser communications link.

*

Natasha entered her flight deck to find a raft of warning lights accompanied by a low-pitched alarm.

"Right on time, Captain," said her co-pilot.

"I bring all of you luck who set eyes upon me," she quipped in response. "OK, what have we got?"

Before the co-pilot could respond, a second wave of alarms lit up the electronic warfare officer's threat board.

"Shit. I've got a high-confidence Barracuda. We've been painted with search radar," advised her EWO.

Clambering into her commander's seat, Natasha snapped her safety harness into place and then plugged in her headset before calling her loadmaster.

"Looks like we may have a Barracuda engagement; suggest you get the accommodation shipshape. Wait out..." She paused as she realised her navigation displays were blank. "Where's our nav system?"

"Unknown; about two minutes ago we lost space-based telem and then all the ground-based beacons also went out. But the problem isn't with us, all our systems are green. It's strange; the whole lot went out together, like someone threw a switch."

In the passenger compartment Natasha's loadmaster sounded the engagement alarm next to the forgotten coffee on his console. Armoured blast shields slid over the windows, red battle interior lights came on, and the in-flight entertainment systems shut down. Like a forest floor awoken by an animal, movement rippled through the cabin as people realised something was going on that required their attention.

"The Captain's advised we've been painted by a Barracuda. We need to get the cabin prepped for a possible engagement," announced the loadmaster over the PA system, before setting off on a rapid walkthrough of the cabin, checking that the emergency exits had been set to automatic, shaking the last of the deep sleepers awake and ordering them to get their restraint harnesses sorted out and personal gear stowed.

In the rear of the passenger cabin, Corporal Sanchez took a final deep draw of her cigarette and aggressively stubbed it out in the overflowing ashtray mounted on the back of the next row of seats.

"Jesus, O'Reilly. How come when we finally get some R and R we end up getting shot down?" she asked the big, stocky, red-haired Irishman next to her.

"Well, Corporal, look on the bright side. We can increase the squadron's party pot big time with something like this," he replied, pulling out the squadron's betting book, which kept a record of all bets made. "OK, my darlings, these are the odds – two to one: no impact; three to one: impact within a minute; five to one: two minutes; ten to one: three minutes; and twenty to one: longer than three. Finally, anyone betting on no survival can get screwed; I feel lucky. What's it gonna be?" he boomed.

Excited mutterings were rapidly followed by cries for the placement and proper recording of the bets.

On the flight deck Natasha told her co-pilot to give up on trying to reacquire the navigation and tactical data networks and asked her EWO, "What's the story on that Barracuda sig?"

"*Nada*. All quiet, but those bastards have more cunning than a fox when it comes to hunting."

"Agreed. I think it's time we start behaving a little unpredictably," replied Natasha whilst hoisting her shoulder-length dark hair into a bunch and pinning it in place with a pencil. She caught her co-pilot looking at her quizzically.

"What?" she asked.

"Nothing. It's just that I'm always amazed at how women can do that."

"Well, I'll show you over a beer later."

*

The Barracudas now employed their intelligent tactical probabilistic software, evaluating hundreds of options before deciding on one that had a probability of success of 98%.

One of the Barracudas, designated Barracuda-1, accelerated to Mach 7 and activated its search radar; on reacquiring ST-6 it now kept the

4

radar locked on whilst continuously cross-loading the data to its partner designated Barracuda-2. This allowed Barracuda-2 to remain undetected and move to position itself in the most likely path of the evading ST-6.

*

"I've got an active sweep again. Confirmed Barracuda closing at zero-nine-three degrees, speed Mach seven, time to closure: one hundred and thirty-three seconds," reported the co-pilot.

"Initiating ECM," replied the EWO.

With ST-6's large on-board power generation capacity, broadband jamming on multiple simultaneous frequencies could be employed. This would have worked with one Barracuda; however, with two, they simply triangulated the source of the jamming and maintained lock.

"Damn it! Still closing. It's got a lock; somehow seems to be burning through the jam," advised the EWO.

Natasha pushed the public address button. "We've got engagement. I'm going into a high-rate opening turn. Hold tight," she announced.

As the aircraft banked sharply, books and other debris slid along the floor in the passenger compartment. Her passengers patiently waited, their fate, not for the first time, wholly reliant on others.

"Still closing, zero-four-five degrees, Mach seven, sixty-five seconds," reported the EWO.

How is it, Natasha wondered, that a voice could imbue such calm in a situation as serious as this? It's almost as if he was reading the weather.

"Cycle times are decreasing. I think it's got us," continued the EWO.

"I'm going into a stalled climb; on the cusp I want aerial mines and flares. Select manual for both. Let's see if we can't lure the bastard into a trap."

"Selecting manual override for flares, chaff, and mine dispenser," echoed the EWO.

"We'll need to fly her on manual. I don't want any processors in the loop. Disable automatic flight controls," ordered Natasha, making sure that the huge aircraft now only obeyed her commands and would not try and override her as she put the aircraft into an intentional stall.

"Automatic flight controls disengaged," advised her co-pilot.

"I have control," she said as she slid the throttles to maximum and pulled hard back on the force-feedback joystick. With a speed of response that

5

never ceased to amaze the pilots of the Stratocruiser, the nose picked up and went almost vertical as the screaming Rolls-Royce engines pumped out half a million pounds of thrust. Seconds later stall warnings lit up the console.

"This is what they mean when they say engines are at a hundred and ten per cent. Let's give it another few seconds until Morticia comes online," said Natasha, referring to the cockpit voice warning system.

As if on cue a rather husky female voice announced, "Warning, stall. Stall. Stall. Stall."

"Zero-four-one degrees, Mach seven constant, twenty seconds," interjected the EWO.

"Here we go. Mike, get ready to take the rudder. I'll take the elevators and throttles," Natasha warned her co-pilot.

"I've got the rudder," he confirmed.

"Stall. Stall," continued the computer.

"EWO is ready on flares. Ready on mines."

Almost as an anti-climax, ST-6 finally stalled and started to settle backwards, falling tail first.

"Chaff and flares, on my mark… Mark," ordered Natasha.

The EWO punched the discharge buttons, and two recessed pods mounted just aft of mid-ships pumped high-intensity flares and a cloud of metal foil into the surrounding airspace in a pattern designed to closely resemble the radar and heat signature of the aircraft.

As ST-6 continued its lazy fall from the decoys above, the EWO launched the aerial mini mines. These radar-absorbing, eggcup-sized packets of high explosive were fitted with a combination of time delay and proximity fuses and were the latest defence against missile attack. Suspended on small parachutes resembling a child's toy, they formed an aerial minefield through which any pursuing missile had to fly.

Barracuda-1 had just finished evaluating the near vertical trajectory of ST-6 against the stored aerodynamic profile it held in its memory and had cross-loaded the results to its colleague when it encountered the minefield. As Natasha and the co-pilot completed their struggle to bring ST-6 out of its stall, the bright white light of an explosion above them heralded the success of their strategy.

"Scratch one Barracuda," announced the EWO.

As the tactical information screens in the passenger cabin announced the result, a cheer erupted from the rear of the aircraft.

"I hear that," replied Natasha, smiling.

Barracuda-2, meanwhile, having deduced that the aircraft would stall, closed to an intercept position and activated its short-range imaging laser. As the cheers continued and the flight crew breathed a sigh of relief, Barracuda-2 detonated beneath ST-6's starboard wing.

The aircraft shuddered and Natasha's master alarm lit up. The rear-looking external cameras told her the full story.

"Mayday, Mayday, this is Sierra Tango Six. We have been engaged by Barracuda and are going down at reference Bravo Zulu niner-five-six-four," radioed her co-pilot.

The EWO activated the automatic SOS beacon that relayed the position, flight details and the recent events in a burst transmission on the predefined distress frequency. As ST-6 started its death spin, Natasha and her co-pilot went through a sequence of switch-throwing and lever-pulling that initiated the crash preparation contingency procedures.

"On my mark, full release sequence commences: three, two, one. Mark."

Both Natasha and the co-pilot simultaneously pulled two T-shaped crossbars, mounted in the overhead console. A dull series of thuds resounded through the airframe, as explosive shear bolts fired to separate the Stratocruiser's fuselage from its wings, long-range fuel tanks, and engines. She checked the altimeter, which showed 43,000 feet, with a rate of descent approaching 16,000 feet per minute. The spin rate started to increase and Natasha could feel the g-forces building.

"Descent rate good. Good separation. Let's go for the air brakes and secondary release."

"Roger," her co-pilot grunted in response as he reached for a second set of release handles, this time struggling against the g-force. "Air brakes deployed."

Outside the cockpit windows Natasha saw a flash of white light followed by a glimpse of bright orange as the enormous air-braking parachutes deployed.

"I've got green lights on all eight chutes. Forward and aft," she announced.

Even with the elastomeric, energy-absorbent connectors between the parachutes and the fuselage, there was still a loud bang and shuddering as their descent rate slowed to 8,000 feet per minute.

"Go for final separation," ordered Natasha.

A final set of explosive bolts fired, followed by retro rockets that separated the fuselage into one passenger compartment and three cargo modules. A proximity alarm let Natasha know that the minimum separation distances between the modules had been reached.

"CMs are clear. Jettisoning primary air brakes now. Primary brakes detached. Going for secondary. Secondary green," said Natasha, as another series of bangs and groans accompanied the rapid-fire series of commands.

Natasha felt herself pushed deeper into her seat as the main and final set of drogues and then chutes deployed, slowing the descent rate to thirty feet per second. As the cabin started swinging gently beneath the eight enormous parachutes, Natasha could see it was snowing outside. "Nice weather," she mumbled to herself, wondering what was going to come next. As if on cue, applause erupted from the passenger compartment, she smiled to herself, then announced over the intercom: "Ladies and gentlemen, Strato Airways apologises for the inconvenience, and would like to assure everyone that your journey will be resumed as soon as possible. Please brace for impact. T minus forty-five seconds."

As the passenger compartment continued to swing, the applause gently subsided and was replaced with silence. The red emergency lights provided an atmosphere of eerie calm as personnel started to count off the seconds on their watches or pull their body and head restraint harnesses tighter.

"Thirty seconds. Vent the hydrogen cells. Stand by for door jettison," continued Natasha.

"H-two cells vented. I've got a red light on eleven."

"Roger. Try a purge."

"Purge is red. Must be damaged."

"Fuck it!"

More silence, then the escape hatches and access doors in the passenger compartment started to jettison. Cold air charged into the cabin, followed in its wake by gusts of wind-driven snow. Corporal Sanchez, sitting next to one of the hatches, shivered nothing but darkness populated by dancing snow greeted her. Inside, the strobe lights above the escape hatches had come on, and the yellow floor-mounted leader lights had begun their systematic flashing that seemed to call follow me. To prevent flailing limbs on impact, she adopted the brace position by clamping her hands beneath her thighs and pushing her feet to the floor, being careful to allow a one-inch gap under her heels to take out any shock.

"Green lights on all hatches. Twenty seconds," advised the co-pilot.

On the flight deck, Natasha, tired from adopting the brace position, relaxed slightly. As soon as she did, she felt both the descent and swinging stop accompanied by a strange scraping noise. The cabin rolled to the right and through the window she could see tree branches.

"Shit! We're going down into a fucking forest!" shouted the EWO.

"Brace! Brace! Brace! We're going to hit hard and unstable; I say again, hard and unstable," Natasha warned her passengers.

For a few seconds the fuselage didn't move, as the parachutes transferred their load to the forest canopy. The cabin was eerily quiet for a few seconds, before a series of loud cracks announced that their position was only temporary. The cabin rolled to the right and continued until they were upside down. Then the fuselage pitched nose down at an angle of forty-five degrees and dove through the trees. Behind Natasha in the passenger compartment, Sanchez rechecked the locations of the emergency exits, fire extinguishers and escape equipment. A chorus of swearing and shouts accompanied equipment and luggage that had come loose and bounced from seat to seat. A weapon clattered along the full length of the cabin.

In the cockpit, a tree branch punched through the forward window, decapitated Natasha's co-pilot and narrowly missed impaling the EWO in his seat. Plexiglas fragments twinkled amidst blood spray and pine branches.

In the passenger compartment, Sanchez felt the restraining harness automatically tighten as they came to a shuddering stop. Again there was silence before the weight of the back end of the fuselage where Sanchez was hanging upside down overcame the strength that the trees could provide and crashed to the ground. A damaged fuel cell exploded, blowing out a side panel and starting a flash fire in the ceiling. She released herself, dropping down to the ceiling of the cabin, and grabbed a dry powder fire extinguisher.

"Make way," ordered the loadmaster joining her. Using an axe he broke the cladding free, allowing unrestricted access to the bundle of burning wires. Sanchez tackled the fire; the dry powder from the extinguisher, snow and thick black smoke mingled and swirled under the diffuse red lighting.

Upside down in her commander's seat, Natasha surveyed her surroundings. The green glow from the instrument panels highlighted the texture of the pine needles and bits of branch that were now part of her flight deck. Blood, dark, viscous and shining, covered the radio console bringing

9

with it a strong metallic smell that mixed with the fresh pine. A gust of cold wind blew snow through the shattered window. "Jesus," she muttered to herself as she refocused on remembering her emergency procedures. Her training told her she was probably in a state of mild concussion, and with this awareness, she began to feel a little better. She checked her instruments; the fire-warning indicator for the number eleven fuel cell was glowing red, and the smoke and carbon monoxide alarms had lit up for the rear end of the passenger cabin.

"Fire in fuel cell eleven, initiating suppression," she announced, trying to wipe away the blood that had already congealed on the control panels. She activated the powder deluge.

"Fire suppression is good. All fires out. Purging cells with nitrogen to prevent re-ignition."

Satisfied she'd stabilised the immediate threat of fire, she checked out her flight crew. Her co-pilot's torso minus his head remained strapped firmly to its seat. Her EWO Charlie Parkes sat at a contorted angle in his seat behind her, occasionally moaning.

"Charlie, you OK?" she asked the EWO.

"Yeah, just hung up a little and can't move my head."

She tried contacting her loadmaster in the rear of the aircraft but the communications circuit was showing red.

"Comms are down. I'm going to get some help. Be back in five."

"Roger that," he mumbled.

She released the emergency escape hatch positioned over the pilot and co-pilot's seats. The hatch popped and fell away, dropping softly onto the snow-covered ground fifteen feet beneath her. The cold was intense. Hanging upside down meant she couldn't release her harness, so she reached down to her right leg and pulled a combat knife from her flight suit, then slowly started to saw through her restraining harness. As she cut through the first cross-strap she dropped to one side and almost lost the knife. The remaining shoulder strap now supporting all her weight cut into her painfully.

Jamming her legs under her seat to transfer her weight, she cut the remaining straps. She'd already started to shiver in the cold and this made it even more difficult to hold on whilst she thought about her next move. All she had to do now was drop the fifteen feet making sure she didn't either injure herself on the instrument panels or get hung up during the fall. She now understood why they were issued flight helmets even though no one ever wore them. She counted to three, retracted her legs and tucked herself into a ball before dropping straight through the hatch and down into deep snow.

With some surprise that she wasn't hurt, she dusted off the snow and stood up. God, it was cold she reckoned with the wind chill it must be forty below. Small particles of ice, known as 'diamond dust', whipped her face and the wind tore at her flight suit. 'Diamond dust' – she wondered who had thought up the name. Folding her arms across her chest, she tucked her hands into her armpits to conserve warmth. Visibility was no more than fifty feet but she could make out the remains of her aircraft. The fuselage was upside down, its matt black body lying partially broken in the snow, one of the giant orange parachutes snapped and straining in the wind. Trees and branches lay parted and split, revealing the white virgin wood; the pungency of the pine permeated the air even with the wind. The diamond dust continued its relentless attack on her cheeks, and she could feel her chin becoming lumpy and heavier as the cold set in. Pulling up her flight suit collars and squinting in an attempt to shield her eyes she made her way around to the starboard side of the fuselage that was in the lee. She used the splash of the red interior emergency lights to locate an exit; a jettisoned door lay abandoned nearby, already beginning to be covered by its own small snowdrift.

"It's fucking freezing here!" shouted a cockney voice belonging to a Corporal Stacey.

"Well, we are sorry, Corporal. Next time I'll have a word and see if we can get shot down somewhere more to your liking. Now, in the meantime, make sure all the fires are out. I want all of you to help one another out of your harnesses and report to your leaders," her loadmaster ordered.

"Right! You heard the man. Move it!" echoed a voice that Natasha recognised as belonging to Sergeant Major Jones, the squadron's senior NCO.

CHAPTER 2

GETTING IT TOGETHER

If ignorant of your enemy and yourself,
you are certain to be in peril.

DAY 0: Midnight

Natasha clambered up into the fuselage and located her loadmaster amongst the mass of people trying to sort things out. "We need to get some help for Charlie, he's pretty banged up."

"Good to see you, Captain. How did you get out? The entrance to the flight deck is buckled; the Major's down there now, trying to get access," he said.

"Good. We need to be quick. How is everyone back here?"

"We've got one dead, a few injuries. You did well, Captain. Where's the FO?" he asked, referring to the co-pilot.

"He didn't make it. I'll go and see the Major."

Natasha pushed her way past debris and people until she spotted the Major who commanded the squadron she had been transporting; he was directing a group of people armed with crow bars trying to get the flight deck doorway open. "Major Burton?" she shouted above the noise of the wind and general activity, conscious that her voice must have sounded weak.

He turned towards her, trying to recognise who she was.

"Captain. Glad to see you're OK. How did you get out?" he replied with a deep and calming voice that reminded her of her father.

"Dropped about twenty feet; not sure we can bring Charlie, my EWO, out the same way. He's pretty busted up."

"Is anyone with him?"

"The FO didn't make it. Charlie is alone."

Half an hour later they'd managed to force an entrance to the cockpit and get her EWO some medical assistance and Natasha joined the others for a briefing inside the passenger cabin.

Lit by the red glow of the emergency lights, she sat on top of a luggage bin trying to warm her hands. As she looked around she wondered why designers always assumed that emergency lights should only be located on the floor. Did they always expect things to end up the right way? Huddled about her were her loadmaster, the Major, Alex Burton, his senior officers and the senior NCO, Sergeant Major Jones. Jostling for position outside this inner circle were the rest of her passengers.

She could feel the cabin becoming slightly warmer as the snow outside started to dam up the gaps between the seat cushions and pieces of cabin cladding that they'd used to block off the entrances. A cloud of steam from their combined breath hung in the area, mingling with cigarette smoke.

"Put that fucking cigarette out!" screamed Sergeant Major Jones. "Don't you know that one of the fuel cells is leaking?"

As if to mock him, small firefly-like sparks spewed across the floor from a shorted wiring loom.

"All right, listen up," announced the Major. The slight murmuring and shuffling died away replaced by the sound of the weather. "We got hit by what was almost certainly a Barracuda. We've got two dead: Captain Kavolsky's co-pilot and our Corporal Neru. We also have three injured, two seriously, and Captain Kavolsky is missing her six loadmasters who are with the cargo modules that were jettisoned separately from us. Captain Johnson will give us a brief on the injured."

Captain Johnson, the senior medical officer, rose from his squatting position, his lanky frame having to bend in the restricted headroom.

"Morning, everyone."

A discontinuous "Morning" echoed through the fuselage.

"We've got three slightly wounded personnel suffering from head wounds, mild concussion and broken ribs. Providing we can keep them warm, there should be no problems. Two of the team that were around on the port side have mild frostbite; we're treating that, but the message is simple and one that you should not need to be told – be careful out there. That's the good news.

"The bad news is twofold; first off is medic PFC Nancy Strong. She is suffering from severe concussion, high blood pressure and an extremely slow pulse. She has raised intracranial pressure, which means she's bleeding inside her skull. Now, unless we can relieve the pressure by drilling a hole and stem the bleeding she won't last more than another twelve hours. Second up is Captain Kavolsky's EWO, Lieutenant Charlie Parkes. He also has internal bleeding and a punctured lung. Without an op he's not going to make it through the next twenty-four hours either. So, we've either got to get some medical kit, or get them out of here. That's it from our side, Alex."

Natasha noticed how he'd used the Major's first name. Although not protocol they all seemed comfortable with it. Alex now turned towards her.

"Thanks. Now Captain Kavolsky here is the aircraft commander. Can you give us a heads-up on SAR?"

Natasha felt she should stand up to talk to them. As she did she noticed an upside-down galley cupboard dribbling steaming coffee onto the ceiling, its aroma mingling with pine. "We're down somewhere in an area known as the Central Nordboden, just inside the Swedish border with Norway. Basically, we've come down in the middle of one of Europe's largest carbon sinks, a huge forest, or to put it another way, in the middle of nowhere.

"Under normal circumstances, we would expect contact from a SAR team within a few hours. However, things don't seem to be all that normal. Just before the engagement we lost all the space-based nav, telemetry and comms, and shortly after, the ground-based beacons went out as well.

"We've rechecked the satellite status with a couple of handheld GPS units. Result: no satellite availability. Somehow, we've lost, or they've taken out, all our space-based systems. The aircraft's inertial nav systems were on the wings and we lost them during separation. So in summary, we reckon we know where we are to within a radius of a hundred and fifty miles or so; that's an area of about seventy thousand square miles. That's not so good," she reported, feeling a little self-conscious about sounding like a school teacher but taking some comfort that she was being listened to with rapt attention. For some reason she remembered reading a book about a sea captain who'd lost his ship on a reef in the Pacific in the late 1700s. She now knew how he'd felt. She took a deep breath and continued.

"Our automatic distress beacons are preconfigured to talk to the orbital as well as terrestrial SAR network receivers. So far there's been no acknowledgement.

"I got your comms tech, Riggs, to look at our radios; both the single side-band and HF are wrecked, so we've been trying the TACVs. These are handheld UHF sets using a pre-set frequency and code designed to initiate an alarm on anyone receiving. They've got a range of between ten and thirty kilometres, depending on terrain. So far we've heard zip. Possibly the storm, maybe the terrain, it's pretty rugged and mountainous in this region. Then again, maybe there's simply no one around here to listen.

"As you know, the Strat is designed to separate into four modules, us being one, and three cargo modules or CMs. Each CM is manned with two loadmasters. So far we haven't been able to contact any of them on the TACVs; however, we are getting active pings from all three CMs' own location beacons. That means that they must be within a twenty-mile range. The CMs were loaded such that your HQ, engineering, and medical AFVs were in one, combat AFVs in the second and logistics in the third.

"Bottom line is that I'm missing six of my crew, we don't know whether anyone knows we've been downed, we're not too sure where we are, and we can't expect to establish contact until the weather clears or someone happens to pass by. The weather forecast before we left indicated this storm will last another seventy-two hours.

"Sorry. But that's the story. Riggs, anything to add?"

Comms Tech Riggs, standing next to Natasha, adjusted his outsized black-framed spectacles and looked at his CO as if checking it was OK to speak.

"Sir, the Captain's correct, the sets are US. We've even tried rigging up a power boost for a mobile phone. I think we need to get access to the comms gear on the AFVs in the cargo modules."

"Thanks. Keep trying. All right. So apart from comms, we have to keep PFC Strong and Lieutenant Parkes alive, and make sure Captain Kavolsky's loadmasters are safe. Captain Johnson, on the medical side, can we improvise?"

"We've got a basic emergency medical kit only and a few personal bits and pieces. I might be able to stabilise Nancy, but unless we get Lieutenant Parkes to the medical carriers or evacked, his chances are nil."

"So, one way or another we need to get to the medical gear. Captain Kavolsky?"

"Yeah, that's a possibility. Each CM has a beacon. We've got two receivers here, so we should be able to triangulate and get bearings and approximate distances to them. We'll need to send out a couple of teams, one in each direction about half a mile with the receivers to get an estimate."

"So in this weather and terrain, let's say a couple of hours each way to get the locations. If we assume the modules are ten to fifteen miles out, that would mean, even with the best will in the world, it's going to be twenty-four hours before we reach them. With proper snow gear we can get back in half the time. So all up, that's a minimum of forty hours. Captain Johnson, what're the chances of Parkes surviving that long?"

"I can put in a chest drain and load him with plasma. We can use the oxygen from the cabin…" Johnson paused, thinking. "Maybe, is all I can say. I wouldn't give him more than a fifty-fifty chance. At the end of the day it's going to be down to his will to live. We can't move him without a portable ICU, so whatever we do we need to bring the gear back here."

"Understood. Riggs, I want someone glued to the comms. Send a message every ten minutes on the TACVs advising that we have a critical injury and need emergency EVAC. Captain Johnson, try and develop a contingency plan to buy some time. Captain Kavolsky, can I suggest you get with Riggs, Captain Schaefer and Sergeant Major Jones here and get a fix on where the medical module is. The rest of you, get some winter weather gear together. We're going to have to send a team out once we know where the CM is located."

"Right, you lot, you heard the Major. We're not on R and R yet! I want some kit. Snowsuits, thermals, snowshoes, survival rations, lights and comms. O'Reilly, you've always got access to everything; you organise it," boomed Jones.

As Natasha briefed Captain Schaefer and Sergeant Major Jones on how they could get a range and bearing to the CMs, a small heap of clothing and equipment piled up next to them. A tall, red-haired, Irish PFC who announced himself as O'Reilly made his report. "Sarge. We've got six jackets, no trousers, some emergency rations, a few lengths of rope, and a spare TACV for communication. Not much, but with a bit of DIY improvisation it should do. Everyone's field kit is in the cargo modules. We were all dressed for a night on the town, not a survival ex. I know it's not protocol but we're all to blame. I guess the excitement of a bit of R and R overtook us all. Anyway, Sanchez has suggested we make snowshoes

16

from the headrests and the thermal insulation from the air frame. We've connected the seat belts up so we can use them as safety lines. We found three pairs of goggles and we've also got three flight helmets from the flightdeck. Captain Kavolsky, this one is yours," he said, handing the helmet over to Natasha.

"All right, it'll have to do," said Jones.

After suiting up, Natasha found herself leading one group out into the storm. The wind was gusting forty-plus knots and visibility was near zero. Every ten feet they were forced to climb over branches, roots, dense brush and fallen trees or navigate ditches filled with snow. Every hundred paces they stopped to tie a strip of blanket and a strobe light salvaged from life jackets to a tree or branch as a marker. In the darkness, the torches they each carried seemed only to confuse the view as the light reflected off snowflakes being driven across their route.

Half a mile from their crash site they stopped and Natasha checked the receiver beacon. She had to take off her gloves to operate it and cursed the designers who had made the buttons so small. "I've got a bearing of zero-four-seven degrees to the medical CM. Range four miles. Let's get back and see what the others got," she shouted.

"Copy that," agreed her loadmaster.

*

Back in the relative warmth of the passenger cabin, Jones summarised their findings.

"Major. The good news is that the CM with the medical AFVs is only about four miles out. The bad news is the terrain: we're in extremely dense forest, so the going will be tough," he reported whilst knocking snow off his head and shoulders.

Natasha heard Alex sigh as he collected his thoughts.

"OK, we wait until the weather improves or help arrives. At least until daylight. We're not going to risk anyone through Scott of the Antarctic-type heroics. Captain Kavolsky, your people are probably better off than we are now."

Before Natasha could object, a lieutenant wearing medical arm patches pushed her way into their group and addressed Johnson. "Sir, Nancy's pulse is slowing, blood pressure is up again and left pupil's dilated. She's lost consciousness."

"OK, attention please! We're going to have to operate here, soon, and with what we've got. Prep her right side. I'll be with you in two minutes," ordered Johnson before turning his attention back to Natasha and the others.

"Major, Captain Kavolsky, can I suggest we continue this debate in an hour? Sergeant Major, I'm going to need some help and some space. I've got local anaesthetic, swabs, saline solutions, cauterising tools, and the like. But we're going to need to improvise for surgical instruments. I'm going to have to make a hole in her skull, so I'll need a heavy hammer and the equivalent of three drill bits. These need to be small diameter and about a half, five-eighths, and three quarters of an inch long respectively."

Whilst Natasha was still wondering how to respond, Jones swung into action as only sergeant majors can when a situation demands an immediate response.

"Stacey! Get your lot over here. I want all this crap moved out the way. Let's get an operating platform set up, lights, blankets, hot water, and some room for our good doctor and his team to work. O'Reilly! I want this place searched high and low for the tools the good doctor needs. Now, the drill bits are going to be driven into PFC Strong's skull and we don't want them to disappear into her brain, so we need to design some sort of retainer or keeper. Is that correct, sir?"

"That will do perfectly," said Johnson in a tone that belied his surprise at how adaptable NCOs were.

"The rest of you, get out of the way and make some room," ordered Jones. "If it means you lot are going to have to spend some time in the fresh air, well, that's tough." The assembly scattered.

Natasha stood back as, within the narrow confines of the cabin, people bumped into one another while they sorted themselves out. Minutes later, Johnson was presented with a small handheld fire extinguisher, an axe, half a dozen Swiss Army-style penknives, and some steel forks that they had stripped of all but a single prong.

"We've managed to snap the fork prongs to various lengths and filed them as best we can. The penknives though might be better. Sorry about the hammer but it's the best we could find," explained Jones, gesturing to the hand-held fire extinguisher and axe.

"Perfect; let's get them all sterilised," muttered Johnson, looking over his surgical tools before moving to examine his patient, who lay covered with several thermal blankets. His medical team had secured her head between two seat supports using Velcro straps, and shaved a neat square of her blonde hair away. With help from a medic, Johnson donned latex gloves and held them up to be sprayed with antiseptic. Others held flashlights, shining their beams onto the bald patch of Nancy Strong's head.

"Thank you," said Johnson. "If you could just move around a little more and shine them here."

A cloud of steam, generated from the heat of so many people huddled around the tight space, rose to the ceiling of the cabin, condensed and then froze in small rivulets. Natasha wondered whether they would eventually form stalactites.

"We need to make absolutely sure her head is restrained. So could two of you please hold onto the straps? Good. Now, we're going to be doing this on local anaesthetic only and there is a real chance she may become conscious during the op. If she does you must keep the tension. She must not move her head. Understood?"

"Yes, sir."

An expectant tension spread throughout the cabin, as Johnson took a marker pen and inscribed a cross on his patient's scalp. He then selected one of the penknives.

"Lieutenant, if you could hold this at an angle of about thirty degrees, centred on the cross. Ready, everyone?"

"Ready."

"Up a fraction. That's good. Fire extinguisher, please."

Natasha stared in disbelief as someone passed him the fire extinguisher. The shadows cast on the grey walls of the cabin resembled an Alfred Hitchcock murder scene.

Johnson checked the blade's angle once more, then using both hands tapped the penknife with the fire extinguisher. Silent gasps reverberated around the cabin as Johnson examined the results, requested the next size up and repeated the manoeuvre. On the third tap, there was a dull cracking noise, and blood jetted into the air like an aerosol.

Natasha was again surrounded by the metallic smell and associated taste of blood. She felt weak as she remembered her flight deck. Johnson meanwhile calmly examined the results, muttered in a satisfied way and issued a series of staccato instructions to his team. Several pairs of hands became active, passing swabs. The fine mist had disappeared and Johnson stood back seemingly contented.

"Excellent. Very good. Let's fit a drain and keep her warm. Let me know the minute she regains consciousness," he said as he made his way out of the circle of people towards Natasha, where he paused and lit a cigarette. He offered her one, which she accepted. As he lit her cigarette using an antique Zippo lighter, he smiled at her in an almost fatherly way.

"She's stabilised. Now all we have to worry about is your Charlie Parkes. Let's go and have a chat with the Major, shall we?"

*

Natasha and her newfound ally Johnson pleaded their case with Alex.

"I understand. But look at the weather. The chances of making it at all with the clothing and gear we have, let alone in the time available, are minimal. Tomorrow we can review the situation."

Natasha silently screamed with frustration. She had lost one of her crew and was not about to lose any more. Scowling, she spat back, "Yeah, and Charlie? Daylight at this time of year is nigh on non-existent, and Riggs has got squat on comms. By the time the storm is over he'll be dead. We have to go now."

"Alex, she's right. We need to get him to a medical AFV," added Johnson.

She decided to go for broke.

"Major, I should remind you that, technically, I have command; it's my crew that are out there, and you and your squadron are my passengers and in my charge. I'm more than qualified to walk a few miles. I'll go it alone with my loadmaster if necessary. At least we'll have given it a shot. There's no way in hell that we'll get an EVAC in the time available."

"Captain Kavolsky, you do realise that this little trek will be extremely rough? You don't have the training, the conditions are appalling, we don't have the correct gear, and… well, frankly I'm concerned you'll endanger everyone who goes."

"Sergeant Major, what's your view?" she asked.

Jones looked at his CO.

"Speak freely. This is a not a normal situation. Go ahead."

"Like Captain Kavolsky said, sir, it's either try or he'll die. I don't see there's any other way. It'll be tough. But we've been through worse."

"I agree," added Captain Schaefer.

"All right. I surrender. But… Captain Kavolsky, you will obey orders out there. You will not give them. Deal?"

Natasha caught Schaefer and Jones exchanging a look and a smile that seemed to suggest they were enjoying themselves.

"I'll go and get the kit organised. We'll meet at the rear of the cabin," said Jones, leaving them.

Alex and Schaefer went to check on the communications efforts. Johnson took Natasha to one side.

"You know, we've just completed two, back-to-back, three-month tours. The only R and R we've had was spent in a muddy hole at the bottom of a mountain pass that was shelled almost continuously. Then two days ago we were withdrawn from the line. No warning but a promise of a week's R and R in Frankfurt before redeployment to the central sector," he said.

"I heard. OK, I'll take it a little easier on him from now on, but I do have a duty to my crew and passengers. What's he like?" she asked.

"Well, most of us just call him Alex. He's forty-two years of age, and considered by many to be rather old to still be on active front-line duty. But his seniors think his experience and aptitude as a front-line commander are invaluable. Frankly, I don't think Alex himself can envisage life in the army out of the field. His command includes men and women from a dozen nations, each of them personally interviewed and selected. He takes pride in the fact that despite the extended combat durations and mission intensities we've experienced, the squadron has an attrition rate that's below many staff headquarters units. Anyway, enough rambling; the important thing to realise is that he's doing what he feels is best for us all."

CHAPTER 3

SURVIVAL

Good warriors make others come to them and do not go to others.

The team tasked with reaching the cargo modules assembled by the front exit. Connected together by seat belts they resembled a para-stick getting ready to jump. They each had been paired with a buddy for the mission. Natasha's was a beautiful but tough-looking Puerto Rican girl called Corporal Sanchez.

As they shuffled towards the exit, Natasha came face to face with the Major and realised she felt slightly guilty about the earlier confrontation.

"Thanks, Major. I hope we'll see you soon," she offered.

"It's Alex. And good luck, Captain," he said.

Natasha pulled the top of her glove aside and looked at her aviator's watch. Its temperature probe was indicating minus twenty degrees Celsius. At minus thirty-seven human skin begins to freeze. She did the maths: the forty-knot winds outside would drop the effective temperature to minus thirty-eight. As she exited the shelter of the fuselage it was so cold that it hurt to breathe. She remembered reading somewhere that there were microscopic hairs in the back of the throat and she could feel these freezing. They had four miles to cover to reach the medical cargo module.

*

They moved one deliberate step at a time in the deep snow, pausing to check out the terrain in front of them and gathering the strength for the next. Every so often one of the team signalled with a tug on the belts that he or she needed to adjust their improvised snowshoes or clothing. Natasha began to wonder if the Major had been right. She glanced at her watch, almost frightened to expose her wrist to the cold. *Shit*, she thought, *we've only been going twenty minutes and it feels like hours.* Visibility was nil; all Natasha could see was the blurred image of Sanchez one metre in front of her. Ninety minutes later, they stopped, and a message was shouted down the line.

"We'll rest here."

Natasha looked around in confusion; she couldn't see any sign of shelter, but then she was pulled and pushed into a small rock outcrop that opened up to reveal a natural culvert with a roof made from several fallen pine trees and a snowdrift. She crawled inside and joined the others, huddled together.

"Put your arm around me, Captain," said her partner Sanchez. "Helps keep us both warm."

"We'll rest for fifteen minutes then move on. We've covered about half a mile. Pass it on to each of your buddies and confirm," shouted Jones.

Natasha's heart sank. That was the same distance they'd covered earlier when they'd established the CM's location. This journey though had felt ten times more difficult. They'd be out for another six or seven hours.

During survival training, she had been told how hypothermia was not an unpleasant death. "It's just like falling asleep. You get so cold that you start feeling warm and sleepy," her instructor had said. Well, at least she wasn't at that stage yet, she thought. It's too painful now.

"Captain. You get that? Fifteen minutes' rest. We've done half a mile," said Sanchez.

"Got it."

"Good. We need to check each other for signs of frost nip. I'll check you first."

"OK," managed Natasha, shuffling about so Sanchez could check her using a small pen light.

"You're fine. But keep your face covered. We're all going to get some nip on this little trip so don't worry too much."

Someone managed to light a cigarette and passed it round. There was no more talking. Ten minutes later, they crawled out and restarted the journey.

*

As the trek continued Natasha found herself growing annoyed at the frequency with which they had to detour around impenetrable branches, some of which seemed to take pleasure in tearing at her clothing. She became so tired that she simply fell over some obstacles rather than climb them. She told herself that the good thing was that she felt annoyed. The instructors used to say that anger was a sign that you had more energy left. She could feel snow and ice inside her clothing, and realised how cold she must be when it didn't melt.

As dawn struggled onto the scene with a weak, grey light, the wind dropped and the visibility improved a little. For the first time she could see the whole group. With their homemade snowshoes and clothing stuffed with aircraft insulation and blankets, they looked more like the defeated German soldiers from the Sixth Army in World War Two being marched into captivity after the battle of Stalingrad than a modern elite force.

On the fourth rest stop, they crawled into another hole and someone lit a distress flare and piled pinewood branches onto it. The light and heat in the enclosed space was intense, and she felt the extremities of her body crying in pain as they were exposed to the warmth. She was shivering uncontrollably.

Sanchez checked her over. "You've got snow inside your jacket and we need to get it out. Better to go a little slower than knock yourself out and end up rolling around in the snow. Just tell us if we're going too fast."

Natasha felt angry with herself. She'd insisted on going on the mission and was now slowing them all down.

"Better?" asked Sanchez, having finished removing handfuls of snow from under Natasha's clothing.

"Thanks. I owe you one. I'll let you know if I need to slow up a little."

"No drama. You know, the Romans used to burn pine incense for the gladiators," she continued, changing the subject. Natasha knew that whatever happened she would never forget the smell of pine.

"We've made good progress. Another two miles and we're there," shouted Jones. No one replied. "Wortosky will lead us on the final leg. It's important that you all dig deep for this. Confirm with your buddies."

"Oh great. Wortosky, aka 'The Iceman' – with him leading, you know its going to be rough. He's got antifreeze for blood. Anyway, you understand what the Sarge said?" said Sanchez.

"Two miles. Dig deep. Follow The Iceman," muttered Natasha.

*

24

Four hours later, the Arctic grey light again began to yield to darkness, the temperature fell, and the wind picked up. For some reason Natasha began to feel better, even happy. It took her a while to understand why: she was now hypothermic. She wondered whether that was why she wasn't getting annoyed anymore, but then realised that the terrain had changed. Gone were the trees and branches, it was now a gentle downhill slope devoid of any obstructions. She wanted to stop and sit down but the continual gentle tugs on her safety line from Sanchez in front of her kept her from doing so. The wind accelerated and was now so strong that she had to lean forward to stay upright. Her face felt as if it was being attacked with a needle gun. She tried to adjust the T-shirt covering her face but it was as rigid as cardboard.

She bumped into Sanchez, who had stopped. "You OK?" came the shouted message.

Natasha tried to reply but her jaw muscles would simply not operate. She didn't know, neither did she have the strength to care anymore. A voice deep down inside told her to remember why she was doing this. Her air crew. She held up a gloved hand and made the OK sign.

They continued in the swirling darkness for what seemed like an eternity. Then with no warning, she found herself standing next to cargo module number three as signified by an enormous red number painted on the black bulkhead that was lit up every other second by a strobe.

They found the access hatch stencilled with Emergency Access. Pull Handle and fluorescent markings for emergency crews that read Cut here.

Several pairs of hands pulled the hatch handle downwards. The hatch clunked outwards an inch and then stopped, jamming against a snowdrift. A group knelt down to clear the snow away with their hands. Natasha stood and watched, unable to give any more. They got the hatch open, and one by one they crawled into the battle-red lit interior of the module. Someone pulled the hatch closed behind them.

The hold was so large that the red emergency lights petered out into inky darkness. Their flashlights stabbed out into the gloom of the vast cargo hold. "Where are the loadmasters?" asked Sanchez, looking into the shadows.

"Hello! Anyone here?" shouted Jones.

One of the six AFVs had been flipped onto its side, its smooth belly facing Natasha. She let out a moan as she realised that both the loadmasters' jump seats were directly beneath the overturned AFV. A flashlight beam briefly illuminated a hand protruding from underneath the AFV, its palm opened upwards as if to receive help. Congealed blood lay pooled on the matt black floor.

"They're gone," said Jones in a soft yet final tone.

The rest of them started to sort themselves out.

"Fuck that for a game of soldiers. There's no way I'm doing that again."

"I heard that," said Sanchez.

"Why? You too cold?" joked the trooper they called Iceman Wortosky.

"Fucking A. It's all right for you, you were born in an igloo. Let's get some hot drinks on the go, shall we?"

Captain Schaefer cut into the banter. "Right. As soon as you're ready I want Corporal Wortosky to get the medical gear sorted. Here's the list. Sergeant Major, you and I will collect as much snow gear as we can carry. Corporal Stacey, you dial up SAR using the HF sets in the vehicles. Corporal Sanchez, how's our aviator?"

Natasha lay on the floor, curled up in a ball, shivering. Sanchez checked her over.

"We need to get her sorted out. She's in a bad way."

"All right. Wortosky, get a couple of emergency packs from one of the AFVs. Anyone else in trouble?"

There was no reply.

Wortosky returned with a white bag and knelt down next to Sanchez. He pulled out several containers and a space blanket sleeping bag.

"Captain. I need to get these frozen clothes off you and get you into the bag. Can you manage?" Sanchez asked.

Natasha focused on the voice; it wasn't distorted by the sound of wind. Was she dreaming? She couldn't make up her mind. God, what was wrong with her?

"Give me a hand with her, she's starting to withdraw," said Sanchez.

Together, Wortosky and Sanchez literally broke off some of the frozen clothing from Natasha and wrapped her in the space bag. Jones came over with what Natasha thought looked like a hairdryer. Her vision was blurring. She could hear a voice that sounded like it was in the next room.

"You're starting to withdraw. Don't worry. We're going to hook you up to a warm-air respirator. You'll feel better soon once you regain control of rational decision-making."

Natasha's brain was shutting down; she didn't know if she was expected to say something. Did she need to make a decision? They put a hood over her head and turned on the little machine.

It took about twenty minutes for her core temperature to rise, and when it did, she gradually felt like she had awoken from a deep sleep. Her perception of her surroundings was crystal clear. Her mind seemed sharp.

Sanchez was next to her rummaging around in a bag. She produced a small foil sachet. "Hot chocolate," she explained as she pulled the rip tag that allowed the heating agents to become active. "We'll give the respirator a few more minutes then try some. The first sips will feel cold, then the next few warm and then hotter. Be careful you don't burn yourself," she cautioned.

"Thanks."

"No probs. You were pretty far gone. Strange feeling coming back, eh?"

"Yes. Like diving into a tropical ocean. Lots of colour, and very sharp images."

"I know. Everything gets a lot sharper. Your brain was beginning to shut down, pulling blood away from areas that are not required to keep the main organs functioning, including areas that deal with logical processing."

After a few more minutes, Sanchez removed the respirator and Natasha took a sip of the hot chocolate. She could taste the chocolate but just as Sanchez had told her, it seemed cold.

"You've gotten a nasty bit of frostbite on your right cheek and touches of frost nip on one foot. We need to soak the affected areas; it's going to be a little painful as we warm you up. If it gets too bad, feel free to shout and scream. No more trips for you today. We can't risk refreezing." She tore open a strip of sterile bandage soaked in gel and gently held it against Natasha's cheek.

"No problem," mumbled Natasha, grateful not to have to cope with the return journey. For a moment, she felt nothing and then the pain erupted. She gasped at the intensity.

"Hold it there for fifteen minutes. Scream away if you want, we're all used to it," said Sanchez nodding in the direction of the others.

Natasha spent several minutes getting herself together and adjusting to an environment that was not freezing her to death. She sat with knees drawn up and watched her breath clouding her immediate surroundings. "How's the rest of the team?" she asked.

"Oh, we're fine. Guess we're a little more used to it; bitter experience, I suppose. Half the squadron have got at least one toe missing. Some of the other regiments refer to us as the first of the nine toes."

Natasha smiled, wincing at the pain.

"Here, breathe on this again for a while. It heats air, then mixes it with a mild aerosol that assists breathing. The mix is water-saturated at forty-five degrees Centigrade. It will warm your brain stem and also reduce heat loss through respiration, which accounts for about thirty per cent of your heat loss. I've added a little painkiller. I'm sorry about your crew," continued Sanchez, handing her the respirator.

The interior lights came on, flooding the hold with brightness. As Natasha's eyes adjusted, she could see in stark detail what had happened to her crew. The AFVs had been loaded in two rows. The CM must have also landed end-on rather than horizontally, and the AFVs had broken free of their tie-downs and concertinaed into one another.

Schaefer came over to join them and knelt down beside Natasha. "If it's any consolation," he said, "they died instantly."

"Thanks. It's just that, well, I flew with them for a while. They both have children, young ones. I've met them, been to their birthday parties…"

"Understood. But for now we need to concentrate on getting your EWO back here and raising SAR."

Across from them Stacey clambered out of one of the AFVs. "Captain. The HF sets are gone. Bloody things have been nicked!" he shouted across to them.

"All of them?" asked Schaefer.

"The whole fucking lot! Fucking antisocial that is."

"Oh shit. I remember, they were pulling them as we loaded. That's one of the reasons we were delayed on the ground," said Natasha.

"I guess they were going to replace them with area code compatible sets once we arrived. They sometimes change-out the sets when moving from theatre to theatre," said Schaefer.

"Bloody great!" exclaimed Stacey. "How the bleeding hell are we supposed to talk to anyone? Without them, all we've got are the short-range VHF and the TACVs. They're good for about fifteen miles; about all we can contact are reindeer."

"All right. Forget the radios. Let's get the gear sorted," ordered Schaefer.

Natasha, feeling useless and embarrassed, watched as they assembled the equipment they would haul back to the crash site, and stacked it next to three antique-looking snow sleds, which more closely resembled something from the Alaskan gold rush rather than a state-of-the-art Arctic transportation system.

"I know they look rather outdated but they're the best sleds known to man. The Norse term for them is a *pulk*. Wood and leather. No high-tech materials, no radar signature, and easy to mend," Schaefer advised.

Jones and several of the others carried what looked to Natasha like a large incubation unit out of one of the AFVs and secured it to the third pulk. Schaefer explained it to her.

"It's for your EWO, Charlie. It's a prototype battlefield ICU; we seem to be the guinea pigs for a lot of stuff. We call it the pod. In addition to being able to compress a patient with hydrogen sulphide, it's outfitted with plasma, oxygen and even an automatic defibrillator."

"Pressurised hydrogen sulphide?"

"Yeah, weird. The Doc will tell you, but apparently, apart from killing you, hydrogen sulphide also induces a state of suspended animation. Slows the heart rate down by more than three times, breathing rate by five and drops your core body temp to thirty degrees Centigrade. The gas pressure also helps to reduce bleeding. Anyway, if anything can, it will keep him alive until we can get him back here. You going to be all right here alone until we get back, or do you want someone with you?"

Natasha felt stupid; she had put the rest of them in danger by her determination to come with them. She was grateful for the way Schaefer handled the situation.

"No. I feel like a bit of an idiot. You'll need all your team. Go ahead. I'll be fine."

As Schaefer walked away, Sanchez came across, now dressed in a snowsuit. Natasha noticed her eyes following Schaefer. Sanchez knelt down to check Natasha again, and they exchanged one of those eye-to-eye contacts. They both smiled, Natasha wincing again from the pain in her cheek.

"Yep, I know, classically good-looking African American, with the build to go with it. Nearly six foot two inches tall. Born and bred in the back streets of Harlem, New York City; came up the hard way. Battlefield commission in the early wars, taken out of the line for command training, and returned as a captain within two years. Cute, eh?" said Sanchez.

"You take care," offered Natasha.

"We'll catch you later. Stay warm and apply more of the gel every hour. We're going to kill the power to save battery life," replied Sanchez.

As they left and closed the hatch, Natasha was sure she could hear some of them discussing her. "She's all right for an officer," she thought she heard. At that moment she didn't think she was.

With only the red emergency lights for company, Natasha shone her flashlight around the module's interior, before letting the beam rest on the position where her crew lay crushed. Things had developed at an unbelievably fast pace, and she wondered how she would cope in an environment that was completely controlling her. She remembered another time when she'd had no control; she'd been a fast ground attack pilot and had fallen foul of a commanding officer who wanted more than just an expert aviator. Her rebuff of his continual advances had resulted in her being classified as unfit for combat and relegated to tankers. On that occasion she'd maintained her professionalism, and determination to be the best. It had taken her two years but she'd finally been promoted to the new Stratocruisers. *Well, I guess if I could beat that bastard I can beat a bit of weather,* she mused.

She adjusted the warm compress on her cheek, pulled the thermal bag around her, curled into a foetal position and let herself be swallowed up by a dreamless sleep.

*

Natasha awoke with a start, as Sanchez shook her.

"Good sleep, Captain?" she asked.

"Jesus. You're back already. Is there a problem?"

"None. I guess you were just exhausted. We went, we conquered, and now we're back. Looks like you're gonna be fine though. Not too bad at all," she said examining Natasha's frostbitten face.

Schaefer approached, casually brushing snow and congealed ice from his snowsuit.

"Evening, Captain, everything all right?" he asked.

Natasha nodded, deciding to dump the various blankets she was covered in and get herself together.

Schaefer continued, "We brought Charlie back with us. Captain Johnson is attending to him. He's not in too good a shape, I'm afraid, but at least with the medical kit we have here he stands a chance. The Major sends his best. We're going to send another team back to the crash site with more gear and bring the rest of them back and set up this module as our base. We're also prepping another team to go and contact the other two cargo modules. We've still got no contact with anyone on the outside."

"Oy, you lot! Stop gaping! I want those poor bastards taken outside," shouted Jones, referring to Natasha's dead loadmasters. "Let's get some chain blocks on the AFV and get it back up the right way."

Johnson and three others were carrying the battlefield ICU containing her EWO Charlie Parkes across to one of the medical AFVs.

"Give me five minutes to say hello to Charlie and I'll be ready. If that's OK with you?"

Schaefer nodded. "I understand. We'll get something hot to eat and drink, then get you booted and spurred. You'll be leaving with Captain Crockett. Weather is getting worse. But this time you'll have the right kit and Sanchez reckons you'll be OK if you keep covered up."

Natasha strode over to the AFV where she'd seen them take Charlie.

"How is he?" she asked.

"Hanging on is about all I can say; it's a miracle he's lasted this long. We're setting up for a rapid scan and then surgery," replied Johnson.

Natasha stepped back as two medics lowered the ICU into a recess and started booting up a control panel.

"Let's get this crap out of the way and the theatre ready," ordered Johnson.

She took her cue and backed out as people started pulling storage canisters out of the AFV to make room. Jones, Sanchez and Schaefer were sitting on a container eating MREs and she went over to join them.

"Here, try this, Captain," offered Jones, handing her an MRE.

"Thank you, Sergeant Major," she replied, studying the label that proclaimed the contents to be spaghetti bolognaise. As she opened it the smell of the food overwhelmed her; she was starving. Without pausing she wolfed the contents down, scraping out the packaging.

"You want another? I think we've got some rice pudding here as well," asked Schaefer smiling.

"And hot coffee," added Sanchez.

"Great. Thanks."

"Corporal Sanchez will take you to see a rather large, red-haired gentleman called O'Reilly to sort you out some snow gear. Make sure you also get some more gel for your face. Don't want you freezing up again. Meanwhile Mr Jones and I are going to see if we can work out exactly

31

where we are using the microwave radar. We might even be able to plot you a friendly route to the other CMs. When you've finished with O'Reilly come back over," offered Schaefer, tossing his finished MRE into a trash container.

"You sure you want to go out again?" Sanchez asked Natasha after the others had left.

"No. But I have to. They're my crew out there."

"I'll take you to see O'Reilly. He's over in that engineering AFV," she said, pointing to the vehicle around which equipment and supplies were being sorted and manifested.

As they made their way across the module, two banks of powerful floodlights lit up the hold. Next to one of them stood Captain Grant, the squadron's engineering and logistics senior officer.

"Give me the fuel status," asked Grant in a tone that was quiet, yet which somehow everyone heard.

"Zip," came the response from one AFV after another.

"It's SOP for all fuel cells to be vented of hydrogen prior to flight, to minimise risk of fire and explosion," offered Natasha.

"Oh, this is just fucking great, no comms and no fuel!" shouted a voice.

"All right, you heard Captain K. This means we're going to have to rely on the dry cells. They can power the basic systems only and are good for about forty-eight hours. So I want strict rationing. Get HQ One parked up on the leeward side outside. Leave enough room for the igloo and access to the side hatch. Let's also get some solar panels up; I know the sun is shit but every little bit of power we can make will help," ordered Grant.

"By the looks of things I'll be lucky to get that far. The diagnostics are showing the bloody dry cells are knackered," replied Stacey.

"Christ almighty. Check the others and see if we can cross-charge from another vehicle," muttered Grant.

They left Grant to his problems and went over to meet O'Reilly. The big Irishman was looking slightly flustered, as he directed the sorting of a mound of snowsuits and other gear.

"Captain. A pleasure to meet you. Bastards never pack anything; they just throw it all in here and leave it for us poor souls to sort out. Half the stuff hasn't even been washed. Anyway, we need to get you kitted up a little better than the first hike. You ever done this before?"

"Last night," replied Natasha.

"Roger dodger. I'll give you a quick brief on the gear. Nothing too complicated for this trip. The two most important things are not getting your underclothes wet and dehydration.

"So, don't wear too much, that way you won't sweat. Don't get snow inside your suit and don't fall into a lake; finally, drink a lot of fluid. You obey these rules, you'll be fine."

"I can honestly tell you that I'm looking forward to sweating," interjected Natasha with a passion.

"We're gonna go with the basic G9 snowsuit, water carriers, sensor and comms packages."

He tossed Natasha what looked like a baby romper suit with an inbuilt nappy that fastened with the largest poppers she'd ever seen.

"These are your undergarments; they go next to your skin. Nothing else. You can change back in the combat team room in the AFV."

Two minutes later and she was back wearing the romper suit and shivering. "God, it's cold."

"Aye. But don't worry; you'll soon warm up when you get going."

Natasha noticed O'Reilly's gaze lingering on her a moment too long. At thirty-four years of age, with long, dark hair and brown eyes she was quietly attractive, possessing a figure that was enhanced by her flight suit rather than hidden.

"Shall we get on with it?" she asked with a smile.

O'Reilly blushed a little before continuing.

"Yes, Captain. Sorry. Now, this is your fluids, local environment, and biometrics monitoring harness. Here, turn around... These two silver sacks here contain mineralised water. They hang under your armpits to stop them freezing and also act as a heat sink. To drink, all you do is suck through either of these plastic tubes. Keep the tubes tucked away; they have a habit of icing up. If they do, don't try and bend them, they'll crack; just use an MRE with a self-heat charge from your rations to defrost them. Don't forget about them; you must keep hydrated."

O'Reilly paused whilst Natasha got herself sorted out.

"The sensors feed data to a little program that controls reactive fibres in the snowsuits. The suit fibres open and close depending on how hot you are. Most of us disconnect it, some love it. Now, next thing are the socks and the G9 over-suit."

33

He handed them over, then waited while Natasha pulled on the socks then the soft zebra-camouflaged snowsuit. Zipping it up, she was glad of the warmth.

"What about all this?" she asked, looking at the flaps that hung down from her behind.

"Aye. That's for ease of access if you need to answer the call of nature. You don't want to have to undress in this weather. The large poppers let you undo everything with your gloves on."

Reaching down behind her, he pulled the flap between her legs and secured the waist belt. "That's it. Better?"

"Terrific. I actually feel comfortable."

Behind them a bitterly cold wind blew snow swirls into the cargo module as the main doors were cranked open by hand, and the first of the AFVs drove out into the snow, its electric drive and rubberised tracks eerily quiet.

"Now, the next thing is Cyclops," continued O'Reilly handing her a combat helmet. "This is one of your most important bits of kit. It keeps your head warm. It contains all your comms, protects your ears against explosions, and it processes and displays all the data from your personal, the squadron's and for that matter any other unit's data link. Lastly, not that we'll be needing it, it's got reactive gel as well as nano-fibre armour, so it'll stop most infantry rounds."

She took the helmet and looked it over; it felt light and was slightly soft to the touch.

"Why's it called Cyclops?"

"It's the camera package," he said, pointing to the mini cameras arrayed around the helmet in a crescent shape. "On the Mark One versions they were combined centrally, like a big single eye."

"Yeah. They moved it when they realised it was a great aiming point for snipers," added Sanchez.

Natasha studied the sensors. "Wow, they've issued you the germanium NVGs. Is it true you can read graffiti on a wall and even recognise a face in the dark?" she said with surprise, referring to the enhanced night-vision gear.

"Almost. We got lucky; we got thirty sets. Anyway..."

He picked up a small box and data line and connected it to the rear of the helmet. "This unit is your PLD or personal location and data unit." He handed Natasha a small box about the size of a packet of cigarettes. She flipped open a cover revealing a dark grey display and toggle switches.

"It's got all your controls. You simply toggle through the menu like this…" he explained. The display lit up in dull red letters. She scrolled down the menu.

"Jesus. This is impressive."

"Aye, that it is. You can customise to your preference, so for example you can enhance your hearing capability, warm up the suit, whatever takes your fancy. Most of the guys turn it off; the snipers love it."

"What about the visual feeds?"

"Similar, you can customise as you want. We'd need an hour or two to run through all the pros and cons. For what we're doing I think you just need to know the basics; all-weather night and day vision, navigation and fluid intake. We'll set up the display through your snow goggles," he said, sounding like a shop assistant.

Natasha finished getting the goggles and helmet sorted out, and tried out the infrared feed.

"I feel like a Cyborg," she said.

"Well, we're not as bad as the Rangers, those really have gone over the edge. We ran into one company of them in a bar about six months ago. The freaks had gone for augmented reality big time. Several of them had one eye retrofitted with an artificial unit and most had implants to enhance hearing. Come on, I'll take you back to Captain Schaefer; he's over with Captain Crockett," said Sanchez.

"I heard rumours that he is a direct descendent of *the* Davy Crockett."

"One and the same," replied Sanchez, as if this was all that needed to be said to describe the man.

Sanchez led Natasha through a large tent that had been inflated to connect the CM with one of the AFVs now parked outside.

"Neat, eh? We call it an igloo. Insulated, quick to deploy, and resistant to small arms fire as well as chemical and biological agents," advised Sanchez.

"Does it make hot chocolate?" quipped Natasha.

Schaefer was seated at a navigation console together with a tall man with blond hair wearing a raccoon-tail fur hat.

"Captain Kavolsky, I'm Captain Crockett, 2IC to Alex."

"Feeling more comfortable?" asked Schaefer, looking up from a screen.

"Definitely. O'Reilly did a great sales job."

"Yeah, he's special. You ever need anything, anywhere, he's your man. Anyway, you are just in time. We're using the microwave radar; it's not got too much of a range but we should be able to map the area, and if we've got sufficient features, use the AFV's database to work out where we are," explained Crockett.

"Bingo. We've got a ninety-eight per cent match. Thank God for that," said Schaefer, zooming out to show their position on the screen. "God, we are in the middle of nowhere. Well, we certainly chose a great place to get shot down. There's nothing for a couple of hundred miles in any direction."

"What about the routes to the CMs?" asked Natasha.

Crockett uploaded the coordinates and studied the display. "Here you go. I suggest we do them one at a time. The first is over open terrain, down at this lake here. We could be there and back within eighteen hours. The second, though, is going to be a lot tougher."

"How are we getting on with trying to contact SAR?" asked Natasha.

"Riggs is building an HF set. But the problem is that without the carrier codes we'll be like a civilian station. The military nets will ignore us. So we'll broadcast on the usual SOS frequencies and then get the civilian SAR to patch us through. The Major's told us to plan for the worst. No rescue within the next hundred hours."

"Sounds sensible, the air force SAR will start a search based on our last known location and follow our flight plan. But with this weather they'll take their time," acknowledged Natasha.

"Great. What an R and R this is," moaned Sanchez in a theatrical tone.

DAY 2

Their mission to the second cargo module had been a failure. Sitting on benches in the rear of an HQ AFV, and still clad in their snowsuits, they held a debrief over hot drinks. They'd found one of Natasha's crew, Master Sergeant Bill Franks, sitting upright in the snow, frozen solid, still attached to his seat, harness and a part of the airframe with the position beacon. There was no sign of the cargo module.

"Alex, there was absolutely nothing left except for the loadmaster and his flight seat. Strangest thing. I can't for the life of me figure out how he ended up like that. The module was nowhere to be seen, no wreckage, nothing," said Crockett.

"He looked like he was just sitting out there enjoying the view," added Stacey. "It was weird."

"Captain, I'm sorry. I understand that he had three young boys and a pregnant wife," said Alex looking at Natasha.

"He did," replied Natasha, impressed that the Major had taken the time to find out a little about him.

"Well, here things have got stranger. Not only have we not been able to contact anyone on HF, but we can't pick up any signal. TV, radio, nothing. It's like we're in a black hole. Riggs has been going slowly crazy," Alex continued.

As if to echo what Alex had told them, someone opened the door to the communications room and they could hear Riggs curse as one of his team continued the marathon session of calling on the TACV. "Mayday. Mayday. Mayday. Any call sign. Any call sign. This is Sierra Tango Six. Please acknowledge. Over," he repeated again and again.

The door closed again and they got down to the business of planning the next trek to the last CM. Schaefer was in mid sentence describing a possible route when the door to the communications room flew open and one of the techs announced that Riggs had made contact.

"Station calling Mayday. Station calling Mayday. This is November Whisky One Two Two. Come back," a deep Texan drawl boomed out of the speakers.

Natasha could see Riggs punching buttons to lock in the signal; the thermal blanket he'd been wearing around his shoulders for added warmth had slid to the ground.

"November Whisky One Two Two. This is Sierra Tango Six requesting priority relay to SAR. We are down at grid Bravo Zulu niner-five-six-four. I say again; this is Sierra Tango Six requesting priority relay to SAR. We are down at grid Bravo Zulu niner-five-six-four. How copy?"

Everyone instinctively looked up at the ceiling as if expecting to see an aircraft overhead. Riggs waved his hand to make sure he had some space as people crowded in around him.

"Sierra Tango Six. We copy your last as requesting priority relay to SAR at grid Bravo Zulu niner-five-six-four. We have a signature from your beacon. Relay has been made. Advise that all comms are HF only at present."

"Roger. Copy that. Sit rep follows. Sierra Tango Six has no – I say again – no access to orbital comms or HF. Beacon and TACV only. Beacon and TACV only. We have two E one VAC and nine nine survivors. I say again, we have two E one VAC and nine nine survivors. How copy?" said Riggs, letting them know that the medical evacuation was a priority one.

"We copy your last and confirm SAR relay on HF only and request for two E one VAC. Over."

"So. No one's got orbital-based comms," said Crockett.

"Shit, I'm losing the signal. God knows why," said Riggs as he flipped switches.

"Tell them that this is very urgent; we are looking at hours," said Alex.

"November Whisky One Two Two. Please relay SAR that E one VAC needed Romeo Foxtrot November."

"Roger. Romeo Foxtrot November. Stand by for SAR relay."

Everyone held their breath as they waited for the response; when it came the signal strength was weak.

"This is November Whisky One Two Two. SAR confirms receipt and will advise. I say again…"

"Fuck it! I've lost the signal again. What the hell is going on here?" exclaimed Riggs in a tone of desperation.

Despite this, there were cheers and smiles all around. When they died down Alex spoke.

"Great news. But we need to be careful. The weather's not exactly perfect for an EVAC. Let's check over the rations status and revisit our power demand profiles. We need to extend our one hundred hours by another fifty."

"I agree. There's no way anyone could put down in this. By the way, what does Romeo Foxtrot November mean?" asked Natasha.

"Right. Fucking. Now. But at least they now know we're here," interjected Schaefer.

The night brought more of a storm, dropping the temperature to minus fifty degrees. They played cards, smoked, read, and generally did what all soldiers did best in the field: complained about how they were treated.

Natasha, having checked on Charlie Parkes, her injured EWO, went and sat with Riggs as he continued to listen out for any traffic. He was rubbing his temples when he suddenly sat upright and clicked his fingers. He flicked a switch and handed her a headset.

A cut-glass, classically British, female voice broke through the surrounding static and background noise.

"This is the BBC Northern Europe. In an unprecedented escalation of the war, Supreme Allied Command today confirmed that all navigation and communications systems have been severely affected by the electromagnetic pulse or EMP attacks of the past several days. Allied governments denounced the attacks and cautioned that they were a serious escalation and would be considering an appropriate response. In further, apparently associated developments; it was also confirmed that several military and civilian communications centres had been attacked by Brotherhood special forces and sponsored terrorist groups.

"On the northern front, the northern sector reported little or no activity in the past twenty-four hours whilst in the southern and central sectors a major armoured push has resulted in lead elements of allied cavalry advancing more than twenty miles without resistance. On the southern front…" The signal faded.

"Where did the signal go?" she asked.

"God knows. This is weird; maybe it's the EMP damage. Sometimes I get a carrier signal and almost as soon as I lock on it vanishes. It's like someone is jamming. I don't know, maybe it's just the weather or the terrain," he confided.

"Could it be jamming? This far out of theatre?" she asked.

"No. It can't be. I don't know. I'm tired. It's weird."

"Well, at least we know why we lost our nav and comms," she said.

"I got a recording of the broadcast. We can play it to the Major. How's Charlie?" he asked, changing the subject.

"'Critically stable' I think was the term Captain Johnson used," she replied.

As if on cue, Johnson joined them. "Captain Kavolsky, would you like to join Alex and me for a whisky?"

"Great. We just recorded a bit of a BBC transmission. You guys might want to hear it."

DAY 7

The storm lasted for another four days, preventing them from attempting any journey to the last cargo module. To keep warm, log fires now burnt continuously in the cargo module. Everything now smelt of pine and wood smoke.

They had rations for only a few more days. The wave of euphoria that had swept through them when they made contact with the allied aircraft had evaporated. They had had no other communication and apart from the one BBC news broadcast had not picked up any other radio traffic, civilian or military. PFC Strong was making a rapid recovery from her operation but Charlie Parkes had died during the fifth night.

The mood in the cargo module was one of sustained depression, punctuated with the occasional bout of black humour.

"I think we're going to have to do this by ourselves. Something is seriously wrong. All the standard protocols seem to have gone out the window. If we wait here, things are only going to get worse. We need to self-rescue," Natasha confided to Alex.

"I agree. Can I suggest you and Captains Schaefer, Grant and Crockett get together and come up with some options?"

It took them several hours of discussion but Natasha felt they had a workable plan.

"We've checked the database. There's a military comms ground relay station about sixty miles east. It's unmanned, but Riggs says it's EMP hardened so he should be able to still talk to just about anyone in the world from it," offered Schaefer.

"Now, we don't have enough of everything to get us all there, so we're proposing a two-leg expedition; we'll hook up with the third cargo module and hopefully pick up my crew and additional food. The team will then split up. Captain Grant will ferry supplies back here. Captain Schaefer and I will continue on to the relay station," summarised Natasha.

"It's a pretty big complex, so we reckon there should be food for maintenance crews and the like. It might also have vehicles. So getting back we hope will be easier than getting there," added Schaefer.

"Good, I like it. You get the pick of whatever rations and gear you need. The storm is easing so plan on leaving tomorrow. One last thing: I know it's low risk but with what we've heard about attacks on comms centres you'll go in hot," said Alex.

"I'll sort out a hunting party. Hodgetts and Stacey are up for it. See if we can get something fresh to eat this side of Easter," said Crockett.

*

Ex-Royal Marine Corporal Hodgetts was the squadron's lead sniper. With a black woollen hat covering his bald head he lay prone, looking through the scope of his LR-51 sniper rifle. *Four bloody hours*, he thought to himself, *and nothing*. It was as if the land was devoid of anything but themselves, wind, snow and trees. His left leg had gone to sleep and his right elbow kept cramping. Just as he had got to the point where he could bear it no longer and would have to move, a red dot lit up on the top right edge of his weapon's scope. The scope used a bio-chemical sensor matrix, based on the same chemical compounds as a frog's eye, and it was able to detect, and track, fast- as well as slow-moving objects. The processors had picked up a combination of heat and movement. A warning tone in his earpiece confirmed that the target was not foliage but animal. He gently took up the pressure on the trigger until the scope confirmed that it was now tracking the target and automatically zoomed in. He could make out the outline of a moose. It stood still, sensing that something was near but unsure as to where the danger lay; warm steam streamed from its mouth and nostrils. Hodgetts adjusted his position, bringing the crosshairs onto the target. Headshot, 300 metres through the trees: not a bad challenge, he thought. The scope advised him where it thought the aim point should be based on analysis of the air density, humidity, wind speed and direction. He used his thumb to engage a toggle switch on the stock and adjusted the crosshairs again for the true wind velocity he felt was acting. He checked his breathing, slowly exhaled, and fired. The weapon recoiled against his shoulder just before the muffled crack echoed through the forest. Through the sights he saw the massive animal roll over against a tree, before its legs crumpled and it slumped onto its side in the snow.

"Hodgetts here. Dinner's served," he advised through his throat mike. "Gonna need a couple of strong hands."

One kilometre east of Hodgetts, Stacey finished using the Orga, an oversized drill bit, to cut a series of holes through the surface of the frozen lake. Stacey prided himself on his fishing skills, which he had honed since his teenage years in England. Hole by hole, he carefully lowered his hooks into the bright turquoise waters.

"Oy! You two make sure you pack the holes properly. I don't want them freezing over. We'll never get our catch out in one piece," he shouted to his colleagues. In between comments about the odds of catching anything, they followed his instructions, ramming pine branches into the holes to keep them from icing up.

That evening, under a star-filled sky, their spirits soared as they roasted their catch of freshwater pike and moose on open fires. Natasha and Sanchez sat together enjoying the entertainment. Someone had turned the antlers from the moose into a headdress, which Hodgetts now proudly paraded around the campfires looking like some ancient caveman.

"The Beast Feast," Stacey had announced as he oversaw the cooking of the fish and moose, which he'd augmented with MREs that he explained had been modified using a personal recipe.

"Anyway, even if you don't eat moose or fish, you need to try it; it'll get your bodily functions operating again," he told them all.

"God. Anything to unblock my bowels. Those bloody MREs have got me so bunged up I feel like I'm gonna burst," said O'Reilly referring to the constipating effects that the energy enhancing additives in the MREs had.

"Charmed, I'm sure," said Sanchez.

"Ma'am, would you care for a tipple?" O'Reilly asked Natasha, holding out his hip flask.

"You can be a gentleman," Natasha remarked, with a chuckle.

Alex, Crockett and Johnson joined them, and together they sat and watched the sparks rise from the fires into the air and spoke about what they'd do when they finally reached civilisation.

"I'm going to call my folks and then have a steak, salad and a glass of wine," said Crockett.

CHAPTER 4

THE RELAY STATION

Don't go into another's territory at an unfavourable time.

DAY 8

Natasha, together with Captains Schaefer and Grant, and Sergeant Major Jones, ticked off the specialists they would need for the mission.

Despite her baptism in winter trekking, Natasha did not feel she could contribute much to the discussion on how best to tackle the route planning, so she sat back and listened as the others debated the fine details. She was happy that they agreed a route, which, although longer, would cross glacial plateaux and lakes rather than the alternative of dense forests and ravines.

"Good. Now we've nailed the route, how are we going to navigate?" asked Schaefer.

"The route's featureless for the first forty klicks, so the microwave radar probably won't be any use. I guess we'll have to do it the old way: compass and bearings," said Jones in a voice that sounded like he was looking forward to the challenge.

"There might be another way," offered Natasha. "We've got a bunch of radio beacons we use to mark out field runways. They generate a narrow angle directional signal, line of sight. You stray off the line and you lose the signal. Each one is good for a range of about ten to fifteen klicks. I'll talk to Riggs; all we'd need to do is retrieve the aircraft receivers. They're in the avionics bay back at the crash site."

"We could use the Cyclops gear to key off them; that way we don't need the aircraft receivers. Let's get Riggs to have a look. It would save us a trip back to the crash site," said Grant.

"Sounds like a plan. If anyone strayed outside the beam width, an alarm could sound to traverse either left or right," continued Schaefer, picking up on the theme. "All we'd need to do is then measure our straight line-distance, and cross-check with altimeters. All in all, even in whiteout conditions we could make progress."

"I like it as well. But, even with the beacons, I want us prepped to do this the old way as well. Maps, laser ranging, altimeters, sextants and the good old compass," finished Jones.

"You sound almost nostalgic," said Natasha, realising this was the first time she'd felt like laughing in a while.

"I am. In the old days on night-ex in the Welsh hills, all we had was a ragged paper map, compass, stars, and sometimes they gave you a watch."

"Thank God for technology," said Natasha, which prompted a chuckle from the others.

*

After eating, they started loading the pulks for the journey. O'Reilly and Stacey exchanged a series of muttered curses as they surveyed the piles of equipment sitting in the snow.

"We're like a group of fucking Eskimo gypsies. How the hell do they expect us to drag around this lot?" moaned Stacey. "Captain, look at this!" he pleaded to Natasha, testing her response.

"Well, I'll haul the G9s," said O'Reilly making a show of stacking the lightweight snowsuits on the back of one of the pulks.

"That's not funny. Look at all this. We're going to need to find a reindeer team; we shouldn't have eaten that one last night, we could have put it in harness," said Stacey.

"It's as bad as bloody selection," retorted O'Reilly, referring to the entrance tests they each had endured to be selected for the mountain squadron.

"Well, at least this time you're not carrying bricks! Get this sorted!" growled Jones. "Stacey, yours looks like a bloody train wreck!"

"Right, Sarge," responded Stacey using his best appease the Sergeant Major's wrath voice.

As they readied the pulks, the wind started to increase and within an hour was gusting sixty knots. Once again they retreated into the module to wait.

"I've got the BBC again!" shouted Riggs, relaying it to a series of loudspeakers.

"... the death toll from today's nuclear strikes against Hamburg in Germany, Newcastle in England and Pittsburgh in the United States is believed to be in the millions. Multiple warheads delivered airbursts each in excess of ten megatons, almost simultaneously at 1535 hours GMT, on all three cities.

"This is the first time since 1945 that nuclear weapons have been used, when the United States dropped bombs on Nagasaki and Hiroshima respectively. The combined power of those weapons was only forty kilotons, one twenty-fifth of what has just detonated over Pittsburgh. The bombs themselves were all believed to be F cubed or Fission-Fusion-Fission types that generate large quantities of residual radiation; consequently, there is widespread concern that the death toll will double within the foreseeable future.

"Rescue and medical services in the cities report being overwhelmed by the destruction, with fires raging out of control well over thirty kilometres from the epicentres of the blasts. Initial responses from allied governments are calling for immediate, massive retaliation, and have given orders for evacuation of all major population centres to rural areas. Some cities are already reporting widespread panic as people queue to leave ahead of officially organised efforts. We are now going live to Pittsburgh to talk to a Sergeant Morrison who is one of the ground team commanders trying to coordinate rescue efforts. We apologise in advance for the quality of the broadcast, but the loss of communications satellites and disruption to terrestrial-based communications means bandwidth has been restricted to allow for priority military and government communications."

There was a burst of static and then silence before another voice continued.

"Hello, London, this is Peter Winette on the ground at Pittsburgh. I'm standing here in a radiation suit, next to Sergeant Morrison from the Pittsburgh National Guard about thirty-two kilometres from what was once the centre of the city. The scene before me is one of utter devastation. It's like the gates to Hell have been opened and the contents have been allowed to flow out. I'm on Interstate 376 and even here, some seventeen kilometres from the epicentre, there are fires raging all around me, exploded vehicles, wrecked buildings, burst gas mains, shorted power lines, and a thick layer of

45

smoke and dust for as far as the eye can see. Above us, there is an enormous pall of dust from the initial airburst and one can still see the remnants of the mushroom cloud. Damage is being reported as far as another ten kilometres from here. The Ohio and Monongahela rivers seem to have vanished. This city of bridges looks like a monument to mankind: the Smithfield, Panhandle, Liberty, Birmingham and countless others are gone..."

The signal faded for a second or two before coming back.

"... and only an occasional pier remains in what looks like a pool of black mud. The city centre has been completely flattened; there is absolutely nothing left. The interstates I279 and I579 are littered with burnt-out vehicles. The fireball from the detonation has been estimated to be nearly five kilometres across; with the airburst occurring beneath the cloud cover, there have been untold numbers of burn victims up to thirty kilometres away from the epicentre. Earlier we witnessed horrific scenes at a kindergarten school with more than two hundred children suffering from second-degree flash burns." His voice faltered as he choked back his emotion. "Oh boy, I'm struggling to put the scene here into words, the loss of life is almost inconceivable, it's a tragedy..." He paused again. "Sergeant, can you tell us what has been going on since the early hours of this morning?"

A New York accent replied, "Our base went to CBRN or chemical, biological, radiological and nuclear alert about ten minutes before impact and we headed for the shelters. We thought that we were the target. With the space-based systems out, we had lost our early warning system and most of our missile defence capability. I know from the guys on the base that at least one of the incoming warheads was brought down, but the number of decoys was so large that the defences were overwhelmed. After the impact, we were told that the target had been downtown Pittsburgh, and basically got whatever we could together and came down to try and help. We set up an aid station here, upwind of ground zero, and a lot of the guys have been driving in and out of what's left of the city to try and bring out survivors. Once we get them here, we're scrubbing them down and giving them what medical treatment we can."

Peter Winette cut in: "What I can tell you is that there must be at least two thousand people sitting in the cold air around me, many suffering from horrific burns, and some are already showing signs of advanced radiation-related injuries. We have no doctors and only a handful of people who are medically trained. Sergeant, what are your thoughts and emotions at this time?"

"I honestly don't know. A mixture of sorrow, anger, despair and a little determination to try and save who we can. There's a little boy who we brought out earlier…" He stopped and the listeners could hear crying in the background.

Peter Winette cut back in: "Sergeant Morrison, on behalf of everyone we wish you the best of luck. In the meantime, we can tell you that it's also now started to rain, which will add to the fallout here and compound the almost unimaginable misery. This is Peter Winette, live for the BBC near ground zero in Pittsburgh."

"Thank you, Peter," said the London anchor. "What Peter did not tell you is that the Sergeant's wife and young son were visiting his mother who lived in Pittsburgh at the time of the strike. Furthermore, he and his fellow soldiers have exposed themselves to more than three times the lethal dose of radiation during the day rescuing survivors…" The signal faded.

"Hold on, we lost the signal again, here… got it," said Riggs.

"We're now going live to Newcastle in northern England, where similar scenes are being reported…"

This time Riggs couldn't recover the signal. Natasha didn't think it mattered that much anyway. What else could they be told?

*

The squadron gathered around Alex who stood on top of some empty containers in the cargo bay. Despite their depleted power supplies, someone had directed a spotlight onto him that lit up his breath in the cold air. Natasha looked around; they were watching their commander with expectant faces, and in that moment she thought she finally understood what leadership meant.

"Now, I know that none of you come directly from any of those cities, but has anyone got any relatives or loved ones in them?" he asked. No hands went up and Natasha could see some of the tension drain away from his face.

"We all have relatives and loved ones in other major cities, and you heard that they're starting evacuation. In exercises, this normally takes two to three days, providing comms and transportation haven't been disrupted.

The disruption we've heard them talk about seems fairly low level, so evacuation times won't be impacted.

"I doubt there will be any immediate additional strikes; the attacks happened some twelve hours ago, and if these were the first of a nuclear offensive, then why wait before launching more? Why not go after everything in one strike? Why they've targeted these cities, I don't know. They're not primary, not even strategic or critical industrial centres. I think there is a degree of brinksmanship underway, and our enemy is waiting to gauge our response. It will take our various governments at least a day to agree this, and it will almost certainly be proportional, but probably not larger.

"I'm sorry I can't give you much more than this but clearly things have shifted very dramatically. If you want to talk about this further, please feel free to talk to your NCOs, your officers or me."

DAY 9

The dark grey light that pretended to be day matched their mood after the previous evening's news. Even the wind seemed depressed, barely managing the enthusiasm to drive some of the large limp snowflakes into their eyes as Natasha and the others waited in line for Jones's inspection before their departure.

Altogether there were eighteen of them, including Corporal Sanchez, who after the first trek, Natasha now counted as both a friend and mentor. They were an odd-looking bunch, she thought, as she looked down the line. Riggs, the comms specialist with his outsize spectacles; Sanchez, the tough, pretty Puerto Rican girl; Schaefer, the tall, well-built captain; O'Reilly, the huge Irishman; and Stacey, the little cockney. Alex had raised their state of alert, and Schaefer had given her a crash course in basic weapons, introducing her to the newly issued assault rifles and the plastic ultra-lightweight 5mm ammunition.

"I know it might seem a little over the top but I don't like the unknown and right now we're in the middle of a lot of it," Schaefer had told her as he ran through the various protocols on what she should do in the event of contact with the enemy.

Natasha had been told that within thirty minutes of starting she would be sweating from the effort of hauling their loads, but as they waited for the order to start she was shivering and stomping her feet to keep warm, although this time she took some comfort from the fact that she wasn't the only one.

"Good morning, everyone. Let's do a final buddy check and then saddle up," said Jones, finishing his brief inspection.

Although she considered herself a competent skier, Natasha had never pulled a sled, and had to psych herself up for the journey. Sanchez had briefed her on the hard work that would be required, especially that involved in righting pulks that overturned. Each pulk was hauled by two people who were known as the tractors. The lead tractor-man was fully harnessed, whilst the second had a waist belt. A brakeman skied behind the pulk to act as a brake and if necessary stop the assembly from overturning. The fourth member of each pulk team kept point about 10 metres in front to warn against dangerous ground. Every hour they would each rotate positions.

DAY 10

Natasha checked her route map again. After reaching the lake, the plan was to follow it for about 10 kilometres before swinging north along a narrow valley that led up and onto a plateau. From there it would be more or less a direct traverse to the relay station. Weather permitting, they were confident they would be back within five days.

As she took her turn as the lead tractor in the harness, she toggled the setting on her polymer goggles, enhancing the level of contrast. She liked the goggles and wondered why so many, including Jones, still favoured sunglasses. As far as she was concerned the less she had to carry, pack and remember the better. It felt good to be able to move without spending 30% of your energy just overcoming wind resistance. In the milder weather they had established a rhythm and a steady pace.

As they descended she felt the temperature drop.

"You feel that?" asked Sanchez.

"Yes. It's got colder."

"We're on the lake. It's a bit like a big cold sink."

A low-level beep from her headset broke into her reverie to warn her of the need to take on fluids.

"Let's take five," ordered Jones.

Natasha unhooked herself from the harness and went to join Schaefer and Jones who were surveying the landscape. As she walked across she noticed one of the troopers called Stram simply staring at the snow. "You OK?" she asked.

"Fine, Captain. No probs."

Apart from the occasional squeak or crunch of snow as someone moved around, there was silence. Two of the troopers whose name tags read Tolstoy and Pavla lit up cigarettes. Natasha had been told that they came from Russia and Poland, and were renowned as world-class climbers. They were apparently envied for their celebrity status in the wider world, where they were featured in extreme sports, and more recently fashion magazines. The squadron had nicknamed them the ballerinas, although O'Reilly liked to refer to them as the *Men In Tights*.

That evening the moon appeared in force for the first time. Sanchez told her it was a good omen. They discussed the nuclear strikes and their worry that the war was escalating.

DAY 11

They found the last cargo module just after midday. It had slid down a steep tree-covered slope. Wrecked AFVs, equipment, trees and other debris lay strewn over the slope like a set of children's toys. Deep snowdrifts and depressions surrounded the pieces where the storms had eddied around them.

"Jesus, it must have landed higher up and then taken off like a toboggan," said O'Reilly.

"Well, someone's home. I can see smoke," advised Sanchez.

"Sergeant Major, let's fire a flare. Let them know we come in peace," ordered Schaefer.

A few seconds later, two figures appeared from the trees, waving and jumping up and down. Natasha didn't wait. She took off down the hill by ski. One of her loadmasters, Corporal Raven, slid down the snow-covered slope to meet her.

"You OK?" she gasped.

"Yes, ma'am. We could hear you on the TACVs but for some God-unknown reason you couldn't hear us. We didn't have a clue where we or you were. Bottom line is we thought it best to wait it out."

DAY 15

Whilst her loadmasters joined the team led by Captain Grant to ferry food and any salvageable equipment back to Alex, Natasha and Schaefer led the rest of them on towards the relay station.

Initially, they made good progress, but another storm, more vicious than anything they'd experienced before, had enveloped them whilst they'd been traversing a wide-open plateau. They'd had no option but to snow-hole.

Natasha looked around the shelter. It measured 3 by 3 metres and had a domed roof. They'd carved recesses for bunk beds, two on either side of the room. In the centre space between the bunks, they'd dug a deeper hole that acted as a well, trapping the heavier dense cold air. A candle flickered in a small shelf in the ice above each bunk, and this maintained air flow through a section of plastic pipe to the surface and also monitored the level of oxygen. A small ante-room allowed them to relieve themselves.

As the first day passed and the storm continued, they'd amused themselves by digging interconnecting tunnels between the separate shelters and enlarging them into what O'Reilly described as "an architectural wonder that rivalled the Vatican".

DAY 17

The second day in the shelter came and went. Each of them had seemed to relish some time with their own thoughts. In her sleeping bag, Natasha drifted in and out of dream-filled sleep or lay awake listening to the howling wind outside and gazing at the ice crystals above her bunk that glistened like a matrix of stars in the candlelight. She concentrated on rediscovering her childhood memories, and having selected a few even managed to rejoin them and string together a few sequential days. Now, not only could she recall breaking her arm after challenging her elder brother to a jumping contest on their bicycles, but also the day after, when she went to her best friend's party with her arm in plaster dressed as a fairy, and the day after that doing her maths test.

DAY 19

A little like waiting for a train that had been delayed for hours, there was a huge sense of relief when the storm finally passed. Sanchez used a shovel to lever the ice block covering the entrance out of the way, and cleared several feet of loose snow to one side before sticking her head outside.

"The weather's good, and believe it or not there's some sunlight!" she called back to them.

Natasha scrambled out of her sleeping bag and followed Sanchez outside into the fresh air. The daylight felt sharp and her eyes took a while to adjust and focus on the landscape. Around her the others emerged from different exits and jumped around like Arctic foxes.

"I think we'll have breakfast on the terrace this morning," joked O'Reilly, heaving a rations bag out and onto the snow.

Tolstoy, wearing just a pair of shorts, proceeded to make a display of stretching his muscular body.

"Hey, Sanchez," called Ryan. "Enjoy the honeymoon?"

"Oh yeah, everything a girl could ever have wished for," came the retort.

"Let's eat. Then we'll sort ourselves out," ordered Schaefer.

Finished with breakfast, they tried without success to reacquire a signal from the directional radio beacons.

"Probably buried," said Jones, giving up.

"Riggs, see if you can raise Six," Schaefer ordered, referring to Alex's call sign.

Riggs plonked himself down next to Natasha and set up his radio gear.

"Sierra Tango Six. This is Relay. How do you read?" He paused to repeat the request several more times, receiving nothing but silicon silence in return. "Zip. The batteries seem fine. But I'm getting an error message on the code again. Something is screwing up the encoder. I'll try the old Microsoft fix-it routine. Pull the batteries, and reboot."

Jones surveyed the landscape. "Well, it's a long shot but we might be able to get a position fix with the radar. There are a few features."

Natasha watched as they set up the little radar and turned it on, its dish turning one way and then the other, mapping the horizon around them. Jones studied the results. "Probability match of ten per cent. Not enough features. We're going to have to make a detour. We need some better terrain for a fix."

Showing little surprise at the news, Schaefer turned to Jones. "We'll take Tolstoy, Pavla and Stram. One pulk."

Jones called them over. "Right, listen up. We've got to get a better fix on our position, so you are gonna be the stars of this little epic. You three, Captain Schaefer and me are going on a little mountain-climbing trip," he said, pointing to a range of inhospitable-looking mountains with jagged grey ridgelines, from which plumes of snow were blowing horizontally into the sky.

Pavla and Tolstoy gave them a quick briefing, explaining how the ridgelines that crossed the valleys would form gullies filled with deep snow, making a difficult climb. Instead they recommended that the preferred route should be the crests of the ridges, which although looking harsh and windswept with exposed grey and black rock, would be easier. Natasha didn't envy them the trip.

"Captain Kavolsky, give us two days. That should be more than enough time. If we're not back by then, try and backtrack to the beacons and re-establish a route."

*

"I'm glad I'm not part of that little trip. I hate climbing," said Stacey, watching them depart.

Natasha's earphones buzzed and a computerised voice announced she had flash data traffic from Corporal Sanchez. Natasha looked quizzically at Sanchez who was just a few metres away before tapping the receive icon. She heard Sanchez's voice: "I reckon it's time for a silent rave. A little bit of retro rock and roll to warm you up. Get ready for some Puerto Rican girls."

Natasha laughed as "Miss You" from *The Rolling Stones* started playing and each of them began dancing in the snow.

DAY 20

Schaefer and the others returned the next day.

"We're thirteen klicks to the south-west of the relay station. Six uphill and seven down. Once we've done the uphill bit to hill 1829, we just take the next valley to the right and follow it to the end," announced Jones.

"Bloody hell, we were nearly eight klicks out in our estimation. We would have ended up in the wrong valley," commented Sanchez as she ran another check on the data.

"I like it; what a mind fuck that would have been. We should try something like that on a few recruits as part of their basic," Tolstoy said.

"Let's program the remaining beacons. Then as Mr Tolstoy seems so energetic he can lead the next leg," replied Jones.

"Comrades," announced Tolstoy in his best Russian voice, "it will be a pleasure to lead you."

Natasha exchanged a smile with Sanchez as she waited for the banter to kick off full time.

"Oy! O'Reilly. Could you haul number two for a while?" asked Stacey. "It's killing my shoulders."

"Oh, Mr O'Reilly, could you pull mine? I'll buy you a bottle when we reach Hamburg," quipped Ryan.

"You're on," replied the Irishman.

"Bloody typical, every time in life I get anywhere near getting something it gets taken away from me," moaned Stacey.

"Well, at least I can see. This is the first time in days I haven't been misted up," said Riggs as he adjusted his large-framed spectacles.

"Should have come with me and Pavla to that laser optician in Kiev. Best thing we ever did. Isn't that true, Pav?" said Ryan.

"It was. And the nurses took care of us."

"Yeah, and risk your eyesight evaporating completely. No way," replied Riggs.

"I agree, you need to watch it; they say that if you have it done in summer like you did, then the winter temperature will distort your eyeballs and you'll deform your retina. You noticing anything?" added O'Reilly.

"Bollocks," replied Ryan in a slightly worried tone.

"It's true!" interjected O'Reilly. "I had me left one done and it's fucked. Every time I go back to Ireland in the winter I have to wear a patch."

"Well, hopefully you will be OK for the next day or so; the weather looks more settled," said Sanchez.

Natasha noticed Stram again; he remained quiet and not engaged.

*

They reached the crest of Hill 1829 just as the temperature plummeted. As soon as they stopped moving, each was shivering. Natasha could hear the powder snow beneath her skis squeaking.

"Jesus. That's minus thirty-five and no wind chill. God, this place is cold," she muttered.

"We should crest the last rise, over there," advised Jones, pointing to a horizontal line that bisected a steep-walled valley they were working their way along. "After that it's downhill."

"I thought you said this hill was the last one?" said Stacey.

"Yeah, well, didn't want to get you over-excited. You know, all burnt out…" said Jones.

"What do you think, push on, or spend the night here?" asked Schaefer.

"Well, as much as I want a warm bed, I'm not sure about the terrain further up, not to mention the avalanche risk. All in all, I would suggest we stay put here," replied Jones.

"Agreed," responded Schaefer. "Stacey, let's get one of your famous English cups of tea. We'll dig ourselves another bed for the night. You and Sanchez will take first watch. I'll take the second with Ryan, Watkins and Riggs the last."

Natasha was impressed. Schaefer, despite having already made a long trek to get the position fix, had still put himself in the line for a watch, and furthermore had taken the worst, the middle one.

"Bloody marvellous this tea," said Stacey taking a sip. "Reminds me of me mum's."

"Where does she live?" asked Natasha for no reason.

"She moved to Newcastle from London last year," he replied thoughtfully.

"Oh God, I'm sorry. Why didn't you say anything earlier?"

"Didn't really want to bother the Major with my woes. I reckon he probably has enough on his plate already. Anyway, not much anyone can do about it, is there?" he said moving off to get his kit sorted.

"I guess not," she muttered, mulling over Stacey's character, then continued, "I'm worried about Stram. He's been withdrawn for days now," Natasha told Schaefer as they sipped their tea.

"Yeah, I know. I guess he's not as good as us at hiding our emotions. We'll have a chat with him later."

The night was cold but peaceful, the only noise being a distant avalanche that rumbled its way down some chute. Even a lone star managed to make an appearance, noted Natasha.

DAY 21

"I want penetration patrol marching order from now on. I know the chances of engagement are low, but with everything so fucked up, I don't want any mishaps. Stacey, you take point. Stram, cover, and Watkins, you're tail-end Charlie," ordered Schaefer.

Stacey led off, with the others following with a minimum of thirty feet separation. At midday they stopped and instinctively turned to face the east where the grey clouds had parted allowing sunlight to stream through and caress the landscape. Despite the sub-zero temperatures they took a moment to unbutton the necks of their snowsuits, roll down their hoods and remove their balaclavas to suck up the weak but discernible warmth.

An hour later Natasha, Sanchez, Jones and Schaefer lay prone on a ridgeline, like a line of children spying on their parents, and surveyed the relay station now just 700 metres away.

"Jesus. It's taken a pasting. The antennae are toast and the helipad looks like it's taken a bunker buster," said Jones.

The antennae array, which had originally been located along the top of a cliff-like ridge, now lay scattered randomly around the base of it, the older, larger dishes resembling discarded china plates, with one embedded vertically in the snow. The area where the helipad had been had the look of a burnt-out campfire.

"What the hell is going on here? How come an installation this far behind our lines has been knocked out?" muttered Schaefer.

"I suggest we drop down to the tree line and move to the north across the valley. We can enter the station using the lower access doors at the base of the cliff. But I'm worried about mines. If they've taken the trouble to hit this place then they sure as hell will have expended a little more effort to mine it," said Jones, recording the scene onto his PDA.

"Agreed," said Schaefer.

Jones downloaded his video survey to his navigation package and merged it with the 3D terrain map. As the others gathered around, he sketched out an approach route then cross-loaded it to the others' PDAs.

"There's a lot of animal tracks, some are moose. At least that means that the probability of mines is less," said Sanchez.

"Thank the good Lord for that. I was beginning to think we were the last living things out here," said O'Reilly.

"What about ground forces?" asked Natasha, feeling a little worried she was asking a stupid question.

"Possible. We'll treat the approach as advance to contact. Two teams, with cover. Captain Kavolsky and I'll lead off with Sanchez and O'Reilly. Once we are in, Stacey will follow with the rest. Pavla and Tolstoy, you two stay with the Sergeant Major to our right and provide cover; that way we should be able to cover both the station and the tree line to the east. Let's break out the mine detectors," said Schaefer.

There was no banter as they set off towards the relay station in single file, each following in Schaefer's ski tracks. Natasha's heart rate was racing as they moved slowly forward sweeping the area in front of them with the electro-resonance mine detectors searching for signs of either metal or plastic. Every 2 metres Sanchez inserted a chemical odour probe into the snow, designed to detect explosive vapours.

*

Beneath them, and out of range of the detectors, lay nearly 2,000 anti-personnel and anti-vehicle mines classified by the allies as APMs and AVMs.

Each mine possessed an acoustic, electromagnetic and pressure sensor. The data from these was then amalgamated and shared across all the mines using an ultra low frequency wireless net. Using three air-dropped beacons as reference points, a map of the area was generated that enabled any changes in the field strengths of the sensors to be analysed and interpreted by means of distributed tactical intelligence software. The minefield effectively became an organism. Tracking Natasha and the others as they made their way to the relay station above, it quickly verified that the disturbance was not animal. Sufficiently interested, the tactical software then went on to determine that the intruders did not possess any vehicles and were most probably a scouting party whose mission was to evaluate the damage done by the earlier airstrike. After reviewing possible courses of action the software decided to let the group continue unhindered and then wait for the main repair team.

*

They reached the base of the rock formation, which housed the main service entrance to the relay station. Large matt black steel blast doors with Air Force Property – Restricted Access – No Unauthorised Entry stencilled in yellow letters greeted them. To the right of the doors, embedded in the dark rock, was a keypad. A small red light winked at them at one-second intervals.

"Well at least the place has still got power," said Natasha.

"O'Reilly, can you run a bypass?" asked Schaefer.

O'Reilly inserted a key card connected to a small black box with a screen. He studied the output and grunted. "Standard codes. Jesus, they never learn." A few taps later and the door lock status went green. He pushed the door open command but got no response.

"It's going to need a hand job," he said with a smirk.

"Ha ha," said Sanchez; "so you shouldn't have any problems doing it, then."

They cranked the doors open manually, then made their way into the lower access and storage area. Half a dozen snowmobiles, and quad bikes for the summer months, were neatly lined up against the concrete walls. Further inside, the floor sloped downwards into darkness. Sanchez switched on a flashlight and slowly swung it across the dark void. The light beam illuminated stacks of grey packing crates, several banks of liquid hydrogen storage tanks and a mass of cable trays and pipe-work.

"Let's find the generators. See if we can get some light. Second Team, call back," said Schaefer into his VHF boom mike.

"Go ahead," replied Jones from the opposing ridgeline.

"You can send the second team across. Use our tracks. Set up a safe corridor beacon your end I want to be able to track out the way we came in," said Schaefer. The beacon would allow the team to retrace their exact entry route in the event their tracks were buried in a fresh snowfall.

"Roger that. Ryan, Leone, Watkins and Riggs will lead off, thirty-foot intervals. Stram, Stacey, Peters, will follow. I'll keep Pavla and Tolstoy this end. We'll need a few minutes to get the beacon set up," confirmed Jones.

*

As the second team moved towards the relay station, the minefield re-evaluated the situation against what had been expected, and determined that this second group of people was the repair team and should be engaged.

From its memory, the minefield determined that Riggs, Stacey and the others were following the same track as Schaefer had used earlier. Using this knowledge, and the speed and separation of the new targets, it was a simple computation to determine the line of closest approach to individual mines and the optimum timing of engagement.

*

From the entrance of the relay station, Natasha and Sanchez provided cover against any threat as Stacey and the others made their way across the open ground. They could hear Schaefer and O'Reilly meanwhile setting about getting the station's power up and running.

"The APUs are over here," said O'Reilly, referring to the suitcase-sized fuel cells that powered the auxiliary power units. "Got it. We've got the instrument lights ... okey-dokey... and then, as the Lord said, let there be light," he announced.

Just as the lights came on, a rapid series of explosions erupted, forcing Sanchez and Natasha to duck down for cover.

"Jesus H. What the fuck did you do, O'Reilly?" exclaimed Sanchez.

"Nothing. I just got the power up, that's all. Everything's good down here," he called back.

Natasha looked out over the area where the second team had been approaching the station. A dozen balls of black smoke were rising into the pale sky, accelerating as they gained height. Beneath each plume was a circular patch of dark snow about 5 metres in diameter with striations stretched out like a child's drawing of a starburst. Bodies, now clad in pink

59

G9 snowsuits, lay around, contorted into impossible positions, their limbs bent at reverse angles. Body parts including a leg and a bare foot had been thrown further out of the blast circles. For a brief moment her attention remained with the foot as she wondered how the boot and sock could have come off. Stacey and one other looked like they were still alive.

"We've got seven down. Probable delayed-action APMs. No sign of Brotherhood ground forces. Stacey, do you copy?" asked Jones.

"Yes, Sarge. Jesus. I stopped to adjust my binding and the whole place went up. It looks like Stram is still alive… He's kneeling in the snow. I can't see any movement from the others."

Natasha zoomed in on Stram's location; his torso was twitching and she realised immediately that he wasn't kneeling, he'd lost both his legs and an arm. A single shot rang out from Jones's position on the ridgeline, and Stram's head exploded.

Sanchez screamed, "What the fuck is going on?" as she started searching for the shooter.

Schaefer reached out and grabbed her arm. "That was the Sergeant Major's shot. There's no way we could have helped him." Sanchez pulled her arm away from Schaefer and looked away.

"Stacey. This is Captain Schaefer. Hold your position."

"Sir, I'm not going anywhere."

As Natasha looked at the scene, an eerie and frightening realisation dawned on her.

"Look at the detonation pattern; it's perfect. Multiple and simultaneously targeted along our tracks," she said.

"So where's the controller?" asked Sanchez.

"Sergeant Major, Pavla, Tolstoy, you guys see any sign of a watcher, anything?" radioed Schaefer.

"Negative," replied Jones.

"Why hasn't he finished the job?" asked Sanchez.

"Agreed. You copy that, Sergeant Major?" radioed Schaefer.

"Roger that. So that leaves us with just one explanation; there have been rumours about IMFs. I guess we just ran into one," he replied.

"What?" asked Natasha.

"He's talking about intelligent minefields," advised O'Reilly.

"Any chance it could be part of the station's own security system?" asked Natasha.

"I doubt it, but we'll shut down the power in case. Assuming this is an intelligent field, it allowed us through and then attacked a second larger unit travelling along the same tracks."

"Jesus, it's classic facility or area-denial tactics. Let the scouts pass and knock out the main group," agreed Sanchez.

"Hey, guys, I'm still stuck in the middle of this thing. It's tried to kill me once and it knows where I am. Also, I'm not sure how long I can stay like this; my legs are beginning to cramp," pleaded Stacey.

Natasha thought through the problem. "It's got to be using a combination of acoustic, pressure and possibly magnetic sensors arranged to detect fluctuations."

"Right. So all Stacey has to do is act like he is not interested in the relay station and it will leave him alone. Like the animal tracks we saw?" suggested O'Reilly.

"Stacey, listen up. We need to convince it that you're not a threat. Take a different route than the one we used. Pick a random one, heading away from the station. We'll also lay down a rolling grenade barrage, moving towards us. I'll put red smoke markers down, the rest of you drop HE. If we can't confuse the sensors, maybe we'll detonate some of the mines," said Schaefer in a voice that tried to reassure.

"This is fucking unbelievable," Stacey replied.

"On my mark... Mark," ordered Schaefer.

They commenced firing; the resulting explosions from the grenades sounded almost lost in the landscape. The minefield remained dormant, but Stacey reached the doors of the relay station.

"Fucking un-bloody believable," he gasped, collapsing next to Natasha.

*

That evening as they sat around the mess table in the relay station, O'Reilly presented them with two bottles of vodka that he'd found behind a cupboard. Sanchez took one and wiped the base of it with her sleeve then checked it, next shook it up and studied the bubbles. "It's good stuff," she announced.

"How do you know?" asked Natasha, never having seen this type of a ritual before.

"Well, the bubbles need to be well-balanced and rise slowly. As for the bottom of the bottle, if it leaves a dark mark like this on my sleeve, you know it's from a factory because the rubber belts that move the bottles around leave a trace. If it doesn't it's probably moonshine."

"Bit like knowing what a good wine should look and smell like," added O'Reilly.

"We can tell you a lot about vodka, and how to drink it. Don't sip it; you'll get drunk quickly because it's always looking for the fastest way to your brain and the lips are closer than the stomach. If you want to stay sober longer than anyone else then drink some olive oil before; it lines the stomach and delays the entrance to the blood stream, and so it goes on…" finished Sanchez, looking at the bottle as if it was going to talk to her.

Natasha shook her head, wondering about the places they must have drunk in to refine their knowledge to such a degree.

"Anyway, it's a great drink to toast our friends that are lying outside," Sanchez continued before starting to regale them with stories about Ryan, Riggs, Stram, Peters, Watkins, Leone and Smith.

Natasha learnt about The Great Caspian Retreat, The Vladivostok Assault, and the Famous Night In Kabul. She realised she felt honoured to be included in the conversation. They spoke to her as if they had decided she was now part of their family and as such should learn their history and customs.

"You know I found out why Stram was acting so strangely. He had just agreed to get married to a girl. I think he said her name was Jenny. Anyway, she lived in downtown Pittsburgh," Schaefer told them.

O'Reilly moved the subject on. "It was a brave thing that the Sarge did today," he said referring to the shooting of Stram.

Natasha noticed Sanchez wipe a tear away and passed her the vodka.

"I know, but it hurt. I've been through hell and back with those guys and now they're just lying out there in the snow. We've drunk tequila and shared dreams together. Today wasn't the same as combat. I didn't get a chance to say goodbye. I didn't even get a chance to share the experience," explained Sanchez.

"What made you run this way and not back the way you'd come?" Natasha asked Stacey, changing the subject.

Stacey took another shot of vodka before replying. "You know, Captain, it was weird, but I didn't trust it – the minefield, that is. It was like it was waiting for me. Anyway, I knew if I went away from the station I was going to have to cross a part of the field that was still fresh; at least the other way a few of the mines had already detonated. Also, I didn't fancy hopping about on one leg trying to pretend I was a rabbit or something. Just isn't dignified," explained the little cockney whilst raising the vodka again.

They sat in silence for a few minutes before Stacey continued. "You know how, before an attack, some of us write letters or notes to our loved ones, whilst some just talk to their mates about them? Well, strangest thing, when I was out there I thought I should but I couldn't, all I could think of were my chances of making it."

There was a reflective silence and they just stared at the gunmetal grey mess table that was littered with paper cups, MRE containers, cigarette butts and empty soft drink tins. Natasha studied the room; it was just as uninviting as any military facility: grey rough concrete walls, steel fixtures and fittings, worn looking and with a unique smell.

"All right. Let's get back to the future. The comms here are toast. So it's Plan B. Prior to the airstrike, the relay station generated its own electricity from solar, converting excess power into pressurised H2 or liquid hydrogen which has been stored in four thermally insulated cryogenic tanks. I think we can get enough fuel back to the Major for the AFVs so we can all drive out of here and get back to civilisation," said Schaefer, calling a halt to the wake.

"Can you run a few sums?"

"We've got snowmobiles and sleds. All we need to do is work out how to get the tanks onto the sleds," added Sanchez.

"We can vent one of the station's storage tanks, dismantle it and get it mounted on one of the equipment sleds. Then decant the H2 from the other tanks," suggested Stacey.

"We'll need to check the H2 vents are still operational. After the air strike they could be buried or damaged; we'd get a build-up followed by a big bang," said O'Reilly.

"That wouldn't be pretty," agreed Sanchez.

Natasha thought about the problem for a moment. Somehow they needed to check that the main H2 vent line was clear so that they could vent off one of the tanks.

"I saw an air compressor in the hanger. We could use that to purge the vent system. If it works for compressed air we should be fine," said Natasha, wondering where she'd got the idea.

"Outstanding. First thing in the morning, let's get to it," ordered Schaefer, looking truly impressed.

DAY 22

The next day another blizzard enveloped the relay station.

"I don't fucking believe this!" exclaimed O'Reilly. "The goddamn weather in this godforsaken place is fucking unbelievable. How the fuck can this keep being so fucked up?" Outside, the wind tore across the open ground at more than sixty knots. Any sign of yesterday's violence had disappeared. Visibility was non-existent.

"Look on the bright side. We could be on stag out there with the Sarge and the others," replied Sanchez.

"Fucking unbelievable," came O'Reilly's measured reply. "Un-fucking-believable."

It took them nearly six hours to reroute the piping and hoses, vent the first of the hydrogen tanks and mount it on one of the sleds.

"Well. That should do us," announced Sanchez, standing back from the assembly with her hands on her hips and looking proud of her work. In front of her was a mass of stainless steel cryogenic hoses and valves connected to the first of the tanks that she'd secured to the sled.

"Let's do it, then," prompted O'Reilly, pushing a small green button and starting the cryogenic pumps.

As the liquid hydrogen was pumped, the stainless steel hoses and valves turned white with ice as the liquid, at minus 260 degrees Celsius below zero, drew heat in from the surrounding air.

"How long?" asked Natasha.

"Well, should be done in a few hours," replied O'Reilly; "any faster and we risk a blockage or worse an explosion. We'll need to monitor the sensors continuously. Any build-up in pressure and just hit the large red mushroom button here. That'll stop the pumps."

They spent the remainder of the day eating, resting and tinkering with the radios.

"Nothing. No military, no civilian. *Nada.*"

"Maybe they took out everything," said O'Reilly. Natasha listened, waiting for the inevitable question to follow.

"What do you think, Captain K?" asked Stacey.

"Unknown," she replied. "Seems improbable that they could have knocked out everything. Maybe like Riggs said, it's just our location, or the storm."

Sanchez continued to play with the frequencies. Suddenly she held up her hand and flicked a switch. "Bingo. We've got the BBC again."

"This is the BBC in London. Attacks continued today on civilian communications centres with emphasis on television, radio and telephone facilities. The BBC continues to broadcast from London and has not been affected.

"The death toll from last week's nuclear strikes is now estimated to be six million, with more than twelve million wounded. Of these, nearly seven million are expected to die from radiation-related illness within the next month and a further million within the year. Evacuation of all major cities is almost complete with no major difficulties being reported.

"The main financial markets have now completed their relocation to alternative sites and trading will begin again tomorrow.

"On the central and northern fronts, allied ground forces continue to advance rapidly with little or no resistance encountered. Despite the terrain, advances of one hundred kilometres have been reported. In the southern sector, allied forces are reported to be engaged in fierce fighting in and around the Dardanelles. A helicopter assault on Gallipoli was reported as encountering stiff resistance, but the 101st Airborne divisional commander expressed confidence that the area, including the straits, would soon be in allied hands.

"In other news, the World Health Organization has confirmed the outbreak of a strain of pneumonic plague in three separate locations. Investigations are currently underway to determine the exact nature of the virus. Those infected have been taken to isolation centres for treatment…"

The signal faded and was replaced with a burst of static and then nothing.

"Shit, what the fuck's going on with this? One minute I've got a good signal and then zip," said Sanchez.

"Oh man, this is fucking unbelievable. Don't we ever learn? It's like a bad dream. Nukes, the plague and now fighting at fucking Gallipoli again. We're better off in this godforsaken place," proclaimed Stacey as he slumped down in a chair and covered his face with his hands.

"Aye. It'll be fucked up all right," echoed O'Reilly.

"The advances they spoke about seem impressive," commented Natasha.

"They do, and we can only guess what preceded them," replied Schaefer in a voice that made Natasha shiver.

"Yep. Bugs, bad air and bottles of instant sunshine, I wouldn't wonder," added Sanchez, referring to the probable use of biological, chemical and nuclear weapons.

"Well, at least we're in the news now. For the last twenty years, in fact since all the bollocks with Afghanistan, we've been the forgotten soldiers fighting a forgotten war. No one thought much about it, even as it spread," said Stacey.

They spent another night in the mess room drinking coffee laced with whisky from O'Reilly's personal store.

Stacey asked Natasha if she thought it was possible the minefield could have modified its mission profile.

"Excuse me! But how the bloody hell could it change its mission profile? It can't be that clever," interjected O'Reilly.

"Well, we can't do a hell of a lot about it. I don't think it's worth worrying about," said Sanchez.

"Oh, easy for you to say that. You wait," replied Stacey with a passion.

"The only thing we know is that it seems to favour large groups. It's like it's putting a value on its ammunition. So one thing we do is go one by one," ordered Schaefer.

"Who's going first?" asked O'Reilly.

DAY 23

As the sun came up the next morning, they looked out over a vastly different landscape. There were blue skies and bright sunshine bounced off the white snow that now covered their dead. They could see Jones walking along the ridgeline in a T-shirt.

Natasha took a moment to ponder what else her senses were telling her was different. After a period of self-analysis she got it. It was the silence. For the first time she could remember, it was quiet. It wasn't so much the absence of the wind that was noticeable, it was more subtle. In fact so subliminal that she almost forgot her train of thought until Sanchez spoke. It was the sound of sound; it seemed to be richer, clearer and more real. She felt peaceful.

"Right, let's give this a go," said Sanchez clambering onto one of the snowmobiles. "You coming, Captain?" she asked Natasha.

Natasha got on behind Sanchez; the seat was big and softly padded. She felt nervous, scared and yet excited as she summoned up the courage for what they were going to do.

"Just put your arms around my waist and relax," advised Sanchez.

She gently released the brake, thumbed the throttle forward and moved slowly out of the hangar and down a slope, towing one of the hydrogen tanks. Natasha checked behind that their load was stable and shouted the all-good to Sanchez. In return she got a thumbs-up, before they quickly accelerated across the minefield. It was over almost as soon as it had begun; as they sped up and over the opposite ridgeline Natasha felt herself go weightless for a second and then settle back down in the soft seat.

"Good morning, Captain," said Jones welcoming her.

Natasha looked back across the snow to the entrance. Suddenly what she'd just done made her feel weak.

"I know," said Jones, "sometimes you don't realise the magnitude of what you've done until afterwards. Have a coffee and take five."

"Well? You guys gonna just hang out?" she heard Sanchez prompt the others over the field radio.

CHAPTER 5

BACK TO CIVILISATION

If the military leadership is wise, the country is safe.

DAY 24

Natasha and the others arrived back at the cargo module at midday. They cruised into the area like jet skiers on a holiday, hauling the trailers of fuel behind the snowmobiles. Alex was standing outside one of the igloos looking pleased to see them.

"Welcome home," he said as the engines of the four snowmobiles fell silent.

Natasha dismounted, stretching her limbs and working out the stiffness. The return journey from the relay station had been blessed with bright blue skies, sun and powder snow, which had softened the memory of the minefield.

Alex held an extensive debrief.

"It's weird, intelligent minefields, taking down our GPS and comms, air strikes. It's like they've leapfrogged several levels in technology without us knowing about it," commented Grant.

"Not only that, they've also managed to deploy it in the field. It's one thing developing a technology, but to produce and distribute it as well. How come we were never warned? What have our intel people been doing?" asked Schaefer.

"Unknown. Since you guys left, we've still had no contact, nothing," replied Alex.

"We picked up a BBC transmission a couple of nights ago. Didn't you?" asked Natasha.

"No. Nothing," replied Alex, looking surprised.

"They must be jamming, it's the only explanation," said Crockett.

"So, we can add that little trick to their box as well. What the hell is going on? No SAR, nothing. It's like we're in a void," complained Grant in an exasperated voice.

"Well, let's look on the bright side, we're not dead and now we've got enough fuel to get us out of here, and I reckon that deserves a celebration," interjected Crockett, lifting the mood.

MORNING, DAY 25 – CARGO MODULE SITE

With the six AFVs and the snow scooters and the fuel, they could now transport all the equipment they'd salvaged, as well as the eighty-nine survivors, 300 kilometres to a regimental base at Nord Jensen which was the home of the 15th Norwegian mechanised infantry. The plan was to travel south-east across country until they met European Route 18, the main highway between Scandinavia and northern Europe, and then just "turn right", as Crockett had said.

*

As the sun set, Natasha and Alex took a walk through the area as the final preparations for departure were being made. She'd felt like a spare wheel until Alex had asked if she wanted to get up to speed with how a ground unit operated. She'd accepted the challenge, although whether out of pride, boredom or the fact that she was beginning to like and respect the Major, she didn't know. She'd spent the day inside one of the HQ AFVs listening to them planning the route, discussing contingencies and tactics, and was now happy to get outside.

Next to the vehicle-access hatches, boxes and crates were piled haphazardly, as people hauled and stacked as much gear as possible into every available space. Cryogenic hoses snaked white and frosty across the snow as they finished decanting the liquid hydrogen from the tanks they'd towed back from the relay station to the AFVs' internal tanks. She noticed Stacey and one of his crew who were working on a set of track assemblies on the AFV she would be riding in.

"Oy! Who the bleeding hell stuck all this lot in my cockpit? I can't see out of the view port, let alone steer. Get some of this bloody rubbish out of here. Sorry, ma'am, but it's bloody typical," he said, noticing Natasha.

"No probs. Carry on," she replied.

"She's a bit smaller than your rig, but Betsy here can go places that you wouldn't believe. My mate Leo here is the one who looks after all the systems," Stacey continued in a proud, almost maternal voice.

"Will we be good to go?" she asked.

"Couple of hours max. Leo's just making a few adjustments to the track mechanisms."

Nearby, a four-man ground crew were prepping the squadron's aerial drones. The two little craft were shaped like doughnuts, some 2 metres in diameter, with the centre devoted to a large turbo fan. Pre-flight cables led back from them across the snow to a panel in the side of an AFV. Alex introduced her to the squadron's air section officer, Lieutenant Byrnes, a squat figure with a small black moustache and unshaven chin.

"Boys' toys," mused Natasha.

"Good evening, Captain. Good evening, Major. Meet Mozart and Beethoven, AKA the Musicians. Eyes in the sky, with a little punch. Top speed of one hundred and forty knots, VTOL, hover mode, and an endurance time of about forty-eight hours. We've got all-round field of vision cameras mounted on the underside and around the main hub. We can go IR, UV, night or day with a thousand times magnification, all motion stabilised with auto tracking, of course."

"Of course. What about payload?" asked Natasha, warming to and egging on the Lieutenant who was obviously proud of his craft.

"Yeah. They've got a sting, hence the logo." He pointed to the silhouettes of violins spitting lightning painted on the machines' matt black bodies.

"Fourteen air-to-air, or air-to-ground, fire and forget or wire-guided missiles, with the usual programmable warheads as well as mines and smoke. Defensive capability is basically run but the systems have on-board automatic evasive routines and because they can move and change direction so fast they're tough little bastards to hit." He continued the pre-flight checks and spoke into his boom mike. "Roger. Let's go for a hover, and deploy the cams on Beethoven."

The little machine spun up its turbofan and lifted unsteadily into the air to about head height and then stabilised as its gyros synchronised. Natasha backed away, both out of respect and a desire not to get covered in snow. A small door in the underside slid open and an array of cameras that looked like a disco-light pod dropped down and spun round a few degrees before stopping and reversing a fraction. In the morning darkness, it really did resemble a UFO, thought Natasha.

"Cams are green? Roger. OK, let's do Mozart," said Byrnes into his mouthpiece.

"Impressive. Who makes them and what do they cost?" asked Natasha, getting a smile from Alex.

"Air War Inc makes them, manufactured entirely in Hawaii and they go for about ten mill apiece. Anyway, we've been talking to your air crew, Corporal Raven, who told us he is not only a qualified loadmaster but also an electronic systems specialist. Also Sergeants Lions and Jenkins who apparently are flight engineers."

"Yeah, on the Strats we were expected to be able to undertake all the infield maintenance and any repairs as well as fly. You know, they could take some of the load if you want?" replied Natasha, looking at Alex.

"Good idea. It's going to be an intensive trek. Why not. Good to see you've polished the briefing LT; you ever think about going into sales with Air War?"

As they moved away, Natasha started to giggle.

"Tell me," said Alex.

"Well, I never thought the infantry were so geekish. It's worse than the air force."

*

They'd been on the move for two hours and Natasha felt like she was back on basic flight training as she slowly familiarised herself with the capabilities of the squadron's air assets and how they integrated with the AFV's own weapons and sensor systems.

She was seated in the combat centre in Schaefer's AFV. Around her were Raven and Byrnes who were flying Mozart, one of the two aerial vehicles, and Sanchez and O'Reilly who were manning the threat and weapons desks. Natasha could talk to each on a dedicated communications link. Sanchez had selected the *Concierto de Aranjuez* by Joaquin Rodrigo as background music, to help her concentrate.

Each looked comfortable in the oversized black leather executive swivel chairs. Seven feet above them sat Schaefer in the commander's chair, which was mounted on a telescoping ram allowing him an all-round view of the outside through an armoured glass cupola.

The compartment was dominated by a myriad of screens, interspersed with switchboards, junction boxes, levers and cable runs. Coiled data and headset cables bounced around as the AFV traversed the rough terrain. Natasha had once visited a fast-attack submarine, and the room had possessed the same atmosphere. Schaefer's telescoping chair hissed a little as it moved up a few inches and swung around.

"Neat, isn't it?" said Sanchez. "They were going to scrap the thing but all the older commanders persuaded them to keep it on the basis that a commander needed to see outside and not just be reliant on sensors and displays."

"Same with aircraft. So I'm ready to learn. What have you got to show me?" asked Natasha with a smile.

"Well, we've got just about every sensor invented and then some. We've got access to both strategic and tactical analysis: when it's available of course. The top board is air threats, middle is ground-based and the lower is subsurface – mines, that sort of thing. At the moment, we're on passive arrays only, looking for electric-field leakage: sound, radio, heat, light, magnetic and explosive telltales. I'm getting feed from the Musicians as well as all the other AFVs," advised Sanchez as she tapped ash into an empty 40mm grenade casing that was taped to the instrument panel.

"Can you show me the feed?"

Moments later, an overhead view of the trail ahead of them emerged on one of the screens.

Overlaid onto the camera feed were the terrain details, rock outcrops, defilades, heights and ranges to points of tactical interest. Even foliage types were shown.

"It's the ultimate in augmented reality; we call it Real-Aug. We keep both eyes on the 'real terrain', so to speak, but one on the sensor feeds' overlays to enhance our situational awareness. As long as you don't rely too much on any one, it works," interjected O'Reilly.

"What are those?" asked Natasha, pointing to a highlighted overlay of their route.

"Oh, they're animal tracks. If you look to the top right of the screen, you'll see the interp. Clever stuff; apparently the software uses a combination of deterministic maths and fractal mechanics to make a call. A bit like seeing one card in a poker hand and then guessing the rest. Can even give you a direction and speed of movement," said Sanchez.

"What sort of animals?" quipped Natasha, not expecting a reply.

"Hold on. It's got a database of what lives where and when certain things hibernate or migrate. They spent a lot on getting trackers and hunters from all over the world to participate in the programming," said Sanchez, tapping the menu. "Here we go: five moose; all female."

Natasha nodded, trying to comprehend the sophistication of what she was witnessing.

"Anyway, we take all the feed and build up a threat map. It even works out where, if you were a bad guy, you would site your armour, mortars or infantry. Gives you arcs of fire based on defilades of known weapons, the whole lot. See?" she continued, bringing up a map that was colour coded.

"Shit," said Natasha, "how the hell do you sort all this out?"

"You get used to it. When they first thought this lot up, they were worried about info overload, especially when you've got adjacent combat teams, satellites and AWACS all peddling their info. But after a while it's just like being a money broker: you go with your instincts. All I do is paint the threats with a priority and give O'Reilly the info. He can then engage, as he wants. I use a colour code to help him out, bit like traffic lights: green is OK, yellow is a possible, red is watch out, and black is death unless you unload quick. I tend to only give O'Reilly red or black - any more and his brain has a breakdown."

O'Reilly grunted. "She's not bad. Only ever really screwed up once. Told me we had a threat of ambush with movement. I pasted the area with aerial mines. Turned out I had destroyed half a dozen sheep."

"There were three, and they were goats," corrected Sanchez.

Facing the rear of the compartment sat the communications officer, Lieutenant Stevenson. "Captain Kavolsky, could you have a listen to this?" she asked.

Natasha joined the pretty blonde who moved a pink cashmere scarf draped over a console out of the way and signalled to Natasha to plug her headset into a jack.

"Nice scarf," said Natasha.

"Present from my husband back in the States. He's convinced the army winter weather gear is rubbish."

Natasha plugged her headset in and watched the monitor play back the signal.

"The airwaves have stayed dead but about a minute ago I got a carrier signal. It lasted for about twenty seconds before it vanished and was replaced with this. It's repeating at ten-second intervals; it's to the south of us. At first I thought it was a nav beacon but now I'm not sure. I reckon it might be a distress beacon. Our database has got no record of a beacon around here and there's nothing in the library that remotely resembles the signal."

Natasha listened to the signal. "Is it terrestrial?" she asked.

"Absolutely. Not moving and ground level."

"Weird. It's not a nav beacon. At least not one that I recognise. It sounds more like a handshake. Like one system trying to connect with another."

"That's what I think as well. But I've got no other signal. There's no one replying."

The signal faded and they were back to silence. Natasha studied the monitors. They were all dead. Nothing.

"Corporal Sanchez, you get anything from the other sensors?" asked Stevenson.

"*Nada.* All green. But send me the range and bearing and I'll log it."

"Will do."

As Natasha unplugged her headset she noticed a Post-it message stuck to a switch panel. It read Property of Riggs – Don't Fuck Up My Settings – please.

Natasha recognised the name as that of one of the two comms specialists who had been killed at the relay station. Stevenson read her thoughts.

"Yeah. Dead men's shoes."

"I'm going to get a coffee. You guys want anything?" offered Natasha.

Designed to cover large distances in relative comfort, the combat team's cabin occupied nearly half the length of the AFV. As well as seating, weapons and ammunition storage, it also contained a galley, toilet and even a shower. A ladder led to an upper deck, which although no more than a metre high, provided sleeping space.

As she waited for the drinks dispenser to do its stuff, Natasha looked around. Some of the troopers were dozing in their harnesses, their heads lolling beneath their helmets. Others were watching movies or reading. Bulkhead-mounted screens relayed the terrain, threat and navigation feeds. But most of their attention was being paid to what looked like a serious poker game around a makeshift table of equipment and stores containers.

A couple of the troopers acknowledged her with "Hi, Captain". She smiled in return and gave them a nod.

*

Natasha spent the next few hours learning how to fly the Musicians and some of the tricks that the little machines could perform. She was deep in conversation with Raven and Byrnes when Sanchez interrupted them.

"Weapons. Threat."

"Go," said O'Reilly.

"Check possible designated Yellow One. Flight, bring Beethoven north two hundred. Mozart to stay on station," she ordered.

"Beethoven north two hundred. Mozart to stay on station," echoed Byrnes.

Natasha watched as her board changed views to the threat display. A possible threat had been identified, shown by a blinking yellow square.

"I'm cross-linking to tac-net now. Could be civilian, but who on earth would be out here by themselves?" said Sanchez whilst sending a burst transmission to the other AFVs updating them with the latest information. "Yellow One is moving. Scout closing to one hundred metres. Visual coming up," she said.

"I'm waking them up. Combat alarm now," said O'Reilly, initiating a low-pitched alarm.

"Weapons. Commander," said Schaefer "confirm all weapons safe."

"Confirm weapons are safe," responded O'Reilly, letting Schaefer know that all weapons were still locked.

"Dismount team. We have a yellow threat, designated Yellow One, prepare to dismount. Break left and right, staggered formation," ordered Schaefer.

The AFV slewed to a halt, nosing down gently as it did so. The side doors and rear ramp opened with a hiss of air and the noise of hydraulics as the high-speed worm gears engaged and cold air swirled into the compartment. Natasha watched on the CCTV screens as two four-man squads dismounted from the AFV.

A wide screen lit up, showing an amalgamated view using each trooper's hat-mounted camera view, weapons status, and position with respect to the AFV and the terrain. They'd taken up positions either side of the AFV, spread out at 10 feet intervals in a skirmish line.

One of the Musicians relayed an infrared image of a rocky outcrop set amongst the trees just to the left of the trail they had been driving along. Atop it was the unmistakable thermal shape of a figure lying prone and holding a rifle.

Natasha wondered if the person had any idea of the amount of firepower that was ranged against him.

"Commander. Threat," said Sanchez.

"Yeah, I can see him. Wait one," ordered Schaefer.

"Hotel One. This is Delta One," came the voice of one of the combat team.

"Go, Delta One," replied Schaefer.

'Yeah, Captain. Corporal Hodgetts here reckons that the rifle is a hunting one. Claims it's a Sharpe's 200, although how the hell he can tell that from the imagery is beyond me."

"All right. So what do we do? Anyone want to go up and ask him what's going on?" asked Schaefer.

"Corporal Hodgetts here reckons we should light a flare. Says that will alert him to the fact that we're not prey and hopefully not frighten him off."

"Sounds good to me. We'll pop one from our position. Weapons. You copy that?"

"Roger. Flare firing forward now," said O'Reilly.

A pop, followed by a bright white light from the parachute flare, lit up the area. Long shadows danced across the snow as the flare descended. The aerial scout camera monitored the man as he moved quickly back into the tree line, and then tracked him as he ran away into the forest.

"Poor bastard; we probably frightened the life out of him. Let's hold our position for another thirty minutes and keep tracking his progress," said Schaefer.

They tracked the man for another kilometre as he continued heading away from them, then feeling a little perplexed by the event restarted their journey.

"Bloody typical, we've seen no one for weeks and when we do, he runs off!" moaned O'Reilly.

DAY 26

Natasha woke with a start and took a few moments to realise she was still in her seat in the combat centre.

"We stopped again?" she asked Sanchez, who was sipping a coffee and smoking.

"Yeah. Big debate going on in the Major's AFV. We're lost, and tempers are getting a little frayed."

Natasha sat up and realised she was desperate to go to the bathroom. In the crew compartment both the toilets were occupied so she decided to return to nature. The cold air made her shiver as she walked down the stern ramp. The daylight, although dim and overcast, still seemed bright and harsh on her eyes. At the rear of the AFV Stacey was cooking breakfast, holding court on his skills and surrounded by a group of about fifteen people. She bypassed them and headed a few metres into the tree line. On her return, she grabbed a coffee and decided to find out what was going on. As she walked up the stern ramp of the HQ AFV she could hear the arguing.

"This is bloody ridiculous," said someone as Natasha entered the cigarette smoke-filled command centre.

Clustered around the polymer map table were a dozen people; the vehicle navigators were all seated, with the senior officers standing behind them. A mass of fingers and hands were pointing to separate parts of the terrain map displayed on the table. Ash fell off someone's cigarette and lay in a heap among spilt coffee and cups.

"Morning. We're lost," said Alex, looking at Natasha and smiling warmly.

"Oh. Why?" asked Natasha, wondering if she was expected to contribute to the debate.

"We're in a maze of logging trails not shown on any of the terrain maps. Some seem to lead somewhere, others are dead ends, and some just go round in circles. We've been wandering about for hours burning fuel."

"Ah-ha," said Natasha, and then paused. "So what we need to do is understand how to navigate the logging trails…"

Crockett picked up on the train of thought. "Yoh… hold on. The loggers. There must be some logic to this maze. They won't only rely on GPS."

"Have we checked for signposts?" asked Alex.

The room remained quiet.

DAY 27

The next time Natasha woke up was to a cheer as they finally emerged from their off-road trek onto a main highway.

"Stacey, you're buying tonight," quipped O'Reilly.

"I will, you Irish bastard, but not before I've had a long hot bath. My limbs are as stiff as hell, the bloody hydraulics have been playing up for the last few miles and Betsy here has been a real donkey to steer."

"Hey, Captain, I checked the base guide book; there's a bar called Naughty Girls near the base in Nord Jensen. Any chance of some R and R?" asked O'Reilly.

"Definitely," acknowledged Schaefer as he unhooked himself from his headset.

"Naughty Girls? That just about sums you lot up. We've just survived what has to be a military first and all you can think about is a lap dance," interjected Sanchez.

"How did you know it's a lap dancing bar?" asked O'Reilly.

"I worked there," replied Sanchez winking at Natasha.

Schaefer opened the stern ramp and Natasha was one of the first out onto the roadway. For a few seconds she enjoyed the quiet, tranquil scene that her senses were delivering, decoupled from all the electronics of the AFV. Her surroundings seemed magnified. It felt good. She shook her head, wondering for an instant whether this thought process would lead anywhere else or whether she would forget it in a few minutes. She decided she would try and recapture and build on it later.

Ahead of her stretched the main road that ran the length of Scandinavia, the E-18, lined either side with trees, their branches heavy with snow. A light ground mist, just several feet thick, provided an almost magical scene.

Schaefer slid down the hull of the AFV and Alex, Grant and Jones joined them.

"Thank God for that. I was beginning to wonder if we'd ever find civilisation again," said Alex.

"It seems like we've been gone for months," echoed Natasha.

"You notice anything strange about this road?" Jones asked.

"No. It's straight and long. But I'm sure you're going to tell us," replied Alex.

"Looks like it hasn't been used in a while."

Natasha looked. He was right. With the exception of their own AFV tracks, there was no sign of any recent use. The weather had been fine for the past thirty-six hours, no wind and no snow, so where had all the traffic gone?

*

Without sufficient fuel to get all the AFVs to the Nord Jensen base, they decided to separate into two groups. Three AFVs led by Schaefer would make contact with the base; the remaining three would wait where they were.

Schaefer's engineering AFV, Echo One, sat squat with a look of contentment in the snow. Its white and gunmetal grey leopard-stripe camouflage seemed strangely at odds but at the same time in concert with the surroundings. Natasha reached out and stroked the hull of the AFV; it felt like ceramic. Schaefer was checking the supports and cabling on the mine detection and sweep assembly, which protruded from the front of the vehicle like an insect's proboscis. The system used a combination of neutron and magnetic resonance imaging to detect mines. If it did, it then employed what Schaefer described as a glorified Van de Graaff generator to fry the electronics in them. The assembly was kept at a constant 2 metres above ground level, rather like a stabilised gun mount.

"Morning, Captain K, you coming with us?" asked Sanchez with a smile, as she clambered out of a hatch and on to the roof of Schaefer's AFV, dragging a signal cable.

"Not this time; Stacey and O'Reilly have persuaded me to stay with them so I can accompany them to Naughty Girls later on. We'll miss you. You almost ready?" replied Natasha.

"Should be ready in thirty minutes or so. The roads up here are built on about six feet of polystyrene foam blocks to stop subsidence in the summer when the frozen topsoil melts. I've got to upload the library for the signature and run a calibration check before we're good. I've become almost paranoid about mines after the relay station, and without our reactive armour, I want the mine detection to be fine-tuned."

"Reactive armour?" asked Natasha.

"Yeah. The AFVs have a void between the inner and outer hulls. It's normally filled with a kinematic gel that's designed to capture high-velocity projectiles from mines and the like. Trouble is that SOP is to remove the gel to save weight during air lifts. So all we've got is air," advised Sanchez.

CHAPTER 6

CONTACT

Adaptation means things like avoiding a convenient route when it is realised that it has features that lend themselves to ambush.

Sanchez checked her threat boards again as Schaefer's AFV Echo One led the convoy of three AFVs at a steady 15 kilometres an hour along the deserted snow-covered E-18 towards the Norwegian army base.

All her boards remained green; there was nothing: no electronic fields, no sign of mines, no data traffic, nothing. She looked at the internal CCTV feed from the combat team cabin. The guys were joking and singing about what they'd be doing in Nord Jensen that night.

Her thoughts turned to Captain Kavolsky. It wasn't often that Sanchez liked an officer outside of the squadron but Natasha was different. She behaved like she was just one of them, no airs and graces, no demarcations.

Her threat boards lit up. Ahead of them was a pass with steep rocky sides. Ideal ambush terrain. She flashed the threat to Lieutenant Stevenson who had replaced O'Reilly on weapons.

"And into the valley of death rode the fools," joked Stevenson, flicking a stray blonde hair away from her face.

"Captain. Threat. I've got a couple of tickles on the mine detectors but well below the threshold, probably some iron in the rocks around here. We're still good to go," advised Sanchez.

"Roger that."

Fifty kilometres away, Natasha had been talking with Alex and Johnson about the continued lack of any sign of people or communications when the contact alarms announced. Together they turned to see the video-feed from the Musicians that showed a burning AFV. Alex flipped a switch and the audio feed from Schaefer and the other AFVs flowed into the room.

"Mike One's KIA. Sanchez is reporting Mark Two Vulcan fire, designated Black One. Location is somewhere at the north-east of the pass. No signs of ground troops or other positions. No e-sig. No signs of any laser targeting. She reckons they must be using fibre optic-based imaging," reported O'Reilly.

*

Inside Schaefer's AFV the incoming fire sounded like a high-frequency whine as rounds impacted the armour. Sanchez again checked the AFV's skin sensors, which were designed to detect laser target designators. They were still green. She checked the audio sensors: the signal was poor but indicated that the fire was coming from the right-hand side of the pass. She spotted a gulley to their left, which looked like it could provide a defilade, and Schaefer immediately ordered the AFV into it. "Driver. Hard left, head for the gulley."

Sanchez felt the AFV shudder, loll to one side and then stop as one of the track assemblies collapsed. An electrical fire broke out and a thick black toxic smoke rolled around the cabin. Alarms sounded and were soon followed by yellow strobes warning everyone that the Halon fire-suppression was about to initiate and that they should don their built-in breathing masks or BIBs. Her eyes were already stinging and her throat felt sore as she fumbled for the mask that was hanging nearby. She forced herself to calm down as she brushed her hair aside to make sure the mask seals were good, then pulled the straps to release the cool oxygen. The smoke and heat from the electrical fires was now intense. The hull shuddered again and this time daylight poured in as the starboard side of the cabin split open, releasing some of the heat and smoke. Next to her, Stevenson hit the emergency evacuation button and the crew escape hatches blew open. On her headset, Sanchez vaguely heard an exchange between Schaefer and Stevenson culminating in the order to abandon the AFV. She released her seat harness, dropped down and groped her way to the floor-mounted hatch. As she did, she found herself hung up on her oxygen and headset comms lines. Fuck it, they must have got tangled up in something. She took a deep breath and pulled off her headset and mask then dived head first into the snow beneath the AFV.

She was alone. As melted wiring insulation dripped out of the hatch into the surrounding snow she tried to work out where the others had gone. Shit! She'd forgotten her helmet. Her eyes were streaming and stinging from the acrid electric-smelling smoke that billowed out of the escape hatch above her and swirled around. There were screams coming from inside the AFV.

*

Natasha felt useless as she watched the feed from Beethoven. The carcass of Schaefer's AFV had still not exploded but it was burning fiercely. Some of the vehicle's crew were moving, some crawling, some helping wounded who were leaving thermal blood trails on the snow-covered road surface.

"Alex, look where Crockett's AFV is; they've got defilade. Can't we use that info?" she asked.

Alex nodded and instructed Crockett to send them the sensor records over the last sixty seconds.

"Got it. Stand by one. We can also use the audio detectors. I'll try and back trace," came the response.

Before they got any further, Schaefer's AFV exploded. Pieces of it were thrown skywards and across the road. Stevenson, who Natasha recognised by her pink scarf, and someone else narrowly missed being decapitated as a piece of track assembly cartwheeled over them. Some of the troopers were firing their weapons uselessly at the surrounding rock faces.

"Get into cover!" she shouted, but her voice sounded squeaky and quiet; it was like one of those nightmares you'd have as a child when you couldn't run away from the danger.

"Fuck! They can't get at Crockett so they're going after the survivors from Schaefer's AFV," growled Johnson.

The surviving crew from Schaefer's AFV were now picked off one at a time. Shredded pieces of red and white-clad body parts were dumped like pieces of meat around the roadway. Eventually, only one trooper remained. Beethoven's cameras magnified his image.

"That's Abrams. What the hell's wrong with him?" asked O'Reilly.

82

Natasha watched the figure; he seemed to be oblivious to the danger he was in and was wandering along the road with his arms outstretched in front of him. He continued for another few paces before his body was literally sliced vertically down the middle, the two pieces falling like salami onto the ground.

"I've got a fix. East side of the pass. Uploading coordinates now!" Crockett advised.

"Beethoven engaging."

Two HE missiles sped out from Beethoven towards a position on the rock face.

"Missiles on target. I think we got one. But I've still got no idea where the western gun is located," reported O'Reilly.

*

At the other end of the pass from Crockett, Schaefer, Sanchez and four other survivors were trapped.

"There's no way we can reach Crockett from here. We'll try and use the gulley and move south. Leave anything heavy. Sanchez, Crest, you two rig a carry bag for Kurz here. Porter, you provide cover. Let's get ready to move," ordered Schaefer.

They set up a makeshift stretcher for Kurz, and as they dragged him onto it Sanchez caught sight of a large piece of AFV bodywork protruding from his stomach. She knew he wouldn't make it unless they could get him to Johnson.

They started to move along the shallow gulley dragging Kurz behind them on a makeshift sled made from the AFV escape hatch. It was hard work: they couldn't stand or even crouch, so they had to lie on their sides and push down into the snow with their boots then heave Kurz several feet forward before repeating the process again.

They'd covered no more than 20 metres when Sanchez's foot punched through the snow and her boot became entangled with a cable.

"We've got mines. Remote controlled," she announced.

"Oh, fucking great. What the fuck are we supposed to do now?" said Crest.

"Disarm them," she replied, already digging out a smooth white cylinder from the snow and breaking the fibre optic bundle that connected it to its host.

Ironically, it was Sanchez's efforts that forced the artificial intelligence system controlling the mines to respond. When it detected Sanchez disabling some of the mines it reasoned that if it did not attack them now, then the mines would be lost for no gain.

The mines were designed to be propelled into the air before exploding and spraying the area with ceramic darts. The mine closest to Sanchez hit a rock overhang and was deflected before detonating, leaving her badly concussed but alive. As her eyes regained near focus, she found herself staring at someone's lower abdomen and legs. The upper torso was missing. She picked up an empty helmet and tried to activate the communications gear before realising that the signal and power cable ended in thin air, the transceiver and battery pack had disappeared.

She slumped back against the gulley side; further along she saw Crockett's AFV bomb burst out of the gulley, before crashing over the wreckage of Mike One and leaving the pass. *Well, at least some of the guys have got out,* she thought as the sound of more explosions echoed around the pass then died away. Then the effort of staying conscious became too great, she gave up and slipped into a welcome blackness.

CHAPTER 7

ESCAPE AND EVASION

So unless your heart is wide open and your mind is orderly, you cannot be expected to adapt responsively without limit.

The sound of crunching snow woke Sanchez from unconsciousness; she was lying in the gulley at the side of the road. The sun had dipped below the horizon and the snow had developed that early evening crust that felt jagged and unforgiving. It was the type of snow that broke under foot, and although she couldn't see where the sound was coming from she knew instinctively that whoever was making it would not be friendly.

Involuntarily she felt her grip tighten on her weapon. Strange, she thought, she couldn't remember having picked it up. Slowly, she brought the weapon up to her chest and checked its status display. It was green, full magazine, set to automatic on five-round bursts, soft targets. Standard trooper selection. She selected single shot and slid the safety to off.

The sound was coming closer, and she worried that the warm air from her breathing would be seen. Should she hold her breath? No. She decided that breathing through her nostrils would be OK. Very slowly, she turned her head towards the direction of the sound. From her vantage point, lying just below the level of the road, she could see several pairs of airborne-style combat boots with white camouflage trousers tucked into the tops. The boots moved, picking their way through the wreckage and debris from her AFV that littered the road. She watched as a pair approached the body of a trooper; they paused and then kicked it to check for life. The body absorbed the kick like a sack, and the boots moved on.

The boots paused and were joined by a second pair, like two dancers, the crunching of the snow providing the rhythm. They stopped at another body. From the pink scarf that lay on the snow Sanchez knew it was Lieutenant Stevenson. Again, the boots kicked, but this time the body recoiled as Stevenson curled up into a ball. Her pretty face turned towards Sanchez and for an instant their eyes met and Stevenson winked at her. The boots moved backwards a step and paused. A second later Stevenson's head exploded as a single shot rang out. Brain matter and blood sped towards Sanchez but dropped short on the snow. Stevenson's face no longer existed; a tangled mass of blood and blonde hair was all that remained.

There was a low guttural exchange of words that Sanchez could not understand and then the boots started to move again, but this time away from her, 5 metres then 10. Then, just as she started to relax a fraction, the boots stopped and angled back towards her location. She fought against the urge to immediately engage; she needed to think the situation through. How many more of them were there? Where would they be? Which way should she bug out? For some reason she remembered what Stacey had said after the minefield, how he had decided to follow the route that had already expended some of its ordnance. She would go north, back the way they'd come into the pass.

As she tensed her muscles in preparation to move, she felt a movement next to her left foot, lower down in the gulley. Meanwhile the boots stopped again; it was almost as if they could sense her presence. Careful not to attract attention, she turned her head very slowly to see who was touching her foot. Schaefer met her gaze. She put a finger to her lips to be quiet, then pointed to her left and held up two fingers indicating that at least two soldiers were close. He nodded in acknowledgement. She held up a trigger finger, followed by a single finger pointing to the northern end of the pass. The boots started again; they were coming directly towards her. She signalled Schaefer that he was to provide cover for her, then held up three fingers signifying on the count of three.

As she reached zero the boots stopped. She rose to a kneeling position. One bad guy wore a white balaclava, the other a black one. She tracked her weapon left a few degrees until she had White Balaclava in her sights. He reacted, first his gloved hand moved to activate the throat mike: then stopped as he decided instead to go for his weapon. Mistake, thought Sanchez, as she fired a single shot. Both white-gloved hands went up to the throat as he tried unsuccessfully to prevent his balaclava changing colour to dark red. Next to her, Schaefer fired a five-round burst and Black Balaclava dropped into the snow. Sanchez stood and looked around the pass; there was no one else standing, just bodies and debris. She checked behind her in the gulley to see if anyone else from their AFV had made it. It was just her and Schaefer.

"You good to go?" she asked Schaefer.

"Yeah, I'm good," he replied as he got to his feet, working out the cold from his limbs.

"We'll use the road. We got hit with robot sentries and I'm sure our friends would have stood them down before venturing in here but we need to move quickly; they will send another team or turn the bastards back on. So let's go," she said giving him a pull up on to the roadway by his harness.

Together, they moved north along the roadway as if they were in a drill. "Fire and manoeuvre. Fire and manoeuvre," her instructor used to yell during her boot camp days. Zigzag 20 metres, swivel, hit the deck, roll to the right or left, scan the area, pick your targets, scream "Covering fire", fire three to four shots, wait for your partner to arrive and then do it all over again. It was hard work, but at least she wasn't in full battle dress; all she had was her personal belt with ten magazines of ammunition and her survival kit.

They cleared the area where her AFV had been destroyed and she did her best to ignore the dead: some whole, others in pieces.

They'd covered 700 metres and reached Lieutenant Lefevre's AFV wreckage before they were engaged. "Covering fire!" screamed Schaefer. It was her turn to sprint. She rose from behind a large section of the AFV's wreckage, her legs growing tired. She started zigzagging towards an imaginary line just behind where Schaefer lay prone, now shooting at someone behind her.

She slipped and went over backwards. "Shit!" she shouted, before rolling to her right as incoming tracer flew past her. She could see half a dozen figures at the southern end of the pass. She got her breathing under control, selected her targets and screamed, "Covering fire!" letting Schaefer know he could move.

By the time she reached the northern end of the pass and took cover, her lungs felt like they were going to explode. Incoming rounds were cracking against the surrounding rock faces. She tried to calm her breathing down. Her lungs felt sore. She held her breath and counted to three. Feeling more in control she searched for targets. The sights picked up a thermal image and then movement behind some wreckage about a hundred metres away.

Schaefer had about 40 metres still to go. "Covering fire!" she yelled. A click came from her weapon. Shit! She'd not only forgotten to count the rounds remaining but also not checked the weapon status display. She saw Schaefer starting to get up. "Reloading!" she managed to scream. Schaefer heard her and dropped back down again.

She ejected the empty mag, fumbled in her belt for another, then paused. *Calm down*, she told herself. She carried on talking to herself. *Take your time reloading. Don't slam the mag in; it may look good but more times than not it won't engage properly and you'll have to do it again. By that time you could be dead.*

She checked the magazine wasn't full of snow or ice, tapped it against the side of her weapon to make sure all the rounds were hard up against the back-stop and aligned, then gently fitted it into the weapon. She heard it click into place, pulled back the slide that lifted the first round and let it run forward into the chamber. A green ready light came up on the weapon information screen together with the number and type of rounds in the magazine.

She had two bad guys in the open, the rest moving along the gullies either side of the roadway. Fuck it, they'd almost got Schaefer in a crossfire. She selected full automatic, then yelled at Schaefer, "They've dispersed, wide screen, I'll go full auto, you take the left. You copy?"

"Copy," he shouted back.

She yelled, "Covering fire!" then emptied a magazine in an arc from the centre of the roadway to the right.

Schaefer flew past her still firing wildly behind him before diving for cover.

"Thank fuck for that," she heard him mutter, out of breath.

They now just had to manage one last dash then they'd be out of the pass and could get off into the forest. Sanchez took a series of deep breaths trying to get as much oxygen into her blood as possible.

"Last evolution, then we'll break left to the west and into the trees. Ready?" she asked.

"Let's go."

She rose and ran weaving towards the end of the pass, dodging one way and then the next, trying not to be silhouetted against either the walls or the entrance to the pass. A hundred metres further along they left the road and entered forest. The going was tough; a thin layer of frozen crust covered nearly three feet of powder snow. Every step they took punched through the crust and they had to work hard to move.

"We've gotta put some distance between them and us. We need to go before the rest arrive. There were certainly another three or four who came into the pass," said Schaefer.

"I'm good to go. Those bastards will have to get through this just like us," managed Sanchez between breaths.

They continued heading away from the road, ignoring the noise they were both making, knowing that each pace they covered would take them closer to safety. After nearly an hour Sanchez's legs were no longer responding, her thighs had gone beyond jelly. It was now dark.

"I need a break. Anyone who's made the effort to follow us this far deserves to kill us. They'd have earned it," she said, simply sitting down on the surface of the snow, her legs still embedded several feet.

"You got any night-vision gear? I lost mine somewhere along the way and my WINSS is trashed," asked Schaefer.

"*Nada*. Left everything in the AFV. But the WINSS on this is good."

Sanchez powered up her WINSS, or weapon integrated navigation and night-sight system. As part of their mission prep, she'd uploaded the maps of the area and marked on them the location of the ERV point, major landmarks and possible refuges. Every hundred steps she'd entered a way point into the memory. She looked at the display. "I reckon we're about two klicks off the highway."

"Let's take ten and do an equipment and ammo check," he suggested.

In addition to their weapons and about a thousand rounds of ammunition, they had the usual assortment of survival gear: sewing needles, thermal blankets, signalling mirrors, flares, matches, two mini hydrogen fuel cells for torches and weapons, water-purifying tabs, three chocolate bars, some high energy tabs, a pack of Superman pills designed to keep you going on adrenaline for a few hours, a red penlight, three compasses, and a first aid kit.

Sanchez looked at the WINSS again.

"I suggest we keep going on this heading then swing north-east to join the E-18. Here, have a chocolate bar. I'll lead?" she offered, standing up and cramming a chocolate bar into her mouth.

With only one night-vision screen it was difficult going. Every 200 steps they stopped, partly out of exhaustion but also to execute a watch and listen stop for five minutes. Four hours later they broke out of the trees onto an open rocky plain. Here, they made better progress, as the snow was only a couple of inches deep. They'd been moving fast for three hours when the night suddenly got darker. Sanchez cranked up the gain on the WINSS and looked out at the sky.

"Fuck it. There's a storm coming. We need to buckle up," she said, disconnecting part of her equipment harness and offering one end to Schaefer so he could attach himself to her.

"Another storm, well, that's a twist," joked Schaefer as he tied himself off.

Within minutes they were in a blizzard. Reasoning that their tracks would soon be covered, they pushed on. Sanchez was beginning to hurt from the cold when her WINSS system went blank.

"Piece of crap WINSS is out. I knew I should have brought my assault weapon but I left it with Captain K," she muttered as she tried to reboot the system without success.

"With these clothes, we're going to get into trouble here; we can't build a shelter on this plateau," he said, referring to the fact they were only wearing their standard combat gear and not the G9 snowsuits.

"I know."

"How far before we get back into forest?"

"I reckon we've got six more klicks," replied Sanchez.

"Let's move. I'll navigate."

Within an hour, Sanchez knew she was beginning to suffer from the first stages of hypothermia. The day's events had sapped her strength and now the weather was draining what she had left. As she self-diagnosed, all the signs were there; a loss of will and a dreamlike state started to overtake her. She'd been trudging along behind Schaefer, blindly trusting his judgement, when an inner voice told her to stop and check. She grabbed Schaefer and ordered him to stop. He just stood there and gazed at her; she could see he was withdrawing from reality. She had to put the compass down in the snow she was shivering so much; the lanyard was too short so she had to kneel down to check their direction. "Stand up and wait!" she ordered Schaefer, frightened that he would sit down and not move again. She wrote down in the snow the direction they were following three times before she convinced herself that Schaefer had been leading them due south instead of north.

She took over the navigation again and they backtracked north, the weather got worse, visibility was nil and her mental state deteriorated until all she could think about was putting one foot in front of the other. At some point she resigned herself to die; she had nothing left. She was about to undertake her last step and then give up and just sit down in the snow when she collided with a wooden door. Schaefer stumbled into her and then collapsed. She fought the urge to just sit down and join him and instead some inner voice told her to find the handle and get the door open. She groped around the door frame and was rewarded with the discovery of a thick loop of rope that held the door in place. Part of her brain told her to find the knot and untie it, then another voice told her not to be stupid; there wouldn't be a knot. She lifted the rope and the door blew inwards with the wind. With the last of her strength she dragged Schaefer inside.

She found her penlight on the end of a piece of parachute cord around her neck and turned it on. She pulled Schaefer to one side and closed the door, latching it with another rope, and then looked around. A wood-burning stove sat in the centre of the hut; she checked it and found it full of kindling and logs, ready to go. She removed her gloves and searched for a flare in her survival pack but it had disappeared. "Fuck it," she muttered. She checked Schaefer's pockets but they seemed to be just full of snow. She looked around again and spotted a book of matches sitting next to the stove. The match heads were exposed, and a large strike surface was duct taped to a wooden upright nearby. She picked up the matchbook, trying to control the shaking of her hands, then giving up, just held the shivering matches against the strike surface. They flared into a bright white light and as gently as possible she laid the burning matches in the kindling. Within seconds, the fire had taken hold. She left the grate open, allowing as much warmth and light as possible to flood into the room.

"Good. We've got warmth and shelter. Next thing is to sort out Schaefer," she mumbled to herself, self-testing her capability to speak and reason.

There was a wooden bed along one side of the hut covered with old grey coarse blankets. She dragged Schaefer onto it, propping his legs up against the wall so his brain received as much blood with as little work as possible, then started checking his vital signs. For a few minutes she thought he'd died. She couldn't find a pulse. She shone her penlight into his eye and the pupil constricted. He was alive, just.

She stoked the fire and then set about finding a metal pot to boil some water. It wasn't perfect but steam was steam. As she waited for the water to boil she fought the temptation to fall asleep by managing to find a cigarette in her smock. As the water started to steam she checked Schaefer's combat clothing. It was remarkably dry, just a few handfuls of snow, which she scooped up and tossed on the floor and then covered him with a pile of the coarse grey woollen blankets. Finally she placed the boiling water under the bed where the steam would percolate, and got under the covers with him. Neither the howling wind nor the angry banging of the door as it thudded to and fro against the frame registered with her as she dived into sleep.

*

Sanchez dreamt that she was in a tree house in a forest. A wind was howling. Beneath her, a pink scarf blew across the snow. She tried to reach it but couldn't climb down because there were wolves with bright red eyes surrounding the bottom of the tree. A man dressed in black was hacking at the base of the tree with an axe.

She awoke with a start. Fragmentary images of the engagement and their escape burst into her mind. She was hugging her weapon and it took a moment to remember where she was. The red glow of her penlight was still on and she recognised the grey blankets she'd pulled over her earlier. Schaefer was next to her; he was breathing deeply and regularly. Thank God. She could hear the wind whining and the hut's wooden door rattling; the storm was blowing itself out. She got up and restocked the fire before crawling back into the bed.

Next time she awoke the wind had died away. The hut was dark, silent, and smelt of wood smoke. She felt warm. Schaefer had his arm around her and was gently stroking her hair.

"Morning, Captain," she said.

"And you."

She turned her head to face him, and before she could stop herself very gently kissed him on the lips. He responded with a passion that surprised her. She would always recall the strange sensation of his mouth being so cold and then warming as their tongues explored one another. It was as if a wall had been blown in as they gave themselves up to one another. Untapped reserves of energy were let loose. They fought to get one another's clothes off. Ignoring their weapons, and the tangle of buttons, harnesses and straps, he managed to open her combat smock. The cold no longer seemed to feature as he pulled her thermals up, his fingers finding her breasts. She opened her legs and pulled his hand down between her thighs. She felt him rubbing her pubis through her combat trousers and felt the warmth start to emanate. She undid his belt, pulling his trousers roughly down but not managing to get them over his boots. The wind picked up and the door started to rattle again.

He finally managed to undo her trousers enough to push his hand down inside them. Her heart rate and temperature soared as his hand first touched her pubic hair and his fingers felt her wetness. She moaned slightly as he gently slid a finger inside her, and she held her breath as the excitement she felt was amplified by their surroundings.

As her hand found his penis and she stroked him, the door blew open. They continued for a minute but the room temperature fell rapidly. Schaefer pulled away from her embrace and hopped across to close the door with his trousers wrapped around his boots. He hopped back to the bed and burrowed under the covers to find her. The roughness of the old woollen blankets compared to the smoothness of his skin made her senses tingle.

He knelt between her legs with a blanket over his shoulders and looked at her. She still had one of her boots on, with one leg of her combat trousers bunched up to it. His chest looked smooth and supple. Supporting himself on both hands he entered her. She rolled him over and climbed on top of him, pushing down and grinding her pubis against him. She arched backwards, her combat smock open, her thermals pushed up, teasing him with her breasts. She felt their bodies' coldness slowly being replaced with warmth and then heat and sweat as they started to move rhythmically. The emotional trauma of the last few weeks and the preceding months' combat somehow enhanced her pleasure as she leant forwards, and pinning his arms by his sides and pushing down on him, cried out in climax.

Next time she woke up the room was dark, the fire had gone out and the wind had stopped. She slowly extricated herself from Schaefer and then groped around the floor for her penlight. She looked around the hut. In the centre was the cast-iron wood-burning stove from which rose a metal chimney. There were two beds, and a table with no chairs. The décor was finished off with some shelves that looked like they'd seen better days and upon which sat an antiquated radio, even older-looking snowshoes and an assortment of tins and provisions. Her stomach rumbled in anticipation, reminding her of how hungry she was.

She looked around for some more wood for the fire but apart from two lonely-looking logs, there was none left. She'd need to venture outside. "Wood, fire and then breakfast," she muttered. Schaefer snored in response.

She dressed then pulled open the wooden door only to come face to face with a wall of snow. As she dug an exit using one of the old snowshoes, the first rays of bright sunlight broke through. Outside it was a clear blue sky, no wind. Scrambling out and up onto the surface, she had to squint in the sunlight. Around her were pine trees and giant snowdrifts; the only part of the hut that was visible was the chimney stack. She lay on her back looking up at the sky for a few minutes before deciding she should start digging out firewood from the log pile stacked neatly against the wall.

With an armful of logs she returned to find Schaefer awake, lying in bed, his head propped up on one arm.

"Morning, Captain," she said.

"Good morning, Corporal," he replied.

"What's the plan?" she asked.

This was the fork in the road, she thought. Is it a combat thing or is it real? She waited for his response.

"You know I've dreamt about this moment for the last fourteen months," he replied.

"And the plan?" she asked, feeling elated.

"Well, phase two is getting back to the squadron. But before that, it's breakfast. I don't know about you but I'm starving."

They examined the tins of food.

"I can't read Norwegian, and some of the labels have disappeared from old age, but we do have what looks like vegetable soup, tuna, corned beef, beans, sardines, carrots and potatoes," said Schaefer.

"Sounds good. You cook, I'll get the fire going again," she replied with a smile.

With the hissing and crackling of the logs for company, they ate sitting cross-legged on the floor next to the stove.

"When I saw Stevenson executed, I felt like one of those mother antelopes you see on the wildlife shows. You know, the scene when her baby is taken down by a lion or hyenas or something. It pulls on your emotions until something snaps, but you move on, you can't afford to dwell on it. It's the first time I've felt anything like that. I don't know why I've been thinking about it. Maybe it's because for the first time in my life I couldn't do anything but I knew what was going to happen," she said.

Schaefer hugged her in consolation. "And thank you. You saved me last night. I was gone."

"I'll tell you, thank God for the locals, they take their survival seriously. The stove was rigged and ready to go. They had the matchbook ready, the strike surface marked, everything. If they hadn't I doubt I could have gotten the fire going."

"Probably be good if we left the place the same way we found it. Just don't ask me to do the washing up," he replied halfway through a mouthful of a mixture of tinned carrot and corned beef.

"What do you mean you've been waiting months for a moment like this?" she asked, relishing the question, and the response.

"It was in Siberia, outside Archangel. I don't know what happened, it was a bit like someone just threw a switch. You were sitting on a crate cleaning your weapon. As I walked past you flicked a cigarette away. From that moment I just knew I loved you."

"Jesus. That's it! I flicked a cigarette and you fell in love with me. My mother would love that story, true romance. She fell in love with my father when she saw him driving a tractor."

"What about me?"

"What about you?" she teased.

"Well, when did you discover you wanted me?"

"I haven't said I do yet. But if you must know, it's when you walked past me that time in Archangel and I tossed that cigarette away. I saw you smile and I liked it."

"Really?"

"Probably not. But it was your smile that I first noticed."

As the light faded they cleaned their weapons, checked their ammunition and stuffed their pockets with food, matches and kindling. Finally, they cleaned up the cabin making sure they prepped it as they had found it, ready for its next visitor.

"I'm not too sure where we are but I reckon if we head north-east for another six to ten klicks we should reach the E-18. All we then need to do is hike the remaining fifty klicks and we're home. We've got another forty-eight hours before they close the ERV, so we should be fine," she said.

"Well, at least we've got snowshoes," he replied, pointing to the antiques hanging on the wall.

*

There was no wind, and even though it was dark the going was infinitely easier with the snowshoes. Sanchez took point as they came within a kilometre of where they hoped they would meet up with the E-18. She noticed the snow becoming firmer and she guessed that she was now on a track.

The next thing she remembered was a bright flash of light on her retina and then trying to sit upright. She was badly winded and her vision was distorted. She must have fallen. She forced herself to calm down. First things first. Check your breathing, test for broken bones. She moved each limb in turn, then not trusting just this check, also ran a hand over each arm and leg. Next she focused on her head; she could feel warm blood on her face, her jaw hurt and she had at least one loose tooth. The blood was coming from above her left eye, which she now realised was almost closed. She scooped up a handful of snow and pressed it against her forehead, and could feel the blood flow slow in response. She was trying to remember who she was with and what she'd been doing to end up like this when Schaefer slid down next to her.

"Jesus. One second you were in front of me the next you were gone. You dropped almost twenty feet, straight off an overhang."

"Tell me about it. I knew I should have slowed. I felt the ground change, I should have known. Must be losing my touch," she replied, beginning to recall the event.

"I hope not."

She managed a painful grunt in reply.

"My head feels like it's been in a fight, I can hardly move my neck and I've got some mild concussion. Can you have a look?"

Schaefer flicked on the penlight. "Shit. You're not going to enter any beauty competitions for a while. Nasty cut over the left eye, your cheek's banged up and bleeding. Looks like you head-butted that rock. We'll need to get you stitched up soon. You want anything?"

"No, not yet. Give me five to get myself together. You know, for a moment I couldn't even remember who I was with."

96

"That's just because you're fickle. Try and move your head from left to right," he said moving around her and checking the rest of her head.

"Shit, that hurts, it's like whiplash, I can't move more than about twenty degrees to my left, but it's OK to the right."

As they stood up she noticed a dull red glow from beneath the snow a few feet away.

"What the fuck's that?" she asked.

Together they circled it cautiously. Schaefer knelt down beside it and scraped away the covering of snow. It looked like a missile that had embedded itself in the ground. He gently wiped more of the snow away, then, gaining confidence, brushed more vigorously. It was tubular in shape and about 2 metres long and 30 centimetres in diameter. Around the circumference there were banks of smaller cylinders.

"I've never seen anything like it. There are very fine wires coming from each of these empty canisters, like a spider's web. It's not a weapon. It's more like a large antennae array."

"Let's get the fuck out of here. This place gives me the creeps. The highway can't be more than half a klick from here."

"This isn't ours," he continued; "look at these markings."

"No shit. Let's go."

They reached the highway thirty minutes later. It was covered in snow with no sign of any tracks.

"Well, nice to see nothing's changed. The place is as empty as it was when we were last here. You ready for a hike?" asked Schaefer.

"I need a smoke first," muttered Sanchez. Rummaging around in her pocket she pulled out a crushed packet of cigarettes and offered one to Schaefer. "You got a light?" she asked.

The sun started to come up.

"It's going to be a nice day."

CHAPTER 8

ERV

The morning means the beginning, the midday means the middle and the evening means the end. What this says is that soldiers are keen at first, but eventually slump and think of going home. So at this point they are vulnerable.

It had been nearly forty-eight hours since their contact in the pass. Their four remaining AFVs were laagered at the ERV in a small clearing set amidst the dense pine forest a few hundred metres off the E18. Here they waited, licking their wounds, sorting themselves out and following standard protocol in the hope that any survivors from the contact in the pass would find their way back.

Crockett's AFV was the only one that had escaped the pass. It was covered in score marks, and pieces of armour were missing or hanging off the vehicle. The rear ramp was open and a team were cleaning the interior that was still littered with bandages, plasma bags, frozen blood and burnt-out electronic equipment. Helmets, G9 snowsuits, body armour and other debris was piled up outside.

They had five wounded, the status of which Johnson had summed up with the following report: "They'll make it; we've got the usual – impregnation with ceramic darts, burns, shrapnel, shock, loss of blood. We're lucky all of the seriously wounded were killed."

In all, they had lost thirty-six. This included everyone from Schaefer's AFV, and ten from Crockett's. Only Lefevre had survived from his AFV after he was blown out of his command seat into the roadway.

The video, voice and sensor data from the Musicians and the AFVs had been amalgamated, and from this they'd put together a post-contact tactical analysis. The technology that had been used to engage them had shocked them and raised more questions.

Alex had explained how the ambush site had been well chosen, a classic choke point, well thought out, and would have taken a while to prepare. Using image recognition rather than lasers for targeting, their own AFV sensors had been rendered useless. They had been effectively blind to the fact they were being tracked and targeted. The main armament that they had been engaged with was a robot sentry using diamond-tipped rounds. With a muzzle velocity of more than 15,000 feet per second and a rate of fire of 2,000 rounds per second, the AFVs did not have a chance-they were literally sawn open. The mood pervading the squadron was one of anguish, tempered with fear. This, Alex had confided to Natasha, was something that he had not seen before.

Natasha had needed to clear her head and think on what Alex had told her. She reviewed her own feelings. Was she frightened? She finished her coffee, stretched, pushing her palms up towards the sun, and for the first time noticed Stacey and her flight crew who were helping repair Crockett's AFV.

"How's it going?" she asked. They were all seated in director's chairs arranged in a semicircle in the snow. Across their laps lay a fibre optic harness they had pulled from the underside starboard service hatch of the AFV.

"Bastard job, this bit. We have to sand the terminations down to five micron or else the junction box won't work," replied Stacey without looking up from his work.

Natasha focused on him as he gently moved the diamond paper across the end of a single fibre. She blew a deep sigh signifying she was impressed.

Hicks, Stacey's technician, looked up from behind his sunglasses. "The new Mark Three AFVs have the fibre optics woven into the armour, no junction boxes or harnesses, just a lot of redundancy. Problem is that it's going to be another couple of years before they're deployed."

"Captain, you think there's any chance there could be survivors?" asked Stacey.

"I've no idea. It was pretty chaotic. You saw the mines detonate in the gulley. What was left of Schaefer's team were right in the middle of it. But if you're asking if the ERV will remain open as planned, then of course. It's SOP; we owe it to them to stay on station," she said.

Before anyone could say anything else, O'Reilly's voice boomed out an announcement.

"Well shit, if it isn't the honeymoon couple!"

Natasha looked around and saw Sanchez and Schaefer being escorted inside the perimeter. She rushed over and instinctively hugged Sanchez, but as she drew back she saw her swollen and battered face.

"Yeah, I know, he's a wife-beater," said Sanchez, nodding in Schaefer's direction whilst managing a grimacing smile.

"Any of the others make it out?"

"No one," said Schaefer. "They executed anyone they found alive. Corporal Sanchez saw Stevenson shot in front of her."

Johnson bored a path through to them. "Corporal, let's get you inside and sort out your face," he ordered. "Captain, I'll see you afterwards."

Natasha went with Sanchez and Johnson to the medical AFV. Inside, she sat on a bench opposite Sanchez and shared a cigarette as Johnson examined her.

"You OK?" Natasha asked Sanchez.

"Honestly? I'm a little frightened; it's not just the kicking we've received though, it's our whole environment. Something has changed the country here. It's almost surreal," began Sanchez, before drawing a sharp intake of breath as Johnson dabbed at the cut above her eye.

"How do you mean?" asked Natasha.

"Hold still for just a while longer please, Corporal," interjected Johnson. "We're going to have to staple your eyebrow, otherwise you'll be bleeding all over the place as soon as your head thaws out."

Natasha remembered her brother getting stitches when she was young. "How many will she get?" she asked, reminiscing.

Sanchez laughed, and Johnson again told her to sit still.

"The weird thing is the wildlife," she continued. "After I fell we were walking along the road, and decided to take five. We bumped into a wildcat and her family in a small den. She just looked at us; she didn't move, there was no attempt to protect her children. Just stared. It was odd; I've never seen anything like it."

"Maybe she was frightened?" said Natasha, handing back the cigarette to Sanchez and blowing out a long plume of smoke that seemed to expand disproportionally into the confines of the cabin.

"No way. The opposite. It was if we didn't really pose a threat anymore. She seemed to be tolerant of us. Like we simply weren't relevant."

As Johnson completed stapling Sanchez's head, medic Nancy Strong arrived. "Ah hah. Nancy. Good of you to join us. I want her X-rayed and scanned. She's got severe whiplash," he muttered. Straightening up to his full height, he rubbed his back and stretched. "I'm going for a smoke, I can hardly breathe in here. Tell Captain Schaefer I'll see him in five."

Schaefer came in and Natasha caught a quick smile being exchanged between Sanchez and him. Maybe O'Reilly was right: a honeymoon couple.

Nancy Strong went into the next cabin to ready the X-ray machine.

"Well? What's the story?" whispered Natasha.

Sanchez smiled. "Yeah," she said. "He took advantage of me whilst I was at a low point."

"You two look good together."

"Thanks, although looking at her now I'm not sure how to take that," commented Schaefer.

*

Sanchez and Schaefer were debriefed. Initially they centred on the actual contact and the execution-style mopping up operations that they'd witnessed. It was Johnson who summarised it.

"Why bother to expend your energy and scant resources on prisoners or nurturing future resistance? Best to eradicate it, the resistance that is, before it can multiply. The body does the same thing when it's invaded."

"Jesus, you make it sound like we're a virus," exclaimed Crockett.

"I think that's exactly how our enemies view us," replied Johnson.

"Is there any chance some of the others survived?" asked Crockett, obviously not willing to accept what Johnson was telling him.

"From our AFV absolutely not. I don't know about Lefevre's," replied Schaefer.

"All right, thanks. No, we're certain from the Musicians' feed that no one except Lefevre got out of his," acknowledged Crockett.

Schaefer then described the object they'd come across in the snow. Natasha questioned him closely and then fetched Corporal Raven.

"What they've described sounds like that WAJIS, or whatever it was called, jamming system we drop-tested a few years back. Corporal Raven, you remember?" she asked.

"It does. It was a wide area information jamming system, codenamed WAIJS; it was developed out of Sandia Labs. The idea was to drop a large number of these units across the theatre of operations. Each would lay dormant, slowly acquiring a map of the wireless communications in its own area. The map would include frequency, volume and type of traffic as well as choke points and redundant routing. It was clever stuff. Each would then share the information acquired with the other units by piggybacking the comms traffic on the networks it was monitoring. Acting together, the units could then optimise disruption by jamming weak points and assessing the impact. The program was shelved because of lack of funding or some other thing."

Schaefer nodded. "It would explain the lack of comms traffic, whilst explaining the fact that we can communicate. We're new to the map and moving around, we're not regular communicators, so we've got no real pattern."

"Any way we can use what we now know to our advantage?" asked Alex.

"I like it. We'll get the techies together to come up with something; we might yet be able to order up a pizza delivery," said Crockett.

Alex laughed, and for the first time Natasha glimpsed the flash of the character that was normally hidden behind the armour of leadership.

"Right. We'll reconvene at 0600 tomorrow for a planning session. Captain Grant, how long before we're ready to move again?" asked Alex.

"Another twenty-four hours, we'll be good."

"Fine. Captain Crockett, tell everyone that we need to be ready to move in thirty-six hours. I know it's a small possibility, but that'll give anyone who did survive a little more time."

*

Natasha sat alone and looked at the night sky. The stars were out in force competing against the moon and the aurora borealis for attention. The air possessed a clarity that only winter and freezing temperatures could make happen. The sound of boots creating an alternating crunching and squeaking noise in the snow alerted her to someone approaching.

"Mind if I join you?" asked Johnson.

"I'd be happy."

Johnson sat down next to her, his tall frame making him seem slightly uncoordinated as he did so. He lit a cigarette.

"Where do you get the fuel for that thing?" she asked, referring to his Zippo lighter.

"O'Reilly," he replied as if she was stupid for asking.

"O'Reilly," she echoed.

They sat in silence for several minutes, each at ease.

"How's everything?" she asked.

"Injury-wise, not too bad. No real drama. But, as I told Alex, I'm more worried about their psychological state."

"He really cares about them, doesn't he?"

"Like a family."

"Has he got anyone?" she asked before she could stop herself.

Johnson blew a long line of smoke out into the cold night air before answering.

"Years ago. She died in an accident just after they were married. He was driving. You two would look good together."

She felt herself blushing. "Can I have a cigarette?" she asked.

"He's been beating himself up over what's happened. You know the thing, he could have planned it differently, used another route, etcetera, etcetera."

She thought about what Sanchez had described and the dead they'd left lying in the snow and shivered realising she'd left her jacket in the AFV. Johnson took his off and gave it to her; it felt warm from his residual body heat.

"The whole situation is different. I think whatever we had done would have ended in much the same way. We need to put away all our guilt in the 'I've fucked up drawer' and open the 'I will have vengeance drawer'," she said, surprising herself with the turn of her emotions.

"I will have vengeance?" he asked.

"Oh yes, by the time this is over I think we will need to."

Above them the northern lights flickered.

*

Jones opened the planning session with a simple yet comprehensive update on the events of the recent weeks and the situation in which they now found themselves. All in all, it was bizarre.

Crockett looked frustrated. "How come they've penetrated this far behind our lines? And what the hell happened to the mountain regiment we were trying to reach, for Christ's sake? That's a major force in anyone's books."

"That means they must be here in force. But why here; what's the significance?" asked Captain Grant.

"Well, we know they've been going after comms. It must be the road. Cut it and you more or less sever communication between the north and south of Scandinavia," answered Alex.

Schaefer stood up and paced the cabin. "But where were their ground troops? They only turned up afterwards. Why hold off when we were getting our butts kicked? They could have finished the job; we could have been completely wiped out."

"Maybe they're waiting for bigger things, maybe busy setting up other ambush points. I don't know," replied Lefevre, who was sitting on a medical equipment container whilst medic Nancy Strong changed the bandaging on his head.

"Well, we're in what I would now call rag order. We can't go south. We've got no comms with anyone and we keep getting chewed up without achieving shit," said Crockett.

"We can't just sit here. We've been AWOL for weeks, not seen another soul, and still managed to get ourselves reamed twice," added Grant in an exasperated voice.

Natasha felt herself getting annoyed with them. She stood up and used what she hoped sounded like an authoritative tone. "Listen to what you've all just said. We know they're targeting military installations and severing communications – that includes roads as well as data links. So let's find a population centre that is not a communications hub and without any nearby military installations. Somewhere that would not be deemed of any strategic or tactical value."

"And then?" asked Schaefer.

"Then we drive into it and ask what the fuck has been happening. Someone must know." She stopped, anxious she may have overstepped the mark but feeling better.

"Anyone got anything to add to what Captain K has suggested?" asked Alex in a voice that suggested admiration as well as a little surprise. No one responded.

"Good. So, let's find a suitable town."

Crockett brought up a map of their location and then zoomed out. Then he highlighted the roads, military installations and communications links. He stopped and clicked on a town called Alfjorden. "This looks as good as any," he said, bringing up some detail. "Population eighteen thousand, nearest military base is over a hundred and fifty kilometres to the east of it. Sits alongside a fjord, but the roadway that goes through it leads nowhere, just on to farms. It's like it's at the end of a spoke. We'll need fuel, but there must be some gas stations around here."

"Alfjorden it is then. Let's get a routing and ingress-egress plan. I also want our tracks covered from now on. Captain Grant, see if you can rig something to trail the vehicles. Sergeant Major Jones, please update the squadron's log," said Alex.

CHAPTER 9

ALFJORDEN

Therefore, those who win every battle are not really skilful – those who render others' armies helpless without fighting are the best of all.

Riding in the commander's chair of the AFV, Natasha felt herself drift into yet another upright sleep; she was getting good at this, it now seemed to be almost natural, and she had even managed to stop herself from dribbling while she snoozed. She let her thoughts go free, and found herself back in her days at college; she wondered where her friends were now.

Stacey's voice in her comms headset ended her reverie. "Milords, ladies and gentlemen… and any Irish aboard, ETA is two zero minutes."

The journey, although without incident, had been eerie; they'd seen no one. It was as if the whole area had fled. They'd stopped at two military fuel depots to replenish their hydrogen tanks; both installations had been abandoned.

As dawn broke, the squadron halted 5 kilometres from the town of Alfjorden.

"This is Six. Screening positions. We'll laager in the trees," commanded Alex.

As the AFV bounced to a stop, Natasha unhooked her hardwire comms link, toggled the switch to short range VHF, then clambered onto the roof of the AFV and slid down to the snow-covered roadway. She landed stiffly, her legs cramped from the drive. On the horizon, the sun hung like a pale orange in a white sky. She liked the fact that she could look straight at it without hurting her eyes.

"God, you're losing it," she muttered to herself.

A gap in the trees offered a glimpse of the town in the valley below. Through her field glasses, it looked somehow softer than the images from the stabilised stereoscopic camera mounted on the AFV. The town was either asleep or deserted. There was no movement, no heat vapour rising, nothing. Alex joined her as Grant's AFV passed them, its tracks throwing up a delicate blizzard of powder snow as it slewed into a gap in the tree line for cover.

"The Musicians are airborne. Let's go and watch," said Alex.

They entered Natasha's AFV combat control centre. Huddling around the displays showing the feed from the Musicians, they watched in anticipation as they moved along the main road into the town before coming up on what looked like a vehicle checkpoint or VCP. A barrier across the road, accompanied by a tired-looking tent and a sandbagged emplacement, announced that access to the town was restricted.

"Lieutenant Byrnes, can you get a low-angle shot from one of the scouts on that VCP?" asked Natasha.

"On the way."

The image stabilised and she captured a still and enhanced the magnification. As it grew on the screens, people jostled for the best view of the monitors. A biohaz sign came into focus.

From the adjacent driver's compartment, Stacey's voice spoke for all of them. "Oh, boy! This is fucking great. This is all we need. Don't tell me this is one of those fucking plague sites!"

"All right, let's continue the sweep," ordered Alex.

"I've got the feed, five by five on all boards. All sensors are good. We've got e-sig, probably from domestic electrical appliances working from battery storage, solar or wind power generators. Nothing worrying," reported Raven.

"Jesus, look at all the cars. It's like they were having a town meeting and left them overnight. The harbour area is backed up for a kilometre," said Byrnes.

"It looks like they've been left for a while," said Natasha.

"The IR sensors are clear, only occasional traces – probably animal. No people out and about," continued Raven in a dispassionate voice.

Ghostly images of the town were overlaid with occasional swirling faint heat traces and electric field markers.

As they completed the sweep Alex called an ops meeting.

"We're going to go in and find out what happened and provide any help we can. Captain Johnson will lead a medical team. Lieutenant Lloyd-Smith's gunners will provide some muscle. We'll treat this as a hot zone. Full CBRN kit. We'll also set up a delousing facility," said Alex.

"I'll take Lieutenant Tsang with me; she's had direct experience of working in a hot zone. Give us twenty minutes to gear up," said Johnson.

Natasha studied the young lieutenant. She'd got to know her through Johnson who'd told her that the thirty-two-year-old Chinese woman was the best combat MO that he'd ever come across. Not only practical, she had a PhD in molecular biology and had received numerous offers from industry. She'd joined the allied forces after both her younger brothers and parents had been killed during the Gobi Desert guerrilla wars.

"I want to go in as well," announced Natasha, preparing herself for a battle of wills as she saw Alex and Jones exchange glances.

"Captain Johnson," Alex said, "please break out some kit for Captain K. Sergeant Major Jones will accompany her. Now, although this place should not be of any military significance, we keep getting surprises. So we'll run close cover with the Musicians. I want to know about anything that emits an e-sig, and equally importantly, I want to know what does not."

*

The team assembled for a briefing in Alex's AFV. Johnson gave the overview.

"Ladies and gentlemen, we don't know what we're going to find. There could well be large numbers of infected and seriously ill people.

"Lieutenant Tsang and I will direct the team to the locations we want to see, and also advise when, where and what tests we will conduct. Our primary objective will be to get into the hospital. It's the regional medical centre, and in the middle of town, on the north-west shoreline of the fjord.

"We will be wearing full CBRN suits and be deloused as we egress. We'll also carry an extra set of CBRN kit for each team member and the usual array of large needles. With the snow and ice the streets will be slippery, so remember to wear the overshoes, otherwise you'll be sliding about like a bunch of penguins.

"All contact with people will be conducted as if they are contagious. The protocol will be simple. We will offer them food, water and medical treatment. They will all remain under quarantine within the town. Now Lieutenant Lloyd-Smith will fill in the practical military details."

The military muscle, as Alex had described it, was to be led by the most junior officer in the squadron, a twenty-two-year-old first lieutenant named Lloyd-Smith. The young Englishman's military pedigree stretched back generations. So far in fact that he had convinced many of the Americans that his ancestors had fought against theirs in the War of Independence. Although young for the command of the squadron's field artillery, he was supported by an experienced gun team led by a squat little French senior staff sergeant, Gyan, who in turn delighted everyone by telling them his ancestors had fought Lloyd-Smith's at Waterloo.

Lloyd-Smith stood with his hands on his hips, and his legs slightly apart, assuming what he obviously considered to be the stance of a leader. Around his neck he wore a pair of old-fashioned Zeiss binoculars that were apparently his great grandfather's. Clearing his throat and surveying his audience, he began. Natasha fought hard to keep a smile from developing, as she noticed a bright blue silk scarf beneath his combat smock. Jones whispered into her ear, "He also wears his spurs when he's riding the AFVs." She shook her head and surrendered to the urge to giggle.

Sergeant Gyan handed out a selection of CBRN packs. Natasha selected a small size, tore open the plastic packing and pulled out the vaguely familiar trousers with integral booties and the separate smock and gloves. The suit had two layers of active carbon sandwiched between two layers of bio-engineered silk impregnated with chemical disinfectant. These were in turn shrouded in layers of a hydrophobic cross-linked silicon oil-based polymer designed to repel any liquid. The material felt dry and smooth to the touch but crunched a little when you squashed it.

Within the confines of the AFV cabin, she was soon sweating with the effort of hauling on so much clothing. She was halfway through when she realised that she would need a larger size. Embarrassed at the fact she was delaying them, she struggled out of the small one and selected the next size up. Jones came past with the respirators and spare filters.

"Take a large one. You'll feel more comfortable. The suits don't breathe so I would also lose your thermals if I was you," he advised.

"Thanks. Guess I'll learn."

"Well, I hope we don't have to go through this too often."

"Make sure all your hair is free of the seal," Sanchez said, pulling some strands out of the way. "Then place your hand over the intake filter and suck in. If you can feel the mask tighten against your face it's good. OK?"

Natasha gave Sanchez the OK sign. The mask felt strange: her eyelashes touched the eyeglass, and the inside smelt like the packaging of new home electrical equipment.

"Comms check," announced Lloyd-Smith over her earpieces.

Sanchez handed her two syringes and an electronic sensor. "Captain, you only use these if told. It's simple- you jam it into your buddy's thigh and push the plunger. If you don't have a buddy you do yourself. Anywhere in the upper thigh is good. Got it?"

"Yeah," replied Natasha, staring in disbelief at the size of the needle.

"Don't worry, you won't have to use it. The juice in the syringes is good for nerve gas agents, useless for most biological, but it's SOP, so we have to take them."

"Thanks."

"Now, this little baby is an CBRN sensor it's great for a range of nerve and chemical agents, radiation, mustard gas, and that sort of stuff. If it sees any it will start whistling and the little red light will start flashing. You can hang it anywhere. Again, useless for bio weapons but SOP."

"Uh-huh. Do we have anything that will be of any use?"

"Your suit. Take good care of it."

*

Outside, the snow scooters were lined up in a row. Alex stood beside them wearing a short-sleeved shirt and fatigue trousers, talking to Johnson. Natasha walked across to join them, still wearing her respirator and feeling slightly stupid.

"You ready?" asked Alex.

"Ready? I feel like I'm back in basic," she replied whilst for some reason noticing the hairs on his arms standing on end in the cold.

"Very good. Let's go bug hunting," muttered Johnson, taking a final puff of his perennial cigarette, handing Alex the butt, donning his respirator, and clambering onto the scooter all in one movement. Tsang, carrying a large yellow kit bag, jumped on behind him and hugged his waist.

Natasha clambered on behind Jones and they followed Johnson as he sped off towards the town, a flurry of snow being kicked up in the air behind them. The pillion passengers reminded Natasha of the young girls clinging to their boyfriends on the back of motor scooters in a Mediterranean village.

They stopped at the abandoned VCP next to which was a noticeboard below a biohaz sign. The board was covered in messages and photos of people.

"Sir. There's a bunch of messages pinned up here, all in Norwegian," announced PFC Cook.

"Thank you, Private Cook," said Lloyd-Smith. "Well at least they're not in ancient Kurdish."

Natasha dismounted and strode up to the board; some of the messages were sealed in plastic bags to protect them against the weather; others had been left exposed. One in particular caught her attention; it was on pink paper and looked like a child had written it. She pulled it off the board, the drawing pins falling into the snow. It was addressed to *Mama og Papa*. The paper had the texture of old papyrus in her gloved hand. A deep sadness started to well up from inside her.

Alex's voice came over the net. "Sierra. This is Six. Get some stills then continue your sweep. We'll find some people to get them translated."

They mounted up again, and like tourists continued their exploration. They approached a crossroads. The first of a long row of wooden-clad buildings that made up the outskirts of the town was a hundred metres away. Lloyd-Smith held up an arm theatrically signalling them to stop.

His team dismounted and took up screening positions across the roadway. They all lay prone with the exception of Lloyd-Smith who stood in the centre of the road surveying the ground with his Zeiss field glasses. He was wearing two sidearms, slung like you'd see in an old Western movie. Natasha noticed Sergeant Gyan shake his head as Lloyd-Smith continued the show.

Finished with his reconnaissance, Lloyd-Smith issued his orders. "Colins, Zimbabwe and Frost. You are on sniper cover with the LR-51s. Sergeant Gyan, you and I can take a walk with Piper and Cook. Break out the mine detectors."

"Why is Sergeant Gyan called Tequila?" asked Natasha.

"I'll tell you later. He's an extraordinary character, the most decorated man in the French army."

"Really?"

"Really."

111

Natasha stood on the scooter's seat to get a better view as Lloyd-Smith executed the minesweeping operation in textbook fashion. Ahead of them and on the hill that led down to the town centre, the road was jammed with vehicles. Snowdrifts covered some completely. Thirty minutes later Lloyd-Smith made his report.

"All clear, Captain."

"OK. Let's get on with our job. Alex, you copying this?" asked Johnson, ignoring call sign protocol.

"Roger Sierra. Beethoven and Mozart still green."

Now travelling along the centre of the road in single file, they stopped for Johnson and Tsang to check their sensors.

Natasha patted Jones on the shoulder and shouted through her mask. "What do you think?"

"God knows. Looks like the *Marie Celeste*," came the muffled response.

"Green on sensors. No nerve, no chems, no radiation. We're good to go," said Tsang.

They threaded their way along the street between the abandoned cars. Natasha juggled her attention between keeping her knees from bumping into the vehicles, looking at the buildings and watching the repeater screens that were feeding images from the Musicians. The reality of the scene before her seemed magnified and yet oddly distant through the respirator faceplate; her own movement emphasised the stillness of the place. A shopping bag lay on the street partially covered in snow; a child's toy pink pig lay on the passenger seat of an abandoned car.

It started snowing again and the occasional flake stuck to her respirator eye lens. She shivered, one of those strange shivers that only affects the top half of your body and mixes a strange sense of anxiety partially offset by a feeling of security and warmth from the proximity of Jones in front of her, and the softness of the scooter's seat. Some of the houses had lights on. She wondered if they should stop and simply knock at a door to see if anyone was in. Many had plastic tape across the entrances, reminding her of TV crime scenes that said Police – Do Not Cross. Some of the tapes were red, others black. Other houses had windows covered with plastic sheeting. She pressed the pretzel on her throat mike.

"Captain Johnson. This is Kavolsky. Not sure whether you noticed but the houses here have some type of warning or exclusion tape across the doors. Like a crime scene."

"Yeah. It's SOP for a contagion. Red is for infected. Black means there are deceased in the building. The plastic sheeting is a poor man's isolation attempt."

Natasha was amazed that there were standard procedures in place for such an event.

"Do you think it worth checking if anyone's inside?" she asked.

Sergeant Gyan cut in. "All stop. We've got bodies in the streets. One o'clock from my pos."

Natasha looked over Jones's shoulder as Beethoven descended to street level, throwing up a cloud of snow from the rotor's downwash. On the pavement outside a Starbucks café, two figures sat on the street with their backs against the wooden hoarding.

"Hold your position. Do not approach," Johnson ordered.

"Roger. Sergeant Gyan, you take Piper and cover left, I'll take Cook and go right. Musicians will move to sentry positions," ordered Lloyd-Smith.

Johnson walked over to Natasha.

"You might want to see this. But check your suits first," he said.

Natasha and Jones checked one another's suits then approached the sidewalk but remained a few metres away as Johnson went forward to examine the bodies. With a reverence he gently brushed the light covering of snow from the faces of the figures. Natasha could soon see that they were an elderly man and woman as Johnson continued wiping snow away whilst being careful not to knock off the spectacles that the old man still wore. Johnson cleared his throat and began his report.

"Alex, we've got one dead male aged sixty-five or so and one dead female approximately the same age. Both have been dead for some time, I would say five days, but difficult to tell. Cause of death looks like hypothermia, they're only wearing raincoats and... God, would you believe it, their nightclothes. Both nasal cavities and the mouth are showing signs of discharge-looks like a combination of blood, saliva and watery sputum. I think Corporal Stacey may have been right: classic signs of pneumonic plague virus. Just going to take a look at their ankles... Yeah, we've got clear signs of pleural effusion. We can't do much of an autopsy with these two; they'd take forever to thaw out. So, Lieutenant Tsang, we'll do a viral swab analysis now."

"Six copies."

"You two can come over now if you like. We're going to perform a little analysis to see what it was that killed them," said Johnson.

Natasha and Jones exchanged glances and then cautiously approached the bodies.

"I guess they were man and wife," said Natasha pointing out the fact they were holding hands. "But why weren't they wearing any clothes? It must have been freezing out here."

Johnson sighed. "I would imagine they came here to die. Hypothermia as you almost found out is a fairly painless way to die. Probably preferable to what they were witnessing around them and what they would have to endure."

Tsang brushed a few snowflakes from her respirator eyeglass and opened up one of the yellow containers. It contained an array of glistening stainless steel and Perspex instruments and what looked like a very expensive audio amplifier. She touched a few buttons and a section slid open, revealing a bright blue light.

"How does it work?" asked Natasha, trying not to sound too stupid.

"Simple. I take a swab from the nasal cavity like so," she said, inserting what looked like a 1950s' ice cube grabber up the old man's nostril.

"The unit uses the polymerase chain reaction to map any viral DNA. This used to take hours, now with the nano tube pumps it takes minutes."

Natasha looked at the bodies again. They reminded her of the time she had said goodbye to her parents. Both had died within months of one another when she was in her early twenties, her mother first from cancer, then her father from what the doctors called a broken heart.

"Oh," she said, in a tone of complete ignorance.

Tsang studied the small screen, then flipped her comms to VOX-ALL.

"Mmmmm. OK. We've got confirmed common flu, pneumonic plague, tonsillitis, and... dengue?"

"Dengue?" queried Johnson, moving in to peer at the screen. "Interesting."

"What, like malaria?" asked Natasha.

"Yes, a little; it's transmitted by mosquito but it's a very different disease. Long incubation period. But we've also got a whole pile of gene fab modules here and other things that neither the database nor I recognise," said Tsang.

"Gene fab modules?" Natasha asked, feeling both stupid and afraid that she was being a nuisance.

"Yeah. The science was started by a bunch of computer software geeks back at the turn of the century who got bored with computing and turned their skills to genetic engineering. By establishing standard sequences of genes that do specific but very simple things you can chain-link them to start building up more complex systems and processes. For example, there are modules that act as a simple switch like a transistor, some that trigger a glow or change colour. You've probably seen the glow in the dark snails? Anyway, all sorts of stuff. Their presence is a sure sign that the virus that we're dealing with is man-made or at least man-modified."

"I wonder what their names were?" Jones asked rhetorically.

"Alex, we're done here. Request permission to continue to the hospital," asked Johnson.

"Sierra, this is Six. All sensors are green. Proceed."

"All Sierra. Check your kit. Respirators tight and sealed. Comms up. Weapons ready. I want own and buddy checks confirmed. We'll move on foot from here," Lloyd-Smith ordered.

In classic infantry patrol formation for built-up environments they now moved towards the town's centre. Gyan and Piper now covered the left, whilst Lloyd-Smith and Cook the right. Mozart and Beethoven hovered just above roof level a hundred metres ahead. The road had been blown clear of snow leaving a layer of shining blue ice beneath and Natasha slipped and had to grab hold of Jones to stop herself from falling. Ahead of her, Lloyd-Smith went down hard, losing grip of his weapon. As he started to get up, he stopped, staring into the open doorway of a pharmacy.

"Oh shit. Six. This is bad. We've got a lot of bodies in here."

PFC Cook stepped past Lloyd-Smith's position and went into the pharmacy. A moment later two shots rang out. Natasha felt herself being bundled to the ground by Jones. "Stay down," he ordered in a calm voice.

"Sit rep," requested Lloyd-Smith recovering his composure.

"Sorry, sir, but there was a dog in there munching on a body," replied Cook.

"Understood. Six, you copy? Captain Johnson, I assume you would like to see?"

"Six copies."

Natasha and Jones sorted themselves out and followed Tsang and Johnson over to the entrance as Lloyd-Smith and then Cook emerged from the inside. Natasha noticed the frightened eyes behind the respirator masks. Jones shone a powerful flashlight around the dark interior. The inside of the pharmacy had been ransacked; there was packaging and containers all over the floor. Lying amongst the debris were maybe twenty people of differing ages. The flashlight picked out grotesque images; some people were in sleeping bags, others were wrapped in blankets or winter clothes, others were just in night clothes. Frozen pools of body fluids, blood, vomit and excrement were spread across the white marble floor interspersed with a light covering of snow.

"Alex, this is bad. They're all dead. These people probably ransacked this place searching for medicines. This is very bad," reported Johnson.

"Do you want to RTB?" asked Alex.

"Negative. We need to get to the hospital."

"Roger that. Be advised that the Musicians have signs of IR spectra and smoke. Probably a campfire across the fjord."

As they moved closer to the road junction of the bridge and the road that ran along the fjord, the jam of cars became worse and they had to climb over several to make any headway.

"Jesus, look at this, it's worse than Katie Freeway in Houston on a Monday morning," said Lieutenant Tsang.

They reached the bottom of the hill and Natasha crossed the road to get a better view over the wall along the fjord. The fjord was frozen and more vehicles were abandoned on the ice. Several miles away she could see the plume of smoke that Alex had spoken of.

"Captain? We need to get on," said Lloyd-Smith, urging her to rejoin the group.

They reached the hospital, a long, box-like, six-floor concrete building. The entrance was set back 50 metres from the roadside on a small rise. Its forecourt, too, was littered with abandoned vehicles. Three banks of large swing doors greeted them. Inside, the gloomy interior was illuminated with emergency lights.

"Six. Piper and I will escort the med team into the building. We'll probably lose video feed, so Sergeant Gyan and Cook will stay on station at the entrance and provide a relay. How copy?" asked Lloyd-Smith.

"Roger. Six standing by."

Tsang came up alongside Natasha giving her a start. "Fucking spooky, eh?" she muttered as she strode past followed by Johnson. Lloyd-Smith and Piper guarded their flanks, panning their weapons from left to right. "Shall we join them?" offered Jones.

Natasha shivered inside her suit.

"Tsang's right. This place is spooky. No heating, just a few emergency lights. What the hell happened here?"

They followed Tsang and Johnson, clambering over a pile of stretchers and their human contents that had been laid out in the foyer. Johnson tripped on an arm that protruded from under a blanket and almost fell.

As Natasha looked at the bodies, her heart rate started climbing and she felt beads of sweat forming on her forehead; one rolled down into her left eye. Shit; thirty seconds ago she had been cold. Now she was starting to overheat. She tried to ignore the faces attached to the bodies. A tap on her shoulder and the reassuring voice of Jones broke through her isolation.

"You all right?" he asked. She nodded.

"Control your breathing."

"Lieutenant Tsang, let's see if we can find the med labs, the ops room or the emergency offices," said Johnson. "Everyone else OK?"

No one replied.

Tsang made her way to the reception desk and swept an arm across the counter, clearing a pile of debris from it to reveal the tabletop floor plan.

"I'm guessing a little with the language, but looks like the emergency room is to our right, the ops room is on the second... the med labs are on the sixth."

"Let's make sure we stay together. I want another suit check please," said Johnson.

Using flashlights they moved along a corridor that led to the emergency room, the beams making the frost particles on the white hospital walls sparkle, and highlighting the white and grey colour of the dead that littered the black and white chequered tiled floor. Stepping over more bodies they reached the end of the corridor where two large swing doors and a sign announced that they were entering the emergency room. Johnson pushed against them but met resistance. Lloyd-Smith and Jones joined him and together they pushed open the door against what turned out to be a dead medical orderly who lay sprawled across the floor on the other side.

"Listen up, everyone. I know this is rough but try and keep control. Control your breathing; focus on the job at hand. Let's continue the sweep and try and find out what happened here. We need to find the stairwell and get access to the offices and labs. Any files, data logs, hard or soft, will be good. We'll start at the top and work down," said Johnson.

They found the stairwell, which was mercifully clear of death, and started to climb. Lloyd-Smith and Piper moved like they were on a house-clearing exercise, darting up each flight of stairs in turn with weapons at the ready. Then shouting all clear before repeating the process.

Johnson called out, "Lieutenant, may I suggest we conserve our energies for a more realistic encounter?"

"Just making sure, Captain," replied Lloyd-Smith, ignoring the advice.

They emerged onto the sixth-floor landing marked Laboratory and were back in daylight.

Johnson and Tsang moved immediately to the main office area and started sifting through a stack of dishevelled files piled up between computer monitors and instrument displays.

Out of the corner of her eye Natasha saw Lloyd-Smith, who'd moved to the window, presumably to look at something other than death, start to convulse. She rushed across to him. He was hyperventilating and grabbed her for support. Jones separated them and then clamped a hand over Lloyd-Smith's respirator intake to seal off the air and halt the hyperventilating. After a brief struggle, Lloyd-Smith held up a thumb, signalling all was well.

"You OK, sir?" Jones asked Lloyd-Smith.

"Yes, thank you, Sergeant Major. It's just that I can't quite take that in," he said gesturing to the scene outside.

Below them was what looked like the town centre's car park, but oddly there were only one or two cars in it. The streets outside were full of vehicles. It took her brain a second longer to solve the enigma. In the snow, row upon row of black plastic bin liners stretched across the area, each containing what she now knew was a body.

"Jesus, that's some morgue. Private Piper, you count the rows, I'll count the columns. Give me VOX priority," ordered Jones.

"VOX priority relay – Sierra Two to all stations," came the computer-generated acknowledgement giving Jones's transmission priority.

"Alex, we must have thirty thousand dead here. Bring Mozart and Beethoven over to the car park at the rear of the hospital."

"Routing the Musicians now. How much longer do you need? Over."

"We're looking for records and data only now. No sign of survivors. Difficult to give a time at this point."

"Roger. Six standing by."

Natasha was emotionally haemorrhaging; things had spiralled out of any reference frame that she could relate to. She noticed a dog gnawing away at a bag close to the back of the building, and could see half a dozen foxes near the perimeter fence clustered around another. Numerous gulls hopped around pecking and drawing off sinewy strands. As Mozart and Beethoven dropped into the scene, the gulls lifted off only to land a few metres away.

Natasha left Jones and Lloyd-Smith and went over to Johnson and Tsang who were trying to get the database systems online.

"You knew all along, didn't you?" Natasha asked.

Johnson nodded. "As soon as we came across the VCP, I suspected."

It took them another hour to download the database for the past month and collect handwritten notes and diaries that lay scattered around.

"Six. I think we have enough with what we've got. We'll do one last sweep here for survivors. Then RTB. ETA three zero minutes."

"Roger. We'll have the delouse ready for you."

Johnson and Tsang led them on a final sweep through the hospital wards. They worked floor by floor.

On the second floor, Natasha was confronted with a brightly painted corridor. It was the children's ward, denoted by a mural of a large owl pointing with its wing to a set of double swing doors. She stopped, not wanting to move further. Jones caught her elbow and beckoned to her that they should leave this to Johnson. She nodded, and together they descended the darkened stairwell, clambered back over the dead in the foyer and went outside. The fading afternoon light was bright compared to the darkness of the building. They found Sergeant Gyan scanning the opposite side of the fjord through his field glasses.

"Column of smoke off on the horizon, at the top of the hill. One o'clock. That's the IR sig that was reported by the Musicians. Someone survived."

"Six. This is Sierra. We've got a vis on the IR sig the Musicians picked up earlier – signs of smoke five miles due west of our pos. Confirm it looks like a campfire. How do you want to proceed?" asked Jones.

"Let's leave it for now, Sierra. Range is outside our envelope."

*

By the time it was Natasha's turn to enter the decontamination tunnel they'd set up, it was dark and she was beginning to feel extremely cold.

"Captain. Your turn. Please take everything with you. There are seven sections. Enter the first section and seal both the doors," a voice that Natasha recognised as medic Nancy Strong told her.

She unzipped the door to the cylindrical tunnel and entered the first of seven compartments. It was lit with a bright UV lamp. Two small cameras and a speaker hung from the roof. The walls, floor and ceiling were studded with half-inch diameter black spray nozzles. She could hear the sound of the small compressor outside that kept the space between the double walls positively pressurised in order to contain any leakage.

A stencilled orange notice on the black wall in five different languages reiterated what Nancy had told her.

After the series of chemical showers, ultra-violet washes, and even chemical vaginal swabs, coupled with what she'd seen in Alfjorden, Natasha was emotionally exhausted and felt relieved as the recycle pumps in the last section of the decontamination unit whined, signifying the end of the process. The exit door was unzipped and Sanchez greeted Natasha, handing her a towel and a thermal blanket.

"You'll be glad to know that your suit was not damaged, and for now you'll stay a part of the human race. Enjoy the tunnel?" she asked, smiling.

"Who the fuck thinks this all up?" asked Natasha, shivering.

"There are some clothes waiting for you in the medical AFV."

As Natasha got dressed, she took stock of her emotional state and decided it could only get better. Sanchez pushed a mug of hot chocolate into her hand.

"What would have happened if you had found damage to my suit?" she asked.

"We'd been told to shoot you."

Natasha laughed but when she looked at Sanchez she wondered if she should have.

"Where's Captain Johnson?"

"He took off with Lieutenant Tsang. They're reviewing the data they collected."

Finished drying, Natasha went to find them. What she'd witnessed had shaken her but at the same time ignited a deep desire to understand.

She found Johnson, Tsang and Alex huddled in the HQ AFV in semi-darkness, engrossed in the recovered hospital files. Without saying anything Johnson slid along the bench to make room for her. As he did, an inch of cigarette ash toppled lazily onto the floor.

"We've been reviewing the video diary from the hospital," said Johnson. "It's a compilation of personal video diaries and one or two comms and data packages networked from the government and international medical centres. The guy on the screen is a Dr Olsen, an intern on the emergency ward. First entry was fifteen days ago, the last was three days ago."

Tsang hit the play button.

"This is a diary of events here at Alfjorden in the hope that anyone finding it will learn from our experiences. Attached to this document are copies of the database, analyses that we conducted, together with several communications from outside centres."

On the screen a face appeared. The doctor looked middle-aged, maybe fifty years old, his face was an opaque white covered in sweat, his eyes were bloodshot, and every second or two he had to wipe mucous and blood from his nose. His voice sounded like it was drowning and he had to stop talking every few words as he coughed.

"With the death of Nurse Jacob last night, I am now the only medic here. I do not have much longer to live, hours at most, and I need to decide how best to help the few patients I have left. The worst thing is the children; how can I keep them from the agony? We've only got two ways to go at this point; either crawl outside and die in the cold or linger inside here with only our fellow sufferers as company. My lungs have deteriorated to the extent that any effort, even breathing, is painful, definite pulmonary oedema, eyesight deteriorated, loss of motor control in hands and legs. Mortality rate one hundred per cent. I doubt I shall have the strength to record again. Make use of this."

Tsang moved the diary back ten days. Olsen was replaced with a female surgeon called Anders.

"Since the first cases yesterday, we've been inundated. The morgue capacity has already been exhausted and our single incinerator cannot keep pace. We've asked for additional ones or freezer trucks from the government but I don't think we're going to get them, so we're starting to store the dead in the car park. The mortality rate is running at ninety per cent..."

Johnson stopped the playback and started reading from his notes instead.

"Apparently on day three, they received a brief from the CDCI... that's the international centres for disease control in Atlantis, Lawrence Livermore Labs, and Stockholm. They confirmed that the virus was a designer strain of pneumonic plague; in other words, man-made, with no known post-infection treatment. They named it APP for Accelerated Pneumonic Plague. Apparently it has airborne capability, with transmission primarily through inhalation, although the tests also showed transmission was possible via contact with your eyes or ingestion, the latter aided by the ability of the virus to stay alive on surfaces and in direct sunlight... a tough little bastard.

"The incubation period is weeks, with no immediate ill effects or symptoms. Then all of a sudden – boom! I reckon this explains what we've seen, i.e. high levels of penetration into the population. No one knew they were infected, at least for a few weeks."

Johnson paused to light a cigarette, then handed the packet to Natasha before continuing; "Some labs in Great Britain managed to isolate one of the gene fab modules that they christened 'The Clock'. Lieutenant Tsang reckons from the report she read that this gene was like a door on a time lock, a gatekeeper if you will. When the countdown hit zero the door opened and APP came out to work. Once released, the onset of immobility seems to be within six to twelve hours, and this is followed by death within a few more hours.

"Oh, by the way, Moscow CDC also found an accelerated aging gene spliced into the APP virus itself. Fairly neat little modification; after going active, the virus will only live on for a little more than sixty hours. It's all very clever, very clean and very fucking business-like. The design enabled massive yet undetected infection rates, followed by a devastating death rate, then whoosh, all stop, just like nothing had happened, and little chance of reinfecting anyone who happens along afterwards."

Natasha sat stunned at what she was hearing but Johnson had more.

"This site is not unique – on day eight they report that they're waiting for release of VX stocks from central government: nerve gas capsules! They had no other way to ease the suffering.

"On day nine here they lost power; apparently there was an explosion in the main switch centre. They lost contact with anyone outside and the radio and TV stations started going off the air. They started to burn furniture to stay warm... there were not enough personnel to move the dead... labs ceased to operate... they were down to giving aspirin to the children, nothing for the adults. The only good news that's reported is that, mercifully, APP seems to cause unconsciousness in the young before death."

"Someone blew up their power distribution system," commented Natasha. She looked at the file directory; one marked BBC News that was dated just eleven days before caught her attention. She pointed it out. "Have you opened it?" she asked.

"No. Be my guest," replied Johnson, lighting another cigarette.

Natasha opened up the file and knew immediately that something had gone seriously wrong. The familiar female voice of the civilian presenter they'd heard several times over the past few weeks had been replaced by a military-sounding official.

"This is the BBC World Service, broadcasting from the south of England. On the home front, sabotage attacks and air strikes continue to target civil and military communications centres. This broadcast will therefore be limited to two minutes.

"Limited enemy air and seaborne landings have occurred at various locations where fierce fighting continues. It is expected that the subject areas will soon be back under allied control.

"The World Health Organization has declared a pneumonic plague virus pandemic. A special United Nations Security Council session has been convened to discuss the origins of the virus. Many areas are reporting that medical facilities are being overloaded. Authorities, however, continue to work on isolating the virus and remain confident that a vaccine will be forthcoming in the near future. All people not engaged in essential services are requested to remain at home or in their temporarily assigned quarantine areas until further notice. Non-compliance will result in the arrest of offenders.

"The Congress and the US Senate have agreed to suspend the Constitution and impose martial law in thirty-nine separate states. This follows similar moves in other allied nations.

"Stock exchanges across the world remain suspended. The royal family and government remain in the capital. The government would like to remind all civilians to refer to their local area wardens for more information on medical, food and water provision.

"All reserve military and essential services personnel have been ordered to report to their muster stations by 1800 hours local time tomorrow.

"In response to the nuclear strikes on our civilian cities, Supreme Allied Command confirmed that a series of retaliatory tactical nuclear strikes has been made along the southern front, in and around the Dardanelles and at selected naval ports in the Black Sea, North Africa and the Middle East.

"This broadcast will now be terminated but will be repeated at unspecified times throughout the rest of today."

Natasha stood up, grabbed a pen and started to sketch overlapping circles and a timeline onto a whiteboard. The fragments of information they'd picked up over the past weeks now fell into a perfectly formed and chilling picture.

"It all makes sense now. One. Introduce a 'sleeping' virus. Two. Set off a bunch of nukes, leading to mass evacuation, hence spreading the virus. Three. Disrupt comms so when the virus emerges, our emergency response will be degraded, and then…" She paused.

"Walk in and take over," finished Alex. "Clever. Very clever. We've been fighting what has effectively been a low intensity war for the past twenty years. Our industry and society have been able to keep pace with the losses and the cost. In fact, many people believed that the war was actually propping up some of the economies.

"Until now, the whole thing had just become part of daily life. We hardly even made the news. Our enemies have exploited our complacency and belief that we had superior technologies, our reliance on specialised finely balanced but non-robust systems and the few people who are trained to maintain them. They raised the ante and have gone for broke."

"Charming. You remember what Hitler said to his senior generals when he was conquering Russia: '*While German methods must be concealed from the world at large, all the necessary measures – shooting, exiling, etcetera – we shall take, and we can take anyway. The order of the day is: first – conquer; second – rule; and third – exploit.*' These bastards may have worked out how to bypass steps one and two and get straight to three. This isn't an escalation, they've instigated total war," said Johnson, blowing a long stream of cigarette smoke into the air.

Natasha shivered as the reality sunk in. "You think about it: our GPS system relies, or rather relied, on only twenty-four primary and eight back-up satellites. Any ground-launched replacements can only come from three sites. Jesus, take those out, or even just a few key people, and it's game over. I remember reading that our major cities like New York and London use terrestrially based wireless comms that rely on no more than fifty or sixty switching stations. You take those out and the whole system stops. Eliminate the few dozen trained engineers who can fix them and you're talking months before they can be repaired."

"Our major hospitals can only support twenty or so ICU cases each. You flood any city with more than a couple of hundred ICU cases or degrade the population of doctors and trained medical personnel by much and we've got big problems," added Johnson.

"Shit, and you know how precarious our power distribution network is. Even with the decentralised push over the past decade it sometimes can't cope with a solar storm," interjected Tsang.

"And so it goes on," said Alex, "but what we've surmised assumes that they can walk in and take over, and that means our defence forces would need to be eliminated. How?"

"Even assuming that military systems were not affected, how long could our combat teams continue to operate with available fuel and ammunition?" asked Natasha.

"Weeks," acknowledged Alex. "And at the end of it, you get our infrastructure and industry largely intact."

"So, what's been our response to this? If we've worked it out then I'm sure others have," asked Johnson.

"We've gone nuclear, maybe biological as well, probably big time. They've gone strategic, full CBRN in response. God, with no GPS, accurate targeting would be impossible, so they'd have gone for overkill," concluded Alex.

They sat in silence, digesting the information. Natasha wondered where this left them.

Johnson flicked his cigarette butt out of the hatchway. His hands were shaking. Natasha put an arm around him and squeezed.

"These fucking idiots. They've finally done it. They've managed to undo in weeks what has taken more than a million years to evolve," whispered Johnson hoarsely, trails of smoke discharging from both his nostrils and mouth with each word like the gas discharge from a weapon.

"So what happens now?" asked Alex, who had been observing them quietly from the doorway.

"I need to upload all the information we recovered. We've got the downloads from the CDC and others that were issued before they lost comms. I'm not sure that we can do much except collate as much data as possible and learn. Fucking hell, Alex, we're talking about a mass extinction event here."

"But at least one person has survived. The smoke we saw… There must be some hope. Where there's one there will be others," said Natasha.

"One, one out of a town of, what, twenty thousand, plus the surrounding area. We counted thirty-two thousand dead. Thirty-two, and that was just the car park! You extrapolate that across the US and we're talking about a remaining population of what? Fuck, about fifteen thousand! That's not enough to fill a quarter of a football stadium."

"And if ten people were huddled around that fire then we're talking a hundred and fifty thousand," Alex said, trying to instil some hope.

"What about the bastards who built the virus?" interjected Natasha.

"Unknown. If it was the Brotherhood, from what we've seen they could have undertaken an immunisation programme. I don't know..." said Johnson, sighing.

"Come on," said Alex, hauling up Johnson by the arm. "We need to talk to the squadron. I'm not sure where we're going from here but I need you. We need to put a briefing together for everyone."

*

Several hours later they started the squadron briefing. Alex stood alone; a powerful floodlight from one of the AFVs was trained on him, picking out and highlighting the snowflakes falling slowly around him. With the exception of the perimeter sentries, all fifty-five remaining members of the squadron, and Natasha's aircrew, were present. They formed a loose semicircle in front of him; some sat in the snow, others stood or squatted on equipment containers. Natasha noticed how before he started talking he took a deep breath and tensed his chest muscles. *I guess he's trying to look strong*, she thought. He caught her eye before beginning.

"It seems a strange way to begin, but well done today. I'm sure you've heard parts or all of what's been found, but this briefing, I hope, will fill in any gaps and bring you up to speed with everything we know or can surmise.

"I think we can be certain that what we've seen is the work of the Brotherhood. We are dealing with an enemy that has revealed a number of technological breakthroughs that until now he has kept well hidden. These have enabled him to execute his strategy of ethnic cleansing on a scale that is unprecedented. His goal is now totally clear. The extermination of our society, and I stress the word extermination. He has dumped what we consider to be basic human values and morality, and changed the rules. I think people like ourselves who have had to fight him for a while already knew this but hoped we could contain him. Others either had no idea or chose not to believe it.

"We underestimated him. He's managed to use a prolonged, low-intensity conflict as cover to prepare for total war, and without the historical clash of conventional armed forces and the collateral damage to material assets.

"We can hope. But I think we must be prepared to accept that what we've found here has been repeated across a much wider arena and other theatres, and this includes places where your families, relatives and friends live.

"None of us have been trained for the current situation. We are in an environment totally or partially controlled by our enemies. The civilian population, certainly in this area, has largely ceased to exist and we have yet to contact any friendly forces.

"Captains Kavolsky, Grant, Johnson and Crockett have prepared a briefing for you. I do not expect anyone to actually come to terms with what you are going to hear. I certainly can't. I hope however that it will give you sufficient information to allow you to start thinking about how each of you, individually and together, is going to respond.

"We've split the brief into three parts: the first is a recap of the current situation; the second is how we believe it occurred; and the last is possible forward plans of action, which at this stage are purely options, no more. No decision is expected from this brief.

"The session is open; questions are welcome at any point. Those on watch will have a separate briefing. We will record all of the proceedings in the squadron's log, and these will be available to all so you can review them at your leisure.

"Captain Grant, if you please..."

*

The brief lasted until the early hours of the morning. Natasha could feel the competing emotions of anger, sorrow and fear jostle for recognition and change hosts as she walked around. To this mix had been added theoretical extrapolations, technical details and challenges, religion and philosophy. She spotted Sanchez, with Stacey, O'Reilly and Hodgetts and decided to join them.

"I reckon it's all those fucking multi-nationals. They never gave a shit about anything but profits. They cut deals with anyone so they could access the big growth areas. They didn't give a shit about where they set up their manufacturing bases. I had a mate who worked for Boeing building wings who told me that security in the new manufacturing plants was a bloody joke," lectured Stacey in a voice full of anger.

"You've got a point, but what the hell were our intelligence services doing? Surely they would have known and flagged it?" asked Hodgetts.

"What, like nine eleven, Iraq and WMD, Iran, North Korea, Algeria, the Arab Spring, ISIS. The whole lot's fucked up; even if they did know, then, like Stacey says, the CEO of Top Secret Technology Company would probably just employ more lobbyists and make a few more political donations so they could transfer their facility, or enter into a nice little joint venture," replied O'Reilly.

"So what we're saying is that we've been fighting for a greedy bunch of bastards who've sold us out by selling our technologies and made a shit load of money doing it," commented Hodgetts.

"None of it matters now. What matters is what we are going to do about it," replied Sanchez.

O'Reilly stood up, dusted the snow off himself, took a long drink from his flask and said, "Well I reckon this is fucking outrageous. I reckon we've been sold out. I'm going to take this to the Sarge. See you later, Captain."

Around them Natasha noticed that all the debates had suddenly stopped; it was like someone had simply turned off the power. She looked slowly around at the groups; some had more than several inches of snow resting on their shoulders and hair, two or three sitting on the ground had been buried to their hips. Warm breath, vapour from hot drinks, and cigarette smoke climbed into the air to meet and mingle with the continuing fall of snow.

Thirty minutes later Alex walked back to the centre of the arena and reiterated what they thought had happened: the introduction of the virus, the nuclear strikes and consequent evacuations of millions of people infected with the virus, the disruption to communications and essential services. He paused at the end, before mentioning that there were many theories as to how this had been allowed to happen and that in his opinion none of these should influence the choice that they now had to make. He offered them three options:

"A, we stay here. B, we move on and try and link up with other allied forces or population centres, or C, we disband the squadron now and take our chances."

The last sentence set off a ripple of movement and Natasha knew they had crossed a psychological bridge.

"We will convene a meet at 2100 hours tomorrow for a vote."

As another round of discussions started, Natasha and Johnson followed Alex out of the meeting area and into the tree line. They continued deeper into the forest, passing a sentry who acknowledged them with a salute before returning to his sensor display. They walked for another five minutes in silence before the going became almost impassable. Johnson placed an arm on Alex's shoulder, stopping him moving further.

"Well done, Alex, you did well," he said. "You've even got me hoping. It's strange how the brain when faced with total and absolute disaster can generate hope from a hopeless situation when given some options."

Natasha didn't know what to think anymore but she needed a respite. "Have you got any of that whisky that O'Reilly always seems to have?" she asked.

Johnson dug into his tunic and pulled out a large silver flask, unscrewed the ornate silver top with a flourish and passed it to her; the top dangling on a chain clinked against the flask in the silence.

They sat down, sharing the whisky and listening as occasional clumps of snow dropped from the heavily laden pine branches. Natasha was sitting between them and could feel Alex's knee against hers. She realised it felt good.

"What do you think they'll decide?" asked Alex.

"They won't disband now, it's too early to have sunk in. Yeah, they've seen this one place, but no one is going to believe that what's happened here really has happened all over. And then even if you can convince yourself it has, then us is all you've got left," said Johnson.

"The biggest problem is going to be later on when it starts to dawn on them that this has happened everywhere. Then the cries for loved ones will start," added Natasha.

The noise of a branch snapping halted the conversation, as Crockett and Grant came to join them.

"The sentry told us where the party was; mind if we join in?"

They sat down next to them and produced more whisky flasks, all of which were the same.

"Am I missing something here or have you all got identical flasks?" asked Alex.

"O'Reilly organised them for us back at Sevastopol; he got a job lot from some Russian colonel in exchange for some whisky," replied Grant.

"Well, I suppose whatever happens we'll never run out of whisky," quipped Johnson.

"Where does he keep it?" asked Natasha.

"That, my dear, is the closest guarded secret in the squadron. No one except O'Reilly knows," he replied.

"What does your friend Corporal Sanchez say?" Alex asked Natasha, changing the subject and taking a long sip of the whisky.

"I left her talking to Schaefer. I guess I'll find out in the morning," she replied, smiling to herself about the hidden romance, but happy that Alex had noticed the relationship she'd built up with Sanchez. She looked at the others as the snow continued its silent descent and wondered if they had families or were just so used to this lifestyle that they could block it all out.

*

Next morning the squadron made their unanimous decision and presented it to Alex; they didn't have to wait until evening. They would stay together until they met up with other allied forces; their best bet, they believed, was the European Allied headquarters in Germany.

CHAPTER 10

RECON

Those who face the unprepared with preparation are victorious.

The Great Belt bridge, one of the longest bridges in the world, lay 50 kilometres ahead of them. By crossing it they would enter Denmark, and in turn Germany and Allied Headquarters. It was the only land route available to them and one they expected to have been attacked.

During their journey they had passed hamlets and small villages, all of which had seemingly suffered the same fate as Alfjorden. Twice they'd come across the remains of military convoys that had been destroyed by air attack, the scattered and charred remains of the crews still lying where they'd fallen.

Natasha had had the time to analyse her feelings and come to the conclusion that she simply felt empty. She wasn't upset and she wasn't annoyed. This realisation disturbed her; she'd always prided herself on being emotional. She asked Johnson about it and was surprised to hear that Alex too had had the same discussion. As for the answer, well, Johnson thought it was a combination of reaching the bottom of the emotional barrel that resulted in a psychological defence mechanism kicking in.

They travelled off-road using the logging tracks through densely forested terrain until they met a glacial valley that led south towards the network of fjords over which stood the bridge. Here, they laagered beneath a 16,000-foot high rock outcrop and waited whilst Schaefer led a recon team along the fjord to the bridge.

It was mid-morning four days later when Schaefer and the recon team returned. As Natasha entered the debriefing room she could not help but notice how exhausted the team looked, their blood-red eyes contrasting with the black and white zebra stripe cam cream worn on their faces and hands. Their combat smocks and trousers were dirty and stained from digging observation posts, and their backsides looked like they had been sliding down mud embankments for the whole time. Their clothes reminded Natasha of her childhood when her mother would scold her for sliding down muddy river embankments near their house.

Alex poured each of them steaming hot coffee.

"Cheers, sir," said Stacey, accepting the coffee. "Mind if I have a seat?"

"Be my guest. Breakfast is on its way," said Alex whilst moving aside to give the shabby-looking group unrestricted access to the narrow benches around the ops table.

"Thank God. First bloody hot food we've had. The Sarge didn't want any nasty little heat sigs," Stacey continued whilst sliding along a bench and leaving bits of pine needle and mud smears on the white surface.

Schaefer and Hodgetts slid in next to him, adding to the organic debris, and took a mug of coffee, each cradling it with care and sighing with satisfaction.

"Sergeant Major Jones will give you the overview…" announced Schaefer, blowing onto his coffee without looking up.

Jones, who had remained standing, scratched at his four days of stubble and plugged a data card into the view screen. As the system booted up, he took a sip of coffee, savouring it like a wine connoisseur.

"Well, sir, it's like you thought: they've set up either side of the bridge and configured it for denial. Airborne units, well dug in. Some signs of previous firefights, a couple of burnt-out old allied Mark Seven Bradley AFVs, and a few field guns, probably local allied reservists. Looks like the fight was pretty uneven though.

"They have arty, MLRS and SAM sites, all airborne portable so fairly lightweight but still able to pack a punch. We didn't see any sign of armour but I'm not totally convinced. The same goes for remote sentries like we ran into before, but the approach roads are sunk within the ravines so there's a possibility that they are hidden in the rock faces."

There was a pause as, in a flurry of exhibitionism, O'Reilly who had dressed himself as a French waiter, together with Stacey's vehicle systems specialist, brought them breakfast.

"I thought you gents would appreciate a good Irish breakfast. Last of the sausages and chips but what the hell."

"I don't believe this!" cajoled Stacey. "You told me before I left we'd run out of sausages. I've been away risking my backside for you and I bet you ate sausages every day; and then to top it all, you turn my crew into cooks!"

"Not every day, just twice," replied O'Reilly with a smile.

While the others tore into their breakfasts, Jones continued his debrief. "They've set up three command centres, all C4I2s."

"What is a C4I2?" asked Natasha, feeling a little out of her depth.

"Sorry, Captain. Our field manual designates a C4I2 as having an integrated command, control, communication, coordination, information-gathering and interoperability capability. I'll link you a copy; it's a good read," replied Jones with a smile.

"Wow," offered Natasha.

"Two are on the south side, one on the north. All up, I would say we're talking regimental strength. Possibly reinforced."

"Shit. Four to five hundred against sixty," commented Crockett, echoing all their thoughts.

"I know what you are all thinking," continued Jones, bringing up a hand-drawn sketch of the area, whilst also managing to lean across the table and grab a sausage from Stacey. "But they've left a back door open. The fjord is frozen," he said taking a large bite of the sausage and scalding his mouth on it.

Alex studied the sketch. "What's the thickness of the ice?"

"About two feet along the shore and six inches at the bloody centre," interjected Stacey, giving them the impression that the obtainment of these measurements had somehow caused Stacey some grief.

"It's enough for the AFVs to drive along the shoreline, but too thin for a crossing," commented Crockett.

"But it should be fine for snow scooters or people to make it the whole way across," added Grant.

"Can we get the AFVs all the way along and up onto the bridge using the ice along the eastern shore?" asked Alex.

"Ice-wise, should be no problem," replied Jones.

"Any signs of other units or activity in the area?" asked Alex.

"Nothing. The only traffic we saw was inside their perimeter. I think they're it. Probably told to hold until relieved, that sort of thing."

"Comms?"

"Heavy but encrypted. Couldn't tell if it was real or just for show though."

"Patrols?"

"Yeah. They send out five-man foot patrols to about five klicks along the approach roads, and parallel with the fjord up to the plateau on the eastern side. About seven klicks to the west. There's a permanent sky cam up; it stays on a racetrack circuit out to about ten klicks along the approach roads but it barely covers a few hundred metres out along the fjord. They've got wireless cams slung beneath the bridge and at stations up to five hundred metres along the shores."

"Mines?"

"All the roads. Staggered. Alternating fifty-metre sections. Usual stuff, APMs and AVMs – not sure if they're networked but almost a cert they're hooked into the C4I2s. The bridge is rigged for demolition."

"Air support?"

"We saw them launch a pair of Stalkers a couple of times, from an area close to the northernmost C4I2, the new Black class, the ones with those three-sixty-degree sensors and tactical AI. We need to assume there's a dedicated squadron; for this size of force, four minimum, maybe six."

"That's a problem. We're going to have to work out a plan to take them down at the off. Now, what's the best way to take a bridge?" asked Alex, in a voice that communicated to them all that they were back on the offensive.

"Both ends at once," came the unified response.

"Great work, guys. Finish your breakfast, then go and get yourselves a shower and grab some sleep. We'll do a strategic level two Chinese Parliament at 1400 hours. I want you all, plus Lieutenant Lloyd-Smith and Sergeants Gyan and Byrnes."

CHAPTER 11

PLANNING THE OFFENSIVE

Without deception you cannot carry out strategy. Without strategy you cannot control the opponent.

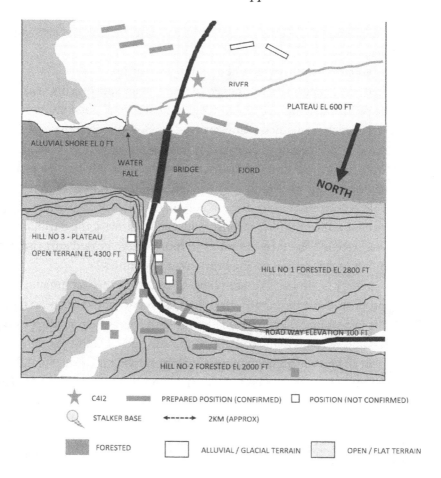

n the HQ igloo, Alex stood before his whiteboard with a crude map of the bridge and the surrounding areas.

There were no data screens, in fact no electronic equipment at all. The igloo was crowded with senior NCOs as well as officers, all of whom were talking whilst waiting for the session to begin. Alex saw Natasha studying the whiteboard and read her mind.

"I know, with all this technology, why are we using a whiteboard? Bottom line is that I like the freedom it gives people to think laterally. They've already seen the detail, and this reverses them out of it, gives them a chance to think strategically rather than tactically. You'd be surprised at some of the things that fall out of these sessions when people are decoupled from all the detail. You ever attended a full-blown Chinese Parliament before?"

"No," she replied, wondering exactly how it worked.

"It's a good process. Everyone's equal, no rank; it captures a lot. Captain Crockett and I will propose a plan, everyone else can challenge it and suggest alternatives."

Jones's voice called them to order, making her jump.

Crockett, the squadron's 2IC, moved to centre stage sporting his raccoon-tail hat. He picked up a marker pen and highlighted several possible approach routes, then gave them a quick synopsis using his Bowie knife as a pointer.

"They are in pre-prepared defensive positions, so normally we would be expected to have a three-to-one numerical advantage for this type of assault. We're outnumbered nearly ten to one, they are dug in and have Stalker-class gunships. Now, notwithstanding this, our objective is the total destruction of the enemy. We have artillery, AFVs, surprise, and a will to exact some retribution."

Natasha watched the faces around the room; they showed surprise but an underlying eagerness to try. She even saw a few smiles.

"The strategy is simple. We are going to decimate their command and control and push them into chaos. It's a little like what they've been doing to us. It's going to require careful coordination, absolute overwhelming firepower, ruthlessness and, as usual, a shit load of luck. Now, Lieutenant Lloyd-Smith here, whom as you all know is a scholar of military history, will further elaborate."

Lloyd-Smith stood at the end of the table and began in his best British officer's accent.

"Well, you all probably know that at the Battle of Trafalgar in 1805, Nelson's ships were outnumbered but performed an extremely bold manoeuvre called crossing the T... This had the result of putting Nelson's ships right into the middle of the combined French and Spanish fleets in such a way that he could fire from both port and starboard. This evened out the enemy's numerical superiority and allowed him to be able to fire directly into a target-rich environment. But..." he paused for effect, "modern-day analysis reveals something else. The real key to his success was the impact of this manoeuvre on the enemy's command and control.

"Now, Nelson's commanders and their subordinates shared a complete understanding of his plan. In fact, through years of working together he and his officers and NCOs had an almost telepathic ability to carry out mutually supportive actions without further orders once the battle had begun. Sound familiar?"

"Sounds familiar," said Sanchez, lighting a cigarette and being rewarded with some laughter.

Lloyd-Smith continued. "It was this, together with the manoeuvre, that, as the Major so succinctly described it, pushed the French and Spanish into chaos. Our strategy will be similar. We are outnumbered but the enemy is positioned in all-round defence. He cannot bring all his firepower to bear on a single target. We will get inside his perimeter with the squadron's AFVs and destroy his positions from within using mobile and locally superior firepower. The only thing we need to ensure is that the enemy cannot react and redeploy. To ensure that, we must eliminate his command and control."

Lloyd-Smith continued for an hour, detailing what levels of degradation of command and control were required and how they could achieve them. They discussed various options and scenarios and after several more hours they had an integrated tactical plan, which Alex summarised for them.

"Lieutenant Lloyd-Smith will provide the AFVs a safe corridor to get up to and onto the bridge by clearing the northern side of the bridge using artillery. Now, by 'clear' I mean the total destruction of the enemy. Total destruction.

"Captain Crockett will meanwhile secure the southern end of the bridge. This will allow the AFVs to penetrate into the centre of their operations where we will sequentially engage and destroy the southern units.

"Captain Schaefer's mission is threefold. Number one, destroy the Stalker base and as many gunships as possible. Number two, knock out the northern C4I2. And number three, mop up any resistance that Lieutenant Lloyd-Smith's barrage leaves, and block any attempt by the enemy to cross the bridge in either direction."

"Sorry, Alex, I counted four elements," said Schaefer.

"Actually, only two. Number three won't be required," interjected Lloyd-Smith making them all laugh.

Alex let them settle down before continuing. "Captain Crockett will take out the two southern C4I2s, secure the bridge from demolitions and provide a southern blocking force for long enough for us to bring the AFVs across.

"Now, the AFVs will act as an armoured thrust. It must not stall or delay during the crossing of the bridge. We must simply punch through anything that's in our way. We will not halt to support anyone, that includes Captain Crockett, Schaefer or any AFV that becomes disabled. I will command the AFVs.

"A lot has to go right here, the C4I2 centres must be destroyed and Lloyd-Smith must clear the northern approaches.

"So, now for our own command and control. Corporal Sanchez will be it. We will rely on her to advise us when the various phases of the operation are complete and when certain elements can move. She'll be positioned on the north-eastern plateau and use signalling flares only. We will stay e-silent and only go hot on comms once the AFVs are across the bridge and engaged. This will maintain our advantage of surprise.

"In addition to this little mission, Corporal Sanchez will be the one who sets up a juicy enough series of targets for our enemy friends to go live and thereby make themselves targets for Lieutenant Lloyd-Smith."

"No drama, Major," replied Sanchez, "I've got a few tricks in the bag."

"We've heard!" muttered someone from the group, which prompted some whistles.

"Corporal Hodgetts," continued Alex ignoring the banter, "will provide sniper cover for Miss Sanchez. You'll be the angel on her shoulder. She's going to be sought-after property so you will need a good position."

"I'll keep an eye on her. Providing Captain Schaefer has no objection of course?" interjected Hodgetts.

This brought more whistles and catcalls.

"Is there an echo in here?" shouted Sanchez jokingly.

"Settle down, people," ordered Jones.

"All right, I think we're now into section planning. I suggest the relevant commanders and section leaders organise these. Afterwards we will hold multiple integrated briefing sessions with the entire squadron. As Nelson did, so shall we. I want everyone to understand and know what one another are doing and why. If one leader is KIA I want someone to step in; if they're KIA I want another, and so on. Lieutenant Lloyd-Smith will facilitate these."

Natasha was impressed; despite what had happened to them, what they'd seen and the fact that they had probably lost their families and friends, their spirit seemed unbroken.

"Right, take an hour, have a coffee. Then get with your teams. I want you all back here with a level three plan in say five hours." As the others filed outside, Alex signalled to Johnson, Schaefer and Natasha to stay back.

"Do you think we can do it?" he asked.

"Yeah, I do. It's going to be messy. But I think we can. It'll be one hell of an operation; something for the staff colleges to study for years to come," replied Schaefer.

"Captain?" Alex asked Natasha.

Natasha swallowed her surprise, not just at the question but at the fact that he was seeking her advice, or was it just reassurance?

"I'm no expert, Major. But I don't see we have an alternative. From what we've seen it's not about winning the war anymore, it's become about us and how we want to and feel we should live. I'm not explaining myself too well, but I guess we're like a family. If we lose this, then we'll lose everything we've got left... Does that make any sense?"

"For the moment, absolutely," said Johnson.

CHAPTER 12

ORDER OF BATTLE

If opponents have no formation to find out, and no gap to take advantage of, how can you overcome them even if you are well equipped?

It was one of those winter early evenings when the moon and sun hung together like old lovers, thought Natasha as she crunched through the snow accompanying Alex on a tour. Final preparations were underway all along their route. Lloyd-Smith's artillery team were on top of one of the AFVs working to dismount the last of two MLRSs, which together with an electronic mortar would provide the artillery barrage required to clear the bridge approaches for the AFVs. Nearby were the sleds that Lloyd-Smith would use to mount and tow his field artillery behind the snow scooters.

Black equipment containers littered the area like large bugs, stern ramps were open and a constant stream of personnel moved equipment, ammunition and weapons to different areas. An atmosphere of professional apprehension permeated the scene.

Natasha spotted Sanchez sitting on a container, reassembling her weapon with practised ease, a cigarette dangled from her mouth. Her face had healed well from the fall during their escape although she still complained of whiplash.

"You good?" asked Natasha.

"Nothing that a warm bath wouldn't solve," she replied, clipping a magazine into her assault weapon, another taped upsidedown alongside it.

"Nice weapon," said Natasha, admiring the non-standard issue assault rifle and sights.

Sanchez blew a long stream of smoke into the air and held the weapon up proudly like a child would show a toy.

"I know. Parallel thirty-round magazines feeding dual barrels, integrated flash suppressor and silencer. I won the sights at a card game with a bunch of deep reconnaissance and prisoner rescue guys nine months ago. They use bio-molecular motion detection that's interlocked with an enhanced IR and UV detection system. It's better than a toad! Hodgetts' has got the same. You ever see that movie of Picasso? He used the glowing end of a cigarette in a dark room to sketch out a horse. They filmed it in slow motion. It was brilliant. Anyway, this makes me feel a little like him, a professional if you will!"

"You not going with a Zute suit?" Alex asked, referring to the active camouflage suits that the sniper teams used.

"Nah. We've got good cover up to the plateau and the things are too restrictive. I guess I like to be in touch with my environment, not be cocooned."

A tall, gangly trooper who Natasha thought couldn't have been more than eighteen years old joined them carrying a box-load of black cylinders. Sanchez introduced him. "This is PFC Williams. He'll be coming with me."

"Pleased to meet you," said Natasha, studying Williams. He had orange unruly hair that looked as if it needed to be brushed by his mother. His kind, almost childlike face looked nervous in the evening light.

Sanchez noticed Natasha's concerned look, slid down to the ground and then whispered in her ear, "He's OK. Just a bit of a rookie. And don't forget I've also got Hodgetts and the boys watching my ass."

"Those the dummies?" Natasha asked Williams.

"Yes, Captain. I've set them to body heat, 36.9 degrees Celsius, with a fluctuation of one degree every six seconds. We've tested them mounted on poles using our own sensors. They look just like a group of ramblers out for a Sunday stroll. Should attract quite a bit of attention," he replied in a voice that sounded to Natasha like it hadn't yet broken.

"Clever."

"You two take care. And best of luck," said Alex.

As they left Sanchez and continued their tour, Alex asked, "How come women always seem to maintain such neatness in the field? Did you see that little stack of tissues in Sanchez's equipment harness? Even if we men carried such things they'd be soggy and crumpled."

Natasha laughed. "I guess we can work on multiple levels."

Crockett's assault team, who were tasked with knocking out the southern C4I2 command centres on the opposite side of the fjord, were assembling for their final briefings and equipment checks. They'd formed up into a long row and one of the squad leaders – Natasha could see it was Corporal Olly – was moving from man to man, forcing each to jump up and down, bend and touch their toes, then twist left and right. With the hundred pounds of equipment that was strapped to each of them, they looked more like astronauts on an EVA than combat troops.

"Loosen that fucking waist strap; you won't be able to breathe on the climb! Tighten the chest harness, Matt! Kennedy, what the fuck is that eyewear? You aren't bloody well going on a safari. Lose the shades!" shouted the little squad leader.

Natasha had met Olly through Sanchez, who'd told her that apart from possessing an extraordinary self-sufficiency and being one of the best infantry section leaders in the squadron, he held in disdain just about all authority outside of the squadron. She'd laughed when she'd told him how Alex had had to intervene on Olly's behalf on several occasions, after senior officers had complained that the man had not responded to their presence in an appropriate manner. She studied him now, standing in front of the others, laden with their gear. His physique looked soft, almost out of condition in comparison.

As if reading her mind Alex whispered in her ear, "What he lacks in physical strength he makes up for psychologically. He is a leader in physical and mental endurance, and able to continue in situations where most would simply give up. He can come across to those who don't know him as laid back and relaxed, almost to the point of being insubordinate and undisciplined. But don't take it the wrong way."

"So I've been told. An interesting character."

"Now, that is Corporal Galeago," said Alex, pointing out a man trailing along behind Olly, and ignoring the general banter as he sharpened a hunting knife.

"He's Crockett's second squad leader, comes from the Basque region of Spain and fiercely proud of his ancestors who fought with the terrorist organisation ETA for many years before the region was finally given autonomous statehood. He possesses one of those extraordinary talents whereby he can channel just about all his strength into any one limb. This makes him quick and agile as well as extremely strong. He's the squadron's Russian arm-wrestling champion. Climbing, judo, pistol shooting, Spanish classical guitar, and hunting in his native Basque region are his passions."

"You love them, don't you?" she said.

"Love? You know, I've never thought about it. But maybe a little."

As Olly got to the end of the row he paused and stared at a pile of equipment that had been abandoned in the snow.

"Where the fuck's Winston and his lot? Jesus, I can't believe they've just dumped all their mortar gear and pissed off. You wait till I catch up with them."

"Corporal Olly, how we doing?" asked Alex.

"We're good to go, Major. Just missing the mortar team. Oy, Winston! Do you mind getting all your shit out of the way? We're trying to get geared up and can't fucking move because of your crap!"

Winston sidled past them on his way to calm down Olly. "Indeed, *mon Capitaine*, we were just a little peckish," said Winston, throwing back his head a little and half grinning.

"And that is Lance Corporal Winston. A keen violin player, he's a slightly eccentric character, often finding humour in situations that are frightening, if not terrifying, for others. But despite his quirks he's got an innate instinct for mortars. The best," commented Alex.

She knew Winston through Sanchez as well, so she decided to tell Alex a few things. "So I've heard. Some of the squadron reckon he is mad; he has a peculiar habit of issuing crow-like screams as he fires his mortars. But he has an almost magical ability to direct fire on positions without the aid of fire control computers, and is trusted implicitly by his fellow troopers to lay down close and accurate suppressive fire."

"Now I'm impressed."

"Why are you telling me all this?" she asked.

"If I'm taken out, I want you to take over command. I know it's debatable but we are in a situation that, like you said; is no longer just combat, whatever happens they'll need leadership but at many levels. Captains Schaefer, Johnson, Crockett and Grant all agree it should be you. Think of the next few hours as a little tour of some of the characters you may have not had a chance to meet. It might help you."

Natasha thought about what he'd just said. Before she could object, Sergeant Major Jones's parade voice boomed across the area.

"All right, listen up. Corporals Hodgetts and Sanchez have departed. Corporal Winston, get your lot shipshape. Jump off in four."

The general hubbub was replaced with quiet conversation as an expectant atmosphere now took over. An owl hooted.

CHAPTER 13

INGRESS

Advantage in a military operation is getting help from the land.

Eight kilometres east of the Great Bridge along the banks of the north-eastern shoreline of the frozen fjord, Schaefer sat beneath the lower branches of a pine tree that was heavy with snow and once again went over what he had to do. He would destroy the northern C4I2 at the end of the bridge, eliminate the Stalker base that they believed was located there and then provide a blocking force to allow free passage for Alex's AFV column to get up onto the bridge itself. Christ! And all without getting killed. Sanchez had been gone for four hours. As he had watched her leave, he'd felt like a teenager parted from his sweetheart over the summer break. Although painful, it was one of those strange emotions that also gave warmth and happiness. He decided to let go of the self-imposed restraints and gently slid into the warmth of the emotion. He looked at the sky; the moon was glowing it was so bright. He wondered if Sanchez was looking at it now. "Damn it. This must be love," he muttered quietly to himself, almost fearful, and yet at the same time secretly hoping that some of the others would hear so he could share with someone this newfound feeling. He made one final check of his underwater rebreather. The oxygen and helium pressures were at full and the carbon dioxide scrubber indicator lights glowed full green. He started checking the underwater scooter systems.

The scooter's diagnostics board lit up with a friendly green status. Satisfied, he flicked the power off, stood, stretched, and then started a slow circuit of his team checking each man was ready. He gave the five minutes to go signal and his team extinguished their cigarettes, emptied coffee cups and hauled their dive gear and scooters to the shoreline before starting to cut access holes through the ice.

Behind them the branches on the pine trees moved, shedding powdery snow into the air as Crockett's team emerged onto the shoreline to join them. In addition to their zebra-patterned snowsuits, body armour and helmets, each was laden with a Bergen that looked like it should topple them backwards if it wasn't for the counterweight that was provided by the equipment that hung from their fronts suspended on their webbing harnesses.

Like two football teams, Crockett's and Schaefer's men shook hands with one another before Jones corralled them into a line abreast along the shoreline.

"We'll catch you on the flipside," said Schaefer.

Jones then signalled Crockett's team to advance, and in unison they stepped out across the ice, heading towards the southern shoreline. Once they reached it they would turn west towards the bridge and assault the southern end of it at the same time as Schaefer hit the north.

As Schaefer watched them move across the ice in line abreast he smiled, amazed that in an age of intelligent super-sensitive sensors such field craft was still adhered to, but then again, he corrected himself, it worked. They would project the minimum profile to anyone who was watching from a position further along the fjord. As the noise of crunching crampons on the rough ice faded, Schaefer turned back to his own team.

"Let's go," he ordered.

SANCHEZ-HILL NO 3

At the same time as Crockett's team started out across the fjord, Sanchez and Williams both lay on their backs just below the plateau on hill number three on the north-east side of the bridge. The 4,300-foot climb had been long and tiring but uneventful; just before summiting, they'd stopped to put on additional clothes in anticipation of a long wait.

Sanchez now watched as her breath streamed into the air above her, slightly obscuring the stars. She checked her watch for the hundredth time.

One minute. She tapped Williams and signalled for him to wait while she went up onto the plateau. Williams gave a worried-looking acknowledgement, his eyes flitting from left to right. Sanchez reached out to give him a reassuring pat on the shoulder and what she hoped was a comforting smile.

She unhooked her webbing harness and backpack, wriggled free and nonchalantly pushed them across the snow to Williams. All she would take with her up onto the plateau would be grenades and her assault rifle.

She gave Williams a thumbs-up sign and then, cradling her weapon, edged her way up the slope; just below the top she took a deep breath and cleared her senses. Then, using her toes and elbows she inched her way up until she could see across the plateau, which sloped gently away from her. The moonlight bouncing off the snow was almost blinding in its intensity as she looked out across the flat white landscape interspersed with the occasional grey boulder.

Before the mission they'd discussed the disadvantage of the moon but in the end decided that as they weren't going to go hot with their electronics, which included night-vision gear, they would be better off with the moonlight than without it. Now, in the open like this, she wasn't so sure. Slowing her breathing, she opened her mouth so she could listen better. Silence was all she could hear. Not even the light wind that she felt against her cheeks disturbed it. She waited patiently, certain that there must be an OP or sentry post somewhere in the vicinity. She started counting to 150 to ensure that she gave herself the necessary time to observe each segment of the landscape before she checked the next. It was all too easy to believe you had surveyed an area thoroughly when in fact you had maybe only spent seconds doing it.

She'd reached 106 when she smiled; it was her sense of smell that confirmed the presence of the enemy. The light wind had increased almost imperceptibly, just enough to pick up a few particles of diamond dust and blow them against her face, but with them had come the unmistakable smell of cigarette smoke. It was close, coming from almost directly in front of her. She dare not use her IR sensor, fearful that even the weak electronic field signature would be detected at such close range. Straining her eyes for a visual, she completed one slow pass across her field of vision. Nothing. She searched again, forcing herself to slow down. The orange glow of a cigarette being inhaled grew and faded. She locked onto the position, keeping her head and eyes still. Then, allowing her field of focus to broaden, she slowly began to distinguish a black slit running horizontally, barely above ground level. It was the window of an OP, set within a small snow mound, almost lost in the surrounding landscape. She reckoned it was about 50 metres away, with the slit about 2 metres wide and only 10 or so centimetres tall. She'd been lucky; to the right of it was a great visual marker: a large boulder. She christened it Bertha.

She continued her survey of the area. It looked like the OP's primary function was to watch the approach roads that lay in the passes to the northwest rather than guard the eastern approaches to the plateau. But she needed to be careful; they'd still keep an eye out in her direction and there could be electronic sensors or tripwires. She checked for animal tracks; if they were there it would mean that they probably kept the sensors turned off. She couldn't see any. Again she considered using her own weapon's sensors to check but decided she couldn't take the risk. She would have to simply trust to luck and rely on Williams and Hodgetts to drop anyone before they could get her.

She guessed the OP was probably manned by between three and five personnel. She cycled through her limited number of choices: take out the OP; find a way around it; or stay where she was. The last option was out. Finding a way around it would take time, risk mines and sensors, and render her vulnerable. She checked her watch again; she had ninety minutes before Lloyd-Smith would let loose his artillery barrage. Decision time. Well, fuck it, she thought, they obviously weren't expecting her, and if she could take out the OP she would have an unrestricted theatre of ops, as Schaefer would say.

HODGETTS'-HILL NO 1

Hodgetts' sniper team comprised himself, Wilcox and Strachan. "One spotter and two shooters," as Hodgetts liked to refer to the make-up. They were armed with LR-51 individually customised sniper rifles, capable of firing accurately over a distance of more than 3,000 metres using fin-stabilised armour-piercing ceramic rounds.

They had spent six hours getting into their forward firing position, from which they would provide cover for Sanchez on the opposite plateau. Their approach had taken them within a body length of some of the enemy positions. Hodgetts now had a decision to make; the heat and visual camouflage suit he wore, known as a Zute suit, had started malfunctioning.

The suit used a probe driven into the ground to disperse his one hundred watts of body heat, and it had failed. As a back-up the suit had two chemical heat sinks but these were now full as well and the inside temperature of the suit was becoming unbearable. He either had to dump the heat using a vent or pass out. If he vented, he'd expose himself to the enemy but also the potential of being hit by Lloyd-Smith's barrage.

CROCKET SE SIDE OF FJORD

Reaching the south side of the fjord, the twenty-man assault team turned west and headed in single file along the boulder-strewn shoreline. To their right, out on the ice, a pack of silver and grey wolves trotted along in single file in the opposite direction, their coats shimmering in the moonlight.

"I thought wolves' eyes didn't shine at night?" whispered Olly.

"Course they do; it's because of their cone structure. It's different somehow from ours," stated Winston with some authority.

"Hey, shut the fuck up with the biology lesson," ordered Jones.

"Yes, Sarge."

Jones found the visual identifier he had been looking for: a large glacial boulder with two smaller ones perched rather unnaturally on top. He signalled a halt and the column knelt in unison, as if they were paying homage to an ancient king, each having to lean slightly forward to counter the weight of their Bergen.

Jones dumped his Bergen, then donned his Cyclops. He set one lens to IR and kept the other as standard to preserve half of his night vision. He scanned the rock face ahead of him; it seemed completely unoccupied, just large granite slabs weathered smooth with water erosion. He reached inside his breast pocket, pulled out a close-range IR remote controller and sent a coded command ahead of him. Instantaneously he saw the pre-positioned IR strobe start flashing; he took a second to note the position, then sent the shut-down command to the strobe, turned off his own sensors and continued ahead to the spot where he had seen the strobe.

"How's life?" he asked the deserted area around the location of the strobe.

"Fucking great!" came O'Reilly's voice. "We've got a little problem.

They've set up a remote sentry about a hundred metres up ahead around the next bend, covering the approach to the bridge. Bastards were down here earlier today fixing something or other and resighting the cams."

"Shit."

"Aye, but as we say in Ireland, 'all's not lost just because you've lost'. You can go up and over. About fifty metres back is a ledge that starts at ten metres and runs right above the RS; you can drop down about a hundred metres past it. From there on, you've got a clear run to the waterfall."

"What about the bridge cams?" asked Jones, still trying to decipher the proverb.

"No problemo, you'll be in a blind spot this side of the waterfall."

"Got it. Once the attack goes in, get yourself to the ERV or the bridge."

"Aye. I'll be sure to hold up me hand to hitch a lift."

As Jones left, he didn't see O'Reilly reach inside his tunic to touch his lucky bracelet and whisper a silent prayer to God and his ancestors.

It took an hour for them to bypass the remote sentry but once clear they moved rapidly to the bottom of the frozen waterfall that rose 600 feet up to the southern plateau, the ice shimmering with a mixture of pale blues, greens and milky whites from the moonlight. From its base, they could just make out a section of the great bridge. A single, lonely-looking cloud had turned up to celebrate their arrival. Quiet reigned, the only sound the trickle of water from the frozen waterfall running across the boulder-strewn shoreline.

As they made ready, fixing crampons and sorting out their kit, someone's weapon dropped with a clatter against a rock, breaking the silence. Tension crackled through the team as they waited for a response. There was none.

"Stop dicking around and get on with it," whispered Jones.

"I don't fucking believe this. The whole of this godforsaken country is frozen, apart from the one place we've gotta climb. All we need now is to be bounced halfway up; what a mind-fuck that would be," muttered Olly.

"Oy, Olly, thought you didn't believe in global warming?" came a voice.

"Fuck off," came the response, followed by a raft of sniggers.

"Keep it down and hurry it up. At the rate you lot are going it'll be summer before we get going," said Jones, cutting across the banter.

"Well, it'll be sunup in ten or so hours," someone muttered.

"Knock it off. Let's get moving."

"Fuck. There's no way I'm going up with the Body Lite on. I'd rather risk changing at the top," whispered Olly, referring to their body armour, which despite being lightweight was a long way from allowing full freedom of movement.

"Your call. But we're going to be a little exposed at the top. Contact might be fast."

"Cheers, Sarge," came a chorus of voices, as most of them dumped their armour.

SCHAEFER—20M BENEATH THE FJORD

A kilometre past the waterfall, and beneath the frozen surface of the fjord, Schaefer let go of the power throttle on his underwater scooter and waited as he and the scooter settled gently towards the muddy bottom. He could feel the communication ropes connecting him to the others go taut and then slack as they also stopped. It took a moment to get used to the silence after the high-pitched whine of the electric propellers ceased. As his left knee touched the bottom a flatfish sped away from him. He pulled off a glove, feeling the cold waters immediately caress his hand, and turned on his navigation display. Through the clear water the display shone brightly. Only a few specks of cloudy sediment drifted upwards across his line of vision from where he had touched the bottom. The navigation system told him they should be within a couple of hundred metres of the bridge. He checked his rebreather status: all systems were green and the primary carbon dioxide scrubber, helium and oxygen tank levels told him he had another three hours if required. He shut down the display and tugged on the communication line to let the others know they were good to go again. A few seconds later, two tugs told him the rest of the team had understood and were ready. He powered up the scooter and let it tug him gently off the bottom.

Three minutes later he halted again. With the clear water he used laser ranging to locate the bridge piers rather than sonar. The display confirmed that there was a bridge support directly to his right. He signalled his companions to turn on their hardwired comms.

"Bridge support is fifty metres to starboard. We should see Hodgetts' light stick markers. Acknowledge."

He picked up a handful of sediment and let it go in the water; the current was slightly from his left. He powered up the scooter again, angling it a few degrees to counter the current. Within seconds he saw the first of the blue light stick markers that Hodgetts had laid out. They were spaced at 5-metre intervals along the bottom and veered right before stopping at the base of a massive concrete structure that formed the base of one of the bridge piers. A white noticeboard had been placed next to the last marker. In the blue light Schaefer could just about make out the scribbled message: The Shadows welcome all who follow in our footsteps. This is the last pier before the shoreline. So, go up, turn right and you will have arrived.

Schaefer's team assembled in a semicircle around him, swaying in the gentle eddies that spun off the pier. Schaefer and PFC Iceman Wortosky would be first up.

Using controlled breathing, they adjusted their buoyancy and drifted up towards the ice above, being careful not to ascend too fast. At a depth of 15 metres they stopped for a thirty-minute decompression. Schaefer took several minutes before he could get his buoyancy under control, cursing as he bounced up and down a few metres before stabilising. Finally happy, he reviewed the next page of his check list. There was a note from Sanchez: Play no 8. He selected the song from his comms package and Jimi Hendrix's *All Along The Watchtower* started up in his earphones. At the first line he laughed and felt himself relaxing. Across from him the Iceman had fallen asleep whilst still floating in perfect control.

Finishing their deco stop, they ascended to the underside of the ice where Iceman drilled a small hole through it to the surface. Schaefer inserted a periscope and panned around the area. Across the surface of the fjord to the north, nestled in a recess, he could make out the entrance to the Stalker site and to its right the C4I2. He swung the periscope up to survey the underside of the bridge. A series of small black boxes with antennae were positioned along the steel spans. Demolition charges. As the rest of his team joined him, he briefed them on what he'd seen then let each in turn study the view.

Next they moved around to the southernmost side of the bridge pier, which was out of sight of the shoreline, and cut an egress hole. Their equipment went up first, packed in dry bags and labelled with the owner, what was in it and for what use. Each checked their buddy's. Schaefer checked Iceman's, labelled Iceman. Demolition Charges. C4I2 No1 and gave him the OK sign.

With the team good to go, Schaefer lengthened the communication rope that connected him to Iceman, took a deep breath, unplugged himself from his breathing apparatus and let it fall away. Then, using his ice pick, he hauled himself half out of the water onto the ice. Satisfied he hadn't been compromised, he dragged himself completely out and slid across to the deep shadow of the concrete pier pulling his dry bag behind him. After unpacking and checking his weapons, he took a long look around before giving the communication rope a tug. Starting with Iceman, and looking like seals, each of his team popped their head up, looked around briefly, and then slid across the ice on their stomach to join him; their dry suit crackling as the water froze on it.

As he hooked on his grenade belt, Schaefer thought about Sanchez up on the plateau. He looked at the moon and, as she had asked, thought about the Sea of Tranquillity and her, knowing that she too would be watching it. Strange what love can do; it was almost as if this whole thing was a game and somehow he and Sanchez were detached from the reality of it. He snapped himself out of his reverie and checked his team's readiness. Smiling as if they knew what he was thinking, they each gave him the OK sign, their teeth contrasting with the camouflage stripes running diagonally across their faces. Two hours to go. He crept around the edge of the pier and looked across the 50-metre stretch of ice. A 2-metre rise of dark grey alluvial gravel and stone marked the transition from the fjord to the shoreline. The sound of rocks clattering onto the ice caught his attention. He focused on the location from where the sound had come, fixing the position of a bored-looking sentry. Someone came out of the C4I2 entrance, paused as if taking in the night sky and then walked over to the sentry. They started chatting, their breath steaming in the air.

SANCHEZ-HILL NO 3

Sanchez reversed gently back down the slope to join Williams. She tapped him on the arm and signed to him that she was going to take out the OP and that he was to watch her back. Then she drew a rough sketch of the position and shape of the OP.

Williams nodded but looked worried. Electing to ignore the possibilities, Sanchez rolled over onto her back, set the delay counters on three grenades to 2.5 seconds and then selected anti-personnel – close quarters – confined space from the options menu and clipped them onto her chest harness.

Both she and Williams now inched their way up the slope until they could just see over the plateau. Studying the landscape, Sanchez planned her approach to the OP, whilst Williams impressed her by being able to point out the position of the OP within seconds and letting her know where he should position himself to be able to give her cover. They were ready. Now all she had to do was worry about the things she didn't know about and, as she liked to tell everyone, when this was all that was left there was no point in worrying at all.

Next, she removed her helmet, took both Williams' and her spare water containers and poured the contents over her snowsuit and balaclava. The water would quickly freeze and her IR profile would be reduced for a precious few minutes. Controlling her breathing she slowed her heart rate, closed one eye to preserve night vision in case a flare went up, and started inching her way up and onto the plateau, where she experimented with various movements to find the best one to minimise noise. She found the one that worked best was when she used her forearms and toes only, keeping the rest of her body a few inches off the snow.

Now she needed to optimise her speed of approach; too fast, and she risked detection from noise and movement; too slow, and she would be exposed for longer and at risk of being spotted. She decided to increase her pace slightly, whilst being careful not to let her breathing become laboured.

At a distance of 20 metres from the OP she could hear the low murmuring of voices; taking the opportunity she increased her pace again. The wet balaclava had frozen and stuck to the stitches she'd received from her fall with Schaefer. They itched. A light flared in the centre of the observation slit as another cigarette was lit. Another 10 metres would put her behind Bertha the boulder and into a blind spot. Well, she thought, they certainly seemed relaxed, but then reminded herself that things could change in a heartbeat.

Then, without warning, the ground beneath her altered, the soft powder changed to a crust and her left elbow penetrated it with a crunch. To her, the noise sounded like an explosion and she froze, putting her face down into the snow to minimise heat trace, and held her breath. The voices from within the OP continued. Holy shit, she was within 10 metres of the observation slit and knew she couldn't move any further without sounding like someone walking on broken glass. She thought about using her grenades but knew the chances of success were too low.

The base plan had been for her to plant a line of decoys that resembled a patrol, then ensure that they drew fire. This would allow Lloyd-Smith to launch a smart barrage which would target the enemy fire positions.

So now it would have to be Plan B. If she hadn't signalled on time, Lloyd-Smith would assume she'd been compromised and launch a dumb bombardment. This would generate a diversion large enough to give her time to overcome whatever difficulty she was having, and allow her to set up the decoys for a second smart barrage.

She reckoned she had thirty minutes to go, but dared not look at her watch for risk of being detected. She would just have to wait in the open, hope they wouldn't spot her and then move in as soon as the dumb barrage began. She pushed her face deeper into the snow and started counting. Every fifty seconds she tensed each of her leg muscles in turn in an attempt to maintain circulation and prevent herself from stiffening up.

CROCKETT-BASE OF WATERFALL

Crockett made ready his ice picks, checked all his zips were done up and pulled his hood over his head to protect himself against the trickle of cold water he knew would become an issue. He, Jones and the squadron's two specialist ice climbers, Pavla and Tolstoy, would be the first up. They too had dumped their body armour, helmets and other heavy and restrictive gear. They would only carry ropes, pulleys, a silenced ice drill and their personal weapons. The rest of their gear would come up in their Bergens on the end of the ropes. They did a final check of their Bergens, making sure the equipment they needed first was on top.

"The angle's not too bad, about eighty degrees. Providing we don't hit an overhang I think we should be able to do the six hundred feet in under an hour," said Pavla, as he clipped on what looked like gold-plated professional sport crampons.

"If we do hit an overhang, we'll go ahead and secure a pull-you-up," added Tolstoy.

They started up the frozen waterfall, in a line four abreast. Each drove an ice pick into the wall of ice, checked the weight and then drove in a toe spike.

Amidst heavy breathing and showers of ice they slowly moved upwards. At a height of 10 metres Jones signalled for the second team to start. With the noise they were making in the otherwise silent night, Crockett wondered how long they would be able to climb before they were discovered.

Halfway up, he checked his altimeter and set an ice anchor for the dead- man-drop rope. The climb had got steeper as they went higher and was now close to ninety degrees. Despite his best attempts at prevention, cold water had found a way straight up his sleeves and then down his back and legs. But the worst thing was his fingers, which had started to cramp. He'd never really got used to the new ice pick designs, which had a smaller diameter handle grip than the older ones. He signalled to the others to take two minutes' rest, and transferring his weight to his feet, leant back against his harness and tried to work the cramps out of his hands. He smiled to himself as he remembered what his physical instructor used to shout at them in basic training: "Pain is just weakness wanting to get out of your sad little bodies".

He glanced across at the others; they too were wriggling their hands, trying to work out the cramps and get the blood flow back. Ready, they began to climb with more urgency. They worked their ice picks with aggression, sending small showers of ice raining down over the others below. He counted out his left arm swings and did a mental calculation: another hundred and fifty more. At number eighty-two his muscles felt the waterfall angle even further backwards; above him loomed an overhang. He paused and looked across at Pavla and Tolstoy. Without acknowledging any command they accelerated up the overhang, leaving Jones and himself to watch. "Shit," gasped Jones in praise as Tolstoy and Pavla reached the outside edge of the overhang, then turned upside down by placing a leg over each shoulder, and hung by their spurs to rest for a few seconds. Then in a manoeuvre that defied comprehension both pulled themselves upright, drove their picks into the ice and then continued up and over the overhang and out of sight.

"Fuck me," Jones said to Crockett, who was like him staring in awe at the two climbers above them.

"And me," echoed Crockett.

Seconds later, two ropes dropped down, and Crockett and Jones clipped on their drop brakes, swung away from the face and started stepping themselves up and over the overhang.

As they continued over the crest and onto the frozen river surface, both relished the change in weight and with it the change in the use of muscles, and leopard-crawled across to the shelter of the right-hand riverbank.

Panting from the effort of the climb, no words were exchanged as they brushed the sweat and water from their hair and then took turns in blowing uselessly onto their white silk cotton gloves in an attempt to warm up their hands. Then, arm over arm, they started to pull up their Bergens; their forearms were burning and felt like jelly before they'd finished.

Olly's head appeared, signalling that all of them were now up.

"You wait till I catch up with fucking Winston. I swear that bastard was purposefully dropping ice chunks on my head," he gasped.

A few of the crouched shapes chuckled.

"Keep it down. Let's get ourselves sorted," ordered Jones.

Whilst organising their gear and donning their armour, they munched on chocolate and energy bars, the rigours of the climb already just another memory.

Winston and his mortar squad moved into a small recess carved out of the riverbank and started assembling the two 40mm composite-material mortars they would use as close artillery support. As he worked, Winston mentally ran over his preparations. He had contracted O'Reilly a few months earlier to obtain the latest M7 stealth rounds, which meant that radar backtracking of their rounds' trajectories would be almost impossible. Together with their thermal blankets the mortar team would be very difficult to locate. But just in case, he'd told his team to prepare two alternate firing positions each about 50 metres from the other and pre-position rounds at each.

For ranging and fire control without the aid of electronic equipment, Winston had devised a system that used simple trigonometry and optics. Each of the signal flares the assault teams carried had been modified to release a small reflector that would hang 20 metres beneath the flare itself. Whoever fired the flare would need to put it somewhere near the target, preferably directly over it. All Winston then had to do was measure the relative angles between the flare and the reflector with his optics, and they would have a range. Once over the target area, the smart rounds would home in on their targets using their own sensors.

Finished with their preparations, they settled down to wait.

SCHAEFER-C412 - NW SIDE OF FJORD

Schaefer checked his watch. Ten minutes. He gave the signal to move. The moon that was now behind the bridge was casting a deep shadow, which he used as he leopard-crawled on his stomach across the ice towards the shoreline. He carried a silenced pistol, his grenade belt and a combat knife. One of the sentries was still loitering near the entrance to the C412, chatting with someone inside. Laughter rolled across the ice towards him. After each metre of advance he paused and listened, forcing himself not to hurry. As he reached the shore, his heart was thumping so loudly in his ears he thought the sentries must be able to hear it.

LLOYD-SMITH - 8 KM NORTH OF BRIDGE

Deep in a pine forest on the north side of the fjord, 8 kilometres from the bridge, Lloyd-Smith's watch started vibrating again. The first time had been five minutes earlier. Sanchez had not signalled and was obviously having trouble. It was time to launch the secondary fire plan, which would generate enough of a commotion to allow her to get herself sorted out. Lloyd-Smith checked one last time with Sergeant Gyan who was studying the night sky for Sanchez's signal flares. Gyan shook his head in confirmation there was nothing.

Lloyd-Smith sighed, straightened himself and then strutted across the snow to the fire control station, his white combat smock open at the neck to reveal his blue silk neck scarf. His battery team looked at him in expectation; in response he stood with his arm raised before pronouncing, "Gentlemen of the artillery, as that world-famous British Field Marshal Bernard Montgomery, said, artillery lends dignity to what would otherwise be a vulgar brawl." He paused for a second as if to let his message sink in, before bringing his hand down with a theatrical flourish and simultaneously shouting in his best and most dramatic English, "Five salvos. Fire for effect!"

There was a short pause before the MILMS rocked slightly as each of the five salvos of 500 aerial mines and electronic ghosts were fired in rapid succession. Sitting in the control van, one of his team, Gunner Cook, monitored the flight trajectories. With the slight northerly wind Lloyd-Smith had set the parachutes on the mines to open about a hundred metres upwind of the target area. He gave Lloyd-Smith the thumbs-up.

SCHAEFER - C412 - NW SIDE OF FJORD

Three minutes. The nearest sentry was now no more than 10 metres away. They waited, each in his own preferred body position that they had evolved over many operations to prevent cramp. With thirty seconds to go Schaefer switched on the mini heater in his weapon; although the heat signature was a risk, he preferred this to the risk of either a feed jam or a misfire from ice build-up. The green light on the rear of the weapon told him all was good just as Lloyd-Smith's opening barrage began.

"Well, at least Drop Short is on time for once," commented Schaefer, referring to the infantry's derogatory term for all artillery.

CHAPTER 14

SWARM BARRAGE

Stir opponents up, making them respond to you. Then you can observe their forms of behaviour and whether they are orderly or confused.

LLOYD-SMITH' – 8 KM NORTH OF BRIDGE

"End of mission – bug out!" ordered Lloyd-Smith, knowing that even though they'd iced the MILMS with water to lower its heat signature, and were using stealth-cased munitions, they would be quickly targeted by counter battery fire as the enemy deduced the approximate launch trajectory of the incoming rounds. Within seconds they were on the snow scooters and towing away the control and power vans.

"Shoot and scoot," shouted another of his team, Gunner Piper, as he revved a snow scooter in readiness for departure.

"Fire and manoeuvre, Gunner Piper, fire and manoeuvre," corrected Lloyd-Smith, feeling elated.

SCHAEFER - STALKER SITE

The two sentries guarding the entrance to the Stalker site reacted like snakes awoken in the cold, their movements becoming more energetic as the intensity of Lloyd-Smith's opening artillery barrage built. Schaefer rose to a kneeling position, feeling the familiar mixture of fear and adrenaline flood through him. From experience he knew the next five minutes would pass almost in slow motion, but be over very quickly. Some of the squadron called the effect the vortex.

The calmness came and the world slowed as he shot the closest sentry. Iceman killed the second. Together they crossed the ice to the Stalker entrance. From inside the entrance they could hear the sound of turbines winding up. Moving quickly, they entered a wide tunnel carved out of the deep snow. Someone approached from the opposite direction and managed a look of surprise just before Schaefer shot him twice in the forehead.

Thirty paces further on they emerged into an open-air space some 15 by 15 metres, surrounded by high walls of snow. Two matt black Stalker gunships were lifting clear of their service pads, their turbo fans kicking up a whirlwind of snow and their sensor arrays glowing a dull red as they swivelled beneath the hulls. Two more Stalkers remained on the service pads but two other bays were empty.

"Shit. Too late. The bastards are out of their cage," cursed Schaefer.

"Let's follow the control umbilical and fuck up their command centre," replied Iceman, pointing to the control umbilical that snaked away from the service pads into an adjoining tunnel.

Ignoring the two craft lifting off they followed the umbilical along the tunnel to a maintenance area. Iceman shot a technician working at a bench as they continued on into another tunnel. After just a few metres the tunnel opened out to a control room. Overhead screens showed the start-up sequences for the remaining two Stalkers as well as data from the four that were airborne. Schaefer and Iceman killed five flight techs including their commander before the other seven even realised that they'd been compromised. As the survivors scrambled for their sidearms, Iceman and Schaefer shot them as if they were on a house-clearing exercise, each of the threats slumping to the floor in turn, like puppets whose strings had been cut.

Without exchanging a word Schaefer and Iceman now positioned two-minute delay, phosphorous and HE grenades amongst the servers, CPUs, power supply and distribution boxes before retreating back to the landing bay where they dropped more grenades into the service hatches of the grounded Stalkers.

As they made their way out, two enemy came running towards them. Schaefer and Iceman dropped to one knee and fired in unison, as if they were performing a dance. Someone ran from a side tunnel, slipped and hit the ice-hard ground with a thump; a sidearm skidded towards them.

A young woman stared at Schaefer with frightened eyes. He fired twice directly at them and then moved on. Outside they could hear a fire-fight.

As they emerged from the tunnel, one of Schaefer's team approached.

"The C4I2's toast. Trouble is, the bastards are blocking our access onto the bridge."

"Good work. We got the Stalker C and C, but four are out of the nest. Any cas?"

"None."

"OK, let's get ourselves up on to the bridge."

SANCHEZ - HILL NO 3

Sanchez had counted to 1,650 when she heard the rapid series of muffled pops, which she recognised as the sound of aerial mines and sub-munitions deploying from their mother pods. Lloyd-Smith's fire mission had arrived at last.

All across the northern approach roads to the bridge, hundreds of aerial mines and electronic ghost target decoys would now be falling on small parachutes or gliding on mini wings to earth. Several white flashes, followed by sharp explosions, told her that some had already found targets.

It was time. Ignoring the pins and needles in her right foot and the cramp in her left arm, she stood and ran the few metres to the cover of Bertha the boulder. Adrenaline obliterated any fear. She sensed the enemy inside the OP stirring; any moment and they would be at stand to positions, searching for their enemy. She could hear the sound of hurried movement and hushed voices from inside the OP. She selected fully automatic on her assault pistol and engaged the weapon's heater. Then, whilst looking back across the plateau to make sure that Williams had remained on the reverse slope out of sight, she froze in shock. The tracks she had left on her approach were being lit up by the angle of the moonlight. They stood out like luminescent paint. Fuck it. She had seconds before the people in the OP would see them too. She armed a grenade, and a small red light winked twice in response, signifying it was now safe only as long as she maintained a grip.

She held the assault weapon in her left hand and the grenade in her right and stood ready to storm the OP; her heart raced. Her mind ran through the next steps. Shit. From her angle there was no way she could get the grenade into the OP's window: she was right-armed and the throw needed a left. She decided to take a chance; scrambling around Bertha she moved across to the opposite side of the OP that looked over the approach roads.

It too had a narrow slit of a window, and for an instant she sat no more than a metre away facing it. Inside she could clearly make out surprised faces. Frightened that she would miss if she threw the grenade, she leant forward and simply posted it through the slit, then rolled onto the OP's roof. The detonation, although muffled by the snow, was still loud and thumped through the ground into her, the flash that jetted out of the windows temporarily destroying her night vision.

Next she dropped a phosphorous grenade through the same window as before, diving back behind her friend, Bertha the boulder. The muffled explosion this time brought with it the sound of snow sizzling and the smell of burning flesh as the phosphorous did its work.

She left Bertha again and now emptied a magazine into the OP, working the muzzle from side to side as well as up and down.

She waited for sixty seconds and, using her weapon's sights, checked to see if there was any sign of movement. Satisfied, she signalled Williams, who acknowledged and clambered up on to the plateau, dragging their gear behind him.

She changed magazines and checked the area for any response units. Then just as her adrenalin levels started to subside, first one hand and then another punched through the snow no more than a metre from her. They seemed to be grasping at the air as if they knew where she was. Recovering, her mind ran the reasoning and deduced there must have been a sleeping hole running off to the side of the OP. Whoever it was now grasping at the air must have been asleep and had woken to find himself buried. Keeping an eye on the grasping hands that were now trying to dig their way out of the snow, she stood, the hands now either side of her feet. She fired half a dozen rounds down into the snow. The hands twitched, clenched again at nothing and then stopped moving.

Williams joined her, stared at the hands for a moment and then dumped their gear on the snow.

"Shit, I'm glad to be rid of this lot. It weighs a ton!"

Together they moved across to the edge of the plateau where they could overlook the northern passes below. Occasional flashes and explosions still erupted from the barrage and there were half a dozen or so fires lighting up pale yellow circles of snow from direct hits. Suddenly, two black silhouettes flashed past them no more than 10 metres away.

"Fuck. Did you see that?" shouted Williams.

"Stalker gunships. They're after Lloyd-Smith. We're not worth them stopping for at the moment. Come on. Let's set up the dummies; we haven't much time left. There's a small ledge about thirty metres below us – see it? That'll do perfectly."

The dummies they'd prepared were designed to mimic a column of infantry. They each had an IR beacon that generated a heat profile of a human, and which varied slightly over time to simulate a slow walking-like movement. This movement was then made more realistic by placing the beacons on top of thin wooden staffs that had small sails that would catch the gentle breeze on the plateau and create a swaying motion. Sanchez was sure that any half-intelligent sensor below them would lock on to the perceived threat, and expected a fairly rapid and heavy response.

"Shit. I missed the ledge," said Williams in the tone of a young schoolboy, as one of the dummies ended up a few metres further down the steep slope.

"No worries, amigo. It'll look even better from below. Let's hurry. Lloyd-Smith and his team will be setting up their second fire position and those Stalkers will be searching."

Finished, they moved to their left 200 metres, turned on the dummies using a remote and settled down to watch.

It took a little more than ten seconds for the enemy to react. Tracer arced up towards the ledge from at least half a dozen locations. Sanchez patted Williams on the shoulder in congratulations, and Williams, despite looking nervous as occasional rounds flew past their own position, managed a satisfied smile.

"Well, this should give Drop Short something to aim at. Let's send him the invite," said Sanchez.

They fired two green signal flares.

LLOYD-SMITH – 10 KM NORTH OF BRIDGE

Two kilometres to the west of their first firing position, Lloyd-Smith prepared for his second fire-plan. His gunnery team were making up the control umbilical from the control and power vans to the MILMS launcher itself.

"Careful not to overheat the seal rings," advised Sergeant Gyan, as he held the umbilical stab plates slightly apart whilst Gunner Colins played a gas flame over them to make sure there was no ice or water in the connections.

"No worries, Sarge."

"Sanchez says we're good to go," shouted Frost, who was monitoring the sky from the top of a pine tree above them.

"Good. Get down here. We're out of here as soon as we shoot," said Gyan.

Unlike their first, the second fire-plan would use swarm intelligence and smart munitions designed to seek and destroy any identified enemy which were now engaging Sanchez's dummies and the ghost decoys from their first dumb barrage.

A sound like the wings of a large bird followed by a staggered series of muffled explosions rippled across the cold and dense night air, causing them to pause from their work and look towards their previous fire position.

"Well, that didn't take them too long; those are Stalkers hitting our last position," said Gyan.

"Quick. But it did sound a little short," added Lloyd-Smith with a smile, as he continued the ready checks on the MILMS.

"They'll take a few minutes to check out the results. When they find we've bugged out they won't take long to locate us... I'd say we've got three minutes, four at the outside," said Sergeant Gyan, grunting as he snapped the umbilical into place. "Umbilical secure, launcher primed."

The last member of Lloyd-Smith's team, Gunner Zimbabwe, completed lowering the auto loader and locked it into place with a hydraulic thud. "Ready on two," he announced.

Gyan fired up the diagnostics display, gently warming his bare hands by blowing on them as the system completed its boot-up. Seconds later his fingers whirled across the keyboard. Lloyd-Smith took up a position next to him, and the rest of his team gathered at their battery stations in readiness.

"Gentlemen, and of course madam," said Lloyd-Smith, referring to the female Gunner Frost, "your attention please. There's nothing like a little on-the-job education," he said in the tone of a lecturer. "There are times when rapid rates of fire are called for. However, in most instances the weapon systems are poorly utilised resulting in excessive fire being laid down on targets for little or no return. Excessive fire places enormous demand on the logistics chain to keep pace with ammunition expenditure, something that any civilised army abhors. For this fire mission however, rapid fire enables us to unleash a vast amount of killing force onto a target-rich environment in a short time. This is, in effect, a textbook case. Remember it."

"Right you are, sir," replied Frost, shaking her head in disbelief as she finished cross-checking Gyan's fire-control profile.

"Aye, right you are, sir," came the mumbled responses from the others.

The MILMS weapon Lloyd-Smith had elected to use was an electronic Kytusha Mark 7000 multi-barrel artillery piece. One hundred 50mm smart HE rounds were stacked in each of the twenty-five barrels. Each round in turn contained three smart sub-munitions.

Gyan completed uploading their initial position, area map and proposed trajectory, and then hit the Disseminate to all button that downloaded the same information to each and every round. With the diagnostics and error-checking complete, the rounds each acknowledged their status, and whilst Gyan hummed La Marseillaise a string of green lights flared across his status panel. Two rounds had red signatures, for which he acknowledged the abort on launch command for both.

"We've got ninety-nine per cent availability. All systems green. Power is up. Launcher ready," he announced.

"I concur," said Frost.

"Gunner Cook, would you like the honours?" asked Lloyd-Smith.

Stifling his surprise at the calmness of his commanding officer, Gunner Cook decided he'd do his best to emulate him. "One hundred salvos. Fire for effect!"

The master fire computer commenced the electronic firing sequence. The darkness around the gun crew flared a brilliant white and a dull fart, as Frost referred to the sound, reverberated around the forest, somewhat deflating Cook's theatrics and signifying that all twenty-five hundred rounds, each containing three sub-munitions, were now on their way to the target area.

Through a cloud of white smoke Gyan called out to Lloyd-Smith: "Good feedback on the rounds; targets being acquired. Networking is enabled. Auto loader good on all tubes except number three, which has a feed jam."

3 MILES ABOVE NORTH END OF BRIDGE

The first fifteen rounds from Lloyd-Smith's swarm barrage arrived over the target area at an altitude of just over three miles where they each deployed hundreds of winged mini robots. These housed the sensors, mapping, command and control payloads. Acting as a networked swarm, they began to map and assign threat levels to the enemy positions that were engaging Sanchez's ghost infantry and Lloyd-Smith's decoys from his first barrage.

The next fifteen rounds to arrive over the target area were deployed a hundred metres below the first. These carried laser targeting pods, each of which had 196 individual gyro-stabilised lasers powered by a thermal battery. Before energising their lasers, they first checked the atmospheric conditions and uploaded the target data from the command and control network above them. Satisfied that their operating envelopes were good, they then fired up the lasers and synchronised them with the target maps.

With all systems good, the command and control network now instructed half of the 7,500 smart munitions, that were waiting on their parachutes for their individual fire missions, to engage.

HODGETTS' - HILL NO 1

Hodgetts had used the emergency vent in his suit, dumped the heat and then crawled under a rock outcrop covered in a snowdrift a few metres away. It wasn't perfect but it should protect him from IR sensors for a while.

He had tuned his rifle sights to the wavelength of Lloyd-Smith's target designation lasers, and now was awestruck as he watched the hundreds of beams that shone down from the night sky like long hypodermic needles. Some targets seemed to warrant only one beam, others were pinpointed with up to ten. Several beams were moving like spotlights on an ice ring following a skater as they tracked moving targets. He spotted the first of the delayed munitions hanging on parachutes waiting for commands to engage just as the first salvo impacted the area in an increasing crescendo.

"Fuck me. Drop Short's hit the jackpot for once," he muttered.

SANCHEZ - HILL NO 3

Across from Hodgetts, Sanchez and Williams also watched as plumes of snow polluted with orange flame, dirt, rock, pieces of pine tree, and human and mechanical debris were hurled into the air. Sanchez thought the barrage possessed its own musical pattern: some explosions seemed to be sequenced in short staccatos, others were staggered with longer pauses in between, some came in unison, and some in harmony. The tones, too, were different, as ground, subsurface and air bursts each erupted with their own signatures.

A flash followed by a blast front and hot air raced across their position, as a weapon detonated on top of a Stalker that had been only a hundred metres away from them.

"Fuck this. That's the second time one of those things has nearly found us," said Williams.

"Probably back-tracked on our signal flares. But at least Drop Short got our quarantine area correct; there's been nothing on us. Let's signal the good news, and after that, as the shepherd would say to his sheep, get the flock out of here."

LLOYD-SMITH 10KM NORTH OF BRIDGE

After the first wave of detonations, Lloyd-Smith's airborne command and control network reviewed the situation and transmitted a bomb damage assessment report and follow-up attack profile back to Lloyd-Smith at the command van before settling down to wait on the humans to advise if there should be any alterations to its proposed plan.

On the ground, inside the control van, Lloyd-Smith and his gun crew stood around the Crystal Ball which displayed a three-dimensional image of the target area, allowing them to view it from different angles, looking for defilades and hard points.

"It's target rich," said Lloyd-Smith.

"More like bees round a honey pot," commented Piper.

"We need to increase the radar microwave energy along the south-east side. We've got too many shadows," said Gyan.

"On it," said Frost, sending the command.

Some of the shadows now vanished as they walked around the display. "That's the best I can do," said Frost.

"Give me a filter on all high-value hard targets please," said Lloyd-Smith. The display changed again.

"I suggest we tag each one of these with a Mongoose followed with a Copper Head. That way we'll be sure to take them out. We've got more than enough redundancy," said Colins, referring to the Mongoose projectiles which had small actuated fins allowing them to fly to targets that were in defilade.

"Let's do it. Remember we won't be using IFF, so fire the lot. I don't want any chance of a blue on blue once the Major and the guys commence their run," said Lloyd-Smith, making sure that by firing all the munitions he had available, there would not be any chance that his barrage could engage friendly forces.

"Roger. Uploading now... Command verified," said Gyan, watching just long enough to make sure that the command and control network had acknowledged, before shutting down the manual command console.

"*C'est bon. Allez!*" he shouted.

"I agree, Sergeant, we better clear off now," said Lloyd-Smith as his watch started vibrating, indicating that their safety window had closed.

They'd pre-marked their escape route along a narrow forest track with simple strips of tape wrapped around trees earlier in the day, and with the moonlight they didn't need the scooters' lamps. Lloyd-Smith was the last to leave. As he sped away, a series of loud explosions erupted, signalling the arrival of the expected Stalker counter attack. He felt invincible.

ABOVE NORTH END OF BRIDGE

Over the target area the command network adjusted its attack profile according to Lloyd-Smith's command and instructed half of the remaining smart sub-munitions to engage. With the second attack completed, the network now moved into a mopping-up operation, waiting for as long as possible before engaging any remaining targets. In all, every enemy target had been attacked by twenty individual accurate weapons. The kill rate was estimated to be 99.9%. Enemy fire from ground positions had ceased.

SANCHEZ - HILL NO 3

The barrage was subsiding and, apart from the occasional delayed action explosion, it was nearly quiet now. The swarm had done its work.

"Fucking A. Let's go," said Williams.

A sixth sense pulled Sanchez's attention to the furthest western approach road.

"Give me the optics."

"Jesus, what about those Stalkers? We'll get zeroed in a heartbeat if we hang out here much longer," pleaded Williams.

"Just do it. There's something I need to check."

She scanned the distance and in an instant recognised the danger.

"Fuck it! We've got a column of AFVs. Inbound from the west. I'd say ten maybe twelve in total. They're moving fast."

"They'll run straight into our AFVs. Shit, the Major won't stand a chance. We've got to warn them," said Williams, surprising Sanchez at the turn of temperament.

"Or stop them," she replied.

"Say again?"

"Destroy them."

"With what? The swarm barrage is probably spent," replied Williams looking at Sanchez and trying to see if she was serious.

"Nature," she said, pointing to a crack that had opened up in the snowline about a hundred metres below her. "There's a crack in the snowline below us, beginning of an avalanche; if we can mark it there's a chance Hodgetts and his team could drop the whole lot into the valley."

Williams squinted to get better focus. The first signs of an avalanche waiting to happen were unmistakable: a giant slab of ice and snow had slid about a metre down the slope, baring the grey mountain beneath.

"Sounds wicked. How are we going to let him know?"

"I don't know, I'm making this up as we go along. Wait, you mark out the avalanche line with all the IR strobes we've got left. I'll tell him what to do," she ordered, turning on the laser and IR flash on her assault weapon and pointing it in the direction she guessed Hodgetts would be.

Despite the extreme range, an arc of tracer swung up almost lazily towards them from the lead AFV of the enemy column.

"Good, that's attracted a little attention. Let's hope Hodgetts has noticed it too."

HODGETTS - HILL NO 1

As the final barrage stopped, a peace descended around them, broken only by the crackling of timbers from burning pine trees and the occasional moan from the wounded, who, reckoned Hodgetts, were probably still too shocked to start screaming.

Hodgetts waited a further two minutes before feeling sure that the barrage had ended.

"Thank fuck for that. I felt like a bloody turkey at Christmas. Just waiting to be roasted," said Hodgetts.

A line of tracer arched up towards Sanchez's position from the approach road to their left.

"Where the fuck's that from? And what the fuck are Williams and Sanchez doing? They should be bugging out," whispered Strachan who had spotted Williams on the opposite ridgeline dropping IR strobes onto the ledge below.

"Sanchez is signing us in Morse… Fuck me, she says there is an X-ray AFV column approaching from the west. Six klicks. Moving fast. Sixty…" reported Wilcox.

"I thought there were no other units or armour around here," said Strachan.

"The fog of war, eh?" replied Hodgetts.

"What the hell are we going to do?" asked Strachan.

"Wait one," interrupted Wilcox. "She's sending more… Avalanche on my markers… What is she talking about?"

"Clever girl! Look at the IR strobes - see the fracture line just below the ledge? The bombardment must have started a slide," said Hodgetts, drawing a line on his optics display and cross-loading the image to the others.

"Jesus. Got it. All we need to do is wait until the column is below Sanchez and bring the whole hillside down on them. Nice one. We have got to be around to see this; what a goat fuck this will be," said Strachan in a voice filled with awe and a little elation.

"Send some tracer back to her as an acknowledgement," ordered Hodgetts.

Strachan selected Automatic – Tracer Only and fired ten rounds at the line of strobes. As he did, he noticed movement from the south.

"Boys. Threat. We've got movement two o'clock. Six, maybe seven total," he said.

Hodgetts followed the track arrow on his display and panned to the right. A target came up on the scope; he was standing in a small dugout pointing in Sanchez's direction.

"They must have been inside Drop Short's quarantine area. Right, listen up. I'm going to take out the AFV column. Strachan, you look after Sanchez. Wilcox, you're my eyes. I'm going to lay two lines of HE grenades, delayed fuse with synchronous detonation, triggered from the last shot. I'll put the first batch into the avalanche line, the second on that row of deflectors below. See them?"

"Got it. How many rounds and what delay?" asked Wilcox.

"Thirty should do it, twenty on the avalanche line and ten for the deflectors below. We need to destroy the deflectors or the force of the avalanche will be dissipated. If that column is doing sixty, that gives us… six minutes. Three minutes to lay the grenades, one minute to bring the hillside down and a minute to fuck about. Let's go for a thirty-second delay; last two shots will be command signals. Got it?" ordered Hodgetts who seemed to be relishing the challenge.

"Shit. They're going after her," said Strachan in an angry voice.

Hodgetts glanced across at his friend. He knew the emotions that Strachan would be experiencing but trusted him to override them and analyse the situation coolly. The first rule in such a situation was to break up the chain of command. Don't just blast away at everyone.

Strachan liked to run commentaries as he worked and his next words confirmed Hodgetts' faith in Strachan's skills. "Bingo. Senior NCO, three upside-down chevrons. Back shot. Body armour. Armour piercing – anti-personnel selected."

Hodgetts recognised the familiar pause as Strachan took up the first pressure on his forefinger and breathed deeply. "Firing," he whispered as he exhaled and squeezed the trigger. The LR-51 recoiled with a hiss as the flash suppression and silencer vented gas. Without checking for the results Strachan rapidly adjusted his sights to the remaining targets. In all, he fired six rounds in under five seconds.

"I got four. Two left, but they've gone to ground. You have got to be fucking joking. How many more of these bastards are there? New threat. Track right on the ridgeline. Three three zero metres. Then drop five zero metres. Second group sheltering behind a rock outcrop," reported Strachan as he continued his one-man war.

Hodgetts finished synchronising the last of the grenades and chambered the first in the LR-51 launcher. He wrapped the weapon's shoulder strap around his elbow and then, using the laser ranger, measured the distance to the IR strobes that Sanchez had placed. The targeting screen lit up with range and bearings, and he pushed Acknowledge and selected Gyro-Stabilised. Now, whenever he moved, the launcher would automatically adjust its elevation, and provided he remained within the lock of the gimbals all he had to do was chamber rounds and pull the trigger.

"I've got eyes on Sanchez's AFV column. Oh, this is just fucking wonderful. Lead is a Mark 5 MBT. Six zero kilometres an hour," advised Wilcox.

Hodgetts took a look as the MBT rounded a sharp bend; it threw a spray of snow into the air as it slid sideways slightly. Behind it, another six MBTs and several AFVs followed, their barrels pointing to the left and right in staggered attack formation.

As if they wanted to further announce their presence the MBTs fired a salvo bracketing Sanchez's position.

"She's fine and the idiots are helping us; they'll start their own avalanche," said Strachan jovially as he continued to harass the enemy who were closing on Sanchez's position.

Hodgetts fired the first fin-stabilised grenade and ejected the shell casing.

"Two metres below the line," advised Wilcox, as a small puff of snow erupted from the ground.

Hodgetts reloaded and fired again.

"Twenty metres high. Five to the right," continued Wilcox's commentary.

"Ah, bollocks. The gyros have packed up. Do you know, in future, we might as well leave all this tech crap behind and come to war in our underwear. There's fuck all that works. I'll use manual sights," said

173

Hodgetts, flicking up the manual sights and powering off the electronics.

His next series of shots were on target, and he continued until he had laid down two parallel lines of grenades, one at the point where he would start the avalanche and the second amongst the snow deflectors below.

"Ready. How much further have our friends got to go?"

"About twenty seconds."

"Let's get this show on the road then, shall we?" said Hodgetts as he fired the command rounds into the middle of the two rows of grenades, which then initiated commands for all of the delayed action grenades to detonate at the same time.

A wall of snow lifted about 3 metres into the air before subsiding, and for a few seconds nothing else happened. Then the sheet metal and timbers that made up the avalanche deflectors lower down the slope started to slide and as they did a hairline crack in the snow below Sanchez's position began to get wider. The whole side of the pass was beginning to slide in one giant slab. As it picked up speed, the slab broke into separate pieces and then turned into a turbulent rush as it headed down towards the roadway.

With the deflectors gone, the route was now open for the full force of the avalanche to build. Hodgetts could see that, on the roadway below, the armoured column had spotted the danger and slowed. They seemed unsure what to do. The lead MBT stopped, and then accelerated again in a vain attempt to clear the danger area. Above it, trees and boulders were now being picked up and swept forward on the growing wave of snow and ice.

One of the tanks, sensing that it would not escape the onslaught, slewed to its right and tried to drive up the slope towards Hodgetts. It stalled some 30 metres up, its tracks racing and scrabbling to maintain traction. In response, Hodgetts calmly chambered another grenade and fired just to the front of the stricken vehicle. Although useless against the armour, it was enough to dislodge the snow, and the tank started sliding sideways backwards towards the onrushing avalanche.

Ignoring the carnage that was now taking place, Hodgetts turned his attention back to helping protect Sanchez. "Where are they?"

"They've moved round behind her. One o'clock. Five hundred metres."

"Got them. Let's give Snow White some help," said Hodgetts as he spotted her hunters.

Sanchez and Williams crawled back to the ridgeline as more rounds flew over them. She surveyed the pass below. The avalanche had done its job. There was no sign of the armoured column and nothing was going to be able to use the road until summertime.

"We need to let the squadron know we're good to go. Let's give them the six reds. Then we'll bug out; there are some pissed-off people up here. We'll leg it north then double back on a south-easterly track. Leave everything except your weapon. You never know, we might get lucky and hook up with Lloyd-Smith. You ready?" she asked.

"About fucking time," replied Williams, firing the first of the red signal flares.

CHAPTER 15

BATTLE FOR THE BRIDGE – INTO CHAOS

The most efficient of movements is the one that is unexpected.

CROCKETT - SOUTH SIDE OF BRIDGE

Crockett had led his assault group south for 3 kilometres along the frozen river that fed the waterfall, making use of the diversion that Lloyd-Smith's artillery barrage had created. Over the millennia the river had cut a deep course and the frozen surface was 3 metres below the level of the surrounding ground. According to his map, it ran parallel to the bridge road for about 4 kilometres before turning right and heading under it through a culvert. It would be at this culvert that Crockett planned to join the road and launch their assault on the C4I2. Crockett was glad to be using muscles that his body could remember rather than those he'd employed for the climb. Each of them wore reindeer skin covers over their snowshoes, which muffled any noise and provided grip.

Sanchez's signal flares with their magnesium smoke trails lit up the night sky on the opposite side of the bridge. The sounds of a nearby firefight drifted towards them.

"The Sarge has made contact," said someone excitedly, referring to Jones who'd led part of the team off towards the southern end of the bridge as a blocking force.

"Hush it up. You'll get your turn," whispered Olly.

176

Something shiny caught Crockett's eye in a recess off to his left. He signalled the others to halt and moved slowly forwards to investigate. They needed to be wary of sensors and tripwires.

It took him a moment to realise what he was seeing, and even then his brain remained in denial whilst his eyes continued to acquire images. The shining object was a wristwatch. The cutback was full of bodies, some stripped naked, others still with their white combat gear on. They lay in a tangled frozen heap partly covered by snow. They were allied soldiers, both men and women. He moved closer, and wiped the covering of snow away from the closest, a woman in her mid-twenties. He looked at another, a male, this time with a major's insignia on his lapel. He had a neat hole in his forehead. His eyes were open and looked to be full of sorrow.

"They've been fucking executed," whispered Olly, who'd joined him.

"A few look like they've died from combat wounds, but yeah, most have been executed," replied Crockett, thinking about the people who now lay frozen and naked, dumped like refuse.

"Bastards," muttered Pavla.

"Definitely time for a visit from Johnny Payback," said someone.

"Quiet. Let's move on. We've got a job to do and we're falling behind time. We've got to reach the culvert under the main roadway."

They continued towards the culvert in staggered formation, the earlier atmosphere of excitement and fear now replaced with silent aggression. They were 300 metres from the right turn to the culvert when Crockett heard the dull whir of a silenced Gatling somewhere above him. Before he could react, a stream of shell casings fell limply into the snow around him where they sizzled, generating little puffs of steam. In front of him, two of his team seemed to jerk around as if they were being electrocuted before collapsing.

"Stalker! Get to the culvert!" shouted someone.

Crockett dumped his Bergen and then sprinted as best he could on the ice, whilst zigzagging. Someone overtook him still carrying a Bergen, moving in a straight line towards the comforting gloom of the culvert about a hundred metres away. Crockett accelerated, deciding that weaving around on the ice was probably not the fastest way to get under cover. As he reached the dark safety of the culvert he slipped on polished ice and ended up careering along on his back. Others piled in behind him, some colliding, some falling over one another. For a few seconds they lay there, each just panting for breath.

"Who's missing, apart from Gilberto and Paul?" asked Crockett, getting his breath back.

"I saw Trevor go down," said Olly. "Poor bastard was carrying the fucking GPMG and slipped. That fucking Stalker just hovered five metres off him and then opened up. It was like it was fucking taunting him. And since when did they put silencers on those bastards?"

"Anyone else hurt?"

"My knee's gone," said Pavla.

"You all right to move?" asked Crockett.

"Drop of morphine and I'll be fine."

"Equipment? Anyone else lose their Bergens?" asked Crockett, looking around and discovering he was the only one who'd ditched his.

"No, sir, that's an officer's prerogative," said Olly.

"Thanks," replied Crockett, feeling embarrassed. "Get some signal flares and set up fire positions at both the entrances. We've got to move on the C4I2 or we're stuffed."

Crockett studied the interior; the culvert was constructed from grey concrete encrusted with watery ice. As his eyes adjusted to the gloom he spotted an aluminium ladder that he reckoned would lead to a service hatch in the roadway above.

"I'm going to check out that access ladder."

Pushing the hatch open an inch, he let it rest on his head, then creased his eyes against a flurry of snowflakes and looked out. He was in the centre of the dual carriage roadway, between the traffic crash barriers. From below, the echoes of small arms fire reverberated around the culvert as Olly and the others took shots at the Stalker. Crockett slid down the ladder.

"That fucking thing's evil! It just sneaked down to have a look and then fucked off as soon as we opened up," shouted Olly, sounding almost indignant.

"The hatch leads into the central roadway reservation, between the crash barriers. We don't have much time; they'll have a reaction force en route and if we sit and wait, we're going to end up getting penned in. We'll get Winston to lay some smoke and decoys. I'll go out of the hatch with Andrews; the rest of you lose as much kit as possible and then bomb burst out in as many directions as you can; give them too many targets. Then we'll regroup. Corporal Olly, I want you to go north and link up with the Sergeant Major. Pavla, wait here and then see if you can get yourself up on to the road for the squadron to pick you up," said Crockett.

JONES - SOUTHERN BRIDGE APPROACHES

After leaving Crockett at the top of the waterfall, Jones had led a squad across open, slightly undulating ground towards the southern end of the bridge. They'd moved pepper pot style, dashing 20 metres forward before going to ground, waiting for thirty seconds and then moving forward again. They were sweating and Jones was glad of a break as he took the time to reconnoitre the area. Galeago's squad was out in a skirmish line on his right flank. From the noise of the firefight alone Jones knew he'd already made contact. To his left was Crockett, and another firefight.

"Let's move; the bastards will have a quick reaction force. Any luck and we can bushwhack them en route. Fletcher, Macnie, Tucker, we'll move to our left a little and set up the GPMG on the reverse slope of that rise. Medic Rider, get ahead of us a little, you can be our eyes and ears," ordered Jones.

CROCKETT - CULVERT 2 KM SOUTH OF C412

Lying on their backs in a drainage ditch between the crash barriers, Crockett and Trooper Andrews fired the signal flares requesting a fire mission from Winston. Within sixty seconds, smoke canisters, flares, and flashing UV, IR and electronic decoys started falling around their position, accompanied by dull pops and hissing noises. The air around them soon became thick with smoke, interspersed with magnesium light and flashing lasers. They could hear the Stalker engaging what they hoped were decoys.

"Let's go," said Crockett, grabbing Andrews. A sixth sense more than anything else warned Crockett to go to ground in the drainage ditch in the central reservation of the roadway. He could hear the unmistakable sound of snow scooters approaching. They stopped. Then came shouted commands. Crockett signalled to Andrews to cover the right-hand side of the roadway and then set two grenades to Personnel – Open Ground-Detonate on Impact Plus Two Seconds.

Lying flat in the drainage channel Crockett could make out the first pair of boots walk past, squeaking in the thin layer of loose snow. *Point man*, he thought. Ten metres behind them should be the rest. He waited, then sure enough ten pairs of others followed, moving in single file. He checked with Andrews who signed to him that he also had ten on his side. He waited for five seconds to make sure there was no tail-end Charlie and then, taking a deep breath, he stood up and gently tossed both grenades into the centre of the procession, before diving back into the drainage ditch. As soon as he hit the ground the grenades detonated. Even with the noise of the explosions he could still hear the ceramic darts and splinters strike the metal crash barrier above him. He leapt back up to engage any remaining targets. There weren't any. All that remained of the column was a mess of tangled bodies and two separated legs. On his right Andrews opened fire. Crockett turned to help, but before he could it was over. Andrews had fired a hundred armour-piercing anti-personnel rounds in just under two seconds into the ten enemy. He changed magazines and signalled he was good.

Crockett clambered over the crash barrier shaking his head in an effort to clear the ringing in his ears from the grenades, and whilst Andrews covered him, walked through the dead administering double shots to each body before moving on. He felt no remorse.

He carried out a quick search for any useful intel or equipment. The enemy looked mature and experienced, physically in their prime, somewhere between twenty and forty. He examined a face; it looked rested and well fed. He checked several others; they looked the same. Their weapons were state-of-the-art airborne. They wore full body armour and comms packs and each had the equivalent of Cyclops on their helmets and a PLD on their forearms. Several of the PLDs were on, their dull red battle-status lights lit.

"Let's get their PLDs; we can use the IFFs for a while at least," said Crockett referring to the Identification – Friend or Foe beacons that were part of the PLD setup.

"Jesus, looks like they've still got access to GPS… How the hell are they getting this if all the sats have been knocked out?" asked Andrews.

"God knows. We're bloody lucky though. Winston's decoys must have lit up their threat displays like a rash, otherwise they would have nailed us in seconds. The Stalker seems to have fucked off as well."

He picked up a helmet; the blood inside had already congealed and was starting to freeze. The earpieces crackled; someone was probably requesting a sit rep. "Grab the helmets. We'll use their scooters. We can hit the C4I2 before they know what's happened."

Several bright flashes and the sound of a renewed firefight arced across the air from the direction of the bridge. The voice in their headsets was becoming more agitated.

Reaching the snow scooters, Crockett studied the unfamiliar controls and pushed a few buttons without success before Andrews, who had somehow started his, pulled up alongside and showed him how to start it. Crockett then turned sharply to face south, twisted the throttle to maximum and accelerated rapidly to nearly 60 miles an hour, leaving Andrews behind.

A vehicle checkpoint or VCP came into view ahead, blocking the road and access to the C4I2. He wondered exactly what he was going to do. Should he stop and engage it, drive through it, or crash into it? The VCP was built up from hard-packed ice berms draped with grey and black armour blankets. The berms were organised in a staggered chicane formation, forcing any vehicle to slow down to navigate them. He could see six or so sentries, some turned to face him, but their weapons were still slung.

To the right of the VCP he could now make out the C4I2 igloo, festooned with antennae. Steam rose from a second nearby igloo. Half a dozen snow scooters and a small Scorpion AFV armed with a 20mm canon were parked in front.

The voice in his stolen headset was beginning to sound hysterical. Crockett pulled to a sliding stop just 10 metres in front of the VCP and calmly got off, dusting snow from himself and pointing to his ears signifying he was having radio difficulties. The sentries continued to look inquisitively at him even as he slowly raised his weapon and fired into the middle of them. Andrews sped past him, sliding through the berms with skill. As Crockett changed magazines he could see more soldiers rushing from the second igloo. He took careful aim and fired. Two went down. A third clambered up onto the top of the Scorpion. There was no way he could allow the Scorpion to start roaming around. He fired, missed, and fired again. This time the figure slumped, rolled over and fell off.

OLLY - SOUTH SIDE OF BRIDGE

Olly, who'd escaped the culvert and the Stalker, threw himself down behind the crest of a small rise next to the road and, ignoring protocol, fired up his Cyclops. With it he had a perfect view of the southern end of the bridge. The bad news was that there were two full platoons dug in around it, supported by a Scorpion. Two more platoons were moving on foot from the east to reinforce them. He saw Jones's squad taking up positions a few hundred metres from the road, and to the right of him Galeago's team strung out in a skirmish line.

"They're going to get chopped up before they get anywhere. And more to the fucking point how come there's a Scorpion parked there?" he said to himself. He tried his radio. "All stations. All stations. This is Olly. Have two bandit platoons, numbers sixty plus, and one Scorpion at Charlie Papa Two. Also have two bandit platoons numbers eighty plus moving east to reinforce. Squawk once to acknowledge." He repeated his message twice more but got no response.

"Fucking typical. No one's listening," he said to himself.

He dropped his Bergen and pulled out an anti-tank missile. He didn't dare use the laser ranger as the Scorpion would probably have a laser detector on it, so he made the best estimate using basic field-craft, which was his thumb. It was 700 metres to the Scorpion, and 400 to Galeago. The status lights told him the diagnostics were good. Next he switched on the target acquisition system, selected Visual Recognition and uploaded the range and bearing. Scorpion probably Mark 5 Eskimo, the processor advised. Olly didn't know what mark or type the Scorpion was but felt satisfied that the processor seemed to know. Launch now. Launch now, warned the system reminding him that the target was live and would become more dangerous as each second passed. Olly released the safety and pushed the button.

For a moment nothing happened, then the protective end caps popped off and with a *whoosh* the missile left its launch tube and went vertical. Olly immediately displaced and moved to a location 50 metres further towards the bridge. He'd just reached it when the sound of a large explosion boomed out. Getting his breathing back under control he checked the impact site. The Scorpion was on fire. Next he turned his attention to the infantry. He'd use Winston and his mortar team for this. He didn't think he could target the dug-in platoons around the bridge without endangering Galeago and Jones but he could target the two moving to reinforce them. He pulled off his gloves to adjust the delicate sights on his grenade launcher and selected a UV marker and a red signal flare, then programmed the marker to advise Winston's incoming smart rounds that the surrounding 180 metres were to be considered hostile. Tying the shoulder harness around his forearm he clamped the weapon against his shoulder, checked the wind direction, and fired. The red signal flare lit up just about where he wanted it. Happier, he waited for Winston to do his stuff.

GALEAGO - SOUTHERN BRIDGE END

As Olly's missile detonated, Galeago went to ground. While he tried to work out who was firing at what, a red flare burst on the other side of the road. Thirty seconds later, two salvos of smart anti-personnel rounds detonated a few hundred metres to the east of him with the sound of Chinese firecrackers.

"Who the fuck fired that?" asked Galeago.

"Must be that fucking lunatic Winston," said one of his team.

"Jesus. Right, let's move up to the road and see what we can see. Whatever was under that barrage is now clean so we should be good. Hold your fire unless I tell you otherwise. We're still stealthy and I want to keep it that way as long as poss."

Reaching the road they could see what Winston had been targeting. The remains of a sizeable force lay scattered around. A burning Scorpion AFV sat to one side of the road. To their right the bridge approaches were protected by a VCP with revetments and trenches running off either side. Just over a hundred metres in front of them two figures were dragging a wounded comrade towards the VCP.

"Bingo! Let's see where they take him," whispered Galeago. Fifty metres on and the small group disappeared into the ground.

"We owe Winston. We would have run smack into that lot," said one of his team.

"Listen up. We need to clear the VCP. There'll be a wildlife run or drain that crosses under the road. We'll pop up and give them the good news."

It took them several minutes to locate a tunnel built for wildlife that emerged close to the VCP.

In the tunnel, Galeago gathered his team close to him. "OK, guys, no more fucking about. We're going to go noisy. We'll put two sets of HE, phosphorous and anti-personnel grenades into the entrance. Staggered timing, each twenty seconds apart from the last. Six blasts, then we'll bomb burst into the middle of it and get bloody. Fix bayonets."

Together they launched their grenade barrage. Galeago checked his watch and counted off the explosions. The enemy would soon work out that there was a regular interval between bangs and would keep their heads down until it expired. It was this interval that Galeago was relying on to get him into the VCP.

"Now!" ordered Galeago. He ran the hundred metres and jumped down into the nearest trench, landing on something soft that turned out to be a body. Bits of phosphorous still burned in clumps and the place smelt of burning flesh and explosive.

The trench separated into two, the main one leading towards the bridge, the right towards the VCP.

"Cossack, Smelly, Picard, you come with me. Picard, you run point. Wallace, Rider, go to the right," ordered Galeago.

As Galeago followed Smelly and Picard around a bend, an explosion, followed by a blast wave of hot air, knocked Galeago and Cossack backwards. Seconds later Smelly staggered towards them clutching his groin, half moaning and half shouting, "Fucking bastards. Those fucking bastards," before collapsing next to Galeago.

Galeago looked at his wound. "Smelly, keep pressure on it. Cossack, go get Medic Rider."

Galeago left Smelly to check on Picard. He found him upside down against the trench wall. He looked intact. As Galeago checked him for a pulse someone landed on his back and an arm circled his neck. *What the fuck?* thought Galeago as he instinctively leant forwards bringing the attacker's weight with him, before reversing the movement, flinging his head backwards, and being rewarded with the knowledge that the back of his helmet had connected with a nose. The arm around his neck lost its grip and Galeago reversed his motion again, this time bending forward, unsheathing his combat knife and grabbing the attacker's wrist.

The attacker flopped to the ground, splayed out on his back. Galeago, still holding the attacker's wrist, now drove the knife into the exposed armpit until it came to rest against bone. For a moment neither moved; so

Galeago pulled it back an inch and then pushed it back, this time twisting in the process. His victim shuddered, cramped and then went still.

"Next time shoot me!" said Galeago as the adrenaline subsided.

CROCKETT - SOUTHERNMOST C4I2

Crockett regained consciousness and found himself lying outside in the snow next to Andrews who was missing the lower half of his body. Thick, black, acrid smoke from electrical fires swirled around him. As his body started to tell him he was in pain, he recalled what had happened. He and Andrews had taken out the C4I2, then during their withdrawal had been hit by a heavy calibre weapon of some kind. He pulled himself into a sitting position and leaned back against the exterior wall of the C4I2 igloo. His face felt cold and he realised he'd lost his helmet. His legs hurt.

The wind picked up for a moment and the smoke cleared, giving Crockett an unrestricted view of the area; dead soldiers lay around the VCP, several snow scooters were on fire. A Scorpion AFV was moving slowly along the roadway towards the bridge. It reminded him of one of the wolves they had seen earlier.

He felt colder. He knew he was losing consciousness; he looked up at the night sky, where the constellation of Orion's Belt shone brightly, hanging like the sword of Damocles above him. A shooting star raced across the sky. He closed his eyes for a second, succumbing to his tiredness. An inner voice was screaming at him to wake up, warning him of blood loss. He forced himself to open his eyes; Orion's Belt had moved about twenty degrees to the right.

"Jesus, I'm losing it. You need to get yourself sorted," he said as forcefully as he could to himself, and in the process learnt he'd lost his hearing.

He examined his legs; the left was broken at the ankle. He could feel something embedded in his inner right thigh just behind the assault armour. He pulled his gloves off and probed the wound; the warm, sticky, slippery feeling on his fingers told him all he needed; he was bleeding and quite badly, the blood pulsed rather than flowed.

Fuck it. The ankle would have to wait. He took his Bowie knife and cut the straps holding his leg armour, easing it gently away to reveal the problem. A piece of plastic was sticking proudly out of his leg. Should he pull it out or leave it? It must have cut an artery; if he pulled it the bleeding could get worse, the artery might even sever and retract. No, it was better to leave it. It was tourniquet time. He felt for one of the inbuilt tourniquets in his combat trousers. It took him three attempts to secure it, using his knife as a lever to turn the straps until they bit deep into his muscle. It hurt but the bleeding seemed to have stopped.

Next he looked for his weapon. He saw the tip of either his or Andrews' under what was left of Andrews' torso. He pulled it free, fighting the urge to vomit in the process. He needed to get annoyed so he could call up some energy. He thought about the executions they'd seen and welcomed the sensation of aggression flowing back into his consciousness.

He was about to start crawling across the snow to the road, when the Scorpion reappeared and took up position at the VCP. Well, if there was one thing left he could do, it was to make sure it got nailed. Fumbling in his equipment harness he pulled out a pack of flares. He tried to remember which colour was the signal for an anti-armour barrage. Was it red? His vision started to blur. He emptied the whole packet onto his lap. Not trusting his memory, he'd taken the time to mark the individual flares before they'd left. He picked up one marked R then P – shit, red was anti-personnel – then he saw what he wanted, G-A, green – armour.

He fired the flare and sat back. The Scorpion's turret started traversing, searching for the source of the disturbance. It was, he thought, just like a wolf, sniffing the air for a wounded prey, its sensors seeking him out. Crockett tried to lift his weapon but he realised his strength had gone; instead he simply stared at the predator and waited. Well, he'd taken out the C4I2, that was good. He started to count down the final seconds of his life.

WINSTON – SE SIDE OF BRIDGE

Just after they'd displaced to their third firing position, Winston saw Crockett's flare burst.

"Well, I don't fucking believe it, we've had more business, nasty though it is, in the space of thirty minutes than we have had in the last thirty days! Target designated as Delta. Range 3,460 metres, bearing two seven

186

five degrees. Confirm range ready," he said checking his map. His team confirmed, before he continued:

"Two salvos, triple AM. Select the rounds." He would launch aerial anti-armour mines.

"Tube one ready."

"Tube two ready."

"Well!" crowed Winston like a wolf howling into the night sky on adrenaline. "Let's groove."

The mortars fired.

"Tingle as you mingle. Let's groove tonight! Let's burn clean. Displace. We'll pick up Punch and Judy and go and join the Sarge." He continued howling at the moon.

CROCKETT - SOUTHERNMOST C412

Crockett didn't hear the dull series of plop sounds as Winston's mines deployed around the Scorpion. But he did manage a smile as he watched one fall almost impossibly slowly on its parachute towards the Scorpion that seemed unaware of the danger that was descending. The mine made contact, ignited and then burnt its way through the hull before disappearing in a cloud of white smoke. A second later the Scorpion flew apart like a computer-animated mosaic.

Crockett slumped back onto the snow. His hand touched a piece of smouldering Scorpion wreckage. Although it burnt him, the new pain was a respite; it jarred him back into consciousness and also gave him satisfaction that the wolf was dead. His leg started to really hurt from the tourniquet; he wondered about morphine but knew it would be the end if he took it. He decided he would make one last effort to get to the VCP so he had a chance of being picked up. He crawled across the snow, scolding himself for forgetting his gloves, his hands now freezing. He reached the VCP and propped himself against one of the berms facing north, then activated his WIAB, or wounded in action beacon, that would let the squadron know that they had a wounded comrade in the vicinity. Whether they could pick him up or not he didn't know and didn't have the energy to even worry about it.

JONES - SOUTHERN BRIDGE APPROACHES

"Oy, Sarge!" shouted Olly, feeling pleased with himself as he skidded to a halt next to Jones.

"Corporal, you trying to let the whole planet know we're here?"

"Sorry, Sarge, but Galeago will need some help; they're pretty well dug in around the southern end of the bridge. Two platoons, I reckon. I took out the Scorpion, and Winston pasted a couple of platoons, almost a company, moving in from the east."

"So that's what was going on. What about Captain C?"

"It's bloody chaos. We got bounced. C's gone after the C4I2 with Andrews, the rest of the team's pretty busted up and being hunted by a Stalker; the bastard thing seems to be alive."

"Right, we'll deal with the bridge first and hook up with Captain Schaefer. After that we'll go find out how Captain C is getting on."

CROCKETT - SOUTHERN C4I2

Crockett tried to focus on what looked like a snow scooter. He tried to arm a grenade but all he could now move were his eyelids. He waited resignedly, as the scooter slid to a halt a metre away.

"Jesus, Captain. Looks like Custer's last fucking stand," said a voice he recognised as Pavla's.

All Crockett could muster in return was a grunt.

"Can you move, sir?"

"No. The C4I2 is US. Can you fire the signal?" managed Crockett using the last of his energy.

After firing the signal flares to let the squadron know that the southern C4I2 had been cleared, Pavla examined his captain. "God, sir. You're busted up. You're lucky to still be alive. You've severed an artery. It's too badly torn up for me to clamp it and the blood clot agents will be useless on something like this. We're gonna have to keep the tourniquet on and get some plasma into you."

He searched through what was left of Crockett's personal kit and found the small package of freeze-dried blood crystals that each of them carried. The crystals were produced from freeze-drying the individual's own blood. When mixed with the plasma that Pavla carried, the reconstituted blood was as good as that which the patient had lost. Pavla checked the label on the crystals to make sure it had Crockett's name, then mixed them into the plasma.

Moving behind him, Pavla slipped an arm under each of Crockett's armpits and then on one leg, and with a strength and balance that few men could have managed, got Crockett onto the scooter. He set up the plasma bag, taping it to the radio antennae on the snow scooter, and then pushed the needle straight through Crockett's battle dress and started the plasma pump; a green light told him it was working.

"Sir, you've got to try and stay conscious. We're leaving, going cross country for ten klicks, then we can try and sort you out a bit more. You good with that, sir?"

There was no response so he shone a torch into his captain's eyes. The pupils at least were still responding. He tied Crockett to the backrest of the scooter using webbing straps. He had a lingering concern that the plasma feed would ice up, and he didn't know how long the tourniquet should be kept on in the cold, so he wrapped the drip in thermal sheeting and put the bag between the seat rest and his captain in the hope it would stay liquid. That was about all he could do.

JONES - SOUTH END OF BRIDGE

Jones and Olly hooked up with Galeago just as Pavla's signal flare burst.

"That's Captain C. That's both the C4I2s out. What's the situation here?" asked Jones. The trench was littered with bodies and Rider was trying to stabilise Smelly.

"Bastards are dug in. Roberts, Picard and Wallace are dead. Cossack's up ahead on point," reported Galeago.

"What's his status?"

"Priority one, grenade went off next to his nuts; his groin's pretty badly torn up. He's on plasma and co-ag. I need to get him out of here quick though. He's got sixty minutes," advised Rider.

"Well, you'll have to keep him alive for a while longer. No one's getting out of here until we can open up this side of the bridge," replied Jones.

"Sarge, what about your leg? You're bleeding," said Rider.

"The leg's fine. What we need to do is open a route up for Schaefer to get involved pronto."

Several mortar rounds detonated ahead of them, showering them with snow and rock fragments.

"Right," started Jones, "Olly, you take a squad and move to our right. I'll get with Galeago and Cossack and push along…"

Before he could finish, Cossack appeared, lurching drunkenly from side to side of the trench before collapsing. Blood was streaming from both his ears.

"His eardrums have burst. His balance has gone," said Rider, turning his attention to his new patient.

Winston and his team arrived, dragging several equipment containers.

"What the hell are you lot doing here?" asked Jones.

"We ran out of rounds and thought you could do with some help. We've brought Punch and Judy, thought they might help, being this is a road and all," replied Winston, then asking, "Sarge, is your leg all right?"

"I don't remember you being my mother, and if anyone else asks me if my leg is OK I'll rip their head off. Get Punch and Judy set up and on to the bridge. After that you can help out your colleagues, Messieurs Olly and Galeago here, to clear these shitbags out from this end of the bridge."

"Aye, aye, Sarge. Oh and by the way, we saw Crockett's signal. His end is good," replied Winston.

"Corporal Winston… good work," offered Jones.

"Nasty business," commented Winston.

Jones's facial expression even under the camouflage zebra stripes echoed what they were all thinking. Winston was weird.

SCHAEFER - MID-SECTION OF BRIDGE

Schaefer and his assault team had fought their way up on to the northern end of the bridge and had crossed half the length of it before getting bogged down in a protracted firefight that had now evolved into a game of grenade throwing. Schaefer's friend Iceman had died thirty seconds earlier. Schaefer saw two grenades pass one another in opposite directions. Another exploded nearby, the blast knocking the air out of him as if he had been sat on by three gorillas. He checked his limbs for injury and was surprised to find that, although his armoured vest was festooned with darts, he'd not been injured.

Without warning a yellow car sped past him, narrowly missing running him down and forcing him to dive over the crash barrier where he crawled behind a lighting stanchion. The car continued for another few hundred metres before it crashed somewhere amidst the VCP on the southern end of the bridge.

JONES - SOUTH END OF BRIDGE

"There's a car coming across the bridge!" yelled someone.

A yellow civilian car with its headlights blazing came racing across the bridge. Tracer fire reached out towards it and, as the car swerved around a VCP berm, it skidded, clipped the edge of the berm and rolled over, bounced off the burning wreck of the Scorpion and then slid along on its roof towards them, coming to a stop 30 metres away. For a moment there was a lull in the fighting; it was as if a play had been interrupted for a moment due to someone wandering onto the stage. The sound of bagpipes playing came from the car. Then the car door opened and a figure crawled out onto the snow.

"Fuck me, it's O'Reilly!" exclaimed Olly.

"Covering fire!" shouted Jones.

"Christ. Anyone else going to drop by?" Jones asked as O'Reilly reached them and relative safety.

"I thought this might be the easier way to the RV; didn't fancy a trek all on me lonesome. I was all right until fucking Schaefer's team shot me up. Didn't even have time to get the car heater on. You any idea how fucking cold I've been?" poured forth O'Reilly.

Jones decided to ignore him and instead gave him an order. "Don't make yourself too comfortable, you can set up the jammers; I don't want those bastards blowing the fucking bridge after all the hard work we've done. I want that bridge sterilised, understood?" he said, referring to the radio frequency jamming devices that would prevent any wireless triggering of the demolition charges on the bridge.

"It'll be as sterile as my grandmother's toilet seat. By the way, is your leg OK?" replied O'Reilly.

SCHAEFER - MID-SECTION OF BRIDGE

Schaefer was still in cover behind the lighting stanchion; several of his team had mustered nearby but they were pinned down. As he waited for a chance to get back into the fight he watched from ground level as a bizarre scene was being played out nearby on the roadway. The squadron's two autonomous mini bots known as Punch and Judy were engaged in a battle with three enemy mini bots.

The enemy bots were arrayed in a spearhead formation whilst Punch and Judy had positioned themselves behind some rubble. A game of hide and seek was underway. The bots, each no bigger than a remote-controlled toy car, surged forward and backwards in short bursts, executing occasional pirouettes and throwing little flakes of snow and ice off their tracks as they tried to acquire fire solutions.

Judy darted forward into the open, bouncing to a stop, its missile launcher twitched to the left several times in quick succession, and then fired what looked like a child's firework. A small white flame accompanied the 2-inch missile as it sluggishly emerged from the barrel before starting its short flight. One of the enemy bots exploded, sending chunks of plastic body, little components and processors up into the air. Schaefer could see though that Judy had paused a moment too long to verify her kill. Before she could retreat to cover she was engulfed in a hail of Gatling fire, and disintegrated. Punch now retreated past Schaefer like a frightened puppy, steering around debris whilst its small electric motors whined amongst the general noise of battle. The two remaining enemy bots followed, ignoring Schaefer, who'd become a low-value human target. They slewed to a stop 5 metres past him, their Gatlings jinking in short steps, rocking their small chassis backwards and forwards. One of the enemy bots opened fire, spraying a fountain of mini shell casings into the surrounding snow.

Schaefer wondered just how advanced tactical AI had become. The bots' tactics seemed to be evolving before his eyes. The white-clad figure of a squadron trooper clambered up over the side of the bridge onto the roadway interrupting his thoughts. He recognised the self-confident gait as belonging to Olly.

"First of the Ninth!" shouted Schaefer, hoping Olly and his own team could hear him and not engage one another. Olly spotted him and waved as he nonchalantly jogged up behind one of the enemy bots, kicked it over onto its side and fired half a dozen rounds into its underbelly. The remaining enemy bot turned to face the new threat that had eliminated its companion, and in that instant Punch seized its chance, darted out from behind its cover and fired two missiles into the side of the enemy machine, killing it and producing a cloud of black smoke.

Olly meanwhile executed an exhibitionist dive over the crash barrier to join Schaefer whilst Punch drove off looking for more prey.

"Good to see you. What's the story?" Schaefer asked Olly.

"Well, the Sarge, Galeago and the boys are slogging it out on the south end but there's a platoon-sized unit well dug in. We took out their armour but I don't think we're going to be able to displace them. We've taken the southern C4I2 out but lost contact with Crockett. There's still a Stalker lurking around somewhere as well. O'Reilly's setting up the signal jammers to stop the bridge being blown."

"All right. We've cleared the bridge up to here. And the rest of the boys have dug in on the northern end, but if we don't bring the AFVs across now we're going to get bogged down and lose the initiative. Let's signal Alex."

"I agree. Wow, Captain, your vest looks like a porcupine. You're a lucky bastard," commented Olly.

"Just about. There was even some fucking lunatic who tried to run me over in a car."

As Olly launched the signal flare he pondered on whether to let Schaefer know who the culprit was but decided the information was probably redundant.

NATASHA - NE SIDE OF FJORD

After Olly and Schaefer's signal flare, Alex gave the order to the four AFVs to move.

Natasha was commanding the medical AFV, which they'd modified to allow them to fly the Musicians from. Ahead of her was Alex whose AFV had been outfitted with an electronic flail system for mine countermeasures.

Natasha shouted to Stacey to let him know they were good to roll. The AFV lurched forward from their laager under the trees and swung right to start their run along the shoreline towards the northern end of the bridge. She felt both excited and scared, the experience being similar to her first solo flight.

They'd worked hard on their ECM after the events in the pass. At Natasha's suggestion, Lieutenant Byrnes' team together with her flight crew had modified the visual and heat signatures of the AFVs by relocating radiators, heat exchangers and electronics, and strapping empty equipment containers to the sides and roof. In addition, each AFV now towed a sled that carried a ghost projector, which mimicked the original AFV's electronic, magnetic and heat signatures. Finally, Byrnes had come up with a device which he told everyone would be the subject of a patent that would make his fortune. He had mounted a Faraday cage at the centre section of each AFV. No more than a long, thin wire wrapped dozens of times around the AFV and held away from the body by plastic spacers, the cage could generate different electrical, magnetic and thermal fields to confuse AI recognition systems.

"ECM online. Threat is green. Two thousand metres to the on ramp," reported Byrnes.

They closed the distance to the bridge to a thousand metres before they encountered their first remote sentry.

"All stations. Permission to go loud," radioed Alex, signifying that they could now activate all their electronic systems.

"Roger," Natasha radioed back, wondering whether she should retreat to the interior of the AFV or stay in the armoured observation cupola. She decided to stay. It was like she'd been told: a good place to get full situational awareness.

"Release the sled," she ordered.

She glanced behind her and smiled as the sled started to draw fire.

"We're clear of the sentries. Five hundred metres to the ramp. Boards are green," continued Byrnes.

"Hold tight, everyone!" advised Stacey, warning that the exit from the frozen smooth surface of the fjord onto the bank at the foot of the bridge's access ramp was going to be rough. Natasha could see he'd decided to take the bank head-on rather than sidestep it. Her navigation threat monitor lit up with warnings to reduce speed but Stacey kept going and Natasha trusted his judgement.

The AFV hit the bank and reared backwards, slowing slightly before going weightless, the sensation being accompanied by a sudden silence as the vehicle's tracks momentarily left the ground. With a shudder of hydraulics, the noise of which reminded Natasha of a hard landing in an aircraft, the AFV reconnected with the ground. A fire extinguisher broke loose of its mount, equipment bins burst open and a cheer erupted as Stacey then threw the AFV through a hard ninety-degree left turn hurling the fire extinguisher and whatever else was loose around again. A grinding noise from something or other followed by a loud bang reverberated through the vehicle.

"We're on the bridge access ramp. We lost part of the number four drive assembly. I'm going to shut it down; we'll only be capable of sixty plus klicks an hour," advised Stacey, sounding quite proud of himself.

"Launch the Musicians," ordered Natasha.

"Musicians airborne. Data feed online, cross-linking now," advised Byrnes, confirming that Mozart and Beethoven were now airborne.

"Make sure you stay in the Major's tracks," she ordered Stacey.

"Too bloody right," came the reply.

Byrnes uploaded the tactical display showing the positions of the Musicians and started piping *Wagner's Ride of the Valkyries* through the internal comms. Natasha smiled. As the data feed was cross-linked, she could see Schaefer's team strung out along the central crash barrier engaged in a firefight about halfway along the bridge.

"Byrnes, you see Schaefer?" asked Natasha.

"I'm on it."

Natasha watched as Byrnes sent Beethoven off to their right, put it into a steep dive, levelled out at about 70 metres and then commenced a shallow dive running along a line parallel to Schaefer, carpeting the positions with anti-personnel mines.

"All stations, this is Hotel Two. We've hit a mine. One drive out," reported Grant who was commanding the rear AFV.

"Hotel Two. You OK?" requested Alex.

"Hotel Two. Still good to go. You push on. We'll catch you up," replied Grant.

"Roger that. Mike One, can you task Mozart with cover?" requested Alex, asking if Natasha could use Mozart to protect Grant.

"Mike One confirms," replied Natasha.

"Thanks for that. We'll see you later. Out," replied Grant.

They passed Schaefer's team who even managed to give them a wave as they sped by, showering them with snow. Then her master threat board went red as a Stalker appeared from beneath the bridge and came up alongside Grant's AFV, raking the side of it with fire.

"Shit. The bastard must have been hiding under there," said Byrnes.

With extraordinary flying skill, Byrnes dived Mozart under the bridge and then emerged on the other side within metres of the Stalker.

"Gotcha!" he said as the sights locked onto the Stalker, the glowing heat signature from its Gatling leaving an IR trail in the cold air.

The Stalker exploded. "Splash one," he said calmly, obviously relishing the chance to fly like a fighter pilot.

But behind her Grant had slowed down even more after the Stalker strike and was showering the area around it with sparks from its damaged track assembly. Natasha's threat boards lit up again. This time Beethoven's sensors had picked up two laser target designators emanating from the southern end of the bridge; these were echoed by alarms from Grant's AFV indicating that he'd been targeted.

"Am engaging," reported Byrnes as he fired two missiles from Beethoven on a reciprocal course towards the origins of the lasers.

JONES - SOUTH END OF BRIDGE

From his position 2 kilometres away, Jones watched through his Cyclops as Grant's AFV tried to shake off the laser designators. The trouble was, he didn't have room to manoeuvre; to his left the road was mined and to his right was the crash barrier. Jones could picture the frantic scenes inside the AFV. They would be trying to close the distance to the enemy, driving through the danger as fast as possible. Two friendly missiles flew past him following the lasers and exploded. Before he could celebrate though, his Cyclops flared as Grant's AFV struck another mine. This time the AFV slewed across the road, leaving a track mechanism on the roadway, glanced off the crash barrier and then contacted with two more mines. The first blew the left forward drive assembly clean off, sending it arcing over the bridge to the fjord below, the second went off directly beneath the crew compartment, lifting the AFV a metre off the road and flipping it on to its side. Pink hydraulic oil from a ruptured line jetted out from the vehicle in a stream over the snow.

Jones's Cyclops whined, signifying that it had detected another laser target designator operating on a non-friendly frequency. He tapped the search key and his eyepiece responded showing two more lasers emanating from the east.

"Fuck. The bastards have flanked us. Enemy lasers at eleven o'clock. Suppressive fire. All units, I say again, suppressive fire at eleven o'clock!" he screamed.

Kneeling, he raised his weapon to his shoulder but knew it was too late. Just as the emergency hatches on Grant's AFV jettisoned, two missiles detonated against its exposed belly. A hydrogen fuel tank exploded, lighting up the bridge. For a moment the noise of the fighting died down as if in latent respect, then started again with double the intensity.

Only a single track assembly remained of the AFV. As Mozart and Beethoven started strafing runs on the enemy positions, Olly and O'Reilly jogged up to him.

"Sarge. What are your orders?"

"Fuck this. We've done enough. Time to bug out."

CHAPTER 16

RV

Roll rocks down a ten thousand foot mountain and they cannot be stopped. This is because of the mountain, not the rocks. Get people to fight with the courage to win every time and the strong and weak unite. This is because of the momentum, not the individuals.

Natasha left the stuffy warmth of Alex's HQ AFV to get some air. A weak sun hung above the three remaining AFVs that sat in a state of exhaustion laagered in a loose circle. Igloos had been set up and camouflaged with pine tree branches.

She walked slowly around the AFVs looking at the damage. Alex's had been hit several times with light anti-armour rounds. Its zebra camouflage paint was scarred black where the rounds had detonated, and there were dark holes in some of the armour panels. Her own medical AFV was missing most of its sensor arrays. She looked at the cupola and was surprised to see it badly scarred from small arms fire. She couldn't remember being targeted. The last of the engineering and logistics vehicles had a badly damaged forward track assembly and had lost its multiple rocket system completely.

The sounds of Beethoven's fourth symphony drifted from an igloo. Natasha tried for a second to remember how she knew it was the fourth, or for that matter Beethoven, before her concentration was broken by a familiar voice.

"Well, looks like everyone's real pleased to see us," said Sanchez, marching into the camp with Williams.

Natasha rushed across to Sanchez and gave her a hug. "Is that your weapon or are you just happy to see me?" she joked, getting caught up on Sanchez's assault weapon.

"He's been asking everyone every ten minutes about you. You better get over there and put him out of his misery. He's in the Major's HQ," she whispered in Sanchez's ear.

Johnson joined them. "Good afternoon, Corporal. Everything OK?"

"Who didn't make it?" she asked, ignoring his question.

"Here's the list," replied Johnson handing her his e-pad.

She studied the list of sixteen names and a lone tear rolled down her camouflaged face, as her shoulders started to shake. Natasha put an arm around her.

"Hey, they're heroes and they won't be forgotten. You'll hear about it later but Crockett saw some pretty horrible shit. They've been executing prisoners, civilian as well as military. Tomorrow we're heading south," said Natasha.

"Where's everyone else?" Sanchez asked, regaining her composure and looking around.

"The youngsters are still recovering from an almighty drinking session. Us elders? Well… I guess we're still trying to come to grips with what we achieved. Hodgetts told us about the armoured column; with that, Lloyd-Smith's barrage and the damage the AFVs did, we reckon we broke an armoured airborne regiment. Six hundred killed plus twenty or so vehicles destroyed. Anyway, like Captain K said, I think you should go and see him. He's lost without you. Come and see me afterwards for a check-up," said Johnson.

As Sanchez made her way over to the igloo, Natasha felt tears welling up in her eyes. Johnson noticed and put an arm around her.

"It's normal, don't worry. It's your body suffering from adrenaline withdrawal. It happens to them all at some time," he told her.

"You know, when I gave her a hug, I suddenly remembered I've got a dog. Her name's Mai Mai; that's Chinese for My Little Sister. God knows what has happened to her. I left her with the base sergeant." She continued sobbing uncontrollably.

*

After the debrief, Natasha accompanied Sanchez to the medical AFV for a check-up. Inside, Pavla lay in one of the beds next to Crockett, who was snoring.

"Jesus, Captain C's pretty busted up," remarked Sanchez looking at Crockett, who'd lost a leg and was bandaged heavily on both his arms and his remaining ankle.

"Yes, he is, and if it wasn't for Pavla here he wouldn't have made it," said Johnson.

"I'm just happy the plasma didn't freeze, sir," said Pavla.

"What?" asked Johnson.

"The plasma transfusion I rigged for the Captain here. I'm glad it didn't freeze."

"Oh. You needn't have worried about that. Since about ten years ago all the plasma for mountain troops has been laced with glycol proteins. Basically it's antifreeze, clever stuff, it's expressed from polar fish. That's why fish in the Arctic can survive without their blood freezing."

"Oh."

"Not to worry. You did good, Private. He's alive. And that's what counts. We'll need to get him a motorised prosthetic leg from one of the hospitals; once we've got that, all I'll need to do is find a neurosurgeon to make the connections and he'll be like new."

"You know one who lives round here?" asked Sanchez sarcastically.

As Johnson checked Sanchez, Natasha joined medic Nancy Strong who was administering doses of painkiller to another patient she didn't know, and seemed fully recovered from her injury sustained during the Strat crash.

"How's it going?" she asked, feeling slightly regal but telling herself that as Alex's successor she needed to get to know everyone.

CHAPTER 17

BARREN LANDS

There has never been a protracted war from which a country has benefited.

The journey through Denmark and into Germany was as lonely as it was uneventful. They saw no one as they made their way towards the Allied HQ, south of Frankfurt. It was here where they hoped they would meet up with other units. All of them reasoned that any units such as themselves would ultimately seek out headquarters rather than disband. Several times they picked up encrypted military radio traffic they didn't recognise, but no civilian broadcasts.

Natasha retained command of the converted medical AFV and the Musicians. Crockett, Johnson and Sanchez rode with her.

They gave Hamburg, the site of one of the nuclear strikes, a wide berth, and travelled across farmland as much as possible. Even in the countryside the extent of the sabotage that had occurred was evident. Power transmission lines had been draped with silver foil, shorting them out and overloading the adjacent grids; there were toppled microwave and cell net communications masts, and aerial deployed mines on road junctions. Oddly, the land and buildings still looked tended, and in many instances lights flickered, powered by windmills and solar panels.

As they continued south the weather grew milder and for some reason the crew in Natasha's AFV took to singing at every opportunity. Johnson told her that they were beginning to accept that their previous lives had finished, and that the singing was a deep-rooted human mechanism of bonding with their new and only remaining family. Natasha told him she thought he was pushing things a little far, to which he replied that she was still in denial and would eventually join in. It had taken her a few minutes to realise that he was laughing but as she thought about it she became more convinced that it wasn't a joke.

There was increased talk of the executions that Crockett and his team had discovered at the bridge. Sanchez summarised what these meant. "Simple. It's ethnic cleansing. Nothing more, nothing less. They don't want us around."

There was now more rain than snow, and for the first time since she could remember she heard birds sing. But with the milder weather came the stench of death. Domesticated farm animals had died in their thousands. Cow carcasses lay in fields in abundance, having died from thirst or lack of milking. They saw a group of horses who had managed to escape their enclosure, munching on grass by the side of the road, one of which still had its reins and a saddle on. Packs of wild dogs and foxes escorted by flocks of crows trotted across fields and along the roads. Natasha wondered if her dog would be amongst them.

"Jesus, what's going to happen in springtime?" she said.

"How do you mean?" asked Sanchez.

"Well, lots of farm animals, like sheep, often need assistance nowadays to give birth. Without it they'll die."

"That's sad. To die with your baby like that," said Sanchez.

They continued on in silence for a while longer before Natasha remarked, "You know, on a completely different subject, have you noticed that the birds only really sing when the sun's out? I mean, it's obvious and everyone knows it, but... well, I've only just really discovered it."

"Yeah. In the Urals, when we were in static fortresses, we used to talk about it a lot," replied Sanchez.

As they moved deeper into Germany their excitement rose when they came across a series of power transmission lines that were live.

"Well, something or someone is producing a lot of power," remarked Sanchez.

"Fuck, will you look at that!" exclaimed Byrnes, bringing up on the repeater screens a view from Beethoven 5 kilometres to their west that showed a glittering maze of silver towers and pipework, interspersed with bright lights.

"That's the nuclear power station at Kleps," said Crockett, checking his database.

"Spooky," commented Sanchez.

Byrnes had taken apart the enemy PLD that Crockett had recovered from one of the dead Brotherhood soldiers on the bridge. He asked Natasha and Crockett to come and have a look at what he'd found.

"I think I know how they've been managing to navigate without GPS. This is very neat stuff. They've used extraordinary magneto resistance or EMR. Neat. Really neat. It's based on nano-sized piezo-static sensors, the type that was used in data read and write mechanisms on the old hard drives. But this is super sensitive; I'm talking nano-Tesla sensitivity to magnetic fields…"

"Can you give us the short version? You've completely lost me," interjected Natasha.

"It's the same as birds use. They've mapped the earth's magnetic fields, then used this to measure them. Throw in some terrain identification shit and *voilà*, you have a nav system equal in accuracy to GPS and absolutely independent of satellites and all the rest of the support systems," replied Byrnes with the patience of a teacher trying to help a pupil.

"Impressive. But I thought the mag flux lines varied? And what about local disturbances, you know, from things like other electrical gear?" asked Crockett.

"That's another neat part. This circuit here…" he said pointing to a magnified scan, "is like a noise cancellation device. It effectively maps fluctuations that are not considered terrestrial and generates an opposite field. The other impressive thing is that you can't jam it. It's analogue, not digital. Neat, uh?"

"Jesus. They've been busy little bees. Genetically engineered viruses, the ability to knock out our satellites, distributed jamming, intelligent minefields, and now this. Wonder what else we'll come up against?" mused Natasha.

*

Natasha could now feel a real bond between her and the others. She had started to get to know them as individuals. Part of her told her to try and restrict and contain this feeling of becoming part of a family. Another part of her told her to welcome it. She spoke to Sanchez and Johnson about her feelings and was surprised when they told her that all of them had been through the same at one time or another; she'd started to recognise the age-old camaraderie that developed amongst soldiers. Sanchez, though, pushed the conversation further.

"You like him, don't you?"

"Who?"

"The Major, of course." She laughed.

"You know, Corporal, there are times when…" She gave up mid-sentence as Alex and Schaefer joined them.

"Are you two up for a foraging mission?" asked Schaefer.

"Foraging? For what?" asked Natasha.

"We're getting concerned about food supplies, not to mention fuel and other basics. Some of the troop haven't brushed their teeth with anything except alcohol for days and some are worried about getting lice for lack of soap. We need to resupply."

"Nice. OK. We get the message. We'll do a scavenge," replied Natasha.

"Quite how you achieve this will be up to yourselves; however, I have it on good authority that Stacey and O'Reilly would add a certain degree of flexibility to your capability. Lloyd-Smith has offered to provide security," said Alex with a smile.

They selected a hypermarket facility 50 kilometres north of Frankfurt. Whilst the rest of the squadron laagered in a forest, Natasha led Lloyd-Smith with his gun team, Sanchez, Stacey and O'Reilly, to the hypermarket, which was a complex of large single-storey steel and concrete warehouse-style shops set amidst an enormous empty car park carved out of a pine forest. Lloyd-Smith set up a forward operating base on the edge of the forest whilst Sanchez, O'Reilly, Stacey and Natasha entered the hypermarket.

"I reckon we should pinch a couple of them quad bikes, take 'em back to the LUP," offered O'Reilly, pointing to an outdoor sports shop.

"Good idea; we can use them to tow food and the like," said Natasha feeling childishly guilty.

Having sorted their transportation, they entered the supermarket in search of food and other basics. It had been looted in the not too distant past, the windows were broken and debris lay about in the forecourt. Inside, the lights were still on.

"Jesus, what's that smell?" asked Stacey pushing an enormous shopping trolley.

"Rotten milk, I reckon. Look at the state of this place. There's no food left at all in here. The whole place has been cleaned out," moaned O'Reilly in genuine disgust.

"Fuck it, there must be something. They can't have taken the bloody lot," replied Stacey.

"Yoh. We've got e-sig. Your twelve o'clock – thirty metres," said Sanchez who was monitoring any electrical field fluctuations within their vicinity.

They immediately dropped to the floor in amongst piles of washing detergent boxes and stared down the aisle ahead of them. For a few seconds they saw nothing, just an empty aisle. Then a robotic shop assistant called a Ballbot glided around a corner and came down the aisle towards them.

The 2-metre-tall, cylindrically shaped machine, which moved on a ball, came gliding around the debris and stopped in front of them, before deploying its tripod stabilising legs.

"May I be of assistance?" it asked in German.

"Yer what?" replied Stacey.

"It wants to know if we need assistance," translated O'Reilly.

Natasha found herself silently laughing at the scene.

"Oh, you speak English. In that case may I be of assistance?" stated the Ballbot.

"Yeah. We're looking for toothpaste," replied Stacey, keeping his weapon trained on the machine.

"That'll be aisle six. The blue sector. Is there anything else?" it replied.

"Yeah. You could come with us. We've got a lot to get."

"Certainly. The customer is always first. Please follow me."

"Jesus. The bloody thing must still be recharging off the solar panels. Probably had no customers for a while."

"It must have gone bloody berserk when this place was ransacked. I thought they worked security as well?" said O'Reilly.

"Yeah, but what's it gonna do? Take our pictures and report us?" said Stacey.

They followed the Ballbot as it detoured around discarded items and led them to what they wanted. They completed their shopping tour loading up trolleys with toiletries, detergents and any remaining food and other consumables that they could find or thought might come in useful. Satisfied, they then took as many newspapers and magazines as possible and with the help of the Ballbot downloaded all the available news pods from the digital news stand.

"I reckon we should get some music players and any music we can whilst we're here. There's no telling the next time we'll be able to get any," said Stacey.

O'Reilly found the sweet shop relatively intact. "Sweets or, as the Americans would say, candies. The guys will be happy with these," he announced.

The Ballbot followed them out of the store for 10 metres or so complaining that they had not paid and warning them that it had pictures of them and they would be traced. Natasha apologised but to no avail as the Bot explained to her the charges and fines she now faced.

Lloyd-Smith drove up to them on one of the quad bikes and O'Reilly gave him a small box of sweets, which Lloyd-Smith sniffed deeply.

"Can you smell that? Reminds me of when I was little," he said, as if talking to himself.

"Do you reckon this is all right – I mean taking all this stuff?" asked one of Lloyd-Smith's gunners in a worried voice, pointing to the mass of shopping bags.

"I'm sure no one would deny you, Gunner Zimbabwe. I'll leave a note telling them that the King's own have borrowed the supplies until further notice," replied Lloyd-Smith.

*

They got back to the squadron in the early evening. That night whilst Johnson and Natasha sat with Alex drinking fresh coffee, Johnson told them how he'd noticed that people seemed as interested in the news of sporting events they'd missed as they were in the spread of the virus and the fighting.

"You know, I'm not sure if this is good or bad. Is it denial or is there some sort of mental healing process going on?"

"Probably a bit of both," said Alex.

"I think the saddest thing I've heard is from Sanchez. She and O'Reilly were asked to see if they could download any podcasts from family members by some of the troop. Against all the odds she managed to find one from Frost's family on the hypermarket server. She's struggling with what to do with it."

"Give it to her," said Alex, "it's her property. We'll have more and more such instances. There's digital fragments of all our lives scattered around the planet on various servers."

206

The news articles that covered the virus were a short chronicle of the demise of society. *Web Crippled*, announced one, citing sabotage missions on major hubs and switching stations. Some of the front pages covered some of the more bizarre goings-on. *Pope Holds Multi-religious Mass in the Vatican* read one headline, going on to explain that the Pope, several rabbis, prominent Muslims, Hindus, Buddhists and even fringe religious sects had led a joint mass for more than half a million people in Saint Peter's Square. Another reported on a meeting of the Jehovah's Witnesses and other Armageddon-based groups who'd seen their numbers swell by more than a hundredfold since the outbreak of the virus. One sect claimed the virus was extra-terrestrial and had been delivered by aliens who were also responsible for the sabotage of the power and communications systems, as well as the nuclear strikes.

A foreign weekly reported an upsurge in attacks on immigrant populations throughout Europe, Eurasia and the Americas, as vigilante gangs took revenge for what they considered acts of terrorism.

"God. They were en route back to the Dark Ages," commented Crockett.

The last pieces of news contained numerous notices and advice to the civilian population: boil all drinking water for thirty minutes; if a member of your household becomes infected then advise your area representative and make sure your home is marked accordingly, then await assistance. Stay in your assigned area. Do not go to hospitals or medical centres, as these are already overstretched. If someone dies in your family, then please bury them (the specified dimensions of a grave were included); if burial is not possible then seal the body in a body bag or, if you do not have one, place it in a freezer or incinerate it. Do not panic buy. Canned foods only should be consumed.

There were numerous calls for volunteers to assist in the delivery of food, medicine and the VX nerve gas capsules that could end it all. Retired medical and engineering personnel were called on to help maintain vital systems. Natasha thought the saddest call for assistance was the one that Nancy Strong found, which called for people to open their homes as orphanages.

One paper apologised to its customers for the brevity and lack of colour in its hardcopy issue, blaming it on the shortage of ink, but carried as a headline the death of a prominent rock star.

Reports told of looting for food, bottled water and medicine as well as the usual luxuries.

Royal Navy Subs Launch Nuclear Strikes – The Empire Strikes Back! screamed the front page of a British newspaper.

"Do you think the crews of the subs are still out there?" asked Natasha.

"God knows. But if anything was isolated from APP then it would be naval vessels," replied Johnson, leaving Natasha wondering how many vessels there could be and what the average complement would be of each.

Natasha found that everyone had different views.

"Do you reckon anyone in our outfit would know how to make any of this?" asked Stacey referring to a tube of toothpaste he had purloined, and changing the subject.

"Good point," replied O'Reilly. "We should get our hands on as much as possible. It'll be worth more than gold in the future."

"The last twenty years of this bloody war has been the biggest deception since those fuckers fooled our intel community into believing that we should invade Iraq and Afghanistan. They were plotting this for decades, I reckon," said Galeago.

CHAPTER 18

ALLIED HEADQUARTERS

If you have no ulterior scheme and no forethought, but just rely on your individual bravery, flippantly taking opponents lightly and giving no consideration to the situation, you will surely be taken prisoner.

Natasha had volunteered to lead a small reconnaissance party to make contact with headquarters. "I don't want to risk what's left of us charging down a road somewhere only to get bushwhacked again," Alex had announced.

Her team, comprising Jones, Lloyd-Smith, Hodgetts, O'Reilly and Byrnes, lay in a long line like schoolchildren watching a movie on top of a ridgeline that overlooked a valley surrounded by heavily forested hills, just a few kilometres from the HQ.

She watched as the sun rose gently above the eastern hills and started its long process of burning off the thick white mist that hung in the valley, glowing with a sympathetic gentleness. It would have been beautiful, she thought, if it wasn't for the plumes of black smoke and the rumbling of heavy artillery, which were almost disguised by the sound of thunder coming from some way off to their right.

"Fucking great," moaned Hodgetts; "how come wherever we show up we find trouble?"

"Well, at least this time it's still happening. Normally we seem to arrive after the fact," replied Lloyd-Smith, squinting as he tried unsuccessfully to focus on the hills on the opposite side of the valley. He gave up; it was too far to make out anything using his nineteenth-century binoculars.

"Nice antique," said Hodgetts.

"Yes. They were a present from my father on the day of my commission. They've been in the family for generations," replied Lloyd-Smith with pride.

The sound of artillery drew closer accompanied by what looked like white and red electrical storm flashes raging within the mist below them. Natasha felt the hairs rise on her neck as she was enveloped in an electric field.

"Jesus!" muttered Byrnes. "That static, noise and light, that's a PBW. I thought it was thunder and lightning."

"What?" asked Hodgetts.

"Particle beam weapon," clarified Jones.

"What, like a ray gun?"

"Yes. Just like a ray gun."

"I bet they belong to those bastards," said O'Reilly with a scowl.

"I know of two allied units that had them on trial, so maybe they are ours. But, more importantly, for once there's a fight going on and we're not too late," interjected Jones.

"Lieutenant Byrnes, let's get Baby ready and have a look," said Natasha, edging back from the ridgeline.

The aerial drone known as Baby was no larger than a model aeroplane but could transmit high resolution imagery.

Within minutes they'd set up the launch ramp. Byrnes revved the little single engine to max, checked the thrust reading on the hold back to make sure that the engine was generating sufficient power, and then pressed the release button. Baby flew off the ramp, dipped, narrowly missing O'Reilly's head, and then rose steeply into the air.

"Energising N-RIM now," advised Byrnes.

Baby shimmered as the negative refraction index material that coated it began to polarise and Baby became invisible.

"I love it when it does that, just like the Klingon Bird-of-Prey in *Star Trek*," continued Byrnes, cutting the thin hardwire control line. "All systems green. We're on burst transmission, visual spectrum."

"How's the reception, any frequency jamming?" asked Natasha.

"Five by five. No jamming so far. We'll drop down a bit, then go IR."

Lloyd-Smith and the others joined Natasha at the console, jostling for the best view of the screen, which at that moment showed nothing but a lot of mist and cloud.

"Should have ground visual in a few seconds," said Byrnes.

The mist and cloud vanished and was replaced with a picture of muddy rolling fields and the occasional patch of snow, upon which an assortment of armoured vehicles were vying for position. Byrnes zoomed in; they could see troop concentrations, some running across the fields in skirmish lines, others running clustered behind AFVs.

"Jesus, will you look at that... Looks like at least a battalion engagement, maybe more," said O'Reilly.

"A real ugly brawl," said Natasha, watching Lloyd-Smith.

Byrnes requested the tactical analysis package for a breakdown. A situation map popped up overlaying the camera feed. Friendly forces were shown as blue, the enemy red. Different symbols marked infantry, artillery, armour, even suspected C4I2 centres and infield commanders were tagged. The allies were being pressed back along the valley from left to right.

"My God, our chaps are fighting for their lives; they must be outnumbered three to one," exclaimed Lloyd-Smith. "We need to help."

"Can we get any audio?" asked Natasha.

"I doubt it," said Byrnes, plugging in a cable that ran out to a parabolic dish. His fingers danced across the keypad as he tried to sync the decoder with the frequency hopping signals emanating from the battlefield below. "Nah. They're on encrypt. Sorry."

"Jesus. They're fucked. Look at that column en route from the south. They don't stand a chance," said O'Reilly.

"Fuck, I can't just sit here. What can we do?" asked Hodgetts.

"Nothing," said the calming voice of Jones. "We let them fight it out. If we show ourselves we will jeopardise the whole squadron. We wait and pick our fights when we have the upper hand. This is a different ball game now." He reached across and flipped the power switch to off.

"Oy, Sarge. You can't do that. We can't leave them," pleaded O'Reilly.

"The Sarge is right," said Natasha. "All we're doing is torturing ourselves."

*

That night, depressed, and listening to the battle die out in the valley below, they camped under the trees, sipping from O'Reilly's never-ending supply of whisky.

"I wonder how many other of our units are left?" mused Lloyd-Smith.

"I wouldn't have bet on any until we saw this. The good news though is that we haven't seen any sign of air power, and that means the Brotherhood must be having some home troubles themselves," said Jones in a tone of reassurance.

"That's great, Sarge. But we can't just keep wandering around Europe hiding for the rest of our lives. We need to hook up with some of our guys and get the fight going," commented Hodgetts, passing O'Reilly's flask on to Natasha.

"Patience. We watch, we learn and then we decide," said Jones. "I'm off to bed. O'Reilly, you take first watch, then Hodgetts. Go easy on the hooch; I don't want to wake up with bad company."

Natasha clambered into her sleeping bag. She took a moment to reflect on how she was now used to going to bed wearing boots and sleeping with her weapon. A heavy artillery barrage started in the valley below, drowning out the whispers of the others.

*

Dawn brought a grey and overcast sky; the artillery barrage had again given way to the sound of advancing thunder and a light drizzle. Natasha had slept with her head in the open air, the ill-fitting hood of the sleeping bag not providing any cover. She awoke stiff and damp, her hair was cold and wet, and her feet felt itchy inside her boots. Raindrops started to spatter on her sleeping bag. She struggled out of it and tried to get her circulation going by doing a few stretches. She looked around for the others. Jones and O'Reilly were lying together looking over the ridge; Lloyd-Smith was also getting himself sorted out, looking around before relieving himself shyly behind a nearby bush.

She crawled up to the ridgeline and tapped Jones on the shoulder. "You guys want some coffee?"

"We'll get it; take over here for a few minutes, there's no sign of anything moving, at least not yet anyway," said Jones handing her the optics.

"Apart from the storm," said Natasha.

"That's life. You want latte or espresso?" asked O'Reilly.

"Just warm and coffee-like will be fine," murmured Natasha, her attention drawn to some movement on the valley floor below.

"You see anything?" asked Lloyd-Smith, noticing Natasha concentrate. He focused his binoculars in the general direction that Natasha was looking in.

"Thought I saw something over by that farmhouse, about two klicks at your one o'clock," she said.

A light drizzle reduced their vision whilst weak plumes of dark smoke rose from a hundred points. Wrecked vehicles lay scattered.

"Do you know that this is the entrance to the plains of Germany that stretch all the way south to Karlsruhe? This area was once the preserve of huge tank armies that faced off against one another during the Cold War from 1947 to about 1990. My great-grandfather was a battery commander here, and his father commanded a tank regiment," said Lloyd-Smith, as if reading an obituary.

"Well, the place has certainly lived up to its history."

"Here, have a tot of this with your latte," offered O'Reilly, crawling up next to them, a thermal flask of coffee in one hand and his hip flask in the other. "It'll keep the ghosts at bay."

"Thanks," said Natasha, taking a small sip from the hip flask. She felt the liquid warming her and slightly stinging the back of her throat. "God, that's good. Makes you glad to be alive."

"Aye, that it does."

"What the hell…?" said Lloyd-Smith tensing up next to Natasha. "Oh, Jesus! Next to the farmhouse. Two o'clock."

Natasha handed the flask back to O'Reilly, sat the coffee down on the damp grass and refocused the powerful optics on the farmhouse. Hodgetts and Jones came up alongside them. Near the farmhouse the smoking hulk of an allied command and control vehicle lay on its side. A number of dead around it. She panned right, looking for whatever Lloyd-Smith had seen; about 10 metres away a cluster of four quad bikes sat parked. A group of enemy soldiers were standing in a circle; they seemed to be laughing and joking, pointing at a bundle in their midst.

She ratcheted up the zoom for a closer look and engaged the software to eliminate the loss of vision from the rain and drizzle. For a moment she struggled to make sense of what was happening, but as the image became clear and stabilised, she involuntarily let out a deep anguished moan. The bundle in the centre of the circle was actually four people: a woman and three men. The woman lay on her back whilst one of the men held her hands above her head and another held her ankles. The third man was standing over her and cutting off what few clothes she had left on. The woman tried to struggle. Natasha could see she had long dark hair that hid most of her face, but for an instant her features were visible and, even through the terror, it was clear she was pretty, probably no more than twenty-five.

The man at her head pulled her hair viciously, forcing her to remain still, whilst the other finished cutting her combat trousers away leaving her naked with the exception of her boots and underwear. He gestured and said something to the surrounding group. Two men chucked away their cigarettes and went to help the others. Now one man held each of her arms and legs apart, spread-eagling her on the ground. The man who had been removing the girl's clothes and looked like he was giving the orders knelt down between the girl's legs and stroked her face, then ran a hand up the inside of her thigh caressing the skin before roughly pushing his hand beneath her panties and tearing them away. He turned to face his friends holding them aloft like a scalp.

"Fuck this, I'm going to drop the bastards," said Hodgetts chambering a round in his LR-51 and quickly selecting the range and correction factors.

"Stand down, Corporal," ordered Jones.

"Sergeant, I cannot stand down. If you're concerned I'll give away our position I'll move."

"I say again. Stand down, Corporal."

"Jesus, Sergeant Major," joined in O'Reilly, "we can't just sit here."

"Stand down, Corporal," said Natasha. "We will not achieve anything by drawing attention to ourselves."

"Well, at least let me go down there and try to help. That way they'll never suspect we're outsiders," pleaded Hodgetts.

"Otherwise what the fuck's the point of carrying on at all?" added Byrnes, silencing them all.

Natasha and Jones looked at one another, both recognising that with all that had gone on before, this tipped the balance. They nodded their agreement.

"All right. Lieutenant Lloyd-Smith and I'll go with the Sergeant Major. The rest of you stay here and provide cover. O'Reilly, you're mobile strategic reserve under the command of Lieutenant Byrnes," said Natasha.

"OK. You heard the Captain. RV will be back here. If for some reason we get separated, ERV will be back where we left the quads. We'll maintain a reception committee for forty-eight hours. Understood?"

"Yes, Sarge."

"Good. There are nine of them and probably more of their mates nearby: that's more than us so we need to be quick and hard. Right, let's go," ordered Jones.

"Where the fuck's Lloyd-Smith?" asked Byrnes.

"Oh shit, the stupid bastard's halfway to his death! Let's catch him up before he gets us all killed," exclaimed Jones with a sigh, as they spotted him clambering down the steep slope towards the plains below.

Natasha and Jones scrambled and slid their way down after him.

A kilometre onto the plain, the intensity of the battle they'd witnessed became apparent. They jogged past three enemy Scorpion AFVs still in their diamond-shaped attack formation. The driver of the first lay slumped half in and half out of the forward compartment, which had been torn open by an anti-armour round. A trooper sat leaning against the front of the second, a half-smoked cigarette still between his fingertips; his face showed signs of a peaceful smile even though the top half of his head was missing, revealing his brain. Charred and dismembered torsos lay scattered around.

They picked up the pace, closing the distance on Lloyd-Smith who was now about 300 metres in front of them.

"Nice work," panted Jones, referring to a destroyed enemy AFV.

"Yeah. Though it looks like one of our guys got the same treatment," said Natasha pointing to an allied AFV that had been blown in two, its stern ramp open.

"Did you notice how many different allied unit insignia there are?" asked Jones, getting his breath back.

"Yes, I guess they're a collection of remnants. Like us, looking for friends."

"I wonder if Alex suspected what we'd find?" Jones posed.

They caught up with Lloyd-Smith who had gone to ground next to an abandoned 100mm cannon, scanning the farmhouse through his binoculars.

"Lieutenant, you ever pull a stunt like that again and I'll have you flogged," said Jones, ripping the binoculars away from Lloyd-Smith and stuffing them into his combat smock, as if this was punishment enough.

"Sorry, Sergeant Major. It won't happen again."

"All right. Now we're in this mess we'd better make the most of it. We'll make our way round the south side of the farmhouse and through the main gate. We should be able to get within a few metres of them before they know we're there," said Jones.

A kilometre further on they slowed to a walk as they approached the shallow depression, at the centre of which stood the burning two-storey farmhouse and assorted outbuildings. Smoke billowed from the farmhouse's windows and a gaping hole in its roof. They moved in single file down a narrow farm track picking their way past shell craters, their boots occasionally sinking ankle deep into the soft mud that interspersed sections of still frozen ground. Jones led the way, followed by Natasha and Lloyd-Smith. A low stone wall surrounded the farmhouse and the outbuildings. A wooden gate was open, next to which lay the overturned allied command and control vehicle she'd seen from the ridgeline. They passed a howitzer, its barrel pointing forlornly skyward as if looking for a friend; its dead four-man crew lay amidst ammunition containers and discarded shell cases.

"Looks like they got hit from behind; they must have been trying to turn it," commented Lloyd-Smith.

"What now?" asked Natasha, ignoring him.

"I'll go left with the Lieutenant here and break up the party. Captain, you work your way round to the right; that's the way they'll probably try and bug out. So, anyone tries to come past you, drop them. *Anyone.* Got it?"

"Understood," replied Natasha and Lloyd-Smith in unison. Natasha thought they probably both sounded a little like schoolchildren.

"Check your weapons and spare mags."

Lloyd-Smith made a show of fixing his bayonet.

The wind direction gently swung towards them and they were surrounded by smoke and the smell of burning wood. For Natasha, the smell triggered a long-lost memory of bonfires with friends in the woods.

Ready, they moved in a spearhead formation into the stone-flagged courtyard in front of the farmhouse.

Natasha went right to circle the house from the opposite side as Lloyd-Smith and Jones continued to the left. She passed an armoured jeep covered in rubble and burning timbers that had crashed into the side of the farmhouse. A deep rumbling thunder rolled up the valley. Natasha looked past a leafless tree that stood guard over a dead soldier and up towards the darkening sky. Smoke swirled around her. The heat of the fire from the building was intense and the timbers seemed to be crackling in anger. Red hot embers drifted past her before settling in muddy puddles. Another round of thunder was accompanied by a series of small explosions that blew glass from a window as small arms munitions detonated from the heat. As she neared the end of the building she could hear the sounds of laughter, a coarse, hard laughter interspersed with the cries of the victim. She shivered; her senses struggled to process the conflicting inputs and turn them into action. The rain intensified a little.

Next to the farm wall, two more dead allied troopers lay propped upright in a sitting position and stared directly at her. Their weapons, an anti-tank missile launcher and a GPMG, sat on top of the wall, below which lay discarded ammunition cases. If it wasn't for their gaping chest wounds she would have thought the troopers were just taking a rest. The raindrops landing on her combat smock were getting larger and more frequent. *I'm going to get soaked*, she thought, before realising what a bizarre concern it was.

An old tractor sat halfway between her and the wall. Doing her best to ignore the hyena-like laughter, she sprinted across to it, crawled underneath and took up a firing position between the two front wheels. She concentrated on setting up an arc of fire, imagining from which direction the enemy would come, how fast and where they would head to.

She selected ceramic armour-piercing rounds and set the weapon to five rounds per second automatic. This would allow her to take on anyone at close range even with body armour without having to worry about going for a head shot. Next she set out two spare magazines, careful to avoid a puddle of muddy water, flipped the safety to off and waited. The rain ran down the engine cowling of the tractor in a stream and onto her face, washing away her tears as the laughter continued. Her mind finally sorted out the conflicting emotions that she felt. Anger won out. Something familiar yet out of place caught her eye. It took a moment before her brain, having instructed her to look again, interpreted what she was seeing. A detached human face lay in the mud. It looked completely intact, like a Halloween rubber mask; she could make out the stubble on his chin, and sandy-coloured hair. Raindrops spattered around it. She looked around for the accompanying body or head but neither were there. What the fuck was taking the others so long?

Some 2,000 metres behind her on the ridgeline, Hodgetts, Byrnes and O'Reilly watched Natasha disappear behind the farmhouse and now followed Lloyd-Smith and Jones as they made their way around the near side. Byrnes watched through his optics as Jones turned to face him and gave a signal to them to engage.

"Right," said Byrnes, seeing Jones signal. "We're on. First down is the bastard who's on top of her. Second down is the sentry who's the only shitbag between them and the Sarge and the LT. Then it's a free-for-all with a priority for anyone who's a threat to our people."

Next to Byrnes, Hodgetts flicked his sights to manual. Ignoring the glimpse of the girl's terrified face and the numerous hands that pawed her breasts, he made final checks for crosswind, air pressure, density and the rain. Then he settled the cross-hairs on his target and pinged the range. The gun's sensors downloaded the data to the round, which in turn responded with a green go light.

"Hello, fucker. My name's Johnny Payback," he whispered, taking up first pressure and then breathing out as the rifle recoiled with the first shot. He reloaded whilst his mind visualised the small fins deploying from the ceramic bullet now speeding towards its target.

Byrnes and O'Reilly reported the result.

"Fuck! His head's gone. What's left of him is down."

Hodgetts was working robotically, following O'Reilly's instructions as he moved from target to target. The rifle recoiled again, and as a spent shell casing rotated into the air past O'Reilly, he was already reloading again.

"Stomach shot. Sentry down. Still moving. Others looking around..." commentated Byrnes.

As soon as they saw the results of the first shot, Lloyd-Smith and Jones charged out from behind the cover of the farmhouse. Yelling and screaming, they hurtled past the sentry just as he went down, and continued straight towards the group that surrounded the girl.

Lloyd-Smith smashed into them knocking one over in a shoulder charge; his momentum carried him forwards and without consciously meaning to, bayoneted a second man, the bayonet glancing off the man's sternum before sinking deeper into his chest. Lloyd-Smith twisted the blade and let out a roar that had its roots in some primeval DNA. But as he tried to disengage the bayonet from the chest, the man came with it, and he lost his footing and nearly fell backwards into the mud. He remembered his father telling him that if he ever found himself in that situation he should dislodge the blade by firing a round. He fired three and pushed the man off to one side.

To Lloyd-Smith's right, Jones stood in a classic forward-leaning fire position, almost as if he was on the range, and calmly fired double tap head rounds into two of the men who were still kneeling in the mud holding the girl's arms above her head. Blood, brain and bone fragments flew through the air and then plopped into a nearby puddle.

Lloyd-Smith lunged again with his bayonet at the stomach of a man to his left who was trying to flee, and narrowly missed. Before he could re-engage, the man's head disintegrated as a round from Hodgetts found its mark. Four men remained, which became three as both Jones and Lloyd-Smith put three rounds each into the same target.

The remaining three who had been positioned to one side of the girl started running towards the rear of the farmhouse. Jones cursed as his shots went wide, and then nearly shot Lloyd-Smith who, still screaming, now chased after them. One of the three slipped and went sprawling on his back. Lloyd-Smith, seeing the man's predicament, stopped screaming and now walked casually towards him. The man held up his hands in surrender. A gesture that Lloyd-Smith ignored as he drove his bayonet into the man's throat.

"Fuck! Did you see the Lieutenant?" asked Byrnes, from the ridgeline. "He's an animal!"

"Shit," muttered Hodgetts, as his latest shot went high and he realised he wouldn't get another chance at the other two as they had disappeared around the rear of the farmhouse.

Natasha had heard the firing and screaming and waited nervously. From her ground-up view beneath the tractor, she saw mud splashing from combat boots. She fired, twice, then three times, the weapon running upwards a little at each burst. A body came sliding across the mud towards her. Another pair of boots veered off to the left away from her and towards the wall. Crawling out from beneath the tractor and rising to a kneeling position to engage the runner, she fired two more bursts, missing both times. She cursed at her lack of skill with the weapon but then relaxed as the man dropped like a rag doll from a shot from one of the others. She turned her attention back to the figure she had shot who was writhing on the ground, and walked over to him; he had no weapon and both his legs were bleeding badly. Natasha studied him for a moment; he was about thirty years old with deep brown eyes. She didn't feel any emotion as she fired straight into his face. Across from her, Jones approached another man

219

clutching a stomach wound. The man looked up at Jones as if expecting help. In response she saw Jones shake his head before shooting him, firstly in each elbow and then each kneecap.

Natasha and Jones jogged back around the far side of the farmhouse to the girl they had come to save. They found her sobbing, lying beneath the headless body of the man Hodgetts had shot. Jones grabbed the torso's equipment harness and dragged the body off the girl, letting it flop into the mud. The girl curled up into a foetal position. Natasha felt angry, dizzy and nauseous. Lloyd-Smith arrived and tried to comfort the girl.

"It's OK now. We're allied forces. It's over. You're safe now," he said as he took off his combat smock and placed it over her shoulders. The girl started to shudder violently.

Natasha pushed Lloyd-Smith aside and knelt down. She noticed the girl's watch, whose cover had come loose revealing a pink teddy bear face. Pulling the dog tags from behind the girl's neck and wiping the mud off them she read the name: Lieutenant Sandra Jane Hutchinson.

Natasha needed to make contact with the girl. Should she appeal to the person or go through the military channel?

"Sandra? Listen to me, Sandra. I'm Natasha. It's OK now, we're allied soldiers. You're safe now."

The shuddering continued.

"She's in shock and we need to move. Captain Kavolsky, please check your weapon and mags. Lieutenant, get her some clothes," ordered Jones, whilst swapping magazines and chambering a round.

"I haven't brought any spare clothes," replied Lloyd-Smith apologetically.

"Jesus fucking Christ, Lieutenant. Improvise, adapt, overcome. I'll be over by the wall keeping an eye out. It won't be long before their friends show up," exclaimed Jones as he strode off.

Lloyd-Smith started undoing the headless torso's boots and pulling its clothes off whilst Natasha continued to try and establish contact with the girl. The rain got heavier.

"Lieutenant, we've got to get you dressed and out of here; they'll be back soon," urged Natasha.

Back up on the ridgeline, O'Reilly alerted Hodgetts to a new threat. "Shit, they've got company, three o'clock, about five klicks. Quad bikes, sixteen – no, eighteen men, and… armour, two AFVs following."

Jones who had been keeping watch ran back to Natasha and Lloyd-Smith at a crouch. "We've got company. We're out in the open and there's too many to stop. We go now."

"Sarge, she's in no condition to move, look at her," said Lloyd-Smith.

Jones pulled Natasha away from the girl and lifted her still half-naked body over his shoulders into a fireman's lift.

"You two set up a diversion, get their attention and keep it away from me. But give me time. I'll head back to the others," he ordered.

They both watched for a few seconds as Jones trotted back the way they had come with the girl dangling over his back, her dog tags swaying in the air.

"There's a GPMG over by the wall; we'll use that," suggested Natasha.

On the ridgeline O'Reilly gave Hodgetts and Byrnes a running commentary of the drama.

"The Sarge is going to try and bring her out. The Captain and the Lieutenant are the rear guard."

"Right. Let's give them a hand, then. We need to buy time. We'll take the first two quad bikes at three thousand metres, hopefully the rest will scatter, then we'll switch to the Scorpions," ordered Byrnes.

"… Give me some LRS," demanded Hodgetts, referring to long range ceramic rounds designed for maximum range against soft non-armoured targets.

"Mr O'Reilly, it's time we deployed our strategic reserve, so get your sorry ass down into the valley and help out the Sarge. I'll spot from now on," continued Byrnes as Hodgetts loaded.

"On me way," he said, dumping everything except his weapon on the ground.

Hodgetts' first round went wide and missed the lead quad bike.

"Bollocks," said Hodgetts reloading with aggression. "The bloody things are bouncing around like a yo-yo. Difficult to hit."

He fired a second round, and this time Byrnes watched with satisfaction as the driver's head exploded and the quad went out of control and rolled over. To Byrnes' annoyance the others didn't slow but detoured around it.

"Get the armour-piercing rounds ready, we'll need to slow up the AFVs," said Hodgetts, missing one of the quad bikes again.

At the farmhouse, Natasha and Lloyd-Smith had swivelled the GPMG around to face the growing threat.

"We'll need armour-piercing rounds for the Scorpions. These are just anti-personnel," said Lloyd-Smith.

"Shit, I can't get the damn belt released," Natasha said, feeling panic rising as she fumbled with the ammunition belt release.

"The interlock is engaged. Put it to safe, then push the cocking handle forward then back," he instructed calmly.

"Thanks," she said as the cover assembly popped up.

Lloyd-Smith broke open an ammunition container marked anti-armour and hauled a thousand-round belt of the Big Five O then helped align the belt on the feeder tray.

"Well then, as Wellington once said, 'We'll go out to meet them in the same old way'," said Lloyd-Smith in his best British voice as he snapped the retainer closed and cocked the weapon. A high-pitched tone and green light told them the gun was ready.

"What's going to happen when they realise they're under fire?" asked Natasha.

"Well, they're either going to stop and return fire, drive straight on, or flank us. If I was them I'd send the quads to the flanks and let the AFVs come straight on to us. Either which way we're going to need an exfil plan. Look around and see what we can do."

As Natasha searched the area to devise an escape plan, Lloyd-Smith wiped his blood-soaked hands on his trousers, then checked the optics and adjusted the range setting on the GPMG. Happy, he fired off a test burst, the gun shook on its mount and tracer arced out across the fields in front.

"The Sarge is going well," said Natasha.

On the ridgeline Hodgetts cursed. "Fuck me. Did you see that? The shot was good but nothing happened!"

"I did. Try another," said Byrnes.

Hodgetts reloaded and keyed in the distance and type of AFV. "It's a Mark Six, yeah?"

"Definitely. Range is about thirty-two hundred metres. Speed over ground is sixty klicks."

"Got it."

Hodgetts fired again; the Scorpion kept coming.

"What the fuck? That was a good shot. Clean. We're missing something here, that should have penetrated but…"

"Oh, you brave boy. We've got ourselves a hero commander," interrupted Byrnes, pointing out the commander of the lead Scorpion AFV who had opened his hatch and had his head out of the turret.

Hodgetts chambered another round.

"Good hit. Commander is down."

Lloyd-Smith was now directing his fire at the quad bikes, which, as expected, were flanking them.

"Captain, we need to buy the Sergeant more time. The best way is for me to draw their attention; you fall back and set up a second position."

"There's no way I'm leaving you, Lieutenant; we do this together," said Natasha.

"Captain, I may come across as being rather stuck up, possibly even childish, but the only way we're going to succeed in this, is for you to listen to me. Please do as I say, not as I do."

Natasha pondered the situation and then made her decision.

"OK. Good luck. I'll pull back to the opposite wall and take out the Scorpions with the—"

"Captain, displace now! Get the fuck out of here. I'll hold the line," screamed Lloyd-Smith interrupting her as a Scorpion approached the wall.

On the ridgeline Hodgetts and Byrnes now no longer had a clear line of sight to the enemy. "Fuck it, the bastards are in dead ground; we'll have to wait," said Byrnes.

At the farmhouse, the first Scorpion drove over the farm wall slightly to Lloyd-Smith's right, scattering the stones like a medieval breach. A moment later a second Scorpion crashed through the wooden farm gate to his left. He was caught in a classic pincer movement.

Natasha had been running back towards the rear of the farmhouse to try and set up a second fire position and provide cover for Lloyd-Smith when she realised two quad bikes were wending their way along the muddy track on the other side of the wall parallel to her. She skidded to a halt and turned, only to confront another Scorpion. She stopped, panting for breath, trying to work out what to do next. Things slowed down. The GPMG ran out of ammunition, the sound of rapid fire being replaced with a slowly decreasing whirring noise as the drive train wound down from 10,000 RPM. Lloyd-Smith abandoned the weapon and started to run towards her. As he dodged an empty ammunition case he slipped and went face down.

She watched him push himself up and turn to face the Scorpion. For an instant both seemed to just look at one another, then the Scorpion's Gatling spun up and Lloyd-Smith disintegrated in a mist of red interspersed with white chunks of flesh and bone.

Natasha found herself pressed against the side of the farmhouse. She knew she was trapped. To one side of her were the Scorpions and on the other were the quad bikes. She looked for some cover. There was none. The sound of crashing timber attracted her attention. Further along was a window through which smoke was billowing. Taking a chance, she ran low and without pausing dived headlong through it, landing on what felt like an old sofa. Keeping her eyes closed and holding her breath, she crawled along the floor until she found the wall of the room, then moved along it searching for a hiding place away from the heat. A sharp crack from an exploding timber showered her with sparks, stinging her face. She could smell her hair protruding from the protection of her helmet starting to burn and could feel the heat of the floor through her gloves and knee protection; her hands and knees began to blister.

Her hand touched what she recognised must be a door frame; the door was closed. She groped around it and found a sliding bolt; she could picture it in her mind, one of those old types. Rotating the bolt she slid it first to the right, which was the wrong way, then to the left. She pushed the door open, immediately noticing the cool air. The fire hadn't penetrated. She crawled through the doorway and closed it before daring to open one eye, then remembering her goggles she pulled them on. She was in a kitchen; a vase of wilted yellow flowers stood on a table. A dead soldier lay in the middle of the floor. She took a breath, and even though the smoke in the room was not thick, it still stung the back of her throat and caused her to cough. A roof beam collapsed, landing a few feet away. Dust, debris and burning bits of timber billowed into the air around her. She retreated along the wall finding a recess in the thick stonework, curling up inside just as another section of the roof came down, blasting red hot embers into the room. Reflexively, she withdrew deeper into the recess for shelter and found a half-height wooden door. She turned the thick ring handle and pushed against the door, which opened revealing a dark, cool space. Crawling inside, she closed the door and flicked her penlight on. A stone spiral staircase wound down into darkness. Another crash next door made her mind up for her. Shouldering her weapon she descended the stairs that led to an earthen-floored cellar. Adjusting the penlight to enlarge the beam she looked around the cellar. It was piled high with wooden crates. The sound of more burning timbers crackling above her, mixed with the sound of water dripping down the walls from the rain, made for a strange combination. As she searched the cellar looking for an exit, the beam caught for an instant what looked like a pale human face peering out from behind one of the crates. Natasha jerked the light back but whatever she'd thought she had seen had gone. Several explosions in the room above pumped a shockwave into the cellar accompanied by dust and debris from the ceiling. Her hunters must have thrown grenades into the house to be certain it was cleared. Someone screamed an order. She hoped it meant that the house had now been declared clear. Allowing herself a respite, she sat down with her back against a rough wooden support and unstrapped her helmet and goggles and pulled her gloves off. She wondered how Jones was getting on. Had he managed to save the girl? She checked her weapon; the magazine was empty. She changed magazine then turned off the penlight. Jesus, Lloyd-Smith had died outside saving her. She buried her face in her hands and rubbed her eyes, then cursed her stupidity as the soot stung them. How long should she wait before moving?

A small scuffing noise a few feet away made her sit up with a start. She opened her mouth to hear better and waited. The sound came again and she pictured someone wearing jeans sliding across a sandstone floor on their bottom. Turning her penlight back on, she whispered, "Hello? Anyone there? I'm an allied soldier. *Bonjour, je suis une soldat allied; parlez vous Anglais?*"

Jesus, I'm in Germany and I'm speaking French, thought Natasha struggling to remember any German. Maybe the noise was from an animal. She was beginning to feel stupid when a little girl's face peered round the side of one of the crates and stared straight into the penlight's beam. She was no more than eight years old, with shoulder-length blonde hair and a dirty-looking face.

"Hi," said Natasha, turning the penlight on herself and trying a smile.

The girl moved out from behind the crates and took several steps towards Natasha. She was wearing wellington boots and a pink ski jacket with fur around the collar.

"*Vous êtes Américaine?*"

"*Oui*, American – where is your family – *ou est votre famille?*"

"*Sais pas.* I do not know. Papa told me to stay here, *Papa a dit moi, restez ici.*"

"You speak English?"

"A little, yes. Miss Stenzil at school teaches us."

"Well, she taught you well," said Natasha realising simultaneously that her mouth was very dry and she was a little light-headed. Shit. She was dehydrated. Her water pack was empty. "Is there anything to drink here... water?"

"I have Coca-Cola," offered the girl, disappearing again behind the crates and re-emerging with a bottle.

Natasha drained the bottle.

"What's your name?" asked the girl.

"Natasha; what's yours?"

The girl smiled. "Mine is Natasha as well but everyone calls me Nat, and this is Gertrude," she added, showing off her teddy bear. "Would you like another drink?"

*

It was three o'clock next morning before Natasha dared to venture outside. The night had been full of the sound of thunder and heavy rain but it was quiet now. The smell of charred timber and flesh lingered in the air.

"I'll take you to my friends; you'll be safe with them," she said, and the girl nodded.

"But Papa told me to wait here for him."

"I know, but there are a lot of bad people outside. I think Papa might be with my friends; they are soldiers. It's going to be wet outside; do you have a hood?"

The girl nodded again and pulled out a hood from her jacket, picked up her teddy bear and took hold of Natasha's hand. The trust somehow shamed Natasha but she put the thought to one side.

It had gone well as they'd made their way across the valley, and it wasn't until they'd reached the base of the slope that Natasha, Jones and Lloyd-Smith had descended earlier that Natasha heard the high-pitched wail of quad bikes.

She scrabbled for traction, slipping backwards several times before catching hold of a tree root that she could use to pull herself up with one hand whilst using the other to haul up Nat. The section of slope they were on seemed a lot steeper than the one they had descended earlier. She needed to get rid of some weight so she dumped her weapon, equipment harness, water bottle – everything except her survival belt. The sound of the quad bikes receded and she relaxed a little, but still managed to lose her footing several times as they continued to climb. The rain started again. They reached a ledge and crawled along it for a few metres before Natasha decided to rest. Her lungs were bursting from the effort and her right shoulder was cramping with the effort of holding on to the girl.

"Don't worry, we're almost there," she said.

"OK," responded the little voice.

As they started to climb again Natasha lost her footing once more and almost ended up sliding out of control to the bottom.

"Fuck it!" she screamed in desperation.

"It's all right. We'll make it," the girl reassured her.

Suddenly the darkness was turned to daylight as a white ice light lit up their position. Natasha froze; then turned slowly and knew they were finished: a Stalker was hovering a hundred feet away. It was just sitting there, taunting her like Olly had described. The beam from the ice light darted backwards and forwards between the two of them as if it was undecided who was to be engaged first. When the Gatling slung beneath it whirred, Natasha grabbed the girl and started to climb desperately. Gunfire pierced the sound of the rain and spurts of mud erupted from the wall in front of her, accompanied with a sound like a slap. Natasha pulled her little companion up towards her but her weight seemed to have doubled and the tiny hand seemed no longer to be grasping her own. Natasha looked down praying that she would not see what she knew she would. The girl's head flopped around at an odd angle, her blonde hair was sodden with mud, and the teddy bear that had rested in her backpack was no longer there. Natasha let out a primal scream: anger, rage and sadness mixed into one.

She let go of the girl and without thinking carried on climbing the slope, not looking back. She made it to the top and crawled into the trees. As she lay on her back panting for breath, she wondered why the Stalker had not killed her as well. Was it really that evil? Was it programmed to destroy morale as well as simply eliminate targets? Guilt swamped her. If she had left Nat maybe she would still be alive; what right had she to have taken responsibility for her? With the rain dripping down from the trees onto her face, she waited for her spirit to survive to take back over. It took a while, and help came from the strangest of places. The voice of her survival instructor lurched out of her memory. "Given up, have we? Well, get up and face it!"

She ran for more than three hours through the forest, twisting her right ankle in the process. Then as the first signs of a sunrise broke up the night, the rain stopped. She wished the sun luck; it now only had to overcome the thin mist that wandered amongst the trees and held the dampness close to the forest floor and it would be warm.

She estimated she had travelled 25 kilometres and should be within 20 of the ERV. She glanced at her watch; the others would only wait another few hours before pulling out. There was no way she was going to make it. She stopped and slumped down against a pine tree.

The guilt had left her, and now she couldn't work out if she was angry or defeated; the two emotions danced with one another, each courting the other. She decided she would toss a coin to see which would win out. For the last hour she had resisted the increasing pressure on her bladder, remembering her survival instructor's words: "In the extreme, resist the urge to urinate. It's your very own hot water bottle and contains a lot of latent heat that your body has generated. One piss is about two hours of survival." God, she was getting confused- that was for hypothermia not tiredness.

A bird flapped in the trees above her, the branches noisily responding. A crow squawked. An animal moved somewhere in the undergrowth behind her and a branch snapped. She looked around at the ground where she sat; thick, soft moss covered large pieces of grey granite. A pine cone lay a few feet away. She remembered the time after the crash when Sanchez had told her, "The gladiators used to burn them before battle."

Her survival instructor came and stood next to her again. "Well, well. It's just not your day, is it, Captain?"

She needed water. To her right lay a muddy puddle. A bird hopped up to it, stuck its beak into it several times in quick succession, shook its head, glanced at her and took off.

She looked at her survival instructor hoping he would help. How come, she wondered, his jump boots were always so clean, when everyone else was covered in mud from head to foot?

"I know it looks bloody horrible but remember that the dirt sinks to the bottom," he said referring to the puddle of water. "So all you need to do is find a straw and drink from the top; it's good clear rainwater and you won't get sick. And remember, drink every thirty minutes when on the run."

"It's been hours, though, and I don't have a straw!" said Natasha.

"So improvise, adapt…"

"Yeah, yeah, I know… overcome," she said to herself.

She fished out a white linen handkerchief from her combat smock, a present from her grandmother, then dipped it into the puddle and sucked at the moisture. She repeated it again and again until she felt the inside of her stomach start to get cold.

"Well done, Captain. Now remember, when you think you've given all, you have to dig again, there's always more. It's all in your mind. The German Sixth Army that surrendered at Stalingrad were marched into captivity in Siberia; the big fit guys died faster than others. It's not the body, it's the mind."

She tried to check her compass but her hands were shaking so much she couldn't read it. Her eyes stung. "Come on! Get a fucking grip!" she shouted at herself, placing the compass on the ground so she could read it.

She started to walk, and then jog. Her ankle was hurting and she thought about popping two of the superman pills from her survival pack. They were a powerful combination of painkillers, cocaine and speed. No. She would only use them after another 10 kilometres. She retied her combat boots as tight as she dared and continued. She found a track that emerged onto the riverbank. The water sped to her right. "Fuck, why the hell did I drink from bloody puddles when I was so close to the river?" she asked herself.

Water swirled around a pile of large rocks, in the middle of which a large oystercatcher delicately moved, its long beak searching for food. It paused, looked at Natasha, then made a *kleep kleep* noise before continuing its exploration.

How the hell did I know that was an oystercatcher? And why is it here when we're nowhere near the sea? she asked herself.

Then an image of little Nat wearing a pair of pink wellingtons wading out into the river so that the water was just below the top of the boots jumped into her consciousness. She recognised it as a game she used to play with her parents. "I'm losing it," she said to herself.

"When you are near the bottom of your will to carry on, you will remember things long forgotten," replied her instructor.

"Thanks."

She decided to take two of the superman pills. Within ten minutes she felt ready to go again. She started running, her ankle didn't hurt and she felt good.

It was two more hours before her ankle hurt again, and she could feel her muscles cramping. She wondered whether to take another superman pill. She stopped for a drink. She could smell chlorine from her body. Jesus, she was now sweating urea. How much further did she have to go? Fuck it, she couldn't remember. When was the last time she'd done a distance check? She smelt smoke, wood smoke. She looked up at the sky to see if she could see the source and then smiled; she was within sight of the power transmission lines.

*

She'd made it to the RV; Jones and the others had waited for her. Sandra, the girl they'd rescued, had died the previous night.

"Did she ever say anything?" she asked Jones.

"Nothing," he replied. "I think she just gave up."

"You've got the thousand-yard stare," said Jones.

"What?" she asked.

"It's a look that you get once you've been through hell. You ever seen the eyes of an animal that's just been killed in a hunt?"

"Yes, once. They looked alive but vacant, not focused on anything, just staring."

"That's them. Welcome to the club."

They spent the rest of the day resting and dividing up Lloyd-Smith's possessions. Jones gave Hodgetts the old binoculars.

CHAPTER 19

THE MUSIC CLUB

Everyone likes security and dislikes danger.

The squadron now debated again where they should go. No one had any idea. They had no plan. They were beginning to fall apart emotionally.

"The only thing that's keeping us together at the moment is ourselves," commented Johnson.

It was dark humour that rescued them when O'Reilly suggested that they should at least continue south towards wine country. If nothing else they could drown their sorrows and maybe visit some of the places they had friends or relatives.

They were 20 kilometres outside the town of Heidelberg in Germany when an IFF detection alarm lit up.

"Looks like we have a friendly beacon," advised Sanchez.

Natasha, holding on to the grab bars as the AFV swayed around some object or other, peered at her repeater screen. She halted the AFV, jumped down from the vehicle and ran back along the muddy track to Alex's AFV behind.

"We've got a friendly beacon. Looks like air force. Bearing zero one zero. Somewhere inside Heidelberg. Do you want me to interrogate?" she asked.

"No. Hold on the interrogation; we want to stay passive. How far before we can get an exact location without going active?"

"Should be able at the next turning, about another ten minutes."

"Roger that. Let me know."

After negotiating a series of narrow farm tracks, the Bavarian medieval university town of Heidelberg finally came into view dominated by church spires, with the setting sun in the background creating a washed-out red and grey sky. Natasha halted again and joined Alex and the others.

"So… Any thoughts?" asked Alex after they were gathered at the rear of the column.

"I say we go in and evaluate what we've got," offered Natasha in what she hoped was a decisive voice.

"I agree. If there's a chance of anyone being alive it'll help morale. They need something. A peg in the wall, so to speak… Something that they can relate to," said Johnson.

"Risks?" asked Schaefer.

"Apart from the beacon, no active e-sigs," replied Natasha.

"I agree with the good Dr Johnson; I think we need to take a look, Alex," said Crockett.

"OK, we'll treat it as a SAR mission. Captain Kavolsky will lead. Captain Schaefer will provide escort. One AFV. The rest of us will wait here for you."

*

Just before midnight and using Schaefer's AFV, they edged closer towards the town.

"The beacon's definitely in the town. I put it almost in the main square. Whoa! We've got varying e-sig," said O'Reilly letting them know he'd detected a varying electric field, which meant that whatever was generating it was actually doing some work.

"You sure?" asked Sanchez, checking O'Reilly's screens.

"To be sure I am. It's continuous and on the same bearing as the beacon."

"Mil spec?" interjected Schaefer, questioning whether the fields were of military origin.

"Negative, looks civilian. There are multiple stable sources… probably lights, that sort of thing, but there are definitely one or two sources fluctuating – or under variable loads from something. Maybe just pumps or something but it's worth a look."

"All right. Captain K, I'll drop you at the end of the high street. From there you just walk straight ahead for a couple of hundred metres and you're in the square," said Schaefer.

"Sounds good," replied Natasha.

Natasha felt a mixture of excitement and impatience as the stern ramp was lowered with a whine of hydraulics. Dressed in their black city assault suits, she followed her team down the non-slip ramp and joined them in a U-shaped defensive perimeter. Each of them knelt on the cobbled street, their Cyclops streaming enhanced visual, audio and thermal data. The cobbles glistened in the cold night air and Natasha reached down to touch them with her fingertips, which protruded from her black gloves. The touch of the stone provided something real amongst the stream of digitally enhanced sensor data. She could hear the whir of servos on the AFV roof as the weapons on the AFV jigged fractions of an inch backwards and forwards driven by the computers that were minutely adjusting their aim to match imagined threat probabilities. Finally the noise stopped as the computers, happy they had reached an optimum state of readiness, froze the weapon positions.

Natasha's Cyclops showed the direction of the beacon and the e-sig. Both were straight ahead. She thought she could hear music and turned up the audio gain on her Cyclops. It was. Thinking it must be one of her team she raised an arm to indicate she wanted their attention.

"Anyone playing music?" she asked.

No one was.

"You all hear that?" she whispered.

"Yeah. Sounds familiar. What the hell is that song?" replied Galeago.

"That's live music. They sound quite good," said Winston.

"Yeah, if you like that sort of thing," said Sanchez.

Natasha checked her audio direction finder. The music was coming from the same direction as the e-sig.

"Hold your position."

Natasha studied the high street. It was narrow with numerous side streets and crammed with wooden-framed medieval buildings, their walls bowed and distorted from settlement over the centuries. The atmosphere was like a late Sunday night, subdued after a busy weekend and waiting for the start of a new week. The thought made her realise that she didn't even know the day of the week. She knew the date but the day no longer seemed to matter.

She surveyed the street in more detail; nearly all the shops were smart boutiques, many of their doors were open and some windows were broken- shards of glass shone amongst the cobbles and on the flagstone pavement.

A black cat with green eyes crossed the street ignoring them. Discarded packing and goods lay scattered around and a lone shoe stood in the middle of the street.

The music stopped, and Natasha cranked her audio gain to maximum. For an instant she thought she heard laughter before a new song started, stopped and then started again. It sounded like a band practising, the drummer a little out of sync.

"Corporal Sanchez, I'll take Corporal Galeago and head down to the square to see if we can find the beacon. Give us a couple of minutes, then you take the rest and see if you can join that jamming session. We'll RV at your location; leave a marker at the entrance."

Several minutes later Natasha and Galeago entered the square, which was dominated by a church and clock tower. Deeply worn stone steps led up to the church entrance, where a huge pair of intricately carved wooden doors stood slightly ajar, guarded on either side by more stone gargoyles than Natasha had ever seen in one place. Next to the doors an aircraft ejection seat lay on its side.

"Let's—" Her sentence was cut off as an ear-piercing scream rose from the darkness within the church. A second later a dark shape flew down the steps, brushing her left leg before racing across the square and down a small alleyway.

"Fuck. That scared the shit out of me," said Natasha.

"Just a vixen," said Galeago. "You get used to them."

"Thanks."

She glanced back up the stairs at the oak doors that hid an inky darkness. It was then she noticed the unmistakable smell of death that hung like rotten meat in the air. She exchanged a knowing glance with Galeago; the church had obviously become a last refuge for the townsfolk and was now a source of food for the local wildlife.

"Jesus. This place gives me the creeps," said Galeago.

"I think ghosts are about the last of our concerns at the moment. Let's check out the seat."

As they started up the stairs towards the ejection seat, there was a loud thud from above them. This time Galeago reacted, diving to Natasha's right, rolling twice and bringing his weapon up to a ready position searching for the threat. Natasha had yet to react before a small parade of metal eighteenth-century soldiers marched out of the clock tower onto a platform to the rhythm of a drumbeat interspersed with nine loud bells. Neither she nor Galeago moved until the soldiers completed their short patrol and entered a second set of doors that swung closed with another thud, returning the silence.

"Well, this place is just full of surprises. What's next, I wonder?" asked Galeago, standing back up and relaxing.

*

Sanchez, Williams and Winston had meanwhile entered a department store from where the music was emanating. They now stood in the women's clothing department where Sanchez had called a halt to try and get a better fix on the source of the music. Toppled mannequins and clothes littered the place, and there was a smell of damp, cigarette smoke and cat urine. A bank of escalators rose within an atrium, which was capped with a domed starlight that let just enough moonlight through to see their surroundings without the aid of their Cyclops. They could now clearly hear music; it was coming from above them. Sanchez was sure it was BB King.

Sanchez signalled to the others to climb the escalators. As they moved towards them Williams bumped into a bucket that stood on top of a pedestal and held a bunch of almost fossilised flowers. It crashed to the floor but the music continued unabated.

"Jesus. Let's get our fucking act together, shall we?" whispered Sanchez.

They paused at the bottom of the escalators, and Sanchez for the first time noticed the state they were in. Their combat smocks looked tired, and their webbing and equipment harnesses looked lived in, resembling faded denim jeans rather than combat-ready clothing. *Jesus*, she thought, *we're beginning to look a little ragtag.* She realised that her own webbing and equipment harness seemed looser; either she had lost weight or it had stretched. Probably both.

As she started up the escalators, a giggle came from behind her. She turned ready to chew out the culprit but instead found herself struggling to stop herself smiling. Both of them were wearing large ladies' summer hats, and Winston was gyrating with a mannequin. *Well, fuck it*, she said to herself, *if we get killed by a BB King-loving musically talented enemy it wouldn't be too bad a way to go.* The sound of bells drifted in from the outside followed by the scream of a vixen. "Jesus. This place is humming," she muttered. The idea of a squadron fashion show crept into her mind.

It would boost morale, and she promised herself that one day they would have one.

On the next floor level they were greeted by a sign proclaiming discounts on musical instruments and electrical goods. Ahead of her was a set of double swing doors, from beneath which a light glowed. The floor was carpeted, and for an instant she felt absurdly uneasy walking across it in her combat boots. She couldn't remember the last time she had walked on carpet; whenever it was, it seemed a long time ago. She was a few steps from the doors when the music abruptly stopped. She froze, and raised her weapon to point straight at the doors ahead. A melee of voices and applause erupted before dying down to a low murmur and another song, this one a recent hit from only two months ago.

She signalled to Williams and Winston to take a position either side of the doors, and braced herself ready for entry. Pulling her weapon firmly into her shoulder, she took three breaths flooding her body with oxygen. She was about to enter when another door opened on her left; she swung around, her weapon at the ready, only to find herself facing a girl in her early twenties who stared back with a mixture of surprise and terror.

"It's OK! We're friends!" said Sanchez in the most unthreatening voice she could muster. She held up a hand, and lowered her weapon as a sign to remain calm. The girl looked at her, understanding but still wary. Then the girl noticed Williams and Winston who remained crouched either side of the doorway still wearing the women's hats; a smile slowly spread across her face.

"Come in," said the girl calmly, and pushed open the door with the sort of flourish that announced they were about to enter a pleasure dome. Sanchez followed her in. Across a large room that had once been the music department, a makeshift stage had been set up, upon which two boys were playing guitars and a girl a keyboard. The girl sang. Next to the stage two other girls stood at a makeshift bar, chatting and smoking. Flashing lights lazily flickered on and off amidst a haze of cigarette smoke. Winston and Williams followed and just stood and watched as the song continued; no one seemed to notice them. When the song finished Winston led a round of applause.

As the applause subsided the two groups stood, simply looking at one another. Sanchez decided to break the ice.

"Uh. Hi. I'm Corporal Sanchez."

Silence.

"We're with the allied armies."

More silence. Powerful emotions were washing around the room. Sanchez could not identify what they were: relief, happiness to find another human being, recognition that they would be safer together, hope, all were there, swirling and tumbling, trying to find an order.

*

In the town square, Natasha approached the ejection seat. A small red light set above a key pad in the armrest blinked every second. She typed in a simple four-digit access code. The red light blinked twice in quick succession and then went out, and a small monitor lit up: 'ARMY AIR FORCE – GS-117. FL LT TOMMY LEE – 249 – W3 – 2 –12'.

"All right, Mr Tommy Lee, where are you?" whispered Natasha to herself. Galeago drew up beside her looking inquisitively at the display just before it went blank.

"We have standard security codes for SAR work. With them you can access certain info. The seat belongs to the army air force, ground support squadron one-one-seven. The pilot is Flight Lieutenant Tommy Lee, he was shot down two hundred and forty-nine hours ago, is wounded code three, which means disabled but not life threatening, and he is within two klicks of here. He last checked in just twelve hours ago," explained Natasha.

"Wow. So what now, Captain?"

"Well, I reckon Mr Lee has either lost, turned off, or broken his personal beacon. Now if I was him, I'd be where the music is. Let's go and join Corporal Sanchez."

Sanchez's visual identifier was an IR beacon that sat on top of a scribbled note. Natasha smiled as she read it. One night only – Sanchez presents… The Rock Apes. First floor, the music department.

*

Upstairs, Sanchez had moved into the middle of the room. Two large batteries were providing the power. Three fridges sat humming in the corner, their price tags still hanging from them. Around the walls were beds complete with side tables, lamps and silk sheets. One of the new three-

237

dimensional holographic video games was projecting its paused image into the air, a three-dimensional spaceship in full flight. In the far corner a small kitchen had been erected accompanied by stacks of canned food, bottled water, cigarettes, and cases of wine and spirits. The room smelt of a mixture of food, cigarettes, alcohol and new appliances.

The door swung open behind her and Sanchez dropped instinctively to her knees in a firing position. Natasha and Galeago came in.

"Welcome to the gig, Captain," she said recovering her composure.

A figure that had been sitting in the shadows out of sight, rolled across the floor in a wheelchair into the light.

"I'm Lieutenant Tommy Lee, Allied Army Air Force, and these people are civilians," said the man in the wheelchair, waving his arm around the room.

"Pleased to meet you, Lieutenant; we picked up your beacon on your ejector seat. I'm Captain Natasha Kavolsky, Allied Air Forces, heavy lift. I'm part of a mountain squadron, the First of the Ninth. We're laagered a few klicks outside town."

"Well, it's good to see someone else."

Natasha thought about what she should do or say next. She made up her mind.

"We're happy to offer you safety with us if you wish. However, irrespective of what you decide we would like to escort you back to our HQ for a debrief; if that's OK?"

One of the band members who was wearing a hooded black sweatshirt jumped down off the makeshift stage and strolled up to Natasha in a fashion that only a youth can manage. As he closed the distance, he pushed his hood back to reveal a handsome face; he had long blond hair terminating in a ponytail, held in place with an elastic band. He spoke with an Americanised European accent.

"Hey, not sure what you guys think you can do here; you arrive like the men in black, some sort of galaxy defenders, yet we're fucked, man, look around you. We're the last; we've lost everyone. HQ and a debrief? For what?"

Natasha grappled with quite how to respond. *I wonder if this is what mothers of teenagers call growing up?* Was he the leader? She decided the best way to continue was to ignore his negativity.

"I understand. All I'm suggesting is that those of you who wish to, come with us for a day; let's talk. If you don't think there is any point then fine, but there's now obviously two groups of us who've survived and there may be more. Corporal Sanchez," she continued, trying now to impose some military authority, "will escort anyone who wants to come back." She turned her back on them and left the room.

Sanchez picked up the thought process. "OK. You heard the Captain; anyone who wants to come, get your stuff together and meet us downstairs in five. Private Williams, double back to Captain Schaefer and warn him we'll have some additional passengers. And lose the hat."

Downstairs, Sanchez joined Natasha. "Jesus. Ponytail there has some attitude problem."

"The younger generation, huh?"

From above them, a melee of shouting and arguments erupted then quickly subsided. The first to appear was Lieutenant Lee who was helped down the escalator in his wheelchair by Galeago and Winston. Various rucksacks followed, dropped from the floor above. After another round of hushed voices and whispering, six people started to struggle down the escalators carrying an assortment of musical instrument cases. Natasha and Sanchez stood to the side as they filed out into the street. One of the girls was carrying a cello, whilst tottering on a pair of blue suede knee-high boots that were ringed with silver chains. She looked like she was going to a Parisian nightclub rather than catching a lift in an AFV.

"Nice boots," remarked Sanchez.

"Thanks," replied the girl, studying Sanchez and Natasha for a moment, and making Natasha wonder who was dressed more ridiculously, herself with a web belt full of 40 mm grenades or the girl with her boots. Jesus, probably neither, she realised.

"You know you can get a pair just up the high street."

"Thanks. Is 'Ponytail' coming?" Sanchez asked.

"You mean Luc? I don't think so," she replied.

Natasha sighed. "I'll go and talk to him. You get the rest back to the AFV."

Natasha went back up the escalators and found Ponytail at the bar nursing a cut-glass wine goblet full of whisky, the half-empty bottle standing guard next to him.

"You OK, Luc?"

"Yeah. Just thinking."

"Well, it's a fairly easy decision, we're hardly kidnapping you, all we want to do is talk. After that it'll be your call."

"I just don't want to leave, that's all," he mumbled, sipping the whisky.

"Why?"

"Because this has become our home, our world. I know we won't be coming back now."

"Hey, listen. Anyone who survived is now living in a new world. Sitting here isn't going to bring back the old one. But that's not really the issue – what is, is that we found you guys because you were emitting a lot of electrical noise. If we can, then some characters that are not based a million miles from here can also, and those guys seem hell-bent on a world without any of us in it. So, without being too blunt, we can't wait around much longer. So make your mind up."

"OK."

"Good. But before we go... can I have a whisky?"

With what looked like a monumental effort he poured her a whisky, then stood up and picked up a ski coat and rucksack. "Cheers," he said offering her a toast.

Natasha took a last look around the room, gulped down her whisky and then threw the breakers on the batteries, submerging the room in darkness.

*

Back at the AFV, Schaefer and the others stared in surprise as the ragtag band of people, musical instruments and the wheelchair came up the stern ramp.

"Jesus Christ, we've found a lost fucking hippy commune," commented Stacey.

Sanchez eventually got them all seated and stowed their rucksacks, although each kept a tight hold of their musical instruments. Natasha decided she would stay with them and sat down opposite a pretty girl with high aristocratic cheek bones, blonde hair (also tied back in a ponytail) and light blue eyes. The girl adjusted the position of the cello case between her knees, looked straight back at her and then introduced herself. "I'm Dominique Lacompte, and these are my friends: Helena Haroldson, she is, or rather was, reading astrophysics and is from northern Norway; that's Isabella Ronaldi – history of art, she's from Italy; and over there is Kitty Wright – art, from the Scottish Islands. The big guy is Kevin Charles – philosophy, from England. And I guess you've already met Luc, who's a physicist from the same town as me. We're all, or rather were, students at Heidelberg."

240

"Well, I'm Natasha and this is my friend Corporal Sanchez. We should be hooking up with the rest of the squadron in thirty minutes or so," replied Natasha, looking each of them over. They looked like they were heading to a gig, rather than being transported to the remnants of a battle group.

"You any good with that?" asked Sanchez pointing to the saxophone that the large Englishman called Kevin held on his lap.

Without responding he undid the case, assembled the instrument, wetted the mouthpiece and started to play *Summertime*.

Sanchez smiled, leaned back against the headrest and closed her eyes. "Take me home, Daddy!" she said.

Natasha too allowed herself to relax for the duration of the song before pulling on a headset and paging Schaefer in the commander's seat.

"Captain, should we be considering quarantine or delousing?"

"Yeah. Been thinking about it, but what the hell for? Are we really going to wander around the planet and never meet anyone? If that's the case then I guess we should all give up now."

"You don't think it's worth warning the rest of the troop?"

"I'll send a burst transmission and ask for some advice."

The music stopped and they all gave a round of applause coupled with calls for an encore. This time the art student called Kitty, who had some of the longest and darkest hair that Natasha had ever seen, lifted her guitar and started playing a classical Spanish piece.

"Ah, just the ticket!" crowed Winston, causing some of the students to quizzically appraise him.

"Where are you from, Dominique?" asked Natasha.

"Both me and Luc come from a small village in the south of France, a place called Saint Christobel. Our families have lived there for generations; we're I guess what you call childhood sweethearts – almost following a tradition."

"What kept all you guys from going home?"

Dominique looked down at the floor, her head swaying with the motion of the AFV.

"We argued about it in the beginning but as the situation deteriorated we decided it was best to stay together in one place. We had everything we needed. When the Lieutenant showed up ten days ago, we discussed it again. But Luc and he reckoned it was best to stay put for another few months."

"Well, I'm glad you did, otherwise we would never have met. You've no idea what the company has been like for the last month or so."

On reaching the rest of the squadron, their guests still carrying their musical instruments were ushered through a small crowd and into the HQ igloo where Alex was hosting a session on logistics plans for fuel and spare parts. As Natasha embarked on the introductions, Johnson burst into the igloo to request blood samples. Alex smiled and held up a hand to signify patience; first up would be a debrief, second would be a medical, he said. Coffee arrived and everyone sat wherever they could amongst the instruments whilst Alex recounted the squadron's recent history.

The first of the debriefs was with Flight Lieutenant Tommy Lee.

"All right, Lieutenant. We're going to record this for the log. It'll also be open for everyone within the squadron and our civilian friends to read. So let's start from the beginning," said Alex. Around him everyone waited like expectant children to hear a favourite story.

"Our ground attack squadron, the One Hundred and Seventeenth, was based just south of Florence. The first sign that we had lost control of the situation was when they managed to take out our space-based assets.

"GPS, comms and surveillance – all went out. One minute they were there, and within an hour we'd lost the lot. I'm still not sure we'll ever know how they did it; we heard rumours they'd attacked us using some type of swarm system – you know, hundreds of small killer satellites that were released from mother satellites. Others said they'd used EMP from high-orbit detonations. I think they probably used both. Anyway, they built on this and instead of waging cyber war, they took the practical approach. First off, they took out any specialist personnel they could get at, then attacked key specific installations with sabotage teams. The transatlantic fibre optic transmission lines, switching stations, that sort of thing. Our comms were badly degraded; we could still communicate but we'd lost integration and data transfer, especially air defence.

"That's when the nuke strikes against the cities happened; we executed mass evacuations to the country in case of more strikes, but instead of more strikes they went after our comms again; they used everything, hacking, jamming, sabotage, the lot. There were hundreds of saboteurs, some say they were sleepers, others that they were air-dropped, that targeted the hardware, switch hubs, data cables, relay stations and server farms. Effective comms ceased. Our governments couldn't get alignment on what the response should be; there was open disagreement. Some wanted to go straight to a full like-for-like response, others wanted to wait. Then came APP. There was disagreement on whether it was connected; the US and some others thought it was. Others didn't."

"It was and intimately," interjected Johnson, handing him a coffee. Tommy Lee nodded.

"Anyway, as strategic services collapsed, each government went their own way. As the effects of the virus were realised, the US and several other countries launched full-scale CBRN strikes that went after both the enemy civilian and military centres. Front lines ceased to exist. With no data, the fighting became more and more splintered as integrated command and control systems collapsed.

"Air and seaborne landings started; there were reported large-scale airborne drops on the east and west coasts of the US, also in Britain, Germany and the Ukraine. Lesser drops occurred in Scandinavia and the rest of Europe.

"Seaborne landings occurred in Greece, Spain and Sicily in Europe and in several places along the western seaboard in the US. There wasn't that much intel available but in general the consensus was that the seaborne landings were divisional in size. The missions seemed to have been to deny transportation routes rather than engage our forces or secure industrial complexes.

"Our response to all these was decided in most instances by the local field commanders. It was chaos. Without GPS there were strikes that went way astray. A day after our CO became infected he ordered us to launch a nerve gas strike against a position in Naples, and a nuclear strike against Brotherhood forces in Turkey. I was assigned to fly cover for the nerve agent attack. A nuke launched independently went off whilst we were over the target. There seemed to be no thought but to inflict as many casualties on the enemy as possible in retribution for our own suffering. What was left of our wing had no idea what had happened to their families, all we knew was that people were dying in their millions. We heard that many of the allies had launched nuclear strikes on their own soil to break up enemy attacks, but I'm not sure anyone really even knew whether the targets were actually enemy concentrations or not. Looking back it was crazy; I remember some of the guys picking random targets and loading their aircraft with whatever they fancied."

"What about your base?" asked Johnson.

"Our base population went from more than twenty-nine hundred to less than ten in a matter of days. The surrounding towns were the same. We lost comms with the outside world completely. I stayed on at the base with what were eventually three other survivors. God, when I think about it, three out of a total of nearly three thousand. Anyway, we stayed put for two weeks hoping that some contact would be made; when nothing changed we each decided to take our own chances. I tried to fly back to the US and see if I could make contact with my family in Canada. We fitted long-range drop tanks, and I took a base guard called Garard who was from Vermont. We got as far as Heidelberg when we were engaged by a pair of A2As that took us out."

Lee shuffled in his wheelchair and took a sip of coffee, then moved slightly away from his audience. When he spoke again it was with a guilty and soft lilt.

"Garard never made it. I guess it takes a little more than a few minutes, training to operate an ejection seat.

"I came down a few hundred metres from the town centre, slid down a roof and busted up both ankles pretty bad. I managed to crawl to a house but couldn't get the door open. That night was the worst I ever spent; all I had was a thermal blanket in my survival pack and the flight suit against the cold. I think if it wasn't for the pain in my ankles that kept me awake I would have died of exposure, that and the church clock bells! It was next morning when I met the others; they were out scavenging for canned food when they came across me. They did the best they could for my ankles; the rest, as they say, is history."

"Any sign of our uninvited friends?" asked Crockett.

"We had a deserter who stopped for something to eat before leaving about two days ago; but otherwise nothing. We had a long chat – you know, the old warrior to warrior type of thing."

"And…?" asked Alex.

"Their commanders are claiming they've had a great victory. That we're finished. The trouble is, apparently, that they too have lost contact with their home command structures. I think our strikes broke them. They're relying on scavenging as much as us."

"Why did they escalate?" asked Natasha. "They must have known that the risk was mutual annihilation."

"According to this guy they didn't have much of a choice. About a decade ago, because of our trade sanctions, they went through a program to genetically modify their basic food staples: wheat, soya and rice. They were confident that the modifications would increase yields and be drought resistant. Apparently it worked well for the first few years: bumper crops and massive yields. On the back of this success they went the whole way. Replanted all their crops with the GM improvements. Then came the last three years. A lot of early rain fell accompanied by an unusually warm period. The result was an outbreak of some pest fly. It turned out that the GM alteration to the DNA had somehow disabled something that normally kept the fly at bay. The result? The fly population thought it was Christmas. The crops were decimated."

"Jesus Christ. You're telling us that this whole thing was kicked off by a fly?" commented Schaefer.

"Sounds plausible. Genes have more than two states, they are simply not just on or off. Physicists have recently drawn parallels with quantum theory; there are a whole number of grey states. Not only that but individual genes are not mutually exclusive, somehow they are linked. It's a bit like throwing a switch to a light only to discover that one in another room also responds," said Johnson.

"I remember some intel about the crop failures. But it was made out to be no big deal," added Alex.

"Well, it wouldn't be the first time Slime got it wrong," said Jones, using the slang term for the intelligence services.

"Anyway, apparently their leaders told them that it was our doing," continued Tommy Lee. "We had somehow unleashed a genetically engineered pest designed to decimate their food crops, we'd released biological agents, sprayed their fields, contaminated the ground water with special drugs. All of this had been done to destroy their civilisation and make them dependent on us."

"Well, it sounds like the age-old political bullshit; if you've got big domestic problems then have a war to take your mind off them," interjected Crockett.

"Well, this guy believed it all until a month ago. Just before the invasion began, his best friend, who was an agricultural geneticist, told him that the whole GM food programme had collapsed because of an inherent design flaw in the gene."

"Great, so we've got one deserter who forgives us whilst the rest are fanatically hell-bent on wiping us out as payback," summarised Johnson.

"I wonder how many are roaming around and what capacity they have remaining?" said Jones.

"And just as importantly, what will they do? If they've nothing left at home, are they going to stay and wreak their revenge?" added Crockett.

"I think we've already seen the evolutionary process at work. Look at what we've witnessed. The executions, everything. It's simple; I think the end game has been reduced to it's us or them," said Johnson, lighting a cigarette.

Natasha thought about what she'd heard. She looked at Alex before speaking; he nodded.

"I agree. They've shown no remorse. I think we're dealing with the equivalent group personality that perpetuated the Nanjing massacre back in the 1930s, the Holocaust, ethnic cleansing, and God knows how many other names history has used for the same thing. If they think we've toasted their homeland then they'll have absolutely no intention of going home. We're dealing with a fight to the death. The only issue is who can wipe out the other first."

"So what's the plan?" asked Tommy Lee, changing the subject.

All eyes turned to Alex.

"At the moment we don't have one. So first up we will continue the debriefs to see what more we can learn. In the meantime I suggest you all go and get something to eat. I'll see you in the morning," he replied, standing to signal that the session was over.

Natasha followed him outside. "Alex, come and listen for a moment. It'll do you good," she said grabbing him by the arm and leading him over to the mess, where the students were entertaining some of the troop.

She felt the stiffness in his arm dissipate as the music found a way into his psyche. The student called Kitty looked at Natasha, her eyes sparking with a brightness that only students seemed to have. What was it her tutor had told her? "You'll leave this college and join the world like a speeding photon. Remember that feeling and you'll never get bored of life."

"God, I wonder what my eyes look like now?" she muttered to herself.

"What was that?" asked Alex.

"Do my eyes sparkle?" she said turning to face him. Before he could reply O'Reilly approached and asked, "Would the Major and the Captain like a nightcap?"

They sat together and enjoyed the music, and it was only when the song finished and they went to applaud that Natasha realised she was still holding his arm.

"They are now," whispered Alex as they gave a round of applause. Natasha could feel herself blushing.

"Goodnight, Major."

"Goodnight, Natasha."

*

"This is incredible," shouted Johnson as he barged into the mess where Natasha and the other officers were having breakfast. The students, Tommy Lee and Tsang followed Johnson into the now cramped igloo all talking excitedly and carrying a whiteboard.

"What?" asked Alex.

"Alex, you need to listen to this," said Johnson with excitement, exhaling a stream of cigarette smoke.

"Go on."

"I'll try and make this relatively simple," began Johnson, pacing around the table. Both Natasha and Alex looked at one another knowing this was a sure sign that whatever was coming would not be simple.

"Heidelberg had a student population of about five thousand. As it wasn't classified as a strategic target, and to reduce logistics problems, the decision was apparently made not to evacuate the population. Indeed, Heidelberg actually took in thousands of evacuees from some of the big cities."

"So far so good," humoured Alex.

"Good. So we know APP was a designer strain of pneumonic plague, engineered to kill. The genius of the design were the splices. The first was the gatekeeper, which kept the nasty part of APP locked up whilst the benign part of the virus that had no apparent symptoms spread widely. The second was the clock, which killed the gatekeeper after a prescribed period unleashing the nasty part of APP that killed you.

"If people had started dying earlier in the infection cycle then quarantine could have helped contain the spread of the virus because people would have gotten ill and been immobilised and not able to travel. However, initially, infected people felt fine, there were no symptoms or warning signals. So quarantines were not set up and this resulted in massive infection rates.

"The medical services were swamped; all the efforts at containment and treatment were way too late. We'd effectively lost the battle before we even knew we were fighting it."

"So I remember you telling us," said Natasha, wondering where this was going but becoming intrigued as Johnson grabbed a marker pen and started

247

scribbling on the whiteboard. She could feel Johnson's excitement beginning to infect the others.

"Now I'll let Lieutenant Tsang tell you the next bit."

Tsang, the young Chinese medic, picked up the baton.

"Now, commonly in medicine, in the gene therapy world we use AAV, or adeno-associated virus, as the transport vehicle to move a virus from host to host. These are harmless in their own right and there's nothing really new about this. Once inhaled, the virus locks on to a targeted gene and then transfers its genetic material to the target gene, altering the target gene's DNA in the process."

"Now, the important thing is that the AAV needs a target gene. Just remember that bit for a moment," interjected Johnson.

"And...?" pushed Natasha and Alex in unison, both obviously not really understanding where Johnson was heading.

Tsang took over again, brushing her long black hair back like a lecturer.

"Please be a little patient while I try to explain this... DNA is effectively a storehouse for genetic information. When a cell divides, the DNA is replicated so that each new cell maintains the same genetic info.

"Very crudely, DNA is organised into segments. These segments are what we call genes. Each gene contains the information required to make a specific protein. The protein in turn is actually constituted from a sequence of amino acids. The proteins control cellular structure, growth and function. An alteration to a particular gene can cause proteins to be over-produced, under-produced or produced incorrectly, any of which may cause disease. This is what APP did. It altered one or more genes, which then manufactured proteins that caused cells to misbehave.

"But what we also know is that genes are interlinked; one gene will, via messaging by something called RNA, also activate or deactivate other genes. It's a bit like us in battle: a command given to one unit will in many instances get passed on to others, often with unknown consequences.

"Like Captain Johnson explained last night, the whole way genes behave is extremely complex; we now believe that genes have a quantum element, they have multiple states, where they are neither on nor off but somewhere in between. The way this all happens and consequently the way cell growth is regulated is therefore still largely unknown. But I'm digressing; for our purposes we don't need to bother with complexity and regulation via RNA and m.RNA and all that stuff, what we need to focus on are the sequences of individual genes. The DNA."

"Now you've lost me," said Alex.

"And me," muttered a few others.

"All right, put another way, for any virus to work, a whole series of genes must be present, so that they can together manufacture the various proteins that cause the cells to do whatever the virus wants them to do," said Johnson trying to help. "You with us?"

"Just," said Natasha. "What you are saying is that it's a bit like a chain of dominoes – for a virus to work, the required gene sequence must all be lined up and present."

"Absolutely!" shouted Tsang as if she'd scored a winning goal.

"But what happens if you don't have one of the genes that are required in that series, or maybe you have a mutated gene, one that stays off when it's asked to turn on?" asked Luc, the student with the ponytail, in a manner that Natasha knew must have been rehearsed for their benefit.

"Well," exclaimed Johnson lighting a cigarette for effect, "then you're a lucky bunny, and you would be classified as being immune. You still with us?"

"Yes, I think so… but I still don't understand where all this is going," said Alex.

Johnson paused for effect, taking a long purposeful drag on his cigarette. "Well, out of the five thousand students resident in Heidelberg, we seem to have a total of six known survivors; that's a major improvement in itself on the mortality rate we've seen in other parts. But…"

"Go on," said Natasha, now suspecting where this was leading.

"But what are the odds of two people from the same village also surviving?"

"Now you've lost me," said Alex.

"Luc and Dominique are from the same village," interjected Natasha, smiling and grabbing one of Johnson's cigarettes.

"Exactly. From what we've seen the odds should be enormous. Somewhere around one in twenty-five million," said Johnson.

"Unless they're missing one of Natasha's dominoes," Alex remarked.

"Jesus, they're both genetically immune," said Crockett.

"Which means there may be others," added Schaefer.

"Indeed. But that's not all. After a little chitchat last night, we also know that all of our student friends from Heidelberg are from small communities with long family histories tied to the same village or area. And that's what triggered my memory," added Tsang.

249

"Something tells me that you're going to share this memory so I can understand the whole picture," said Alex, still looking perplexed.

"The great plague events of the Roman and medieval periods and later in the 1600s killed millions. But across Europe whole villages sometimes remained immune. In those times people attributed this to a whole raft of different theories: the local water, a tree, God, or even witchcraft. The real reason was a mutant gene, I think it was called 169, but whatever it was called, the fascinating thing is whole villages possessed this gene, the reason being that the population was relatively stagnant."

"Or to use another term, interbred," chipped in Luc with a smile.

"You see, gene 169 was one of the first demonstrations of something called a founder mutation, which is a special class of genetic mutation embedded in stretches of DNA that are identical in all people who have the mutation. This was and is exciting stuff because it's part of the solution to isolating ethnic-type diseases that encompass just about everything from malaria to cystic fibrosis. Founder mutations pop up everywhere, some have even used the theory in screening for advantageous genes; endurance athletes for example went after specific types of gene therapy that were shown to help red blood cell count and so on..." added Tsang.

"And...?" said Natasha, deciding to egg them on.

"So the way I see it, is that a large proportion of Luc's village has a very high chance of having survived the virus, as have the others. And if so, Luc's village would be a great place to start," said Johnson.

"Start?" asked Alex.

"The hope of rebuilding. The search for other surviving populations. People!"

Natasha felt herself connect with something. She couldn't describe it. Either which way she felt more alive than in a long time.

CHAPTER 20

THE JOURNEY SOUTH

Nation, army, division, battalion, unit – great or small. Keep it intact and your dignity will be improved thereby. Destroy it and your dignity will suffer.

Excitement and hope permeated the squadron as they started the long journey towards Saint Christobel, the village from where Dominique and Luc, two of the Heidelberg students, came.

Saint C as they'd renamed it was shown on their maps as a medieval town situated on the French Atlantic coast. The route they'd planned would take them across the Alps and then down to the Mediterranean coast, where they would turn east and work their way through the lower Pyrenees towards the Bay of Biscay.

They travelled cold tack with passive sensors only, and no radio comms, whilst Beethoven flew scout on a hardwire umbilical. On two occasions they spotted smoke from a fire, and saw signs that a shop or supermarket had been recently ransacked, but Alex wanted to minimise further risk and maintain their pace so they did not investigate. Tsang and Johnson busied themselves with DNA profiling each of the survivors, followed by the rest of the squadron.

They were deep into the French Alps using the famous Route Napoleon and emerging from one of the long tunnels when Sanchez called an emergency stop.

"Beethoven's got Stalkers."

She cross-loaded the imagery to Natasha in the commander's chair. Outside of the tunnel was a wide valley in which sat arrays of wind turbines, some turning, others stationary. But it was the burning vehicle on the road with dark smoke streaming up into the grey and white sky that dominated their repeater screens.

"I've got a civilian vehicle on fire plus two burnt-out RVs. The RVs are not friendlies and look like they've been there for a while," reported Sanchez.

"O'Reilly, can you run back and tell the Major what the story is. Take a hardwire link as well. Tell them to reverse one hundred metres," ordered Natasha.

"Right you are, ma'am," replied O'Reilly with a flourish, before muttering something about being reduced to a runner.

Sanchez adjusted Beethoven's camera to give a wide-angle view. Above the civilian vehicle a Stalker was maintaining sentry duty over its kill whilst another was flying what looked like a search pattern out to their right. Sanchez widened the view still further and switched to thermal imaging. A small white dot now shone against the cold background of the valley walls.

"We've got a civilian on the run," advised Sanchez.

Natasha felt a cold fear, which was soon replaced by anger as she remembered the night when she would have been one of two small white dots silhouetted on a machine's tactical imaging system.

"What about the recon vehicles?"

"They're dead. Been hit by an air attack by the looks of it. Strange, no other sign of other X-rays, just our Stalker friends," reported Sanchez.

Natasha considered the options. Do nothing, retreat, or engage, destroy and move on. They were well protected inside the tunnel, so the only downside was being engaged by ground forces, of which there seemed to be none. She decided attack was the best way to proceed but was still a little nervous. She consulted her tactical analysis computer. It told her that she needed to establish the level of forces that would be supporting the Stalkers before any decision on engagement could be made.

"Thanks, about as helpful as a mosquito," she muttered to herself. "Corporal, you sure that there are no other X-rays in the area?" she asked Sanchez.

"Captain, we're showing nothing. I know it's strange but either they're really good at concealment or they're not there."

"So... what I'm thinking is this. Either they are there and know we're here and are remaining hidden; or they're not here; or they're here and don't know we're here and can't be bothered to chase the civilian."

"I guess this is what they mean by making decisions with only limited data. Well, the way I see it is that there is a high probability that the Stalkers are alone," muttered Natasha.

Below her, Sanchez shook her head whilst trying to understand her Captain's thought processes.

A green status light came on advising Natasha that she now had hardwire communications with Alex.

"Six. We're showing two Stalkers, no other sign of X-rays. The Stalkers are hunting a civilian. I'm going to take them out. How copy?"

"Roger that," came Alex's response.

Natasha switched her comms back to internal.

"Lieutenant Byrnes, you and your team up for this?"

"Yes, Captain, I reckon," replied Byrnes.

"Do it."

"Mozart airborne. All systems green. I have control," he advised, then cross-loaded the target and an attack plan to the machines and set them in autonomous mode.

Natasha's screen flipped modes and started relaying the Musicians' tactical analysis. She looked at the numbers; the system was predicting a 20% chance of success, which didn't seem much. From her command seat above, she gently kicked Byrnes in the shoulder and mouthed, "Twenty per cent?"

He smiled, and then mouthed back, "Don't worry."

The distance to the first Stalker that was hovering over the burning vehicle was just over 3 kilometres.

Byrnes launched a drone from each of the Musicians before diving rapidly to within a foot of the ground and accelerating to 120 kilometres an hour towards the first Stalker. Natasha ran the mental calculations. The Musicians would close the distance to the Stalkers in about ninety seconds. The drones though, which were much faster and armed with a single missile that had a range of just over a hundred metres, were more of a threat to the Stalkers.

Natasha watched the system now report the chances of a successful mission had risen to 26%.

The nearest Stalker span to face the threat, and Natasha was relieved to see the second break off its human hunt and speed back to support its partner.

"Correct. You should never leave your wingman," said Natasha, fascinated as the game began to unfold.

"Jesus, look at them. It's spooky the way they think; it's like a pair of jackals," said O'Reilly, who'd clambered back into his weapons seat next to Sanchez.

As the drones from Mozart and Beethoven reached the slowly-spinning wind turbines near the burning civilian vehicle, Byrnes intervened.

"All right. Now it's time for a little human intervention," he announced, rubbing his hands together. He flipped the laser target rangers on the drone decoys so they now tracked the wind turbine blades, and reconfigured the gyros and auto pilots to take their input signal directly from the laser ranging units themselves.

"What are you doing?" asked Sanchez in a bemused voice.

"He's reconfigured the drones so they fly in the shadow of turbine blades," said Natasha in an admiring voice.

The Stalkers now seem confused and started to jig from side to side in response to the vanishing act, their tactical software packages trying to assimilate what had happened.

"You're making me feel dizzy, so God knows what you're doing to them," said O'Reilly.

The system now showed a probability of success of 62%.

"Twenty seconds, and the Musicians will be on them. Time for a peep show," said Byrnes, disengaging the laser ranging on one of the drones and switching to manual control.

Within a second the probability of success had dropped to 40%.

"Jesus, the bastards are trying to jam the telemetry link; they must have a station somewhere near. I can't get the continuity on the signal to maintain full control. Well, fuck them." He sent a fire command to the drone to launch its missile, and then flipped control of both back to automatic.

Even though the missile range was inadequate, it did its job, allowing Mozart and Beethoven to close the remaining distance to the Stalkers.

Natasha's screen now showed 95%.

By the time the Stalkers had reassessed the threat from the Musicians it was too late. The two Musicians flew directly over the area where the Stalkers had gone to ground and released their cargo of aerial mines, which homed in on the EM signature from the Stalkers before detonating.

"Outstanding," commented Natasha.

"Well done. Let's go and help our runaway," commented Alex.

"Mozart is en route. Beethoven running cover."

"Any other sign of threat?"

"Negative," replied Sanchez.

As Mozart arrived on station, Natasha's heart sank as she saw the bloody remains of a body shredded by the Stalker's Gatling. She had trouble controlling herself. She wanted to scream.

"Six. Requesting a squad with quad bikes to go and check over the victim," she asked Alex.

"Roger that. Schaefer's en route."

Mozart's audio microphones picked up Schaefer's audio as he checked the body.

"She's dead."

Natasha looked at the camera feed. The woman looked like something out of a medieval peasant scene, in her late thirties or early forties. Her dark hair lay wet and matted across her face and she had a cut above her right eye. Her clothes consisted of woollen stockings, hiking boots, a linen dress and a dark blue ski jacket.

Alex's order jerked her back to reality. "Let's move, Captain."

"Roger. We good to move?" Natasha asked Sanchez.

"Yeah. All green. You gotta put it behind you, Captain."

"Six. We're moving down to the roadway. How copy?" said Natasha to Alex, not knowing how much more she could put behind her.

"Roger that."

They drove off road avoiding the wrecked vehicles.

"Strange, you see the mines? They are all the same. They're Stalker aerial deployed Mark 3 anti-armour," advised O'Reilly.

"You saying the Stalkers beat up their own as well as the civilian? That doesn't make sense," said Sanchez, scrutinising the camera feeds as the rainy drizzle started to intensify a little.

"Maybe they've gone rogue?" offered Raven.

"Olly's been going on about the things ever since the bridge. He's convinced they were autonomous," said Sanchez.

"If the Stalkers thought their command links had been compromised, i.e. they thought that control had been hijacked by ourselves say, then they could have resorted to their own AI. It's always been the big risk with all the AVs. What happens if someone else gets control of the telemetry link? We looked at doing the same with our AVs but decided that the units should simply shut down if the situation arose," Byrnes advised.

"So maybe Olly was right. I thought he was just being over-sensitive," said Sanchez.

"Unknown on that. But software does some strange things. Remember the deep bugs that caused the crisis in the aircraft manufacturers a few years ago? They traced it to a subroutine for the rudder control. It turned out the subroutine had a tag that was the same as that used in a subroutine for the air conditioning fluid low level alarm. What they found was that if the air-con alarm had been triggered and at the same time there was a cross-wind then the rudder would automatically flip in the wrong direction," added Raven.

"Bastards; so now they don't give a damn who they kill," said Sanchez.

"Well, thanks for the cheery outlook," said Natasha.

"Maybe we should try and capture one?" added O'Reilly.

*

It took them several more hours to reach the top of Route Napoleon, where they drove into thick, freezing cloud that sat guarding the descent to the Mediterranean coast.

"Nice weather," commented Natasha just before she was hurled forward against her harness, as the AFV stopped abruptly with a bang and a shudder.

"Fuck it!" exclaimed Stacey from upfront. "We've clobbered a rock or something. Standby."

Natasha, Stacey and his vehicle specialist Hicks dismounted and in the swirling fog went around to the front of the AFV. The track assembly that had been damaged during the bridge engagement had finally collapsed. A pile of boulders that looked to be the remains of an avalanche lay in their path.

"How long?" asked Natasha with a sigh.

"The hydraulics are shot, the gear assemblies are bent, the—" said Hicks.

"So at least the night?"

"Forty-eight hours. And that assumes we can nick one of the tracks off the back end. We're beginning to look like a scrap heap. Look at it, my old Betsy," bemoaned Stacey with what Natasha took to be his most caring tone.

Alex and Jones, looking like apparitions in the fog, joined her.

"Forty-eight hours," offered Natasha.

A wolf howled somewhere.

"This is like a fucking horror movie. Next up we'll be fighting werewolves," grumbled Stacey from under the AFV.

"Sergeant Major, suggest we break out the igloos. Let's set the perimeter a klick out," ordered Alex.

"I'll see if we can't get Hodgetts and O'Reilly to bag a reindeer or something as well," said Jones.

"I bet old Bonaparte never had this fucking problem," continued Stacey. "You know he used this exact route when he entered France to take power for the second time."

Schaefer spotted Sanchez on top of one of the AFVs chatting to a young trooper. On seeing him, she smiled coyly, slid down the AFV hull and purposefully fell towards him. He could do nothing but move to catch her. She giggled as she realised that he'd become aroused.

"You feel that?" he whispered in her hair.

"No. Must be the cold," she giggled.

"Oh Jesus…" he whispered in mock despair, before issuing an order in a loud and authoritative voice so any crew around the AFV could hear. "Corporal Sanchez, I want you and your team in a planning session. It's going to be a long night."

"I love it when you're so cruel," she whispered, giving him a salute.

*

That night, as Stacey and his team worked on repairing Betsy's track assembly, Natasha sat with Johnson and Alex sipping on some of O'Reilly's seemingly inexhaustible supply of whisky.

"You know, I've been thinking," said Johnson.

Alex looked at Natasha with an expression that told her to be prepared.

"We – well, I – have got some hope, but I'm in a delicate emotional state. The route we're taking is one I recognise from ski trips with my parents and later friends.

"Just wind the clock back a few years and I could have been on this very stretch of road. Anyway, what I'm trying to say is that I'm beginning to suffer from an increasing feeling of loss and loneliness. It's like the route is one that the dead have travelled. It's making me feel empty."

"Go on," pushed Alex.

"I can reconcile my feelings but I'm worried that some of us won't be able to."

"Maybe we should take some R and R when we hit the coast?" offered Natasha.

"I agree. I think we run a real risk of emotional dislocation if we arrive at Saint C and find nothing. We need to somehow strengthen our internal bonding but in a relaxed setting, not under fire. I'm not sure if I'm making any sense but I think Natasha is right," replied Johnson.

"No, you're making perfect sense. OK. Two days' R and R once we hit the coast. How does Monaco sound?" asked Alex.

They spent two more damp, freezing nights on the top of the pass before they managed to get the AFV repaired.

*

As they finally emerged from the Alpes Maritimes, the mood lifted. Soon they were driving through the palm green of the Côte d'Azur, and shielding their eyes against the glare of the harsh white villas and the sparkling bright blue of the sea.

"Monaco looks like it was evacuated; it's empty," reported Jones after a reconnaissance trip.

"I wonder why they evacuated?" Natasha asked.

"God knows. Unlikely, but perhaps they thought they were going to be nuked," replied Schaefer.

*

Natasha lay back and let the spring sun gently warm her. Her thoughts wandered like the white clouds in the pale blue and light grey sky above. The colours reminded her of her honeymoon, years before, in Africa, and for a moment, the memories of her husband played out like a movie before her. She'd been a newly commissioned officer when she got married, and together they'd hired a sports car and driven along the Cape. She'd been the one driving when the tire had blown out, sending them over a cliff. It was one of the few periods of time they'd had together.

"I'm done. Shall we take a stroll, Captain?" asked Sanchez.

"You sure you don't want to go back?" asked Natasha.

"Nah. He'll be too busy playing soldier, making sure we are all safe. Let's go and have some fun. We might even bump into the Major."

"What's that supposed to mean?"

"Whatever you like, Captain. Whatever you like," she giggled.

In the cool, sunny, spring weather they walked along the promenade which was lined with palm trees. The street, although covered in branches, sun shades, deck chairs and other debris from the winter storms, still looked like one of the best-kept roads Natasha had ever seen. They passed the Olympic swimming pool which had turned a deep green, and climbed the gentle slope up towards the Hermitage. Here they met Kitty Wright and Isabella Ronaldi, the Heidelberg history of art students. They'd organised a tour of the museum and were followed by a motley-looking combat squad led by Olly.

"Afternoon, Captain," offered Olly.

"Good afternoon, Corporal," replied Natasha, surprised that Olly had taken the time to recognise an officer.

"Thought I'd better let you know that Stacey and O'Reilly have gained access to the most famous casino in the world and… well, later on they plan to host what O'Reilly has proclaimed will be a party to end all parties, courtesy of the NCOs. We've also decided that, as this is a special occasion, the invite will be extended to officers. So ma'am, I hope you can make it."

"Thank you, Corporal. Please relay my acceptance."

The deep throaty roar of a sports car's engine attracted their attention. Lieutenant Tsang pulled up alongside them in an Aston Martin convertible. "I always wanted one of these," she cooed.

"This could turn out to be quite a day," offered Sanchez.

"Indeed," replied Natasha, smiling.

As they rounded a bend they came face-to-face with Tiffany, the jewellers.

Both looked at one another and smiled. "We could get shot for looting," said Sanchez.

"We could, Corporal, we could. Can you get us in without a commotion?"

"Always, Captain, always."

*

Several hundred metres away, Johnson and Alex were strolling along the boulevard around the port.

"I wonder where they all went?" asked Johnson, building a bridge back into Alex's consciousness.

"What?" asked Alex, before realising that Johnson was referring to the famous harbour, that now stood empty of boats.

"Strange, isn't it?"

"I guess they took off to all the remote places the rich go; it must have been a sight to see. The rich, the famous, the beautiful, all setting sail for somewhere else."

"I wonder how many survived?"

*

Natasha walked along the red carpet that led into the casino; gaming chips littered the floor, although the bank, she noticed, which was recognisable by a long line of brass bars, looked intact. The sound of champagne corks popping drew her attention to the main gaming room where a crowd had gathered around the roulette table.

"Captain. Please come and join us. The champagne is warm but so is the company," shouted O'Reilly.

Natasha smiled and took a seat at the table. "What's the house limit?"

"We take it all."

"I'm in," she replied sitting down at the table and dropping a diamond necklace onto the red box.

"Phew… I'll have to check with management."

O'Reilly had set up bank in the main gaming room. From somewhere he'd purloined half a dozen giant silver candelabra which he'd set up around a roulette and several black jack tables. Winston, together with his mortar crew and Stacey, were dressed as bartenders.

"Roll up, you scurvy swine. I'll take any and all bets!" he yelled.

As the party went on into the small hours, Johnson, Natasha and Alex retired to the smoking room, which was an enormous library full of leather-bound books and oversized armchairs. Each held a glass of Napoleon brandy and a cigar. In the gaming room next door they could hear the continued banter and laughter. Then the sound of a band started as the students who had set up shop started playing. Between puffs on her cigar and sips of champagne, Natasha dismantled and cleaned her weapon, with a now practised and mechanical ease.

260

"We'll make a grunt of you yet," said Alex, smiling.

"Yeah, it's tough, but I'm working on it," she quipped, as she disassembled the grenade launcher and gyro sights.

"I heard you've found a way to get the gyros to behave better."

"Not really me, it was Raven. He used a neat little trick we used on the Gatlings we had on the Strat. Same design, same problem. Simple fix. An extra data link that allows the gimbals to maintain feed even when they go into lock."

Alex sniffed his cognac. "God, this smells good."

"Thanks," said Johnson.

"For what?" replied Alex, looking at his friend.

"This."

Natasha finished reassembling her weapon and laid it down on the floor. "Another few days and we'll be at Saint C. That's going to be the real turning point," she said.

"You sound like the good doctor here."

"It's going to be an important time," agreed Johnson. "We'll need to allow them to decide what they are going to do."

Natasha studied Alex and reflected on what she had heard, then stretched out and listened to the music from next door.

"I wonder what happened to the crew of the space station?" asked Johnson, changing the subject.

Natasha relit her cigar without responding and signalling she didn't want to talk about death for the rest of the evening.

That night they stayed in the casino as a massive storm struck the coast, toppling palm trees and hurling signs and other street furniture around the town.

CHAPTER 21

SAINT CHRISTOBEL

*Once people are unified, the brave cannot proceed alone, the timid
cannot retreat alone – this is the rule for employing a group.*

The journey from Monaco to Saint Christobel took four days. They halted
at 1000 hrs at a crossroads on a narrow country road lined with apple
trees in early bud. Just over 2 kilometres away on top of a steep outcrop
was the medieval town of Saint C. Several columns of smoke rose into the
pale blue sky. Not smoke from devastation but smoke from home fires. A
sparkling Atlantic ocean shimmered in the background. Ignoring protocol,
people spilled out of the AFVs to get a better look.

The surrounding land was undulating, and made up of dozens of small
fields interspersed with woodland. A river wound its way across their line of
sight. Vineyards marched in straight lines up the hill towards Saint C, their
routes broken only by craggy rock faces before they finally stopped at a row
of cedar and pine trees standing sentry around a ruined monastery that lay
beneath the shadows of the town's walls.

"I've got movement on optics. Civilians," announced Sanchez in a
triumphant voice.

Natasha, who was in the commander's cupola of her AFV, had to squint
in the strong sunlight to see the image on her repeater. A group of five or so
people were walking along a pathway carrying tools over their shoulders.
The scene looked like something out of a *King Arthur* movie set with the
peasants returning from the fields.

Natasha dumped her headset, clambered out of the hatch and slid down the hull to the roadway to join Alex, Schaefer, Johnson, Tsang, and Luc and Dominique, who'd gathered in the roadway.

"Pretty, isn't it?" said Dominique.

"Like a poem in springtime," replied Johnson.

"So how do we do this?" asked Natasha.

"I'll go," said Luc.

"Mozart will follow you; we'll give you an IR strobe so we can track you. We'll laager here," said Alex.

*

The tension and atmosphere as they waited for Luc to return was evident everywhere. People cracked jokes and laughed almost too loudly. Johnson chain-smoked. Then after what seemed like all morning but was fifty-two minutes Luc returned. He was accompanied by six villagers, all carrying shotguns. As the group approached, four of the villagers remained at a safe distance whilst Luc and two of the others approached.

Dominique ran towards her mother before embracing her.

"Major. This is my father, Dr Heymans… Dad, this is Major Alexander Burton," announced Luc.

"Major. I'm pleased to meet you. Thank you for bringing my son back. And this is the Contessa Lacompte, Dominique's mother."

Natasha looked at Dominique's mother, a stunningly beautiful brunette. She was dressed in a hunting jacket, jeans and walking boots, and armed with a shotgun and what looked like an old Berretta pistol tucked into a cartridge bandolier. She looked like a French World War Two Resistance leader.

"I think we can dispense with the titles under the circumstances. I'm Katie, and again, thank you for bringing my daughter home," she said, holding out a hand.

"I do apologise for our escort," she continued whilst waving a hand at the four men who remained further back, "but the dog packs are getting more brazen, and we've had the odd issue with ambivalent strangers."

"We understand. This is Captain Johnson and Lieutenant Tsang, our medical officers. Without them this would not be happening," replied Alex.

Alex stood back as Luc's father shook hands with both.

"I'm pleased to meet you. Luc's told me about your theory. Now, before we go any further, we're in a bit of a quandary. Some of the townspeople are worried that you may still be carrying the disease. Although nearly fifty per cent of us survived, many did not. They will I think need some sort of persuasion, if that is the correct term."

"Fifty per cent! Wow! Well, as one doctor to another, I think we should have a chat," replied Johnson with a huge smile.

"Afterwards, I think you will be able to put people's minds at ease," added Tsang, also smiling.

The Countess and Dr Heymans left just before sundown. Dominique and Luc elected to stay. Natasha, Alex and Johnson watched people's reactions as this very public family reunion unfolded, and wondered how many of the squadron were thinking about their own loved ones. The atmosphere was a mixture of excitement, hope and sadness.

*

A prolonged series of gun shots woke Natasha early the next morning. Scrambling out of her cot in the AFV she went outside to investigate. The morning was magical; a mist hung close to the ground and swirled around the boughs of trees, and a soft dew glistened on the fields as the sun rose.

"Looks like a shooting party," reported Jones, handing her a coffee.

"Do you ever sleep, Sergeant Major?"

"Sleep 'ma'am' is for officers and other ranks," replied Jones with a smile, offering her his monocular.

On the crest of a hill she could make out ten or so people emerging from the tree line armed with sticks and beating the shrub and grass. Further down the hill and facing them was a line of guns, including the Countess. A boar charged out into the open and all six guns swivelled to face it. She noticed the Countess was the first to fire and the animal staggered and dropped.

"Impressive," commented Jones.

"Very," replied Alex joining them and giving Natasha a wink.

"Mmmm. Beautiful, titled, a leader and a good shot. What more could a man want?" concurred Natasha, feeling slightly inadequate in comparison.

*

An hour later the Countess joined them, interrupting a daily ops meeting. Natasha watched as the men transferred their undivided attention to their visitor.

"Good morning, Major. Good morning, everyone."

"Morning," replied Alex. "Good hunting?"

"Yes," she smiled. "We thought that as it's a special occasion we would celebrate."

"Sounds great," replied Schaefer with an eagerness that Natasha saw drew a jealous look from Sanchez.

"We held a council last evening and it was unanimously decided that you and your…"

"Squadron," offered Alex.

"Yes, squadron, I was going to say men, but they're not all, are they?"

"No, that changed a long time ago."

"As many things. Well anyway, your squadron and of course your civilian wards, are most welcome to make your home in Saint Christobel. Our home will become your home."

"Thank you. It will mean a lot."

"I'm not sure of the best way to do these things. I guess you will need to sort out appropriate billets, if that's the correct term, and all sorts of other practical things."

"Captain Schaefer and Sergeant Major Jones will accompany you back. They can organise the move up. In the meantime, can we offer you breakfast?"

"Thanks. I'm starving hungry actually; not used to crawling out of bed at four in the morning to go shooting for boar."

"Well, it looked to me like you knew what you were doing. Sergeant Major, please let Corporal Stacey know that there will be one more for breakfast, we'll do an officers' table."

"Sir!" snapped Sergeant Major Jones, springing to attention in his best parade ground fashion. Natasha caught the smile from Alex who gave her a wink.

"Shall we go and see if your daughter is awake?" offered Natasha.

"Let's do that."

"I'll just go and put some coffee on," interjected Sanchez sarcastically.

"Thanks, Corporal," acknowledged Schaefer, looking at her inquisitively.

For breakfast, Stacey and O'Reilly surpassed themselves, marching in dressed in chefs' outfits, and carrying silver platters of smoked kippers, butter, marmalade and toast, accompanied by coffee.

"Your highness?" offered Stacey, whilst executing a theatrical bow for the Countess.

They laughed as O'Reilly stood to attention with a silver coffee pot awaiting a command to serve.

"I see you live well, Major," said the Countess putting on an air.

"We stopped at Monaco a few days ago. It had been evacuated completely. Some of the squadron, shall we say, 'borrowed' some of its assets. Would you believe me if I told you that I've never been treated like this before?"

*

For the move into Saint C, the AFVs had to follow a narrow twisting lane that ran parallel to the river. Natasha led the convoy. As they passed the ruined monastery they came upon a graveyard. There were hundreds of fresh graves decorated with ribbons and flowers. The darkened older tombstones seemed to be watching over the new.

The road narrowed more, and Natasha, concerned that they were running out of space, called a halt. She and Stacey dismounted to walk the route. The sounds surrounding them were peaceful: their boots on the gravelled roadway, the gurgling of the river to their right, and spring birds. They crossed a stone bridge and then started the steep climb through a series of switchback curves up to the main gate which was guarded by two towers, topped off with castle ramparts.

"It'll be tight. But at least we're not taking incoming," advised Stacey.

With the exception of knocking a few of the stones capping the bridge's balustrade into the river, the AFVs made it through the main gate without incident. Emerging from the main gate's tunnel they then drove along a deeply rutted, cobbled high street which ran for a hundred metres. It was lined with two and three storey buildings, none of which Natasha reckoned were less than 500 years old. On their left a gallery of shops including a *boulangerie*, bar, café and *parfumerie* was set back behind a row of Roman-looking columns which supported the buildings above. Narrow shaded alleyways led off in different directions.

266

At the end of the high street they entered the town square, in the centre of which a fountain was flowing splashing water into a small pond, surrounded by statues of dancing children holding hands. The far side of the square was dominated by a medieval church and bell tower, around which was a gravel forecourt dotted with pine trees that provided shade for some benches and tables. The Atlantic Ocean carried on sparkling in the background.

Natasha felt like she'd found a holiday resort as she waved at the groups of townspeople who had turned out to greet them. Some of them smiled and waved in return, whilst others looked on inquisitively.

On the right-hand side of the square was the Hôtel de Ville, next to which was a long three-storey building that proclaimed itself to be the Hôtel de Constantine. A row of large double oak doors had been swung open. Above them hung a sign that announced in French and English – *Parking strictly reserved for guests of the Hôtel de Constantine.* Jones, who was standing in the square, directed the AFVs inside.

"Well; this'll do nicely. Wonder if they've got room service?" Stacey muttered to himself as he reversed the AFV into the garage.

"I'm sure they have, Corporal. OK. All stop," ordered Natasha, taking off her headset and clambering down to join the growing number of squadron personnel.

"This isn't a bloody holiday camp! Form up!" bellowed Jones.

The squadron formed up into their sections. Byrnes led all the aviation specialists, including Flight Lieutenant Tommy Lee in his wheelchair. Johnson's medical team formed up on their right. The remains of the squadron under the commands of Natasha, Crockett and Schaefer formed up in the centre with their civilian wards in a line next to Jones. Jones brought them all to attention and each of the section leaders reported in their best parade ground voices that all personnel were present and correct.

"Parade… shun," boomed Jones again. "Saah. All present and correct," offering Alex a crisp salute.

Natasha counted the faces around her. There were thirty-seven survivors from the crash.

"Stand easy," ordered Alex. As the parade relaxed she saw exhaustion for the first time. They looked gaunt, their clothes looked worn out, even their weapons she noticed were losing their finish.

"As you know, we've been offered a home here. On your behalf I've accepted, until one of two things happens…" He paused. "We are either ordered to another location by our commanders or you wish to leave."

He paused again to let what he had said to them settle in.

"Now, until such time as you wish to leave, and make that wish known to your senior officer, you are still operating under military command and should consider yourself a guest.

"Those of you wishing to stay on with us will, before collapsing in a heap, be required to undertake some chores. Captain Kavolsky will organise remote scouting and sensing, Captain Schaefer perimeter defence and Captain Crockett billets and utilities. These will need to be complete by 1600 hours." A low moan followed. Alex paused for a second before continuing. "This is because all of you will need some time to scrub up, so that at 2000 you can attend a welcoming party that is being given by our hosts as thanks for bringing back Dominique and Luc."

As the message landed, Natasha watched as first smiles, then clapping and finally cheers spread across the gathering.

"Parade…! Shun," boomed Jones.

*

At 1600 hours, Natasha joined Alex for a meeting with the Countess and the town's council in the Hôtel de Ville. The room into which they were led was impressive. The Countess sat at the head of a long oak table, surrounded by high-back chairs. Natasha counted fourteen. In addition to the Countess, there were four men and a woman whose ages ranged from early thirties to late sixties, and whom Natasha guessed were the town's elected council. She recognised Luc's father Dr Heymans and gave him a smile which he returned with a wave.

In the corner of the room stood three flags flanking an enormous fireplace: the French, European, and the coat of arms of Saint C. In the fireplace flaming logs crackled happily, and two wolfhound dogs lay asleep on an ancient-looking rug. One of the dogs opened an eye and with relative indifference looked at Natasha. Above the fireplace hung a tapestry showing two knights in a jousting competition. Old oil paintings of either hunting scenes or stern-looking individuals hung on the rough stone walls. Coffee and tea had been laid out, together with some homemade cakes and biscuits.

Alex waited until Johnson, Crockett, Natasha, Schaefer and Jones had found seats before sitting down himself. The Countess began... "Please help yourself to tea and coffee; we're almost out of tea but seem to have an inexhaustible supply of coffee."

As they poured coffee, the Countess introduced each of the council in turn, and explained their roles and responsibilities; these included law, health, utilities, food and security.

After their own introductions, Johnson explained his theory of the virus, and the estimated survival rates. Alex then gave a brief overview of what this meant for society and the present military position based on what they had witnessed and learnt.

"Thank you. Now, I'm sure everyone here will have many questions. But I would suggest that we hold these for the moment and in the meantime decide how best to integrate your squadron into the council's organisation as well as the community. I also suggest we agree some short-term objectives," said the Countess.

"May I suggest four key building blocks. Firstly we acknowledge that the organisation we come up with must be flexible; as the situation evolves so must the organisation, and we have no real way of knowing how it will. Secondly, the squadron loans its medical, engineering and logistical resources to your council for use as they see fit," said Alex.

There were mutterings of agreement from around the table.

"Thirdly... we will establish an integrated defence force, under the squadron's command. This force will include your existing security as well as any other people who are eligible. This organisation will have priority call on any resources."

Alex paused as disagreements were now voiced. "Major, please continue," interjected the Countess.

"And lastly, a new combined group, but under military command, is established to make contact with other communities," finished Alex.

"Thank you, Major. That was clearly and succinctly put. I doubt we will have any objections to the first two points, however the latter I feel will require some debate."

Alex motioned for Natasha and the others to offer any comments.

"Sounds eminently reasonable to me," said Johnson, "but we've been living on the outside and I suspect the townspeople may have a slightly different perspective."

"Well, all I can say at the moment is that I'm very tired. I feel like someone's pulled the plug on my energy reserves. I'll just shut up and listen," said Natasha, reclining in the chair.

"I think the rest of us are with Captain K," added Schaefer.

The Countess opened the debate and introduced the first of her councillors. "This is Robert Caval."

"Thank you. I'm responsible for food supplies – my concern is that establishing contact with the outside is risky for two reasons. First off, many of us are still concerned about infection; and secondly we don't know whether others will see us as a target."

Natasha sat up a little as the athletic-looking woman in her early thirties with close-cropped brown hair spoke up in a strong voice, directing her speech at the council rather than Alex.

"I agree with Robert. Up until now we've only had to deal with dogs, foxes and the odd scavenger. But as salvageable food left in houses, supermarkets and warehouses is exhausted, the situation will change. If we're sitting here pretty, with fields of food and plenty to eat, the less people know of our existence the better. I'm also nervous about the fact that with them," she waved at Alex, "we will become a potential military target."

"For your benefit, may I introduce you to Claudia; she has done an admirable job looking after our security for the past few months," interjected the Countess in a slightly reprimanding tone and pointing out the woman who'd just spoken.

"I disagree with both of you," replied Luc's father Dr Heymans. "The human race as a whole is now on the brink of extinction. We must and I repeat must re-establish contact with other communities or we will cease to exist. There will be other villages like us. We need to find them, and quickly, or we will die."

There was silence in the room as each of them digested what had been said.

A tall and impeccably dressed elderly man now took the floor; standing ramrod straight he removed his spectacles, then walked over to the window with his back to the others. "Let me introduce myself; I am Pierre, I'm sixty-four years of age and have been charged with the responsibility of councillor for justice. I agree with the Doctor. Let me just point something out to you. Around this table two of us are wearing spectacles and I'm sure some of you have contacts." There were some nods, including Schaefer.

"Spectacles get broken, contacts get lost. Is there anyone amongst us who can build new ones? I'm sure there are many more examples of this and the easiest way to fix this problem is to find more people. I also think that, despite how hard we try to hide, we will be found sooner or later anyway. When this happens we will need to be strong – the more communities we tie up with, the stronger we will all be. We're already stronger than we were yesterday and it's because of them, not us."

"I agree with Pierre. If we can establish communication with other communities we can widen our technical skills base. It's either that or eventually we will slip into the Stone Age. I think we all know that modern society is not going to miraculously reappear one morning; it's badly broken and we need to save what's left. How much will depend on how many other people we can get in contact with. Sorry, I'm Michael, a professional engineer maintaining the town's utilities."

"But you're talking about civilians here; we're no match militarily for what is still out there… You heard what they've seen," interjected Claudia. This triggered a free for all with everyone trying to speak at the same time.

The Countess rose and joined Pierre at the window before taking back control of the debate.

"My dear councillors, we will not go forward with the Major's plan until we are in unanimous agreement on all his points. So, I suggest you make yourselves comfortable and go through the elements of the Major's plan, one by one. In the meantime may I suggest our guests take refuge downstairs until we're agreed on a way forward."

As they left the room and closed the door gently they could hear the beginnings of a heated debate.

*

It was just before 2000 hrs when they were recalled to the meeting room. The councillors looked tired. "We've come to two agreements," announced the Countess.

"Two?" asked Alex.

"Yes, two… The first is that we all agree that the proposal made by you should be accepted. The second is that the people of Saint Christobel must ratify this by a vote with a majority of not less than seventy-five per cent."

"The Greeks would have been proud," offered Johnson.

271

"Completely agree," said Alex.

"Excellent! May I now suggest that we vacate this room and join everyone for a long overdue celebration," finished the Countess.

*

In the town square, the boar was roasting over an open wood-burning fire. Trestle tables were covered with white linen, upon which sat steaming vats of potato mixed with cheese, and pitchers of wine. Children ran amongst the tables playing a game of tag called You've Got The Plague.

Dominique, her friends and some of the townspeople had formed a band and were playing on a small stage. Flaming torches had been arranged around an area for dancing. The Countess and her council sat at a head table; she stood and asked for quiet. Slowly people passed on her request until at last only the children made a noise that was ultimately silenced by loud shushing from the adults.

"Everyone, just two minutes of your attention please… Firstly, thanks to the Major and his squadron for bringing Dominique and Luc back to us…" There was loud applause and cheering.

"Tonight the council has been debating what are the next steps for us. After much debate, we unanimously decided to support a plan proposed by the Major… But on the condition that it receives a vote of support from you of more than seventy-five per cent. I will not go into the details now but we will ensure that copies of the proposal are made available tomorrow in the Hôtel de Ville. The vote will be in two days. In the meantime, enjoy!" she said raising a glass of wine.

*

Natasha woke up the next morning with a giant hangover in an enormous four-poster bed in the Hôtel Constantine's wedding suite. Outside, church bells were ringing. Sunlight streamed in through the slats in the shutters and danced across the clean white bedclothes that felt good against her skin. Her memories of the previous evening flashed across her mind. Despite her hangover and a mouth and throat that felt like they had been grit blasted and then vacuum dried, she managed a smile. She felt very comfortable, and this made her realise that she couldn't remember how she had actually got to bed. She also realised that this was the first night she hadn't dreamt of the little girl she'd lost back in Germany. There was a curt knock at the door.

"Come in," she mumbled.

"Morning, ma'am. We took the liberty of assuming you would like a hearty breakfast," announced Stacey, who marched into the room followed by O'Reilly and Hodgetts bearing two silver trays.

"Coffee or tea? We've also got fresh milk."

"Coffee would be great, white."

As Hodgetts poured, she could not but help notice that his bald head had been decorated with drawings of pink flowers.

"We've also got fresh eggs and bread and a selection of cereals, together with fresh strawberries. All compliments of the Countess."

"Thank you. Corporal Hodgetts, you can take the flowers," she said making sure Stacey and O'Reilly could see she was looking at his head.

"Sorry, ma'am?" replied Hodgetts, not understanding.

"The flowers, Corporal. You may take them."

"Yes, ma'am," replied Hodgetts still not knowing what she was talking about but deciding it was just better to agree.

As the door closed she could hear snickers, and she could imagine Stacey and O'Reilly bent double with tears rolling down their faces in laughter whilst Hodgetts still looked at them wondering what was so funny.

In the next room Sanchez woke up in the arms of Schaefer. She lay still for a while listening to his breathing and the church bells.

"You're tickling me," he said.

"How? I haven't moved."

"Your eyelashes are fluttering."

Sanchez got up and strolled across the bedroom to look out of the shuttered windows.

"What are you doing?"

"Just checking out the weather. Thought we might go out for a stroll in the fields or tour the sights of the town." She pulled the shutters open, letting sunlight pour into the room.

"God, that looks good," he said. "Don't move, the sunlight's silhouetting you beautifully. Now just open your legs a fraction. Oh, wow."

She turned and smiled at him. He lay propped up on one elbow and then threw the sheets back to welcome her.

"Jesus, you're a dirty bastard!" she called, running across the room and diving onto the bed.

*

At the morning ops meeting Natasha looked around the table. All of them looked hungover and tired. It was as if their arrival at Saint C had somehow released the remaining reserves of energy, leaving them exhausted.

Alex brought the meeting to order. "Good morning. We've got coffee and fresh milk. So help yourselves. You've all met Claudia here and I thought it would be a good idea to invite her to our sessions so she can see how we operate. Now, this morning at our good Doctor's insistence we've rearranged the agenda. He has something he wants to discuss as a matter of urgency."

"Thanks," replied Johnson, helping himself before continuing. "I've been talking to Dr Heymans. We've put together a list of Christobelians, as we've called them, who moved to other towns over the past few years. We reckon we've got maybe a hundred candidates who are direct ancestors. I want to track at least one or two of them down."

"I think we can guess, but can you tell us why?"

"Two reasons. Firstly, because we think there's a good chance they'll be alive. And secondly, because it will finally put beyond all reasonable doubt the theory that some other influence, like environment, or food or whatever, could have miraculously saved so many from this one town. I know you believe me but some of the townspeople still have doubts."

"And after you've found one or two, what then?" asked Schaefer.

"And then…" smiled Johnson, "I'll go to Paris."

"Paris?" asked Natasha, perplexed.

"Yes, Lieutenant Tsang will explain."

"Yes. In an annex of the Louvre is the EMA or European Medical Archive. We need to get into it and get hold of the technical paper I read associated with gene 169. You see, I remember that the team who did the research actually generated a map across Europe of dozens of towns and villages that were reported to have survived the plague. They did tests on the population and sure enough… they all had this particular gene. If we can find the villages then we'll find more survivors."

274

"Everyone agree?" asked Alex; everyone nodded.

"All right. Put together a team. You'll have the pick of the squadron and the gear. But I've got three conditions. The first is that you make sure you engage with the council, take at least two of the townspeople."

"And the other two conditions?" prompted Johnson.

"Before anyone gallivants off across the countryside, we get Saint Christobel sorted out – we need to at least address the basics and determine what needs to get done and what resources we need."

"How long do you reckon that will take?" asked Johnson, looking a little saddened by the fact that his expedition would be delayed.

"Oh Jesus. Give me a break. We'll know inside a week," replied Alex in exasperation.

"What about the last?"

"Your team will procure and bring back medical supplies we identify in two above. Deal?"

"Deal. Natasha's agreed to lead, and she's been talking to Byrnes about setting up a relay of comms stations so that we can get you sit reps without making a splash. You meanwhile should be able to contact us in an emergency," replied Johnson, jumping up like a child and pushing his chair over in the process.

"Why doesn't it surprise me that you two had already agreed and planned this?"

The final item in the daily ops meeting was the plan for a survey of the town; the idea was to get a mutual understanding of their tactical environment. Robert from the council had been elected as the tour guide.

*

The morning sunshine was bright and a gentle westerly breeze provided the atmosphere of a picnic as they met up at the café in the main square.

"I thought we'd start with health. We can go and see Dr Heymans' surgery. It's right above this café," said Robert.

Dr Heymans now picked up the briefing. "The population was just over twelve hundred before the virus. Now there are just over four hundred, split almost equally between men and women, old and young. I've put together a little database that we can add to. In the short term, we're not too badly off; we should be able to cope with the usual illnesses and injuries that are to

275

be expected. Mid-term we need some additions. Captain Johnson and I are working up a list so we can scavenge the equipment, drugs and if possible the expertise or at least the procedures. The real problem is the longer term; we've no idea how we're going to replenish certain drugs and maintain the knowledge base. We need to devise a plan. That's a major worry but it's longer term."

"And like Pierre so eloquently explained yesterday, that's one of the key reasons we need to establish communication with other communities. We need to rapidly find certain critical, technically competent people if we are not going to slide back to the Stone Age," said Johnson, lighting a cigarette.

"I guess the same goes for all sorts of things. The arts, law, science, and so forth. Maybe I'm being too philosophical but we've built a world where we need numerous people who are highly specialised in an individual skill to come together to build everyday things we now take for granted. God, we even have software designing software. How the hell are we supposed to restart that?" added Crockett.

"Now, Saint C is believed to date from about 1100 BC. Its oldest buildings though are Roman, from around the third century, which have over the years been modified, especially through the medieval era. Economically the town's mainstays were farming and tourism. Michael is our resident engineer and best suited to tell you about the utilities."

"We've got our own drinking water supply from the old Roman wells. We've been using the river and the old mill to drive a turbine that produces just enough power for the freshwater lift pumps and sewage treatment plant. The rest of our power comes from solar and wind. We've got more than we need."

"What about machine shops and spares, that sort of thing?" asked Crockett.

"Nothing. We need to sort all of that."

"Beneath us is a fairly extensive sewer and drainage system."

"I'd like to see it," asked Sanchez.

"Sure thing, there's an access cover by the fountain."

They walked over to the fountain with the stone statues of eight little dancing boys and girls that stood in the centre of the town square. From the small church came the sound of a children's music lesson.

"I remember seeing a picture of another statue that looked almost identical to this in officer school. It stood in the centre of Stalingrad. It was one of the few things that wasn't flattened during that great battle," said Alex.

"Have you read the script, Major?" asked Dr Heymans, pointing to the carved inscription around the base of the fountain.

"I looked but I didn't understand it."

"It's in Latin; a nursery rhyme from the time of the Black Death in the 1600s. I guess it's the French equivalent of the English version... *Ring a ring roses, a pocket full of posies, atishoo, atishoo we all fall down...* or something like that," interjected Tsang.

"Well, that's refreshing," said Natasha.

They opened the cover to the main sewer.

"The main sewer channel runs the full length of the high street about twenty-five feet below us. There are cross channels feeding it every hundred or so feet. It's impressive, built to last," said Michael.

Sanchez got down on all fours and peered into the access shaft.

"Are there many of these access shafts?" she asked.

"At least one either end of every branch. Most of them are in the streets but some are in courtyards. There's probably a few that have been covered over as well. You want to go down?"

"Definitely. These could be a great way to move people and gear around safely if we really got into trouble," added Jones.

Natasha looked at the civilians for any sign of alarm at what Jones was suggesting but they didn't seem to have registered.

"Some of the smaller branches you need to crawl through; the main canal though is big enough to walk through – there's even a walkway."

Leaving the doctors, the rest of them clambered down the access shaft. The tunnel itself was about 10 feet in diameter and covered in a slippery green moss.

"You can see the size of the branch lines, this is about typical. This one comes up next to the main gate," said Michael.

Sanchez and Jones announced they'd seen enough for the minute but would need to make a detailed map of the system and check out every access shaft.

Back in the fresh air they joined the others before Robert led them over to the church, which he explained dated from the sixth century. Around it was the picnic area, which overlooked a sandy beach and the Atlantic Ocean nearly 200 feet below. To their right a row of rock pinnacles broke through the ocean surface and rose nearly a hundred feet into the air.

"It's beautiful," said Natasha.

"They say the king of the world came here to rest for a while," replied Dr Heymans.

"You can access the beach from just over there; there's a stairway that leads down through the cliff itself. But let's do the church and the catacombs this afternoon; I want to show you the rest of the town first," said Robert, starting to walk towards one of the side alleyways.

They followed him like the Pied Piper. Either side of them were medieval buildings that had been extended over time. Some were almost touching above them, whilst others actually met via small archways or bridges.

"You can see how the buildings have been added to over the years. I'm sure that Sergeant Major Jones and Corporal Sanchez will also be pleased to know that most have a cellar and many have interconnecting passageways and tunnels," continued Robert with a little smile.

They stopped for lunch in one of the numerous small enclosed courtyards that was typical of Saint C. Natasha thought the food was heaven. Real bread, cheese, salami and wine.

After lunch and feeling slightly light-headed from the red wine, something which Natasha had never been able to master at lunchtime, Robert now led them back to the church in the main square, which they entered through a low archway buried in the thick stone walls.

"Aren't those snakes carved up there?" remarked Tommy Lee as he guided his wheelchair over a smooth hollow in the stone floor that had been worn to the texture of silk by the years of congregations.

"Well spotted. They are indeed. There's also a dragon. The archway dates from the Dark Ages when the population was still struggling with giving up their pagan religions in favour of Christianity. I guess it was their way of reconciling the two," replied the Countess, who had joined them.

Inside, giant wax candles that had a subtle smell of rose and other flowers lit the church. The interior decoration was plain, lacking the vast painted murals of churches of a later age. Sanchez and Jones were locked in deep conversation about the construction of the church, which to Natasha looked solid enough to resist a nuclear blast.

The alter was flanked by the tombs of six knights and their ladies carved out of white marble. Natasha noticed that both the knights as well as their ladies held swords, and asked the Countess if that was usual.

"No, we don't think so. We think it's probably because of the Viking threat that continued here for several hundred years; probably everyone had to be capable of putting up a fight," said the Countess.

"Now, behind the altar is the entrance to the catacombs, and also what we call the smugglers' tunnel that leads directly out into the ocean. The smuggling really only took off in the early 1700s. I'm sure you'll want to see," she continued.

"Please," replied Jones.

"All you have to do is push my lady with the axe out of the way... like this," said Robert, putting his shoulder against one of the tombs and pushing. With the sound that only stone on stone can make, the tomb swivelled, revealing a staircase down into darkness.

"We used to play hide and seek in here as kids. Well, the brave ones did, anyway," commented the Countess.

"Does Saint C have a priest?" asked Alex.

"That was Father Simon. He died during the first week of the virus. He'd been with us for nearly forty years and was from Nantes. His grave is one of those outside the town. The Countess has taken on his role while we wait for a replacement," said Pierre.

Robert took back control of the tour. "We have to go through the catacombs first; it's a series of passages that extends for several hundred metres."

One after another they squeezed past the open tomb and into the tunnel; the air was cool and slightly musty. Again the stone stairs were worn smooth by centuries of feet. Along the tunnel walls were alcoves in which lay skeletons, some still wrapped in disintegrating linen. Further along, the alcoves stopped and the tunnel widened and sloped downwards quite steeply. The air took on a damp, salty quality and Natasha could just make out the sound of the ocean.

At the bottom of the tunnel, they emerged into a large cave that formed a concealed natural harbour. Reflections from the sparkling ocean outside bounced around the cave's interior.

"At full tide, the mouth of the cave is hidden from the ocean side. It's a fairly impressive secret entrance," said the Countess.

"Perfect," summarised Alex, as he pointed out the four other caves running off the main cave.

"May I ask for what?" asked the Countess.

"We need a place where we can evacuate to if we need to and then escape," Jones added.

"It's a last redoubt. Like the Alamo. A few guys back upstairs at the entrance could hold off a battalion," Sanchez further explained with a voice that told Natasha that she was enjoying rattling the Countess.

*

Two days later the townspeople voted almost unanimously to support Alex's plan. The same day Johnson and Dr Heymans announced they'd delivered the town's first babies since the virus: twins. And it was that night that Alex explained to Natasha, Johnson, Crockett, Jones and Schaefer his deepest fear; that they would, sooner rather than later, have to fight again.

"You know, don't you, that despite all our attempts at maintaining a low profile, it will only be a matter of time before they find us. And I've got no illusions about what we can expect when they do."

"So we need to be ready then," replied Johnson.

*

They increased the pace of their preparations. They explored the cellars and sewers, the homes and shops, they moved bookcases or pulled up floors to reveal hidden or long-forgotten entrances. Natasha wasn't surprised to learn that the children turned out to have some of the best knowledge, showing them hidden passageways.

They held their first meeting with Claudia, the town's councillor responsible for security. Alex started by asking Claudia to give them a little history on her own background, and was surprised to learn that far from being a civilian she was an ex-lieutenant in the Foreign Legion.

"How come?" Natasha asked her, intrigued.

"Ah, I was young and headstrong. I had fallen out with my father who was a wealthy landowner not too far from here. I simply left one morning. By the time of my first leave, which was eleven months three weeks and two days after I joined, and which lasted for eight hours, I had made corporal. I made sergeant in just under two years and lieutenant a year after that. We served in Africa, the Middle East and then the early wars. I received a medical discharge after I nearly lost a leg when a landmine took out our recon vehicle. That was it really."

"She was awarded the Légion D'Honneur, France's highest military decoration. Whilst she was laying on the ground with a shattered leg and God knows what other wounds, she provided covering fire for nearly thirty minutes which allowed her comrades to be evacuated. During this she got shot twice," added the Countess.

Natasha noticed all of the others reappraising her.

"And when you returned, what did your father say?" asked Natasha.

"He'd died the year before. We'd never spoken to one another since I left, although I did find out that he kept an eye on my progress through some of his contacts."

"What was your speciality?" asked Schaefer.

"My unit was principally search and destroy, the usual stuff, underwater approaches, recon, demolition, that sort of thing."

*

That night as Natasha, Sanchez and Schaefer shared a beer, Sanchez asked, "So do you think she's hot?"

"Who?" pretended Schaefer whilst Natasha laughed.

"Don't fuck about, Captain, the Foreign Legion – I'm a hard brave bitch officer lady. You know exactly who I mean."

"Nah. Her hair is too short."

"Supposing she grew it?"

"Well, then she'd be hot," he joked.

"God, if I ever catch you…" She left the rest unsaid.

"Or I you," he responded.

*

Alex now assembled members from the council and the squadron for a war games session. They spent four days and nights huddled around tactical computers, simulating different scenarios, which ranged from rogue elements right the way through to regimental enemy formations.

From these games came the plans, requirements for equipment, and the type and make-up of the force they would need to defend Saint C. It was the equipment requirements that Natasha, Schaefer and Johnson were tasked with procuring.

"Alex, where the hell are we going to get all this?" asked Johnson.

"I've been checking our databases. There's an old Reforger site out towards Mont Blanc," said Crockett.

"A what?" asked Natasha.

"It's an unmanned storage facility that was modelled on the old concept of forward pre-deployment of kit. The idea was that units could just fly in with their personal gear, pick up all their heavy kit in country and then go and fight. It's highly unlikely to have attracted any attention but the kit will probably be second generation if we're lucky."

"Anyway, you guys can now take off to Mont Blanc and pick up what we need. Then you can go and hunt the descendants of Saint C," said Alex.

CHAPTER 22

REFORGER

So an army perishes if it has no equipment. It perishes if it has no food. And it perishes if it has no money.

The entrance to the Reforger warehouse, where thousands of tonnes of prepositioned military supplies were stored, consisted of two massive, rusty, steel-blast doors at the end of a mile-long service tunnel that branched off one of the civilian Alpine road tunnels south of Chamonix.

The bright lights of the AFV cast a long shadow of Sanchez as she closely examined the doors. Freezing cold cave water dripped from the rough granite rock above plopping into the ankle-deep puddles that covered the roadway. A sign on the doors proclaimed that the entrance was Works Access Only.

"Anyone got a wire brush?" she shouted, her voice echoing in the tunnel. "There must be a key pad buried under the rust here somewhere."

After several minutes of scraping, she found a cover under which lay a key pad.

"Let's just hope our Reforger codes are still current," said Schaefer, tapping in the code.

The key pad flashed green, followed by the sound of hydraulic motors and a clunk as the doors started to inch open. Inside, a flashing strobe light gave way to flood lights that clicked on to reveal a large entrance hanger with six numbered tunnels that led off deeper into the mountain. The air smelt of diesel, gun oil, grease paper, damp and explosive.

They parked the AFVs in the main assembly hangar and entered the admin offices.

"I know the odds are small but assuming we've triggered some sort of ingress alarm I'll get Sergeant Gyan to post a couple of sentries at the junction. If there is a reaction force at least we can try and explain what we're doing," said Schaefer.

They made their way to the quartermaster offices that housed some metal desks, filing cabinets, dot matrix printers and old cathode ray display screens. Posters of long-forgotten sporting events and cartoons of world leaders were stuck to the damp, whitewashed concrete walls.

"Home sweet home," said Sanchez.

"Jesus, the records are a mixture of paper and electronic. Some of the kit in here must go back to the Cold War days in the last century," muttered Stacey as he studied a systems operating manual.

"I suggest we grab something to eat and go over the operating procedures and layout for the place," said Schaefer.

Whilst eating, Stacey printed out the weapons and ammunition manifest and handed it to Sanchez who rapidly assessed it.

"We've got no MP sevens," said Sanchez with a sigh, referring to the standard assault rifles the squadron used, as she leafed through the inventory. "But we do have as much ammo as we can carry, including ultra-light, HE, soft and armour piercing rounds; no ceramic though. There are thousands of the old M4 assault rifles and 5.56 ammo. Shall we take them?" she asked Schaefer.

"Yeah, no choice. We'll take a thousand rifles and five million rounds of the 5.56 and another five million rounds of the modern stuff," said Schaefer without looking up from a plan of the facility.

"Jesus. Can we carry all that?" asked Stacey.

"The 5.56 ammo is about eighty tons including magazines, and the rifles about six tons with crates. All up, I think we will need about a hundred and ten tons and a hundred cubic metres in volume, including battle sights, NVG, and all the bits and pieces."

"I'm impressed. You carry all that around in your mind?" asked Natasha.

"Since I was a babe."

"I married a war junky," said Sanchez.

"What about indirect?"

"We've got no third generation mortars or rounds but we do have the old Mark Threes, both forty and sixty millimetre, and lots of rounds," advised Sanchez.

"Take twenty-five each of the mortars with five thousand rounds."

"We've got four and eight mil belts for the Gatlings, all ultra-light. But no compatible missiles or arty for the AFVs."

"Take a million rounds of both."

"You know, I was just thinking, do you think we should adjust the manifests?" asked Natasha.

"What, in case we need more?" asked Schaefer.

"Yeah, or someone else does?" replied Natasha.

"Jesus, I'm not sure how to take that-happy that you think more of us might be still around or scared that you think we'll need all this and then more. Anyway, they're fresh out of Zute suits. But they do have a bunch of smart cam blankets," added Sanchez.

"Excellent, the medical supplies they have here are first rate. All held in environmentally controlled sections. We've got more than we alone could ever use," reported Johnson whilst lighting another cigarette.

"You might be able to stock up on cigarettes as well; you've been chain-smoking since we left Saint C," said Sanchez.

"I know, just impatient I guess," replied Johnson.

O'Reilly arrived with a tray of hot tea and chocolate biscuits. Natasha shook her head in disbelief.

"I'm impressed. You found my favourite chocolate biscuits," said Stacey.

"They expired about five years ago but they were vacuum packed so should be OK," replied O'Reilly.

*

Stacey and Hicks led Natasha into the first tunnel, which ran for a hundred metres before it opened out into a cave that seemed to stretch out onto the horizon. The floodlights steamed in the cold above, and water dripped onto them from the granite ceiling. Natasha felt like a little girl, overawed by the scale.

"Bloody hell, look at this, tank transporters with trailers complete with Gorilla main battle tanks. I remember reading about those when I was a kid," said Stacey whilst munching on an MRE.

"If you like that, you're gonna love this," countered Hicks, pointing to a stack of pallets off to one side. "Prophylactics, fifty thousand."

"Those were the days," said Stacey.

Their first requisitions were six forty-eight wheel trailers and tractors. Hicks walked around one of the tractors. "I don't believe this; these things are driven by diesel, they're antiques."

"Well, the manifest says there's just over a million barrels of fuel stored here, just about enough to restart global warming," advised Natasha. "Stacey, you're going to need to find us a tanker, though, to haul enough for us to get to Saint C."

"We'll also need to take back forklifts, otherwise we won't be able to get all this up and into the town itself. In fact we'd better take three," he added.

"The assault boats we need should be just over there in hangar C," said Natasha, feeling secretly proud she was thinking ahead.

They located the boats, complete with outboard engines still in greaseproof wrappers. They needed forty of the fourteen-man Zodiacs.

Hicks looked at the tech data sheets taped to the boxes. "These things are diesel driven as well. Made in 2009."

"You guys OK alone whilst I go and hook up with the others?" Natasha asked.

"No worries, Captain. Give us an hour or so."

She found Sanchez two levels below hauling a wooden case out onto the floor.

"Now, this is what we need," said Sanchez, excitedly pointing to the side of the crate that was marked FAE.

"What are they?" asked Natasha.

"Fuel air explosives, FAE. Or thermo baric warheads, whatever term you prefer. Jesus, look at this, they've got the lot, RPG right the way through to air delivery. Only a few, but useful."

"I know you want to, so tell me. What's so good about them?"

"Well, they work by first dispersing a cloud of powdered or liquid explosive using a small charge. This mixes with atmospheric oxygen, then a second charge ignites it and generates a sustained blast and heatwave that propagates through the cloud."

"So just like a big bang?"

"Yeah, but the big difference is that the blast wave and resulting overpressure is sustained. Unlike the crap that Drop Short usually fires which lasts an instant, these bangs last an eon. So, for AFVs, igloos, bunkers, all that stuff, you can use a couple of these in close sequence. The first blast will stress the target, then the second will collapse it. I tell you, these babies will give a three mega Pascal over pressure, more than enough to do a lot of damage, and temperatures past three thousand C."

"Nice. I never heard of them."

"And just to finish the picture, after the initial blast the epicentre pressure falls below atmospheric, so the surrounding air then flows back inwards and sucks in any unexploded fuel, which then goes bang again. Sad really, they went out years ago, too brutal, unstable, primitive and most definitely not surgical. All the usual crap that they spin out when the weapons manufacturers want to sell you something else. We found a bunch of these in a Russian storehouse once; Hodgetts and the boys caused chaos with them."

"Why am I not surprised? Anyway, just to let you know we're assembling the transport up in hangar three. Stacey's organising forklifts."

Natasha left Sanchez to it and went to find Johnson and Tsang who were gathering uniforms, boots, equipment harnesses and medical supplies.

"Jesus, can you believe this?" said Tsang pointing to two massive stainless steel doors. "We've got medical supplies on the left and nerve gas and bio agents on the right. Someone had a sense of humour."

They opened the doors to the medical supplies, which slid back with a hiss accompanied by a draft of extra cold air as the positive pressure equalised.

"Wow, there's enough in here to keep a large town going for years," said Tsang.

"Military stores, my dear, are one thing that you can always count on as being well stocked; it's a shame that a lot of the time it never gets to the right place," commented Johnson with a sigh.

*

It took them three more days to complete the loading. Natasha then gave them another free range day for anything else they might need and charged O'Reilly with coordinating it, a mission he embraced with an appetite. The largest additional item O'Reilly located was a Black Hole stealth ground-attack helicopter.

"Jesus, who the hell's gonna fly it?" asked Hicks.

"Captain K says she and Lieutenant Tommy Lee should be able to. I've seen these in action; they're nasty bastards. Anyway, Captain Schaefer's OK'd it," replied O'Reilly, looking at Natasha for confirmation.

"What the fuck are we going to do with chainsaws?" asked Stacey as he surveyed a pile of crates dumped next to his transporter.

"Don't know yet. But as we say in Ireland, you never know until you do."

"Well, there's no way I'm taking this lot in my wagon," said Cook pointing to a pallet of nappies.

"Well, the village has had twins. I thought the mums would be happy."

"Couldn't you find anything we could really use, like whisky or guns or playing cards?"

"Aye, I've got all that. And smokes. Even sausages in a freezer unit."

"Well, thank God for that. I'll take them in my wagon," said Cook.

"Nah, I've got it sorted. I'm gonna take them in one of the Gorillas," replied O'Reilly protectively, referring to the Gorilla main battle tank.

"You have got to be joking. Do you know how much fuel one of those things will use?" Hicks asked.

"We leave in an hour. We can't take the Gorilla but we can get the rest of this stuff and the Black Hole loaded," replied Natasha, taking command of the situation whilst shaking her head with a smile.

She stopped to think a little, then realised what she was feeling; she felt proud, proud of them, proud of her men. Was that right? Was she entitled to start thinking that these were her people?

As the first of the trucks started pumping clouds of diesel fumes into the assembly area, they got ready to depart.

"Oh, very funny," shouted Sanchez as she fired up her threat boards in Natasha's AFV.

"What?" feigned Natasha.

"The nappies."

"Thought you might find them useful."

"Do you know that O'Reilly reckons he found nukes in there?" said Sanchez.

"After we saw all the nerve and bio agents, it wouldn't surprise me, and I guess if we ever really got into a tight bind we could pop back and get one," replied Natasha.

Sanchez looked at her Captain with a face that told Natasha she was not sure whether she was joking.

"And I'm not sure either," muttered Natasha.

CHAPTER 23

DESCENDANTS OF SAINT CHRISTOBEL

When your strategy is deep and far reaching, then what you gain by your calculations is much, so you can win before you even fight.

After delivering the Reforger supplies, they had started their search for living descendants of Saint C. It was not going well. They had visited three of the towns identified as having Christobelians living in them and had found no one. Both Johnson and Heymans were becoming disillusioned and it was only the optimism of Lieutenant Tsang that kept their spirits up.

"Listen, guys, the link is genetic. There's no way on the planet that the population of Saint C has been largely saved because they drink a certain type of mineral water. We haven't found any trace of the people we identified, either alive or dead. And that's good news – the records are old, and they probably moved on at some point."

They were riding in two AFVs; one was commanded by Natasha and carried Johnson, Tsang, Dr Heymans and Dominique. Behind her travelled the engineering and logistics AFV commanded by Schaefer.

The fourth town they entered was the small village of Les Pieds in which a lady called Madame Lebihan had settled after leaving Saint Christobel some five years before. The main street, like the others they'd seen, was devoid of any life except for the usual dogs that trotted arrogantly along it and the spring birds that now sang with a new energy. Sunlight flickered on the tree-lined pavement and the whitewashed buildings. There was no sign of damage or looting, and with the warm weather it was as if the occupants had simply upped and left on a picnic. Only the lingering sickly sweet smell of death and a deep hum of flies that came from some of the buildings destroyed that quaint image.

"We've got e-sig. Domestic. No signs of fluctuations. All the boards are green," reported Sanchez.

"We're looking for a number twelve rue du General Colin. It runs off to the right from the main square," advised Dr Heymans in a tone Natasha found reminiscent of telling a taxi where to go.

"Yeah, got it, mate," replied Stacey.

From the top of the AFV Natasha could see that most of the buildings were locked, their windows closed, with biohazard signs and barriers still in place.

"We'll pull up in the main square. I want options if we need to bug out."

Natasha pulled to a stop in the main square and Schaefer's AFV pulled up alongside.

"What do you think?" Schaefer shouted across to Natasha.

"God knows. Looks deserted. It's strange, I feel like I'm intruding on someone's life, bit like a voyeur."

"We'll set up a perimeter. We'll maintain radio silence unless we've got a problem. Sergeant Gyan, if you please," said Schaefer.

Natasha, Sanchez, Tsang and the two doctors dismounted. Although sure that the APP virus was dead, Johnson was concerned about the potential of other diseases so each wore a full-face respirator connected by a black flexi hose to two large bio-hazard filter canisters on their waists, gloves and over-boots.

"I'll set up a wash station. You know where we are. Stay safe," said Schaefer, waving them goodbye.

Johnson quickly found the address and they stopped outside the cottage's wrought-iron front gate. A biohaz quarantine notice was hung from it. Johnson's and Heyman's shoulders sagged in recognition.

"Maybe she left?" said Sanchez, trying to instil some hope.

They pushed the gate open, which squeaked on its rusty hinges. Tsang yelled out, "Hello! Anyone here? We're allied forces. We're here to help."

There was no response, except from the birds that went quiet.

"Let's check inside anyway," said Johnson in a depressed voice, walking across the overgrown garden. Natasha joined him on the porch, upon which was a doormat with a picture of a dog on it, and next to it a dog's bowl. Two large china pots positioned either side of the doorway overflowed with brightly coloured purple flowers. She used the large brass lion's head door knocker and knocked three times, then again more loudly. For a minute they stood there waiting; there was no reply. She put her ear to the door and listened.

"Shit. I can hear music."

Sanchez moved off the porch and went to a window, wiped some of the grime and dust away and peered inside. "Hey, guys, there's a light on."

Johnson tried the front door and it opened. *La Traviata* greeted them from somewhere inside. They looked at one another as Natasha shouted through the doorway.

"Hello. Allied forces. Anyone home?"

They moved inside, wiping their feet on the doormat. The inside of the cottage was neat and tidy. Photographs of two little girls and a dog in various poses lined the entranceway. Shoes and boots were neatly arranged in a row along the wall.

The music was coming from upstairs. Tsang's weapon knocked one of the photographs off onto the floor. Natasha picked it up and looked at the image of a woman and a man. She was smiling and had her arms around a man in his mid-forties.

"Is it them?" asked Johnson.

"I don't know," she replied.

"It's them," said Sanchez, holding up a bill addressed to Monsieur Lebihan.

"Let's have a look upstairs."

Natasha led them up the narrow staircase. On the landing she paused at a door from behind which was coming the music. The track finished, and she knocked. The music began again.

"Oh shit, this is ridiculous," she announced, then opened the door.

The family, or what Natasha assumed were the family, two small children and the parents, were lying together on a large four-poster bed. The bodies were a black and golden colour, shrivelled and shrunken, almost mummy-like. Next to the children were two teddy bears.

Natasha and Sanchez remained by the doorway as *La Traviata* continued to play and the three doctors examined the family.

"They took VX capsules," said Johnson, holding up the empty packets that lay on the dresser.

"Let's go," urged Sanchez.

"Give me five. I'm just going to take tissue samples from each of them for DNA analysis," said Tsang unpacking her kit.

"All right. But I'm gonna wait outside if you don't mind. I need a change of music," said Sanchez.

They decided not to bury the bodies, and within an hour they were back on the narrow lanes heading towards their next location, another village, called L'Eglise.

"I think we're going to hit the jackpot this time. I can feel it. The Montforts in L'Eglise are both heritage Christobelians, their families go back generations," said Tsang.

Before anyone could reply, Sanchez interrupted: "Commander. Threat. We've got an aerial yellow."

"Say again?" said Natasha.

"Look up at the sky! We've got a vapour trail overhead. Forty thousand plus feet. Heading west. You should be able to see it."

"I'm cross-loading enhanced images. It's a Boeing 987 civilian airliner. I can't get the airline or country of origin though."

"Jesus. All stop!" shouted Natasha.

Ignoring protocol, occupants from both the AFVs had dismounted and were now gazing up at the clear blue sky and the long, white vapour trails. An excited chatter erupted as they debated the origins of the plane. Schaefer clambered up onto Natasha's AFV and together they watched the aircraft.

"Do you think we should try and communicate with it?" Natasha asked.

"As much as I'd like to, our SOP is to only attempt to communicate if we can verify friendly."

"Wonder where they're heading," asked Sanchez.

"It'll be Virgin airlines, to be sure," interjected O'Reilly.

"You wish," replied Tsang and Sanchez together.

They ate lunch on the grass verge under the warm spring sun, the conversation shuttling between the airliner, the Lebihans and the Montforts. As they restarted their journey, Sanchez relaxed the threat level to green and they took the opportunity to open the hatches of the AFVs, allowing the warm spring air to blow gently through the cabins.

*

It was late afternoon and Natasha, numbed by the surrounding scenery, the warm weather and the motion of the AFV, found herself thinking about Alex. It took her a moment to register that Alex had entered her thoughts and analyse why. When she'd done so she was even more surprised to find that she wasn't surprised. She was falling in love with him.

Just as she'd accepted this new reality, the AFV came to an emergency stop sending her lurching against her restraint harness. From below, she could hear various curses as people and equipment collided with one another.

"Sorry about that. But we've got three kids on bicycles in front of us," announced Stacey. "They just shot out of the hedgerow in front of me. I nearly ran them over."

Natasha stared in surprise as she watched the three children ride away along the road as fast as they could, up a small rise and disappear over the crest.

"I'm assuming they'll be the Montfort children," said Johnson with a triumphant voice.

Before Natasha could reply she noticed first one, then numerous sheep appear in the road from the adjacent field. A dog bounded into view followed by a shepherd. From atop the AFV, Natasha introduced herself.

*

That evening they set up camp at the Montforts' farmhouse. As Natasha, Schaefer and Johnson finished the debrief for the Montforts, O'Reilly and Stacey stuck their heads into the AFV.

"Eh, Captain? We were wondering. As today's been fairly special, any chance we can have a small celebration?" asked O'Reilly.

"I don't see why not. Captain Schaefer, any objections?" asked Natasha.

"None. Just one condition…"

"Shoot," said Natasha, intrigued by the sudden soft smile from Schaefer.

"We make it an engagement celebration as well."

"About time," said Natasha smiling.

"Yer what?" asked O'Reilly.

"They're gonna get married," helped Stacey.

"Who? You two captains?" asked O'Reilly.

"No, you idiot, Corporal Sanchez and the Captain," interjected Stacey.

The night grew cool as they set up tables in the Montforts' long barn for their celebration.

"Where is O'Reilly?" Sanchez asked Stacey as he used a large pair of old leather bellows to get the fire properly going.

"He's in the main house cooking. Says he's making an 'Irish Wedding Engagement' stew, whatever that might mean."

They had arranged the seating as a long T-shape with Sanchez, Schaefer and the Montforts at the head. As they sat down, Natasha commenced the toasts.

"Here's to hope and marriage. Hope that we find more people like the Montforts, and marriage… because with two people like we've got here, you just know it's special."

"To hope and marriage," came a chorus of voices.

Someone blew a hunting horn and O'Reilly made his entrance carrying a huge pot of stew. Behind him followed a little black lamb that occasionally butted the backs of his legs causing him to turn around and ssssh the animal.

"I don't believe it! The whole world has gone crazy. How come that sweet little thing thinks you're Mummy?" asked Stacey.

"Well, I don't think it's so strange. It knows I'm a kind, loving guy."

"You horrible demon you. You'd eat the little thing soon as look at it, you would. I'm surprised it's not in that pot."

"That was in another life, my friend, another life. Now I'm reborn. All this has made me think. And I've decided to become a vegetarian."

"Bollocks. You a vegetarian!"

"Well, I am as far as little Joe here is concerned; he's off the menu."

They settled down to dinner, each relaxing.

"You know we've got no guards out, no remote sentries, nothing. If we got bounced tonight it would be all over," said Schaefer.

Natasha looked at the people sat around the tables; it could easily have been a group of friends if it wasn't for the proliferation of weapons that rested against or in some cases on the tables. She smiled.

"You mean we've let our guard down? We're enjoying life? We're being human?" said Tsang.

"I guess we are. It just takes some getting used to," replied Schaefer.

"Well, it's your engagement party. It doesn't happen often. Enjoy it. You know how worried Alex is about the future."

Before Schaefer could continue, another round of toasts erupted from down the table. Then the sound of bagpipes began, with a slow whine and a moan. O'Reilly marched in followed by three troopers carrying trays with bottles of champagne. Joe the lamb trotted along behind. Another round of toasts to the engaged couple, and the Montfort family followed.

*

At breakfast the following morning Natasha joined Dr Heymans, Tsang and Johnson who were busy chatting excitedly. The smell of bacon frying and the sound of O'Reilly singing provided the background.

"So what's the story?" she asked them.

"Well, after finding the Montforts we really need to get our hands on that research paper in Paris. That'll give us the gene sequence and a list of some villages to contact," replied Heymans.

"But we've also got a new part of the plan. It's even better," added Tsang.

"What new part?" asked Natasha.

"The part we've just thought of. Once we get the gene sequence from the scientific research paper, all we then need to do is access and search the European DNA databases that are maintained in Versailles. That way we can get the names of everyone in Europe who matches the required DNA profile. We will have a database of everyone who could be immune, not just the few villages that the paper mentions. And then... well, we can go and find lots of people," advised Tsang.

"There's a few technical hurdles and details to work through, but as anyone will tell you from this troop, all you have to do is improvise and adapt," laughed Johnson.

"You know that, as we find people and the gene matches, we can then enrol them to further the search. The US and the ROW will take longer but at least we have a plan," added Heymans.

Natasha studied them in awe, as she began to comprehend the scale of what they were proposing.

"Wow," was all she could say.

Schaefer and Sanchez sat down opposite them.

"My head feels bad," said Schaefer. "Cognac and champagne don't hurt while you're drinking them but oh boy..."

"Well, it'll hurt even more when you hear what the medical team has cooked up," said Natasha.

"Fried eggs and bacon for the couple?" asked O'Reilly.

"Fantastic. Any coffee?" asked Sanchez.

"Stacey. Coffee over here for the wedding couple!"

The Montforts joined them.

"Captain Kavolsky. We've decided to join you at Saint Christobel," announced Madame Montfort.

CHAPTER 24

FORTRESS SAINT CHRISTOBEL

Being on surrounded ground means there is steep terrain on all sides with you in the middle. So the enemy can come and go freely but you have a hard time getting out and back. When you are on ground like this you should set up special plans ahead of time to prevent the enemy from bothering you, thus balancing out the disadvantage of the ground.

Spring slid gently into summer. Apart from the Montforts, they had no contact with anyone from the outside. They monitored frequencies but the only signals they picked up were either automatic transmissions or encrypted military traffic that they presumed were not friendly. Patrols went out and returned, each time venturing further, setting up passive sensors and enlarging the perimeter.

Only Corporal Vinelli, one of Schaefer's fire team section leaders, had requested to leave Saint C. He had discovered that he was from the village next to where one of the Heidelberg students, Isabella Ronaldi's family, came from. He hoped that by travelling to Porto Cervo in Sardinia he might establish contact with both her family and his own. Isabella herself would remain in Saint C until he returned with news.

Crockett had been assigned with the planning and implementation of Fortress C based on a strategy that Claudia, the ex-Foreign Legionnaire, had come up with.

"If we look like we're a well defended and equipped force, we'll attract attention and eventually we'll be hit with a larger force. However, if we look like a bunch of peasants trying to eke out an existence, we can buy a 'first chance', so to speak. I guess it's a bit like one of those weird fish that look all cute but eat anything that comes near them," she explained.

"But we already are a bunch of peasants," quipped Schaefer.

"Speak for yourself," heckled Sanchez.

From the population they selected 107 men and women to join the integrated defence force. Those selected were either fit, good hunters, had done some form of military service, or just had a specialty that could be useful. The 107 were then stiffened with troopers from the squadron and divided into six combat groups under the commands of Olly, Pavla, Galeago, Sanchez, Jones and lastly Claudia. Each of the combat groups was in turn sub-divided into four-man assault teams. They lined up for their first parade on a sunny morning in the main square, where Jones introduced them to basic parade techniques.

"We won't fuck about with marching and drilling right now but it is important that you all know how to fall into a straight line in your own units," he explained in his best Sergeant Major's voice. It took them several minutes of shuffling around into something that resembled a line.

"Well done. Next time remember how you did it and make sure you can do it in ten seconds. Right, take a seat and we'll begin."

They all sat down, some checking to make sure they wouldn't sit in too dusty an area.

"We've categorised each of you by your responses to the questionnaire you completed. I'll explain as we go. With the exception of Corporal Sanchez's pirates and Hodgetts' lot, you will all be trained for close quarter built-up area fighting.

"For this, we'll be using four-man squads. Each of you will need to know one another's strengths and weaknesses, hence the question about how long and more importantly how well you each know one another. It's not a case of 'oooh I don't like him or her', it's a case of 'I know what he or she would do in this or that situation'. Everyone understand so far?" There were general nods and murmurs from around the group.

"Good. If one of you is killed, any one of your other teammates will need to be able to take over from you. Now, that doesn't mean you all need to be as good as each other in each specialist task, it simply means that you could do the job, not maybe as well but you could do it. We OK with that?"

"Yes, sir," came a consolidated response, which Natasha reckoned had been instigated by Olly who was standing to one side, smiling.

"Now, we'll talk a little bit about the team make-up. We're going to model ourselves on the teams that fought in the longest and fiercest battle that ever occurred: Stalingrad. The team will in no particular order include a marksman, a grenade thrower, a squad automatic weapon, a leader, an explosive entry specialist and a medic. Now, that's more than four, so it means that some of you will have dual roles. Any questions?"

"No, sir."

"Great. This should be easy then. The questions we asked were designed to preliminarily assess each of you for the various roles. For example, if you'd majored in structural engineering or construction, you're probably more suited to explosive entry techniques than a poet. That is of course providing you can work under immense danger and don't have a tendency to panic. Accordingly, if you don't consider yourself physically strong as opposed to physically fit then it would be pointless assigning you to carry the squad automatic weapon.

"All of this is preliminary; there will be many changes for many reasons, not least of which because we often find that certain individuals who on paper don't appear to have a propensity for a particular role actually do. The whys and wherefores of this conundrum are not obvious but are something to do with the fact that all humans are unique and database-type categorisation is often incorrect. Any questions?"

"No, sir!" came back one voice.

"Excellent. Now, after we've taught you, and you've taught yourselves how to rely on one another, we'll then take it to the next level – for this you will need to understand the strengths and weaknesses of the other teams that form your combat group. Questions?"

"No, sir!" came back one voice.

"Is there an echo around here?" boomed back Jones, once more reverting to his parade ground voice.

"No, sir!" came back one voice.

"I'm impressed. Now, with that I'm going to let your trainers loose on you. For training, we have the old farmhouse and its adjoining fields; all the cattle have been moved and we've plenty of room. Posted on the boards over there you will find your teams, currently assigned roles and trainers. Over in the stores you will find your weapons and other equipment. Your first mission is to get yourselves sorted into your four-man teams, pick up your gear and get down to the farmhouse. There you will line up in your teams for inspection. The first team declared ready will get this evening off. The last will get all-night guard duty.

"Finally, the last combat group to assemble will pull guard duty for the next three nights. For clarity, when I say combat group that means all of the four-man teams that make up that group. Your commanders, if you've forgotten, are Lieutenant Claudia and Corporals Olly, Sanchez, Galeago and Pavla.

"Well… What are you all waiting for?"

The market square erupted into pandemonium as they ran across the square to check their names on the lists. There was shouting and yelling as they tried to sort themselves out into their teams. The first of the teams that managed to assemble then rushed off to the row of tables that had been set out with their weapons and equipment. Behind the tables was O'Reilly who had taken on the role of Quartermaster, and Winston and his mortar team who handed out and recorded what and to whom the equipment was issued.

Amidst a lot of shouting and what Jones later referred to as quantum chaos the teams started to set off for the five-mile hike to the farmhouse.

Natasha accompanied Jones and Alex to a vantage point on the crest of a small hill where they could look out over each of the training areas. With the noise of gunfire and the occasional grenade explosion they sat together on a fallen tree and studied the tactical assessment results that had so far been reported. For a moment she let her attention wander; the colours of the countryside looked extraordinarily rich and deep, with fields of rape seed and lavender stretching out towards the hills, broken only by deep green copses of trees. A large beetle emerged from a dead tree trunk, poked about and then disappeared again, and a butterfly hovered near by.

"Do you think the colours of the countryside are getting stronger?" Jones asked, surprising Natasha.

"Yes. They seem rich. In fact they seem richer here than I've ever seen them," replied Natasha.

"Now industry's stopped, the pollution levels have fallen and we've got less dust in the air. Maybe we're actually witnessing global brightening. Either way it's beautiful," said Alex.

Sanchez plonked herself down next to them with a sigh.

"What do you think?" she asked.

"Not bad, the sharpshooters are terrific. Fitness levels aren't too bad. Coordination not bad. It's better than I thought," said Jones.

*

The days rolled into weeks as the training progressed. For all of them, after the fury and pace of the winter the summer rolled past like a teenage one: slow, hot and full of soft memories. The winter belonged to another life, as they worked in the heat to transform Saint C into what the Countess called Fortress C.

They learnt about enfilades, defilades, blind spots, covering, suppressive and killing fire, defensive positions, structural integrity and weakness, camouflage, screens and diversions.

Zimbabwe taught them how to get out of buildings from a height they would never have considered possible.

"When you're fighting in a built-up area, dress for getting out of windows." Blank and confused faces met his gaze. "I'll give you a clue-look at how my webbing pack with ammunition pouches and all the other crap that we're expected to carry is configured. They're behind me; the reason is simple – nothing gets caught. It's little things like this that will make all the difference between getting out of a window in three seconds or five.

"When you let go, remember to turn and twist to face away from the wall. If you don't, when you land your knees will bend but bang straight into the wall.

"When you hit the ground you must roll, as we've taught you, knees bent, over onto the shoulder, minimise the shock to the spine, and roll away from the wall. You roll away for two reasons; the first is obvious, the second is not. It sounds crazy but enemy in any opposing building can range easier off a wall than if you're standing in the middle of the street. So you've less chance of being hit."

The house-clearing exercises escalated from defending against members of the squadron, to attacking an empty house, a house defended by volunteers, and finally to attacking a house defended by the squadron. They practised in night, day and smoke-filled conditions.

They held contests for the best marksman against a range of targets including moving, stationary and situations where enemy were mixed in with friendly forces.

Each person began to feel that they could contribute a particular skill and each began to note who was skilled at what. Some teams soon developed reputations for being adept at a particular task.

"You will start improvising and adapting the tactics and techniques we've taught you. Don't be frightened to do this. Share them with the others and show them to your trainers. We'll all benefit," said Jones.

Gyan held a light machine gun competition that included having to complete an assault course, and a two-mile run carrying the weapon and 2,000 rounds of the heavy old brass ammunition.

"Get your breathing under control, work as a team. The shooter should just relax, let the loader and ammunition carrier do the work. The shooter needs steady hands, so he needs to be relaxed," boomed Gyan above the noise of the firing.

They taught each person basic first aid: pressure bandages, CPR, setting up a plasma drip, and how to use the tourniquets that were an integral part of each of their combat suits.

"Now, it's easy to panic when you see a lot of blood and come to the conclusion that things are worse than they are. Let me show you," said Johnson, as he poured a pint of red-coloured water onto a stone-flagged floor to demonstrate the point.

"For adults, there are three more where this came from before you are in real trouble, so don't panic. It often looks a lot worse than it is. So stop the bleeding, shoot them up with an anti-shock and co-ag and move on. If you think they have lost more than a couple of pints then plug them in to a plasma bag."

Johnson and Tsang put each of the assigned medics through an advanced trauma course designed to treat the most common types of injury they would have to face.

They practised pressure bandaging again and again, using vacuum sheaths as well as field dressings. On one occasion one of them complained to PFC Nancy Strong that he thought he could do it blindfolded he had done it so many times. The next exercise she set them was to do just that. They learnt how to set rough splints, perform CPR, and administer battlefield morphine, plasma and blood, injecting them straight through the combat clothing.

"The needles we use are twice the size of the civilian ones. They are strong and because they're bigger we can get more fluid into the patient quickly – this is important as the wounds we deal with typically are associated with loss of blood volume that causes not only patient shock but the veins to collapse making the insertion of an IV difficult. Now finally, if you can't get a needle into a vein you can use the screw," said Nancy Strong, demonstrating a device that screwed a tube directly into the sternum.

Together with Dr Heymans they were taught anatomy and showed how to fit a chest drain, various immobilisation techniques and burns treatments. Johnson, Tsang and Heymans set up an operating table and using four anaesthetised pigs taught the team artery clamping and suturing techniques.

"This will be one of the most important exercises you will undertake. It's also one of the most dramatic. Burns look nasty but are dormant, so are broken limbs, necks and people who aren't breathing. But stemming blood flow and suturing gaping wounds requires you to get intimate with the patient, who in many cases will be panicking. You'll be covered in their blood and feel the wound. Some of you will feel queasy doing this, others terrified and some will take to it naturally. But I can tell you all this, once you've done this once or twice, the third and fourth times will not seem nearly so challenging and you will get a real sense of accomplishment. Now finally, for those of you who are wondering whether this is cruel, let me tell you that they won't feel anything, and afterwards we'll have a feast to remember them by. But only after you each complete two exercises and then carry the dead pigs back to Saint C using whatever you can to improvise a stretcher."

Crockett taught them explosive entry techniques.

"When you want to get into a building or move from one to the next, don't bother with the doors or the windows, go through the walls. It's perfectly OK to do so providing you don't bring the whole place down in the process," he advised. "To prevent this you need to know how much explosive to use and where to put it. To help you, in Saint C we will colour code each and every point, so you'll know the size of charge."

Teaching the art of sniping, concealment and camouflage was the responsibility of Hodgetts and his sniper Shadow team which had been supplemented by an old Christobelian hunter by the name of Jean-Jacques.

"The basics are fairly simple; they can be summarised as TESSSSSSS, that's like Tess of the d'Urbervilles but with seven lucky Ss.

303

"T is for thermal, or your body heat. Even without a Zute suit you can do a lot. Stand behind an insulated wall, or use your Cyclops to give you a background reading of the surroundings and then pick the one that most closely matches the human body.

"E stands for your electronic signature or e-sig. You generate e-sig from radios, sensors and lasers; we call this splash. So the number one rule is only power up electronic devices when you need them. Learn to rely on your senses. These include your eyes, smell, touch, hearing, taste and yes… gut instinct.

"Now come the lucky seven Ss.

"One is shape – change yours. You might for example be able to use something like a piece of plywood and lie under it on a sloping roof.

"Two is shine, so don't wear sparkly jewellery.

"Three is surface, blend in with the surroundings; if you decide to use that piece of plywood make sure it's got the same texture as the roof tiles.

"Four is silhouette, so on that roof, don't walk across the ridgeline. Don't stand in a window or doorway that's back lit.

"Five is shadow, watch this one.

"Six is sound. If your environment is quiet, don't make it. Plot your approach, avoid surfaces like gravel.

"And finally, seven is smell. Don't wear your favourite perfume. You might think it's stupid but the Vietcong soldiers in the Vietnam war in the last century said they could often track the Americans just by the smell."

Sanchez organised training using both their grenade launchers as well as simply throwing them. She started the exercises with them firing through hoops at varying ranges and heights, and then showed them how to bounce the grenades off walls or other objects to hit a target not directly in their line of sight using delayed fuses. Happy with their progress, she finally introduced them to the 'mother of all grenades', the FAE. For the exhibition, Natasha had joined them.

"Now, there may be a time when you want to bring a whole building down; this is a last resort. The fighting will be confused and there will be a risk that you end up killing as many of us as them. Therefore, this weapon is to be used very sparingly. It's called a fuel air explosive or FAE. Each of you will be issued with one round."

She knelt down and shouldered the weapon. Her target was an old cow shed built of reinforced concrete.

"You need to be a minimum of thirty metres away if the weapon detonates inside the building, outside you need seventy."

She made herself ready. In the silence of expectation the birds sang.

"Fuel air!... Weapon hot. Firing now!"

An instant later a dull pop signified the dispersant charge had fired releasing a mixture of highly flammable compressed gas into the building; this was instantly followed by a deep boom. The heatwave that struck them was accompanied by a hissing noise as the walls of the building bulged outwards. Then the direction of the blast changed and air rushed back past them and the walls of the building bowed inwards before collapsing and bringing the roof down. Plumes of dust mixed with the residue of an orange fireball rose into the air forming a mushroom cloud.

"Jesus," muttered someone from the assembled crowd.

The teams were given sectors of the town that they were responsible for and now trained in. Based upon the exercises, they set about modifying the buildings to maximise their advantage. Access holes were made through walls, some entrances were blocked, others camouflaged, and windows were enlarged and narrowed.

Some walls were lined with cooking foil so that the microwave radars could not see what was within a room.

Some rooms were classified as no-go areas and mined. These rooms were given simple visual identifiers, in this case a red cross painted next to a window or the doorway.

"We need to know every inch of this town and the surrounding countryside. We need to know how to get from one side of the town to the other by at least two routes that are not exposed to a direct line of fire. This will be our great advantage," preached Jones.

Raven, Byrnes and Luc built what they described as the world's first super-hard distributed tactical communications net. They'd gone back in time as Luc had described and used the domestic electricity copper wiring circuits to enable data and voice traffic.

"How secure is it?" Jones asked Natasha.

"What they've done is a little weird. They've integrated each of the transceivers with a language translation program. Isabelle gave us the idea and the program. All the data and the voice telem is translated into ancient Greek. Then translated back again. You've got to enter a three-digit code when you want to receive or communicate. It'll cut off after the handshaking is finished, so if anyone loses a set we're still secure."

"Impressive," commented Schaefer.

At one of Crockett's now famous planning sessions, Michael Hill the engineer from the town's council asked if they could try and build some simple mantraps. There was laughter for a minute before Crockett replied, "Excellent. Rocks and sharp sticks don't show up on sensors."

They built a false roof in the main gate tower and filled it with rubble, then set sufficient explosives in it to bring tons of rock down onto anyone or thing that was below. Mantraps were built, consisting of rubble or heavy wooden logs that were hauled up into the archways and could be released by simply cutting some ropes. The 500-year-old cannonier in the battlements were renovated and quantities of concrete balls manufactured that could be sent racing down the conduits into or onto anyone attempting to scale the walls.

With most of the close defensive network completed, they focused on the surrounding area. On the approach roads they built a vehicle trap, an excavated hole 15-feet deep with sheer sides, which was covered with a wooden matrix floor that supported 3 feet of top soil and a gravel and tarmac road finish.

Hodgetts and Sanchez placed visual range markers in the surrounding areas to provide accurate range estimates for their weapons.

"You can range far better with a pair of binoculars and a preset marker than fumbling about with all the other crap, and you won't have to use anything that gives your own position away," Sanchez told them.

Hodgetts and his sniper team built concealed forward observation posts, whilst Winston set about building a network of anti-personnel mines. Schaefer insisted that any minefield had to be undetectable and be capable of being triggered from within the town, which presented Winston with a challenge.

The area was heavily wooded and the ground between the trees was covered in short grass and moss. It was during a walk back through them that Winston remembered reading about the US 101st Airborne Division in the Ardennes in World War Two when they had been shelled by the Germans. The carnage caused by the shells exploding in the trees, which sent wood splinters shooting through the air, created more casualties than if the shells had exploded on the ground.

He explained his theory to them. "If we hang the mines in the trees, not only will they be more effective, but the distance of them off the ground will render the mines undetectable."

"You're a genius," Natasha told him.

"Indeed I am!" crowed Winston.

"Impressive. All we need now is boiling oil and a catapult!" added Schaefer.

Sanchez ran an exercise where each of them was blindfolded and asked to locate a particular place in the town.

"So what do you think?" Natasha asked Alex after one such morning's exercise.

"Impressive. Anyone who gets inside here is going to have a tough time. So how do you like being a grunt?"

"I'm aching all over. I stink of gun oil and cordite. I love it. Sanchez tells me I could make section leader in a month. All I need apparently is a little toughening up, whatever that means," she said, feeling proud.

"I'm still worried though; the one thing we can't defend against is that they just stand off and destroy us with artillery or Stalkers. How do we draw them in?"

"I know, but at least the Alamo is ready. The boats are in place, we've got fuel and a hospital. I'm meeting O'Reilly in five for a tour."

Isabella, one of the history of art students they had rescued from Heidelberg, who had been helping O'Reilly and Stacey, was waiting at the entrance to the church to escort Natasha. Halfway down the stairway to the cave they found both Stacey and O'Reilly engrossed in studying some graffiti on the tunnel wall.

"Hey, Captain! You seen this graffiti? It's in some other lingo."

"The top ones are Roman. The bottom Gaul," said Isabella, looking at them closely.

"Wow! Do you know what it says?" asked Stacey, obviously impressed.

"The Roman one says Brutus was here. The 17th legion, 3rd cohort. Probably around AD 70. The Gaulist one is a bit more interesting though; it's from a guy called Luc... He's a warrior and he's writing about his sweetheart, someone called Agnon... He's in love and worried about the Viking ship they've seen... He says... her golden hair is like the sun on the ocean in the morning... her lips like..." she paused.

"What?" asked Stacey and O'Reilly in unison, captivated by the story.

"I can't read it. I'll have to get some paper and do a rubbing," replied Isabella in a slightly teasing voice.

"Amazing, isn't it? Soldiers and more soldiers. We're really just the last in a long line of grunts who have been here," commented O'Reilly.

*

With their training and preparations complete, Schaefer organised a passing-out parade. Claudia's group had finished first overall and as such they led. The students provided the music, the score being derived from a Foreign Legion march which was slow and rhythmical. They marched slowly with their arms pointing straight downwards, not swinging.

"The Legion marches like Napoleon's troops did; it's one of the slowest in the world. Eighty-eight paces per minute. Most armies march at one hundred and two. It's almost funeral pace," Alex told Natasha as she watched the strange march.

"Go on," she encouraged.

"The Legion takes – or rather took – all nationalities, from any walk of life. In fact it was fairly common for soldiers who would have fought against each other in wars between their own nations to end up in the same squad in the Legion.

"One of the most enduring legends relates to the son of one of the victims of the Holocaust. The son joined the Legion and was posted to Indo-China. Here he was sent to a squad only to discover that his father's killer, an ex-SS guard, was in the same squad. Anyway, before any retribution occurred the squad found themselves fighting for their survival against overwhelming odds, and during the battle each saved one another's life. It was only after the battle and they'd been withdrawn from the line that the son confronted and then killed the ex-SS man."

After the passing-out parade celebrations Alex, Natasha and the others retired to the officers' mess in the Hôtel de Ville.

"It's been a long day. But we're almost there," Crockett announced before collapsing into an armchair.

"How's the leg?" Alex asked, handing Crockett a large brandy.

"This one's stiff," laughed Crockett pointing to his missing leg.

Jones arrived. "You know, maybe I'm getting too old for this," he said, also collapsing into a chair.

"Tough day, Sergeant Major?" asked Natasha with a smile, handing him a drink.

"It must be. I'm in the officers' mess being waited on by a Captain in the airforce. Olly will be telling them that I've lost it."

"Just don't ask me to take your boots off," she said.

"You know they need repairing, look at them," he moaned, undoing his jump boots and examining the left one.

"Why don't you grab another pair from the stores?" asked Crockett.

"I would but these are custom. Cost me a fortune. One of my legs is an inch longer than the other and the boots were made to compensate," he replied.

"I didn't know. How the hell did that happen?" asked Crockett.

"About twelve years ago. AP round took my lower fib out in Russia. They'd run out of bone extension or some such thing. So I ended up with one leg shorter. The left boot has an insert that equalises my leg length."

Natasha noticed Alex had fallen asleep. Johnson smiled at her.

"Alex?" he said.

Alex grunted a response.

"Starting tomorrow you're going to have a few days off. There will be no arguments or discussions on this. A few days. That's all. We can look after ourselves."

"I know. I know. But…"

"No arguments. Doctor's orders."

"As your 2IC, I concur," added Natasha.

"As Sergeant Major, I do too," said Jones.

"All right. And I guess as soon as I come back off my forced leave, you, Doctor, or Captain or whatever you now are, can go in search of your genes," said Alex with a smile.

*

In the early afternoon the following day, Natasha joined Alex who was stretched out in a field. He was barefoot and wearing shorts, and a T-shirt with a picture of a squirrel on it. Dandelion blossom floated past him on a gentle breeze. She could hear the sound of cattle and sheep from across the fields. The smell of the earth and fields was refreshing; it was a little like taking a shower, she mused.

Without them exchanging a word she lay down next to him and stared up at the sky, squinting against the bright sun that was now almost directly overhead. She let her mind wander back to her childhood and the games her brothers and sister used to play. She tried to keep her thoughts away from the inevitable question but lost the battle and started to wonder where they were now. The intensity of the sun which was piercing her eyelids faded and it was this that alerted her to the presence of someone who was blocking the light. She was in the process of reaching for her weapon before the familiar voice put her at rest.

"Enjoying yourselves?" asked Johnson.

"How did you know?"

"You were both half smiling."

Johnson dropped a rucksack and knelt down beside them. "I've brought you a picnic. We've got some wine, cheese, bread, some salami and… ham. Oh, and O'Reilly found some strawberries," he continued, pulling out a large blanket and spreading it on the ground.

"Strawberries? God almighty. I feel honoured," replied Alex.

"You should be. Here, open the wine. It's a chilled red."

Whilst they ate they discussed the upcoming mission. Natasha loved the way the wine softened the hard bread, and timed her sips of wine to enhance the strong flavours of the food. After chatting about the upcoming mission to Paris, Johnson left them alone.

Natasha smiled.

"What?" he asked.

"Just thinking."

"The T-shirt…" He didn't finish the sentence as she leant across and kissed him. For a second she felt him hesitate before responding. As he did, she pushed him down onto his back and clambered on top of him. His mouth tasted cool and sweet from the strawberries and wine. His tongue explored hers as she stretched out on top of him, pinning his hands above his head. Her fingers interlocked with his as she began to grind her body across his. She felt the grass on her hands, the warmth and strength of his grip. She could feel him stiffen – not slowly but like someone had turned a switch on. She knew that both of them were experiencing the same release of emotions; it was like Sanchez had told her it would be. She stifled a giggle.

His smell and the touch of his hair now combined to unleash an avalanche of sensations. She increased the pressure of her movement against him. She opened her eyes, and amongst the mass of her hair, she saw his were closed. He smiled, and as this broke their kiss, he rolled her over onto her back pushing her T-shirt upwards in the process to expose her breasts and she pulled his head down towards them. For a moment he held back, looking at her body.

She arched her back, pushing herself against him, her hands working their way into the back of his shorts. He moved aside a little and her fingers quickly found and closed around his penis. He lifted himself off her a little to help her as she pulled his shorts off. Rolling him onto his back she took his penis into her mouth whilst gently stroking his testicles. He tried to push her away so he could give her pleasure but she pushed back. Finally, when she thought he would come, she broke contact and smiled at him. He took the opportunity and reached between her legs, pulling the poppers open on her combat trousers, pulling them down around her knees. She giggled, helping him push them further down, then lay back and opened her legs. His fingers explored her, teasing her in repayment for what she had done to him. As she too neared climax she pushed him away. Both of them worked together to undo her combat boots; free of them she struggled out of her trousers.

He lay down on his back and she knelt astride him, guiding him into her. He pushed his hands back up under her T-shirt playing with her nipples. She started to move slowly backwards and forwards. Her breathing quickened, the taste of wine, strawberries, the feel of the grass and the gentle breeze, the fact that anyone could have seen them, and the fact that she knew she loved him all seemed to stack up into one massive emotional mountain. She could feel herself losing control; they climaxed together with a physical shudder that released months of emotion.

They lay there for a while, she on top of him looking into his eyes, listening to the animals and the occasional insect in the fields around them.

"You know, back in Scandinavia when I first met you, your eyes looked like they could spit fire. It's strange I never noticed that they were hazel and you've got little gold bits as well," he said.

"Well, when I met you I thought your eyes looked like a sheet of nano-kevlar armour, impossible to see what was behind."

"Really?"

"Sssh," she said pointing up at the sky behind him. He craned his neck backwards to look. An eagle swooped and came within 20 feet of them before picking up a field mouse in its talons and climbing into the air. "The Native Indians would say that's good luck," she said.

"I'll miss you whilst you're in Paris."

CHAPTER 25

THE DOG JUTES

He will win who knows when to fight and when not to fight.

It was a drizzly dawn several days after Johnson, Natasha and the others had departed for Paris to search for Johnson's acclaimed medical paper. Hodgetts and the old hunter, Jean-Jacques, who Hodgetts had recruited into his sniper team, had invited Sanchez on a hunt. "It'll sharpen your skills," he'd told her.

They lay in a small hide off to the side of a narrow sandy track that ran in a straight line through the trees and up a hill. They were 50 kilometres from Saint Christobel which, although Hodgetts had moaned was "a bloody long way" was, according to Jean-Jacques, the best place to hunt for a particular type of wild boar, one that he said tasted of truffle. Hodgetts lay fast asleep. Sanchez wondered how Natasha and the others were getting on. She was happy her friend had finally summoned up the courage to seduce the Major. She smiled to herself and at the same time noticed a disturbance in the undergrowth to their left. She tapped Jean-Jacques on the wrist who nodded in return. It was the nod of a teacher slightly pleased that his pupil had started to learn.

Several scrapings and rustlings followed before the boar trotted out of the dense undergrowth following a route known only to itself and more recently the hunters. Its small legs seemed to speed up slightly as it moved across the open track, making its way to the safety of the undergrowth on the other side and presumably its bed.

Sanchez tracked the animal, picked her spot, the heart, and then squeezed the trigger. The dart from the crossbow sped across the 20 metres of space and struck the boar just behind its forelegs. It staggered forward for one or two more steps and then collapsed with a thud into the centre of the sandy track.

Jean-Jacques patted her on the shoulder in congratulations, stood up, stretched, rummaged in his old leather jerkin and fished out one of his extremely coarse cigarettes in celebration. Sanchez strained to get up; her limbs were stiff from the long wait and she wondered how the old hunter seemed to remain so supple under the most arduous of conditions. Together they went to inspect the kill, leaving Hodgetts asleep.

"*Ca c'est bon*," muttered Jean-Jacques in his gravelly voice, pointing to the entry wound. He reached down and wiped a small amount of the animal's blood onto his leathery hand which he then smeared across her cheek. Sanchez felt proud. She liked this little hunter who knew every tree and trail in the area, and moved through the country as if he were part of it. It was as if he could sense the animals, not just track them.

She was about to go off into the trees to search for some suitable branches to use as carrying poles for their kill when Jean-Jacques held up a finger to his lips to signify silence. Sanchez froze; a sixth sense told her that whatever had spooked him was not animal.

Silently they both moved back to their hide, leaving their prey on the track. Jean-Jacques pointed to the sky to their right and she looked up to see a flock of birds on the rise and immediately understood. Something had disturbed the birds and this something was probably man. She placed a hand over Hodgetts' mouth and gently shook him awake. They waited looking out along the track. Five minutes passed without anything else happening. But she knew that her senses were rarely wrong and told herself to be patient. After another three minutes, one, then several more black-clad, heavily armed figures crossed her field of vision moving across the track.

Using her optics she zoomed in and started recording. She couldn't identify their uniforms. One of the figures stopped and briefly glanced down the track towards them before continuing.

Three more people, this time dressed in civilian clothes, came into view, escorted by Rottweiler dogs and more black-clad armed figures. She could see that the civilians were prisoners and she felt a wave of aggression rising in her. She had always had a deep mistrust of people who owned such dogs and didn't like the ramifications of what she had seen.

They waited unmoving for another thirty minutes before breaking cover. Sanchez knew that whoever the soldiers were, they were not allied.

In fact the whole thing was weird and slightly sinister. It reminded her of childhood stories about the Jutes and the Vikings, rounding up villagers after a raid.

"Jean-Jacques, you and Hodgetts take this back to the Major. I'm going after that lot to get a closer look."

Jean-Jacques shook his head. "*Non*. We'll track them, you go back."

Sanchez thought about the pros and cons. Hodgetts and Jean-Jacques could certainly track them at a safer distance and Hodgetts was trained in deep reconnaissance. She was already conjuring up a rescue mission in her mind. They would need information on weapons, any base, training and competency of the enemy.

"Do a full recce. We need to plan on getting those people released. No contact. Recce only."

*

It took Sanchez the rest of the day and that night to reach Saint C, arriving just as the sun came up. She immediately went to search out Jones, who was having breakfast.

"Fucking great. First of all we run out of eggs and now you turn up with a story about the goddamn Vikings."

"Jutes, Sergeant Major. Jutes," offered Sanchez.

"Whatever, Corporal. All right, let's go and see the Major," he sighed, leaving the remains of his breakfast.

CHAPTER 26

HISTORY OF GENE 169

In military operations what is valued is foiling the opponents' strategy, not pitched battle.

Natasha was in Paris. As their AFV skirted around the deserted L'Etoile and joined the Champs Élyseés they scattered thousands of birds that were nesting in the tree-lined boulevard. An image of a 1950s black-and-white photograph of two lovers kissing outside a café leapt from Natasha's teenage memories. Even though the street was covered in leaves and branches, the city still had an atmosphere of love and beauty.

"Look at that! I've always wanted to see the Arc de Triomphe. Apparently there's a letter from Napoleon to his Josephine in there," bellowed O'Reilly.

"There is indeed," said Johnson with the voice of a teacher. "He talks about how many generals and guns he's captured at Austerlitz and then finishes it with a *'je t'adore'* to his Josephine."

"Well, look at that, times never change!" shouted O'Reilly again, this time pointing at an oriental carpet store advertising a closing-down sale. "*Les Grande Reductions – Liquidation*! You ever noticed that of all the shops in all the world, carpet shops are always closing down, year after year, even now."

They sped past lines of shops, some obviously looted, others left intact. Natasha noticed a hairdresser's and thought about all the women who had sat there having their hair done before a special night. She noticed a sign to the Metro; it reminded her of a friend she'd had at college who was studying philosophy and used to tell everyone that he loved train stations because that was the one place in the world where people knew where they were going.

The AFV had been stripped and rebuilt for the expedition to enable speed and range. They'd installed additional fuel tanks but reduced the defensive capability.

Johnson and Natasha had picked a multidiscipline team for the task ahead. Dr Heymans, Johnson and particularly Tsang would provide the genetics expertise. Computer software, systems, databases and communications would be looked after by Byrnes and Raven who'd teamed up with Luc Heymans in an apparently inseparable trio. Security and defence were under the command of Schaefer, who had Gyan's squad of Zimbabwe, Frost, Colins, Piper and Cook, and finally the AFV crew which comprised O'Reilly on threat, Stacey as driver and navigator, and Hicks as AFV systems specialist.

The atmosphere was one of excitement, and Natasha smiled to herself. She felt alive and driven by a purpose. *Was this love?* she mused whilst listening to the banter, underpinned by the sound of the AFV's tracks as they softly whined along the cobblestoned boulevard. Faded Tricolore flags fluttered on the Ministry of Justice and other imposing looking buildings under a classic nitrogen blue sky that let big fluffy white clouds sail across it.

But the flowerbeds and lawns of the once-pristine boulevard had now disappeared beneath undergrowth. Weeds had sprung up amongst the cobblestones, some of which had buckled upwards in small mounds. Tree branches and other plant debris littered the boulevard. They slowed down to circumnavigate a deep depression in the roadway which was full of water.

"The city's beginning to die," she said.

"Yeah, the drains are probably clogged up with plant debris and some of the pumps that stop flooding are probably out of service through lack of maintenance or power. Water will back up, it'll freeze and thaw, busting up stonework, more cabling and the foundations," advised Hicks.

They passed lines of expensive boutiques and cafés, some of which now had ivy growing into the foyers, and then rounded the Place de la Concorde and the famous Cleopatra's Needle.

"I remember reading that the last thing that would be left if the human race just vanished from earth would be bronze statues. Amazing, eh? They'd last longer than the radioactive waste we've dumped," commented Raven.

Electronic billboards driven by solar panels still projected images of the latest fashion on some of the buildings. Stacey stopped at some red traffic lights before realising that there was no need. "Blimey. This is weird," he commented.

"Ah... that's the Hôtel Crillon. I was going to take a girlfriend there once," sighed Gyan.

"Supposed to be one of the most romantic hotels there is," added Stacey.

"Are you claiming that you are a romantic?" quipped Frost.

"Yeah," replied Stacey. "I am," he said confidently before accelerating to chase a pack of dogs out of the way.

"We should stop and get some socks," said Zimbabwe as they passed a clothing store. "Nothing seems to have changed on that score. I keep losing them faster than I can replace them."

They sped past a row of airline offices advertising cut-price tickets to exotic islands all ending in 'i', before heading down the Rue Rivoli and pulling up outside the Louvre and the famous glass pyramid. A lone deer looked them over, showing no signs of fear before trotting off.

Despite not having encountered any hostile forces since leaving Saint C, Schaefer still insisted on setting up perimeter security. Johnson, who had grown increasingly impatient throughout the journey, muttered something unintelligible and marched off towards the entrance together with his team. Natasha apologised on his behalf to Schaefer before trotting off after them.

Reaching a broken glass door they descended a wide spiral staircase to the entrance foyer, with glass crunching beneath their boots, only to find their progress barred by a stainless steel portcullis. It took Stacey an hour to cut through it.

"I feel like we're doing a bank heist," commented Johnson as the final bar collapsed with a twang onto the marble floor.

"All in a good cause," offered Natasha.

"OK, let's go. The archives should be down two levels and along past the Egyptian gallery," said Luc Heymans eagerly.

"Jesus, this place gives me the creeps," said Stacey in a voice just loud enough to make himself feel a little more at ease.

"Ah, don't you be worrying, the old pharaohs have been dead too long to worry about the likes of ourselves," reassured O'Reilly as they made their way along the darkened Egyptian hallway that led to the Pan European Technical Archives.

"The archive should be the next on the right," said Luc, studying his museum guide with his flashlight. "Yes, it's here," he proudly announced, shining the torch at the sign and pushing open the transparent blue glass entrance doors.

"I remember reading about this place when I was doing my PhD. It's a human immersion visualisation environment or HIVE. You can manipulate and superimpose very large data sets using three-dimensional representations.

"You can walk around objects, data matrices or even equations to view them from differing angles. There was a lot of criticism when they built it; people couldn't understand why a scientific archive should be established here. You know, next to the Mona Lisa and all that."

"You have to be French to really understand," said Dr Heymans.

"I wonder if she's still here?" asked Natasha, referring to the Mona Lisa.

"I doubt it. The French were pretty good at hiding the contents of this place once before. But if she is, I'm sure O'Reilly will find her," said Johnson.

"Right. So all we now need is power and the reboot manual for the system," said Natasha, looking at the dead screens and wondering how they were going to start.

"There must be a systems control room somewhere," said Raven, marching off into the gloom.

"I'll come with you," said Luc.

"Here you go," announced Byrnes, pointing to a sealed door.

"Ah shit," said Raven. "Right, we're going to have to get some power down here unless you want to bust the door down."

"I wouldn't recommend that; we've no idea whether there's an interlock that could freeze the whole lot," advised Luc.

"Stacey, go and get Hicks and some power sorted," ordered Natasha.

*

Byrnes isolated the archive power net from the rest of the building by exposing the cable conduits in the ceilings and beneath the floor and tracing the cables back to the main breaker panels. He then hooked up two battery cells from the AFVs.

"Right, here goes… and then there was light!" he proudly announced as the auditorium started to glow under red background lights and the systems room lit up behind the transparent blue doors.

"Right, you Irish bastard, time for you to do your stuff," said Stacey.

O'Reilly amazed his audience with the speed with which he bypassed the door security.

"How does he do that?" Natasha asked Johnson.

"God knows. Stacey says he learnt it from his great uncle who was apparently a cat burglar."

"I'll go and get some refreshments. I think it might be a long night," said O'Reilly, marching away like a peacock.

*

Sipping coffee with Schaefer, Natasha stood in front of the wide blue glass window and watched as robot arms moved cube-shaped memory modules from port to port in a precise choreographed motion that only robots make. An hour later the mainframe had booted up and now awaited their instructions.

Natasha left the doctors and the IT team to it and joined O'Reilly, who had cooked a meal under the watchful gaze of the Egyptian statues.

"Incredible, eh?" O'Reilly commented, whilst digging into his food and swilling a Coke he had looted from a vending machine at the main entrance.

"Do you think we should take one with us?" asked Stacey.

Natasha lit a cigarette and waited, intrigued to see how the conversation would turn out.

"Nah. They seem happy to see us. And I guess one day others will want to come and see them as well," replied O'Reilly.

"But what happens if the place floods, you know, like we said earlier, sooner or later the systems will fail…"

"So tell me something, how come Sergeant Gyan is called Tequila?" asked Natasha, changing the subject.

"Well, one day, a long time ago, in a country far, far away…" started O'Reilly.

"We were on an exercise in the Italian Alps. The game was to ambush some units from the 101st Airborne. No big deal. It was meant to be a bit of a holiday…" said Frost.

"Anyway *End Ex* came and we were looking to play, so we decided to drive to a ski resort. Problem was we had no money, or rather very little. So Sergeant Gyan said fuck it, pardon the language, but anyway he—" filled in Stacey.

"… swapped one of the vehicles with a bar owner for ten cases of tequila… And well, you know, the name just stuck I suppose. He lost a stripe over that; took him a year for the Major to get it back for him," finished O'Reilly.

"The good thing was that we were so drunk that we didn't even notice we'd snow-holed for the night. The skiers in the resort couldn't believe it next morning when they were waiting for the lift and we popped out of the snow next to them."

That night, Natasha dreamt about skiing with Alex.

*

Schaefer shook Natasha awake the next morning; she felt stiff from sleeping on the hard marble as Schaefer handed her a coffee.

"We should go and hear what they've got to say. Johnson is clucking like a mother hen," he said.

Together they joined Dr Heymans, Johnson and Tsang who were standing in the centre of the master HIVE. Turandot's *Nessun Dorma* was blaring from hidden speakers somewhere in the room. Projectors shone through the occasional cloud of cigarette smoke generating 3D imagery of a DNA helix. Screens showed streams of the famous four letters ATC&G. Empty Coke cans, discarded MRE wrappers and scribbled notes sat amongst the portable computers and cables that snaked across the auditorium to where Luc, Raven and Byrnes piloted the processing room as they referred to their role.

"Good morning," boomed Johnson, blowing a stream of smoke into the 3D image. He looked excited, tired and sad all at the same time. "I think we need a chat. We've got good news, very bad and some even worse. I'm not sure which you want to start with."

"Any which way you want," answered Natasha, sipping her coffee.

"I'll start with the bad. Ignoring any impact of immunity from gene 169 we think we know how many other survivors there might be. We downloaded and ran an epidemiology program called EPISIMS. It was originally created to enable governments and authorities like the WHO to develop management systems to counter terrorist threats from biological agents, like anthrax and the like, back in the early millennium. These worldwide scenarios were code-named Red Storm. They modelled different quarantine scenarios, such as optimum times to release vaccines, when to shut down air transport, and a myriad of other measures.

"Anyway, we used it to model APP. From the output we're looking at a kill rate that matches our worst fears. In Europe, if you weren't a gene 169 person or isolated somehow, your chances of survival were very slim, around one in a thousand," Johnson said, looking saddened.

"We're just waiting for a few more simulations that look at some variations, such as impact on populations living in the Australian outback," added Heymans.

"Jesus," replied Natasha looking at one of the screens, not able to understand any of it.

1.A.2 Amino acids [23]
Gene Product
tdh YPO0060 threonine 3-dehydrogenase
gcvP YPO0905 glycine dehydrogenase
gcsH YPO0906 glycine cleavage system H protein
gcvT YPO0907 aminomethyltransferase
----- YPO1193 putative pyridoxal-dependent decarboxylase
----- YPO1201 putative amino acid decarboxylase
ansB YPO1386 putative L-asparaginase II precursor
sdaA YPO1771 L-serine dehydratase
putA, poaA YPO1851 bifunctional PutA protein [includes: proline]

"That's it. *Yersinia pestis Orientalis, Y pestis.* The plague," picked up Tsang; "we've also learnt a little more about it during the night. For example, the DNA sequencing was never completed; we've still got about a hundred unidentified genes in the sequence. It's only a few per cent of the total but still a slight concern, as it will impact our estimates of survival probabilities."

"But what about treatment? Surely there must have been some?" asked Natasha, feeling macabre even asking such a question.

"From the available research papers we've found, unless you hit *Y pestis* with antibiotics within twenty-four hours of infection you're dead. The numbers from our EPISIMS run assumed this, but when you factor in the gene fab mods they added to come up with APP, we never really had a chance. Unless you were vaccinated before the outbreak or isolated you were not likely to survive," replied Dr Heymans.

"Any chance that some were vaccinated?" asked Schaefer.

"We've found out that there was enough pre-stored vaccine for a few hundred thousand, and that's worldwide. To be effective it would have to have been administered before infection. Was there any vaccination programme? Probably a few vaccinations for researchers as part of their standard protection if they were working on disease control. But almost definitely no larger programme," replied Johnson.

"What part of the news is this?" asked Natasha.

"That's the bad bit but not the worst. But let Lieutenant Tsang give you the good news first," advised Johnson.

"We found the technical paper on gene 169. That's it," she said, pointing to the 3D image. "It was taken from dozens of graves that they exhumed from about twenty or so villages across Europe. Now, if we superimpose the relevant DNA segment profile of Dr Heymans, his son and a half a dozen of the villagers from Saint C we've also uploaded…"

"They match," summarised Natasha as she watched the various helixes merge into the original.

"We've checked all the villagers. They all match. So what we've proved is that this gene is common to the survivors of Saint C and to the people who survived the plague back in the medieval period."

She looked on in awe as Johnson manipulated one after another of the segments of the double helix signatures, each with a name of one of the villagers, and matched them to one another.

"Wow."

"Yes. And now we've got the sequence for gene 169 we can scan any DNA sequence we have for a match," added Heymans.

"Jesus. So now all we have to do is…"

"Exactly," interjected Tsang, putting her arm around Natasha. "Get to the DNA archives in Versailles and run a match program for the gene across all the stored DNA personal records. We can then filter the matches by geographic region, age, sex… and whatever else you want."

"Do we know any more about the prevalence of your special gene? How many people might have it?" asked Natasha.

"That's the worst part of the news, I'm afraid," Johnson said. "We know from the skeletons that were analysed as part of the research on gene 169 that the gene was around in each of the three pandemics or plague outbreaks that were recorded in written history. The first was between the fifth and seventh centuries, the second was during the fourteenth to eighteenth centuries in Europe and the last was in China in the nineteenth century."

Tsang continued. "The problem is that 169 is a gene that codes for a protein on the surface of white blood cells which act as a receptor for other molecules involved in inflammation. Since the CCR five 169 receptors are turned off, it makes a person resistant or immune to certain viruses because they cannot latch onto the receptors."

"You're talking Martian now," said Schaefer.

"What Lieutenant Tsang is trying to say," interjected Dr Heymans, "is that what we've found… or rather rediscovered, is that 169 is unique to euro-Caucasians. People of African, Chinese, Native American and Asian ethnicity don't and have never had it."

"Jesus," said Natasha.

"So what you're saying is that only white Caucasians could be naturally immune?" asked Schaefer.

"Yes," summarised Johnson.

"I feel sick," said Natasha, feeling weak.

"As do I. But I do believe we need to tell everyone everything that we've found," replied Johnson.

"I guess this also means that unless our enemies vaccinated their whole population then the chances are it may have spread to them as well. God… the lunatics," said Natasha.

"Indeed. As Brecht said 'Don't rejoice in his defeat, you men. For though the world stood up and stopped the bastard, the bitch that bore him is on heat again,'" finished Johnson.

"We've prepped a report for Alex. I think we're done here. If it's OK with you I want to move on to Versailles," finished Johnson, stubbing out his cigarette into an overflowing empty MRE container.

CHAPTER 27

WHAT TO DO?

If you do not compete for allies and helpers, then you will be isolated with little help. If you do not foster your authority, then people will leave and the country will weaken.

Seven hundred kilometres from the Louvre, Hodgetts and Jean-Jacques' surveillance file was being played to Saint C's council and Alex's commanders. The strange group of armed men that Sanchez had tagged with the name The Dog Jutes had established their base of operations in the Chateau Gironde, a sixteenth-century, brilliant white, ornate castle that nestled in a forest 55 kilometres from Saint C. On the screens a series of outbuildings came into view, before the image panned to the right and focused on a courtyard in front of the chateau.

"Jesus, the place looks like a mini version of Versailles," observed Sanchez.

To the rear of the chateau were overgrown gardens. In the background were a series of lakes and statues. Several of the Jutes were patrolling the perimeter.

"It is, it was built by a cousin of the Duke of Orleans in the style of Versailles," said the Countess.

"It's also where I grew up," added Claudia in a voice so quiet that most of the people around the table didn't hear her.

"Say that again?" urged Sanchez, who was sitting next to her.

"It's my father's house. I haven't seen it for years. It's where I grew up," she repeated.

"You royalty as well then?" asked Galeago with a smile.

Before anyone could offer any more banter though, the image on the screen changed the mood in the room.

A young boy in his early teens was dragged into the courtyard and pushed to the ground. Around him stood a dozen civilians, also prisoners, their heads bowed in apparent shame. Two Rottweilers straining against their owners' leashes stood guard over the ensemble. Then a man wearing a long black cape strode arrogantly into view, drew a pistol and calmly shot the boy three times. He then turned to face the civilians to whom he made some sort of a speech.

"Sorry, the audio channel's bust," apologised Hodgetts.

"I wonder what he's telling them?" asked Robert from the council.

"Presumably giving them advice on behaviour," said Jones.

"Well, that didn't take us long. We've only just succeeded in wiping out most of the population and what's left seems to be already fucking each other over," stated Sanchez with venom.

"How many of these bastards are there?" asked Galeago.

"We reckon no more than twenty. Some of them are military, some are not," advised Jones.

"How do you know?" asked Robert from the town council.

"Little things, the way they hold their weapons; the ones that aren't military try and look tough, they wave them around like they're a trophy. Guard positions, that sort of thing. From what I've seen I think about three possibly four are military. The rest are just civilian bullies," said Claudia.

"Yeah, I reckon maybe four," agreed Jones.

"And the civilians?" asked Sanchez.

"Fourteen prisoners," said Hodgetts.

"So what are we going to do?" asked Alex, bringing the discussion to a head. "Let's go round the table."

"We get them out," said the Countess.

"Agreed, and fast. My team can do it tomorrow," said Sanchez.

"Well, to me it's simple. We can either drift through this existence ignoring such things, in which case we're helping establish this as the norm. Or we counter it with maximum force wherever we find it. We must strive to enforce basic rights. It's what underpins human behaviours and ultimately civilisation," offered the legal countenance of Pierre.

326

"And if we get weaker doing it? Say they're better than we think and we take a beating? We could call attention to ourselves and God knows what we'll end up having to face," argued Robert, who as ever remained cautious of any external contact.

Hodgetts told them about Germany and what Lieutenant Byrnes had said that had made them intervene. "Otherwise what the fuck's the point of carrying on at all?" he echoed.

"Get them out. And fast. That way we get stronger by fourteen," said Sanchez.

"I agree," came scattered mutterings from around the table.

The Countess now intervened. "Per our constitution we will not leave this room until we have a unanimous decision. I suggest we take a thirty-minute break. Get your arguments together. All those in favour of some form of intervention can use the ops centre. All those against intervention can stay in here. See you in thirty."

It took them another two hours of heated debate before they finally arrived at a unanimous decision. They would intervene. Sanchez would lead the assault using her newly trained team. She would be supported by Claudia and Hodgetts.

After the meeting Sanchez took Claudia to one side. "You OK with this?" she asked.

"Yeah. No worries. Why do you ask?"

"I just wondered why you were so quiet; you don't seem the type to let something like this go by, and we need you. You know the place inside out. Is there anything I should know?"

Claudia looked away and Sanchez could see tears rolling down her face. "Tell me."

"The boy who was shot. He was my younger half-brother. And..." she started sobbing uncontrollably. Sanchez put an arm around her.

"And one of the soldiers I recognised; he used to be the gamekeeper... A little shit called Arnoud. He... well, let's just say I attracted his attention for a while before I left for the Legion. I'll be fine and my team need the exposure.

"I just can't help thinking that if I'd been more honest with myself I may have gone out to search the chateau for him before and saved him."

"Or ended up a prisoner yourself, or dead," said Sanchez, feeling saddened that the only solace she could now offer in this world was one of comparing one human agony against another.

327

CHAPTER 28

EUROPEAN HUMAN GENETIC ARCHIVES

Confront them with annihilation, and they will then survive; plunge them into a deadly situation, and they will then live. When people fall into danger, they are then able to strive for victory.

It was just after midnight when they reached the Palace of Versailles. They approached it from across the landscaped gardens, driving around the lake and pulling the AFV off into cover in a wooded area alongside what was once a cafeteria. Sun umbrellas and chairs lay discarded and tattered on the ground. Despite the presence of the others, the sight made Natasha feel lonely. It was the same feeling as being the last pupil to be picked up after school. In front of them the palace, grounds and fountains were lit up and the sound of classical chamber music drifted around the statues and across the gravelled pathways towards them.

"Wow. Welcome to the party," said Gyan in awe.

"It's beautiful," said Tsang.

"Where's all the power from?" asked Natasha.

"Versailles was a showcase for a geothermal pilot about fifteen years ago," advised Dr Heymans. "They actually drilled the wells in the town square."

"Do you reckon anyone's living there?" asked O'Reilly.

"We'll lay up here tonight. Cold tack. We'll enter the palace in the morning. And I don't want anyone wandering off on a sightseeing trip. Let's get the perimeter up and then we'll hold a briefing," ordered Natasha.

"I don't like the look of this place. I know we've got no sign of any bad guys but it's lit up like Disney World, and anyone who's around here is eventually going to be drawn to the bright lights. Although Captain Johnson and the good Dr Heymans would argue that's a positive, I'm not so sure. I recommend we approach this like we're taking on an occupied target," advised Schaefer.

"I agree. I know we're impatient but there's no point in ending up dead," agreed Natasha.

"So any update on how long you're going to need?" Schaefer asked Johnson.

"Well, not yet. Corporal Raven can give you an update on where we are with the software."

"I've finished structuring a search program to match the gene 169 formats but it's going to take time. We're talking about some five hundred million personal genetic files, each of those has thirty thousand gene data points. We have to sift through that and match it to nearly a thousand reference points for 169," offered Raven.

"That's a lot of data to crunch," commented Natasha, running the maths.

"How long?" asked Schaefer.

"Running at a hundred gigahertz in parallel mode. A week," said Luc.

"A week?"

"Yes. A week. But that's the easy bit," said Byrnes joining in.

"Why? What's the difficult bit?" asked Schaefer.

"Getting the associated data for the matches. The system's going to be super secure. The laws that were instigated when the database was set up were specifically designed to prevent interested parties gaining genetic information on individuals. Put it this way, it was OK to use the group info as a whole for research and comparison purposes, maybe filtering on sex. But anything more, such as cross-referencing geographic locations, social groups and the like, was regarded as an infringement on personal rights. There were too many concerns that gene mapping would lead to linkages on other issues such as intelligence or propensity to develop a certain disease. All data that in the wrong hands could make someone a lot of money, like an insurance company," said Luc.

"Or lead to elitism," stated Tsang.

"Great. And the solution is?" asked Natasha, beginning to feel that the whole enterprise was beginning to get just too large.

"We don't know yet. We're going to have to see how the data is stored and linked. It'll definitely be there because the police, for example, have long relied on DNA matching and they were eventually empowered to access the database," offered Byrnes.

"What about trying just that?" asked Natasha.

"What?" asked Byrnes, Raven and Luc in chorus.

"I don't know, maybe setting up a dummy DNA match request like the police would use but blank out all the profile data except gene 169?"

"Brilliant!" said Byrnes

"I like it," said Luc.

"So all we need to figure out is how to log in as a law enforcement officer," said Schaefer.

"Well, that and booting up the system and breaching the security," said Raven.

"How long for that?" asked Schaefer.

"Don't know, Captain. Could be a few hours or a few weeks. It depends on the security protocols."

"Jesus. So we're talking anything up to two weeks here," sighed Schaefer.

"Maybe," they replied in unison but rather noncommittally.

"Right. So what are our options?" asked Natasha, throwing the question at all of them.

"Any way you could shorten the run time?" asked Schaefer.

"I think I might have an idea on that. In structural engineering they use something called Cholesky decomposition to crunch big matrices. I wonder whether we could do the same here?" said Luc to Byrnes and Raven.

"A must, I would say, but in the meantime, as our commander Alex would say, we need to plan for the worst. Two weeks," finished Natasha.

Thirty minutes later Natasha sent a message to Alex using the chain of repeaters they'd positioned along their route from Saint C. Arrived. Need two weeks. Missing you. N.

*

At dawn they made their way by foot up to the palace. The DNA archives were housed in the royal chapel.

"Fuck me! Look at this place," said Byrnes as he walked in, his weapon at the ready but forgotten as he took in their surroundings.

Natasha stood in awe as she gazed at the brilliant white Roman columns that supported a curved roof adorned with bright gold and blue paintings. Morning sunlight still managed to flood in through the now dirty windows. On the far side, and above the altar, stood the famous gold leaf organ. In the foreground was what they had come for. On an enormous marble table were three state-of-the-art workstations whose screens flickered with screen savers that depicted the famous double DNA helix.

The only ugliness in the room was the sound of buzzing flies that alerted them to the presence of death. They found seven mummified bodies, all of whom they soon deduced had killed themselves with VX capsules. One body in particular caught Natasha's attention, a woman with grey-blonde hair who sat on the floor with her back against a column. Her eye sockets were empty and her mouth was wide open as if in the midst of a silent scream. Before Natasha could force herself to look away a large black fly emerged from her mouth before lazily taking off into the air. Portable computers, notebooks, food canisters, medicine and morphine vials lay scattered around the floor.

"They must have been a medical research team working on APP," said Johnson, lighting a cigarette.

"You know, I think we might bury them," said Natasha.

Johnson and Tsang looked at one another.

"You are right. I think we're becoming too immune to death," replied Tsang.

"Don't worry about it. As long as one of us remembers not to, we won't forget about being human," replied Natasha.

Schaefer strode into the room with Gyan at his side. "How's it looking?"

"Good. We've found the main consoles," replied Johnson, pointing to the displays.

"How we fixed on securing a perimeter?" asked Natasha.

"We've surveyed the area. The place is enormous. I don't think we can set a perimeter but we can put continuous four-hour watches up on the roof. Three rotating teams with passive sensors. That'll give us some warning if anyone comes near," replied Schaefer.

"Maybe we should kill the power to the grounds and the corridors. It might look nice but it's gonna screw up our passive sensors big time," offered Gyan.

"Won't that attract attention – if someone has been watching the place and suddenly all the lights go out?" asked Dr Heymans innocently.

"Agree. Let's leave them as is for the moment but find the breakers – if we get bounced we'll need to know how to kill the power. I'll take first watch. What about response plans?" asked Natasha.

"Corporal Stacey's going to bring the AFV up here and park it in the stables. That's our ace in the hole. We'll work up some plans but I think we first off need to stay low profile, no unnecessary wanderings outside the buildings, cold tack. All in all, if we get bumped at the moment I think the only option is to bug out," offered Schaefer.

"No. Absolutely not. If we get bumped we have to stand to on this one. This is it, Captain; the data here is the Holy Grail," stated Johnson.

Schaefer looked at Natasha for a decision.

"This is the Holy Grail," said Natasha, taking one of Johnson's cigarettes.

"I'll get something sorted," said Schaefer.

"Good. Now I know that the data is going to be the star of the show, but we need everyone sharp, so make sure everyone gets some rest between watches and does not stay glued to monitors watching progress and chitchatting," said Natasha.

*

Whilst Johnson looked after removing the dead, Natasha went to see how O'Reilly was getting on with setting up the messing and sleeping quarters.

"What a place. This will do nicely," said O'Reilly as they made their way along the Hall of Mirrors, or 'Galerie des Glaces'.

The corridor was 240 feet long, 40 feet high and 35 feet wide. The ceiling was curved and beautifully painted with scenes of kings, angels and warriors, surrounded by heavy gold gilt. Massive chandeliers on long cables hung to within 10 feet of the parquet floor. Between each of the one hundred-plus mirrors sat a statue of a woman holding an oversized candelabra. Ornate furniture dotted the hallway.

Dr Heymans, carrying his personal kit and sleeping bag, caught up with them. "It's impressive, isn't it? You know, at the end of the corridor are the rooms where the treaty of peace between Germany and the Allies after World War One was signed. They're called the peace and war rooms," he told them.

"Apt, I would say. Very apt," commented O'Reilly.

332

O'Reilly finally chose the Sun King's quarters as their sleeping quarters and mess, and when Natasha went back a little later to check on the set-up she had to stifle a smile as she entered the room. Sleeping bags were laid out on the big four-poster beds and, whilst Tsang unpacked her kit, Stacey reclined on a chaise-longue cleaning his weapon's sights and offered his opinion.

"I always knew that I had royal blood. Have you seen the wallpaper in this place? It's silk. I reckon I'll go and get meself a bath – have you seen the thing? It's the size of a swimming pool!"

"You need one," joked Tsang.

"You offering to join me, Lieutenant?"

"In your dreams, big boy. In your dreams," she smiled.

"Nice dining table," commented Natasha looking at an enormous dining table adorned with ornate silverware.

"Ah yes, Captain. Corporal Stacey and Lieutenant Tsang felt that we should perhaps take the opportunity to dine in some style," offered O'Reilly.

"Hey, Captain, do you know where the word quarantine came from?" Stacey asked.

"I do indeed, Corporal, it comes from the Italian *quaranta giorni* which translated means forty days. For some reason that's what they thought was a minimum period to ensure that a potential plague carrier should be confined to ensure they were not infected. Why?" replied Natasha, intrigued with Stacey's question.

"Just wondering. I was reading the report that Captain Johnson put together."

Satisfied they were getting themselves sorted, Natasha started the first four-hour watch from the palace roof together with Piper, Frost and Cook. Each of them was responsible for one quadrant of the surrounding approaches and would rotate positions every fifteen minutes. Schaefer had already mapped the surrounding topography, defilades and most probable approach routes for insurgents.

They'd positioned passive sensors throughout the grounds to monitor thermal, e-sig, sound and movement. As Natasha reviewed the set-up and alarm settings she was impressed. The palace grounds had large infrared, electro-magnetic and acoustic fluctuations, mainly from the fountains, the accompanying music and lights but also from animals. All of these had been recorded and mapped and the surveillance algorithms adjusted to filter them out. Schaefer had also used an old trick that Hodgetts had taught him and recorded the sound of boots on the gravel pathways and dry vegetation. These were now uploaded and part of the surveillance algorithms and would now trigger an alarm directly on their weapons' sights. In theory, all they'd have to do was sit back and wait.

Schaefer had also insisted that the lookouts position themselves directly in front of the large and powerful floodlights that lit up the grounds. At first she thought this would silhouette them, but when she'd gone down to the grounds herself and tried to detect her own team she agreed with the arrangement. The power of the lights simply overwhelmed their profiles.

Natasha settled down on her watch. A shooting star sped across the horizon.

It was just after midnight and they were preparing to stand down and hand over to the next team when the threat receivers in Cook's quadrant lit up and brought them to stand to positions.

"Sit rep?" asked Natasha.

"Dogs. There's a pack that crossed the main avenue; must have found the bodies we buried today. They look like they're digging. Yep, a dog's best friend. Bones."

"Jesus. Poor bastards. Even in death they can't get any rest," commented Frost.

Schaefer arrived with the next watch and Natasha went down to the chapel to see how Johnson and the others were progressing.

"So, how we doing?" she asked Byrnes, who was busy tapping away on a keyboard.

"Morning, Captain, good news, for once we're in luck. It looks like we've got free directory access to all data. We think they must have overridden all the protective protocols during the outbreak. It's going to be a lot quicker than we thought. Raven's got the search routines open already."

"Hi, Captain. I've got a raw data file here. Format's a walk in the park. Top level is personal profile, second is hereditary, third is medical and fourth is DNA gene mapping," reported Raven in an excited voice.

"In effect all we need to do is configure our search program to match the database format and set up an offline storage unit and we're ready," added Luc with confidence.

"It's great," said Johnson still wearing his equipment harness, helmet and carrying his weapon as he'd obviously been so engrossed in getting things underway.

"Jesus, why don't you sit down and rest? You'll burn yourself out. We've a long way to go," Natasha said.

In response, Johnson sighed, pulled out a cigarette and found a large cinema-style chair into which he slumped.

"I know, I know. But this is important."

"All right… we're initiating the search and mapping algorithm. Output will be on the left screens," said Luc.

Natasha looked at the screens. The displays they'd set up were simple:

RUN STATUS	
Total File Entries	636,237,389
Total Number File Entries Reviewed	0
Total Number Deceased File Entries	0
Total Matched for Gene 169	0
Survivability Index	0%
Predicted Number of Gene 169 Survivors	0
Estimated Run Time (days)	6.48
Remaining File Entries	636,237,389
Remaining Run Time (days)	6.48

"How come we've got so many records? I thought the population that had signed up to the database was more like five hundred-odd million?" she asked.

"The records include those of the deceased; the database has been going for some twenty-odd years now," advised Dr Heymans.

"Will it take longer to process?"

"We've set our search program to skip to the next file if the birth date exceeds one hundred years. So there shouldn't be any impact," replied Byrnes.

"Right. Well, I suppose I better get some sleep," said Natasha, settling down on the floor next to Johnson to watch the screens.

"You want a coffee?" asked Johnson in a voice that told her he had no intention of moving.

"I'll get it," she replied, not moving either.

*

As the hours rolled past they settled into a routine with the summary screens in the data centre becoming a ritual of observation as each watch finished and took the opportunity to observe the progress.

"Can we look at what we've got so far?" asked Natasha.

"Sure," said Byrnes. "We've got an offline database already up and running... Here, have a look."

RUN STATUS	
Total File Entries	636,237,389
Reviewed File Entries	127,640,217
Number of Deceased File Entries	12,398,037
Total Matched for Gene 169	156,997
Survivability Index	0.123%
Predicted Number of Survivors	707,497
Run Time to Date (days)	1.3
Remaining Run Time (days)	5.2

Demographic analysis after 5.2 days run time				
Age	Male		Female	
0-18 yrs	9,671	17%	17,283	22%
19-30 yrs	9,102	16%	7,070	9%
31-50 yrs	13,653	24%	12,570	16%
>50 yrs	24,462	43%	41,637	53%
Total	56,889	42%	78,561	58%

Potential survivors	135,450
Families	12,789
Part of families	31,662

"Well, the boys will be happy, there's more women than men. Any idea why?" she asked.

"No idea. It's something that I want to have a look at later. We're also beginning to map out who's where..." Tsang advised.

AREA	NUMBER OF GENE 169 HOLDERS	PERCENTGAE OF TOTAL SURVIVORS	PERCENTAGE OF ORIGINAL POPULATION	COUNTRY POPULATION (MILLIONS)
AUSTRIA	3,352	2.5	0.04	8.6
BELGIUM	2,999	2.2	0.03	11.3
BRITAIN	12,752	9.4	0.02	65.1
BULGARIA	4,746	3.5	0.07	7.2
CROATIA	1,727	1.3	0.04	4.2
CZECH REP	4,343	3.2	0.04	10.5
DENMARK	1,726	1.3	0.03	5.7
FINLAND	1,228	0.9	0.02	5.5
FRANCE	12,056	8.9	0.02	67.0
GERMANY	10,172	7.5	0.01	82.9
GREECE	3,194	2.4	0.03	10.8
HOLLAND	5,236	3.9	0.03	17.0
HUNGARY	2,971	2.2	0.03	9.8
IRELAND	2,636	1.9	0.06	4.6
ITALY	8,410	6.2	0.01	61.0
LATVIA	628	0.5	0.03	2.0
LITHUANIA	700	0.5	0.02	2.9
NORWAY	17,981	13.3	0.35	5.2
POLAND	5,062	3.7	0.01	38.5
PORTUGAL	2,460	1.8	0.02	10.3
ROMANIA	3,735	2.8	0.02	19.8
SERBIA	1,499	1.1	0.02	7.1
SLOVAKIA	1,313	1.0	0.02	5.4
SLOVENIA	1,376	1.0	0.07	2.1
SPAIN	7,484	5.5	0.02	46.4
SWEDEN	11,357	8.4	0.11	9.9
SWITZERLAND	2,287	1.7	0.03	8.3
ST CHRISTOBEL	79	0.1	12.91	0.0
OTHER	1,696	1.2	0.46	2.5
TOTAL	135,205	100.0	0.03	531.6

"Oh boy, impressive, but it makes you feel a little scared at the value of the information we've accumulated."

"Yeah, but the scary thing is what else we've found in the database... Looks like our governments also collated a lot of other information that perhaps they shouldn't have," said Luc.

"Such as?" asked Natasha.

"Oh, little things like medical records, education, occupation, income, voting trends," added Tsang with a hint of anger in her voice.

"I always knew it," said Frost pulling her blonde hair back into a bun and shaking her head in disgust. "Every government there's ever been has never told the whole truth. They're all conniving, power-hungry bastards who are meant to serve us but always seem to end up thinking they rule us."

"Yeah, but thank God they did. Without the data they collected all we'd have is a series of names, instead what we've got is a complete profile. Name, address and skills," continued Raven. "We can target people with specific skill sets in a region, anything from farming to marketing."

"How come some countries seem to have a disproportionate number of gene 169 matches compared to their populations?" asked Natasha.

"I think it's something to do with the great plagues and the way they spread. For example the Vikings, or the Norwegians as we know them now, were almost wiped out by three successive plagues. It was brought back by their mercenaries who were fighting in Constantinople and beyond. Ninety per cent of their population lived by the coast in dense population centres. So just about anyone who was left was effectively immune. The survivors effectively formed the base of the resurgent population. They were the ones with gene 169," advised Tsang.

"Whereas in somewhere like Poland or France, where population centres were more spread out, they didn't have such attrition and hence the proportion of gene 169 carriers had less of an impact," added Johnson.

"You know, I've been thinking about something else," said Luc.

"What?" asked Johnson.

"Well, I think once we've done this we should also check out some of the other centres. For example there is the Global Nordic Seed Bank in Svalbard in northern Norway. It's where they've stored samples and genetic info for many plants."

"I like it. There's probably quite a few such centres that we could access," interjected Tsang.

"Sounds great. But can we finish this one first?" replied Natasha, smiling to herself as she imagined trying to persuade any of the squadron to return to northern Norway.

*

As the days passed, Natasha and Schaefer relaxed their curfew and allowed each of the team a one-hour break to explore the grounds around the palace.

Natasha got to know Frost well during their watches and enjoyed her company. She was apparently something of an expert in French history. One afternoon as they strolled past the enormous maze, the gravel crunching beneath their boots, Frost pointed out a small white house with shutters.

"That's where Marie Antoinette took her Swedish lover, a young count."

"Really, what about the king?"

"Legend has it, he knew. But he'd always struggled to live up to Marie's passion for life."

"Men, how typical!" responded Natasha with a laugh.

"Well, according to Sanchez, I don't think you and the Major will have that problem," laughed Frost.

Natasha blushed. "Does anyone not know?"

"I think we knew before you two did. Come on, let's go and explore."

They went across to the small neo-classical building; the French windows were open and the curtains were blowing gently in the breeze. Suddenly they heard a shriek from inside. Natasha and Frost instinctively brought their weapons up to their shoulders and flicked the safety switches to off. Natasha moved to the left and Frost to the right as they approached the open doors. Another shriek followed by a deep sigh came from inside. They looked quizzically at one another and Natasha signalled Frost to cover her as she used her weapon to move the billowing curtains aside and look inside.

It took her eyes a second to adjust to the gloom inside the room. Johnson lay on his back on an ornate double bed – he was naked. Sitting astride him was Tsang who was bouncing up and down, her long dark hair swaying from side to side. Before Natasha could back out, Johnson looked directly at her and held her gaze for a second before smiling.

"You OK, Captain?" asked Frost as Natasha backed away.

"Fine. False alarm. Why don't we go and have a look at the fountains?" she said as another series of shrieks came from inside. Frost looked at her inquisitively for a moment before realising what was going on.

"Who?" she whispered, smiling.

"Captain Johnson and Lieutenant Tsang," she whispered back.

"Let's walk up to the big lake. It's where they used to have massive firework displays," laughed Frost.

CHAPTER 29

RESTORING SOME HUMANITY

The general who wins the battle makes many calculations in his temple before the battle is fought.

Fifty-two kilometres from Saint C, it was raining heavily with a dark morning sky. Sanchez was 2 kilometres from the Chateau Gironde, sheltering in dense forest. Rainwater dripped from the trees above her onto her combat smock making loud splatting noises. She felt warm, dry, alive, focused on doing right, and in love. Life, she reckoned, didn't get much better. Her personal music stream automatically cut off as a sit rep burst transmission came in. Mozart's 'Symphony No 40', a present from Schaefer, faded as a silicon-generated voice told her that Claudia's team had eliminated the Jutes patrol. Six Jutes were down with no friends hurt.

Sanchez was relieved; she'd a lot of confidence in Claudia but had been worried that her teams had never seen action before and an ambush was a tough way to start combat. But Claudia had planned well. They'd learnt that the Jutes' patrols followed a regular and predictable pattern, moving in close single-file formation, and often looking more like a gang out for some fun rather than a serious military force. Claudia had positioned one of her squads in the undergrowth no more than 5 metres from the track the patrol used, and engaged at close range. On either flank of the ambush team she'd positioned two other squads to catch any runners. Finally, on the opposite side of the track some 20 metres into the undergrowth she'd set up a line of anti-personnel mines just in case anyone made a dash for it into the rough. With the patrol eliminated Sanchez now had tactical superiority, as Schaefer would have said. She turned her music back on and settled down to wait for Claudia and her team to move to the chateau and their forward attack positions.

The music had just re-engaged when Hodgetts tapped her on the shoulder.

"You hungry?" he mouthed.

"Yeah, we got any of the scrambled egg and bacon?"

"For you, my princess," he replied with a smile, handing her the MRE.

It was just over an hour later when the next message from Claudia announced that her team was in position.

"OK. Claudia's in position. Let's get ourselves booted and spurred," she said to Hodgetts and the others. They'd brought with them some Jute-like suits which they'd wear. The plan she would use was based on an off-the-shelf hostage rescue outline she'd learnt years ago. Step one: take out as many Jutes as possible outside the camp. Step two: set up a ring of sharpshooters around the camp. Step three: infiltrate the camp with a sniper team. Step four: launch a coordinated sniper assault and kill all the remaining Jutes.

Another burst transmission arrived. Claudia's sharpshooters had eyes on and were waiting further instructions. Sanchez acknowledged. Step two complete.

Step three was to be undertaken by Hodgetts, Sanchez and Wilcox. Now dressed in black jumpsuits with hoods, they looked to any casual observer just like any old Jute. As they now walked calmly across the gravel courtyard towards the chateau, Sanchez concentrated on behaving like the Jutes she'd seen and introduced a little swagger to her step. They attracted a couple of glances from some of the guards but nothing more; maybe the rain was just too much of a deterrent to make small talk, she thought.

They reached a small side door and entered the chateau. She could smell cooking. Ignoring the crash and clanking of saucepans from along the corridor, they found the narrow spiral stone staircase that Claudia had told them about and climbed up to the third floor. A corridor led past what Sanchez guessed must have once been the servant quarters. Outside the second door, they paused. They finished fitting the silencers to their weapons and making them ready before Sanchez knocked on the door.

"Yeah," came a response.

Bloody typical, she thought, *fifty-odd rooms and this one is occupied.*

"Room service," she answered.

"Fuck off," came the response.

Hodgetts tried the handle, it opened and Sanchez immediately slipped past Hodgetts into the room. It took her less than a second to get situational awareness. The room smelt musty. A fat, naked man in his mid-fifties lay sprawled across a double bed with grey and dirty sheets. A young girl of no more than sixteen years old lay naked next to him. Sanchez fired two silenced rounds at Fat Man, hitting him twice in the forehead. As Fat Man's arm flopped down across the girl's face, she started screaming.

Sanchez left her to Hodgetts to sort out as she crossed the room to the window and looked out through a year of grime at the scene below. The view was perfect; two floors below them and across the main courtyard were the outbuildings in which the prisoners were being kept.

"Please be quiet," she said turning to the girl who had moved herself to the opposite end of the bed from Fat Man and curled herself up into what she remembered Natasha had described to her as the female embryo position. *Jesus,* she thought to herself, *I'm getting used to this.*

"We're here to help. Get something to wear and be quiet," she said in a calm but firm voice. She noticed the girl's face and body were badly bruised. "Fat Man won't be hurting you anymore." Although she doubted the girl understood English, at least the screaming stopped and she now just sobbed.

"Wilcox. Shut the door and lock it. Let's set ourselves up," she ordered, moving back to the window.

She sent Claudia a burst transmission. "One Jute down. Total now seven down. Wait out."

They had to wait another hour before an old ship's bell rang ten times, signalling that the daily parade as they had nicknamed the event was about to start.

In the courtyard below, despite the rain, the Jutes herded some of their prisoners into a line. The Jutes' leader then appeared, escorted by two large characters whom Sanchez thought were probably his personal guards.

"Well, if it isn't Bat Man himself. I'm assuming he'll be number one?" said Hodgetts in a satisfied tone, referring to the man they had seen on the video recon shoot Claudia's half-brother.

343

Sanchez counted the number of Jutes now assembled. "I've got eyes on eight."

"Concur. Plus one in the doorway at three o'clock," said Wilcox, who was scanning the area using his Cyclops.

"Nine total remaining?"

"Agree. Upload and cross-link," replied Hodgetts.

"Atavistic," said Sanchez.

"Say again?" replied Hodgetts.

"Atavistic. It means displaying the kind of behaviour long since suppressed by society's rules. That's this lot."

"Fucking wankers, more like it," replied Wilcox as he cross-loaded targets to both Hodgett's and Sanchez's weapons. Their sights would now automatically track the targets and recognise and record when a target had been dropped.

"I see I've been given all the work to do," mumbled Hodgetts as he studied his weapon display. Wilcox had assigned him four targets and proposed a fire solution that would offer him the best chance of success. Hodgetts agreed with the plan and confirmed with the computer.

"Well, I thought those particular four required a professional touch. The lag between targets one and two could result in dispersal. Don't want any of the buggers going to ground."

Sanchez ignored the banter and sent another burst transmission to Claudia. "We have eyes on seven, all in courtyard. Short window. How many you?"

The response was immediate. "We have eyes on three. Ready."

Sanchez ran the maths. A maximum of twenty to start with; seven down, that left thirteen. Eyes on totalled ten. That was good enough.

She sent a reply. "Execute in thirty seconds. On my mark, mark."

As the thirty seconds ran out, Sanchez fired. Bat Man's head exploded and before he had flopped face down into a puddle she fired again. Within fifteen seconds it was over; her weapon's sights verified there were no targets left.

"All targets down. Nice shooting," commented Wilcox.

She sent Claudia an update. "Seven down. Total down now fourteen. How did it go your side?"

"Two down. One escaped. Total down now sixteen. Proceeding to chateau to secure hostages," came the reply.

"Let's clear this floor. We've got maybe four of these shitbags left. Wilcox, please stay with... What's your name?" she asked the girl, who was now standing watching them.

"Whatever," said Sanchez, opening the door and checking the corridor.

"*Comment vous appelez-vous?*" asked Wilcox.

"Simone," came the reply.

"*Bonne. Restez ici avec moi. Pour un instant,*" Wilcox told the girl.

Sanchez and Hodgetts moved along the corridor checking each room in turn. All were empty. A series of explosions from stun grenades whipped up the spiral staircase as Claudia's team started to clear the lower floors. There were more explosions, shooting, some shouting and finally silence.

An update came in from Claudia. "Ground, first and second floors secure. Three Jutes down. Total now nineteen down. One possible remaining."

Thirty minutes later, with no sign of any other hostiles, Sanchez declared the area secure.

"Are my ears fucked again or can I hear music?" asked Hodgetts as he accompanied Sanchez to the main room, where Claudia had mustered the civilians.

"No, that's Beethoven," replied Sanchez, recognising the piece from some of the music that Schaefer had been introducing her to.

They entered the main living room to find Claudia playing a grand piano, surrounded by some of her team and a dishevelled group of civilians.

"Sorry, but I couldn't resist the temptation; it's been nearly twenty years since I sat in this seat."

"What are we going to do with the dead?" asked Wilcox.

"I want to find out where they dumped my brother and bury him properly," replied Claudia.

"What about the rest of them?"

"Leave them outside," said Sanchez.

"And their pets? They've got four of those black Rottweiler dogs in a room downstairs," he continued.

"Shoot them. We don't want those bastards breeding. But before we do let's start with the introductions."

CHAPTER 30

WHO'S WON?

So what kills the enemy is anger.

Thunder and lightning were making it difficult to hear the communications from the watch on the roof of the Palace of Versailles.

"Say again," requested Natasha, becoming frustrated.

"Nah. Nothing. I thought for a minute we had a hostile e-sig. Probably the storm. The threat matrix is green. I've rain all over the repeater screens and the storms are causing flaring," replied Schaefer from the roof.

"You sure?" she asked him.

"We're running a refresh and historical now. Oh shit. We've got threat confirmed. Encrypted comms traffic, outgoing and incoming. Localised. In the grounds."

"All stations. All stations. This is Six. Stand to. I say again Stand to," ordered Natasha using their radios for the first time.

"Fuck it. Of all the places, why here?" muttered Johnson, listening to the exchange between Natasha and Schaefer from his armchair in the data room.

"It's Versailles, Captain. Just the name warrants a presence," said Byrnes looking up from his console. "Nice trick, though, coming in under the cover of this storm."

O'Reilly, Zimbabwe, Colins and Stacey, who'd been watching a movie about Marie Antoinette, rushed into the chapel pulling on their equipment harnesses and body armour.

There was an unmistakable sound of a grenade explosion.

"Six. This is Alpha One. Ground floor. Main entrance. We've got two plus bandits in the nest. How copy?" reported Gyan.

There were more explosions followed by automatic gun fire.

Natasha tried to make sense of the situation.

"Raven, give me a sit rep," Natasha asked Raven, who was collating and integrating the available data from around the palace.

"I can't get a read on who is where. I'm just getting fuzz. Nothing from Alpha Three," said Raven as he tried resetting the filters to bring them online.

"All stations. This is Six. Listen up. I need a report by station."

"Six, this is Alpha One. Standby. We're trying. Wait out," came Schaefer's voice as up on the roof they tried to make sense of the sensor data streams.

"Six, this is Alpha Two..." The link faded to static.

Their comms sets crackled again as Schaefer reported in. "Six, this is Alpha One. We estimate five only bandits inside palace. Say again five bandits. Two on first floor, *Galerie des Glaces*. Others no known location. No sign of immediate support. Say again, no sign of immediate support."

"All stations, this is Six. Alpha One will stay on station until I give the command to start a sweep down from the top. Alpha Two, if you read, maintain your pos. I will take Alpha Four and sweep lower levels and try and hook up with Three who is not responding. Lieutenant Byrnes will man the centre together with Corporal Raven, Captain Johnson and Lieutenant Tsang. We're going to kill the power. We'll use Cyclops," ordered Natasha.

"Fucking A! It's about time we went hot again. I'm sick of creeping around the place on cold tack," said O'Reilly.

"Captain Johnson, Lieutenant Tsang, Luc, Dr Heymans, pick up your weapons and make them ready. This is your data. Guard it," continued Natasha.

Natasha led O'Reilly, Zimbabwe, Colins and Stacey up onto the first floor. As they entered the Hall of Mirrors they came under fire. Natasha pulled back into an alcove for cover as bullets thudded into the wall in front of her.

"Eleven o'clock. Third doorway," advised Zimbabwe over the net with a calmness that Natasha found extraordinary.

As she tried to work out which doorway Zimbabwe was talking about, there was an explosion and a chandelier crashed to the floor, sending billowing clouds of plaster dust into the air. A golden head from one of the corridor's statues rolled along the floor towards her.

"There's two of them. Three doors up," she replied, spotting a figure retreat into another room further along the corridor. She didn't get a response. She asked for a radio check. Her headset was dead. She checked the status; all the lights were green. They must be jamming. She signed to the others that she and Colins would clear the room, the others should stay and cover.

Zim, Stacey and O'Reilly started pumping rounds into the doorway. Natasha and Colins broke cover and covered the distance to the doorway quickly. Her heart was pounding as she took up position on one side of it whilst Colins bomb burst into the room. Natasha followed him a split second later, rolling to the left before lying prone, searching for targets.

She had just taken in the layout of the huge room, which strangely seemed to contain not much more than a very small antique writing desk with a chair either side of it, when a fin-stabilised ceramic round travelling at more than 2,500 metres a second hit Colins in the chest. The round lost one of its fins as it penetrated his armour and started tumbling about two axes. It continued like this as it passed through his right lung, after which it struck his spinal column and then bounced backwards through his heart before finally exiting the front of his chest and coming to rest on the inside of his body armour.

What Natasha couldn't know was how Colins felt as he'd died. His first realisation that he'd been shot was when his spinal cord deformed from the impact of the round, causing the nerve bundle in the cord to short circuit and his knees to buckle involuntarily. Finding himself lying on the floor with the sensation of pins and needles in his hands and feet, he tried to untangle the chain of events that had occurred. This confusion lasted for a few seconds before the drop in blood pressure from his broken heart drained his brain of blood and he blacked out whilst for some reason recalling with fantastic clarity the smell of a teenage girlfriend's perfume.

Natasha dived to her left and rolled; as she came back up into a firing position she collided with someone, knocking him to the floor, his weapon falling to one side.

"Don't fucking move! Don't you dare," she screamed, pointing her weapon at the figure in front of her.

The figure simply lay on his back and looked at her through his visor.

Stacey, Zimbabwe and O'Reilly rushed into the room. Whilst Stacey checked over Colins' body, O'Reilly and Zimbabwe covered Natasha's captive who lay on his back, unmoving.

Natasha tried her radio again. "This is Six. Alpha Four has a man down. Hall of Mirrors. One X-ray prisoner."

This time she got a response. "Roger. Medics en route," replied Byrnes.

Natasha went over to Stacey. "He's gone," said Stacey, standing up. Before she could reply her Cyclops started whining, indicating she was being painted by a laser target designator. She dove to her right and the warning tone subsided.

"Stacey's down!" shouted Zimbabwe. "Shot came from outside. Sniper."

Natasha looked to her left. Stacey was on the floor clutching his neck. Her thermal imaging registered the regular spurts of blood that erupted as a small white fountain.

A phosphorous grenade exploded in an airburst raining gilt plaster work and dollops of burning phosphorus down from the ceiling. She saw a splash of it land on Stacey's arm and burn through his Nomex suit into his flesh. She could only imagine the pain he was in as the smell of burnt meat penetrated her plaster dust-clogged nostrils.

"All stations, this is Six. Alpha Four has second man down. We've got a shooter outside in the grounds. How copy?"

Through a burst of static she heard Schaefer's calm voice. "Six, this is Alpha One. We have eyes on… one X-ray down in the maze. How copy?"

"Six copies. Confirm shooter down. We need a medic."

Her heart was racing as she and O'Reilly dragged Stacey clear of the doorway and into cover. She slipped on a pool of blood and fell. O'Reilly started applying pressure to Stacey's throat in an effort to stem the spurting blood. A spurt of blood sprayed Natasha's face and the familiar taste of iron brought back memories of the crash. A large piece of one of the broken wall mirrors in the corridor fell down and lay in the doorway, picking up their reflections. More rounds slammed into the floor around them.

"All stations, this is Six. Alpha Four has more incoming. Hall of Mirrors. How copy?" All Natasha got in return was static again.

"Fuck it. The comms keep coming and going."

"Jesus, anyone got any bicarbonate solution for his arm? That fucking stuff is burning right through it," asked O'Reilly.

Natasha checked her personal medical pack and pulled out a toothpaste tube of the liquid that would help neutralise the phosphorous. She squirted it onto the wound, almost vomiting with the smell of the burning flesh.

Her Cyclops whined again and several more bursts of gunfire slapped into the plaster wall next to them, bringing more clouds of plaster dust.

"Zim. Shoot the fucker," shouted O'Reilly as he continued to try and stem the blood flow from Stacey.

"Who, the prisoner or the one who's shooting at us?" replied Zimbabwe from across the room.

"Jesus! Both of them if necessary."

Natasha stifled her surprise as Zimbabwe casually shot their prisoner in both knees before crawling to the doorway where he started to return the incoming fire, the hiss of the silencer belying the amount of outgoing rounds as he emptied an entire magazine into the night.

"Don't you worry, me old mate. You'll be fine. The Doc's en route. You got your crystals?" O'Reilly asked Stacey, referring to the freeze-dried blood. Stacey pointed to a pouch then gagged on his own blood. Natasha could see he was going into shock.

"Stay with me," pleaded O'Reilly.

Johnson and Tsang arrived, diving into the room and cover as Zimbabwe continued firing into the night. Tsang opened the trauma kit.

"Lieutenant, get me the HSS kit and two plasma bags. Mr O'Reilly, please let go of him and mix up two litres of blood and five hundred mils of anti-shock," said Johnson, as he took over from O'Reilly.

Johnson took a scalpel and sliced away some of the flesh around the wound. Natasha could see the blood flow was getting weaker; Stacey was bleeding out.

"Stay lively, mate. Two minutes and you'll be OK. I'm just gonna get your spare blood hooked up," said O'Reilly.

Natasha could see that O'Reilly was crying.

"Three mil tear, jugular. Lieutenant, clamps and a ten-mil HSS. I'll clamp, you insert. Private O'Reilly, you can plug him in now, but no pressure, keep the pump off, we're going to need the artery depressurised whilst we repair it. Captain. I need some light please," advised Johnson in a voice that oozed a calm that only trauma surgeons can muster. Another mirror shattered as more incoming rounds pummelled the corridor.

Natasha held a penlight to the wound as Johnson clamped the artery either side of the tear and then flushed the area with plasma to get a better view of the tear in the artery itself. Tsang then inserted a small white flexible tube into the artery through the tear.

The sound of assault rifle fire echoed around the corridor from somewhere else in the palace.

"Zim. Keep an eye on our friend," said Natasha, referring to their prisoner.

"Don't worry, I've got your backs. The shooter's either bugged out or is down."

"Laser," ordered Tsang as she checked the position of the repair. Johnson handed her the small device and she proceeded to play it across the repair.

"The heat from the laser will activate an array of nano hooks on the tube I put inside the artery which will bind it to the artery wall. It's a bit like fixing a leak. Frequency two. Outer sleeve please, Captain. Now I'll repeat the process, this time for the outer sleeve which will fuse the two halves together as well as deploying more hooks. Simple, eh? The whole assembly will mesh and grow into being an integral part of the artery," said Tsang, giving them a running commentary.

"Good job. I'll stitch and bandage. Give him sixty seconds then adrenaline," said Johnson.

Frost and Piper arrived.

"Glad you two could make it. Can you look after him?" asked Natasha pointing to the prisoner.

"Frosty, you got any plasticuffs?" asked Zimbabwe.

"Of course," she replied, fishing some out of her smock. "I always keep a supply for prisoners," she replied sarcastically.

"Looks like he might need a stretcher, look at his knees… Lieutenant Tsang, could you have a look at him?" asked Piper.

Natasha tried her radio again. "All stations, this is Six. Alpha Four has one SWIA, one KIA, one POW. We have Frost and Piper with us. How copy?"

"Alpha One copies."

"Six. This is Byrnes. We still have nothing on Alpha Three."

"Roger that. We can hear firing from somewhere inside the palace. We need to sort out our shit here then we'll move to try and hook up with Alpha Three. Wait out."

"We need to stop the blood loss. His left knee is busted up pretty bad. But he can wait a moment," said Tsang, looking over their prisoner.

"Well, fuck me, you're a long way from home, mate. Just not your day, is it? You see the unit insignia? He belongs to a regiment called the Arch

Angels. Elite special forces. We ran up against them several years ago in Vladivostok," said Piper.

Their headphones crackled. "All stations. This is One. We monitored some comms traffic, incoming and outgoing. They're plugged into a wider net, but how far away their friends are and what strength, no idea," reported Schaefer.

Natasha studied the prisoner; he was in his early thirties, had a small black beard and jet black, raven-like eyes. He had the shoulder tabs of a lieutenant and was staring at Frost. Natasha started to feel uncomfortable. She remembered what Sanchez had told her about trusting her instincts.

"Don't move!" she shouted. A childhood memory flashed before her, as she remembered once being left alone at night-time when her parents went next door to their neighbours. She managed to convince herself that there were burglars in the house and became so frightened that she'd pretended she was talking to several people in an effort to let the burglars know she wasn't alone.

Then the prisoner spoke to them. "You still don't get it, do you? You've lost. Your society and everything it stands for is finished. All that's left is to finish you off. A mopping-up operation. That's all," he said in deep broken English.

"Mmmm," sighed Natasha. "What you maybe don't realise is that there are two 'mopping-up operations', as you call them, going on. Yours and ours. Nobody has won. Everyone has lost. Human kind is in danger of extinction. A simple truth."

"That's your view," he replied, still staring at Frost as he reached for a toggle on his jacket. Natasha couldn't stop him in time.

There was a blinding light but surreally no sound from the explosion as Natasha's Cyclops automatically shut off audio reception to protect her ears. She found herself lying on her back across the room from where she'd been standing, a cloud of plaster dust floating around the room waiting to envelop her. To her left Piper was also laying on his back but his leg was bent at a strange angle up behind his back and his head was missing. The dust began to envelop her, dropping little flecks of gold from the gilt into a pool of blood. She felt raindrops on the back of her neck; the window behind her must have been blown out, she thought. She checked herself for wounds, each leg and arm, knowing that severe trauma often went unnoticed by the victim for a while. She checked her stomach and head. She was OK. Winded but in one piece. The prisoner's head lay next to her, his eyes still open and a smile on his face.

A figure that turned out to be Frost staggered over to her, leaving a trail of bloody footprints in the white dust.

"I'm OK. It's just my trigger finger," reported Frost, holding up her hand. Johnson and Tsang joined them. Tsang checked Natasha whilst Johnson examined Frost.

"We'll get some regrowth on it," he announced, referring to the regenerative powder that the allies had been experimenting with for a few years based on an enzyme that was taken from pigs' bladders.

"Captain K, you're good to go. Bloody lucky," said Tsang.

"Six, this is Byrnes. We got through to Alpha Three. They're in the King's private staircase, eastern entrance. North wing. Heavy fire. How copy?"

Natasha pulled herself together. "Six copies. Advise Three we're on our way."

"Captain Johnson, Lieutenant Tsang, you take Frost and Stacey back to the ops centre. Zim, O'Reilly, follow me," ordered Natasha.

Natasha decided to move to the north wing outside rather than get bottled up in the corridors. Visibility was barely a hundred feet as the torrential rain coupled with thunder and the occasional lightning flash lit up the palace. The rain mixed with the plaster dust and ran in thick slime down her goggles and neck as she moved along the gravel pathway.

They reached the entrance to the north wing and ducked inside the ornate stone entrance. Almost immediately they came under heavy fire with rounds thudding into the sandstone block walls, sending clouds of dust across the hallway. She withdrew into an alcove with O'Reilly and Zimbabwe on the opposite side. She reckoned there were at least two enemy up on the first-floor stone balustrade that had a commanding view of the entrance foyer and was shielded by thick Roman-style columns.

"This is Six. Stairway entrance. Ground floor. How copy, Alpha Three?"

"Reading you... One... Over," came a garbled message interspersed with hiss.

"Fuck this. I can't hear a damn thing. O'Reilly, you get any of that?" she shouted across to him.

O'Reilly shook his head and pointed to his ears, signalling that he had no comms either.

"Jesus. Fucking. Christ!" she muttered as several more well-aimed rounds broke a stone bust of what looked like the god Neptune next to her. She glanced at her PLD and comms status; it was flashing red then green, as the software searched in vain to find a way to establish a comms link.

"Can you get a clear shot from where you are?" she asked O'Reilly.

"The bastards are good, I can't break cover. I'll try and hit them with a grenade. I reckon I can bounce one off the column. Then you shoot them. You ready?"

"As ever."

O'Reilly's shot was perfect; the grenade bounced off a column and arced over the balustrade before detonating and showering the area with stone fragments and more dust.

Using the dust as cover, Natasha held her breath and stepped into the open area of the entrance hall, her weapon held tightly into her shoulder. Her threat display lit up, indicating a thermal image up above. She fired three rounds and the image tipped over the balustrade and fell to the black-and-white chequered marble floor across the hallway from her. Remembering what Sanchez had taught her, she fired twice more into the body.

There was more firing from upstairs – and then silence.

"Six, this is Alpha Three, how copy?" came Sergeant Gyan's voice.

"Sergeant Gyan. This is Six. Welcome back. Five by five," replied Natasha.

"One bandit down. King's staircase. Entrance clear. Others have bugged out into the royal theatre."

"Stand by. We're coming up to join you. Alpha One, this is Six. Start your sweep. How copy?"

There was no response.

"I don't fucking believe this," muttered Natasha before trying Byrnes and asking him to try and relay a message.

Natasha joined Gyan and Hicks at the entrance to the royal theatre. Gyan manoeuvred a small camera around the door and cross-loaded the feed to Natasha and the others. To the right of the entrance was the stage, to the left rows of plush velvet-covered chairs that formed the stalls. Above were three semi-circular balcony levels, and the royal boxes which jutted out from the sidewalls. The décor was blue and gold, heavy with ornate carvings and Roman columns.

"Nice place for a firefight," muttered Gyan.

Gyan selected split-screen on the Cyclops with thermal imaging and microwave short aperture close range radar on the right and visual spectrum overlaid with UV on the left.

"We've got a target, at our eight o'clock. Three levels up," he reported.

Natasha studied the imagery. "Let's put some grenades up there, I'm sick of this crap. Five AP should do it, DOI," she said referring to the anti-personnel grenades set for DOI, or detonate on impact.

"Brutal but I'm sure the audience would appreciate it," joked O'Reilly as he armed a grenade.

All five of them fired together and then dove for cover as the explosions seemed to bring most of the building down. Giant pieces of gold and blue ornate masonry rained down on them.

"Fuck me, we nearly blew up the whole fucking palace," said Gyan looking at the piles of debris.

"Well, at least our friend is toast," said O'Reilly pointing to a body.

Natasha, looking at the devastation, was also wondering how grenades could do so much damage when Gyan handed her a large piece of ornate balustrade.

"Look at this; the place is built out of papier mâché. It's not stone."

"Jesus. Lucky we didn't fire phos," said O'Reilly.

"All stations, this is Six, how do you read?"

Suddenly Natasha's comms cleared, the hiss of static gone as Schaefer and Byrnes reported in.

"All clear here."

CHAPTER 31

CITIZENS MAKE THE BEST SOLDIERS

Pretend inferiority and encourage his arrogance.

Sanchez was chatting with Jones over a coffee when Olly strode purposefully into the ops room in Saint C. "What's this about an armoured column?"

"Hodgetts' team came running back in about two hours ago. They spotted an enemy armoured column about a hundred and sixty klicks to the east of here. Looked like they were scouts for a bigger force. They're heading in this direction," replied Jones, calmly still sipping his coffee.

"Oh this is fucking great," exclaimed Olly. "First of all we had bloody Jutes and now we've an armoured fucking column. I thought the whole world had been wiped out and we were all that's left. Now all of a sudden anyone who's anyone seems to be turning up around here."

"The Major's called a sit rep in an hour. Grab a coffee," interjected Sanchez.

"How come you two are so laid back about this?"

"Well, in simple terms, we've done everything we can. Unless you can think of something we've forgotten?" replied Sanchez, using the smuggest voice she could muster. It was odd, she thought, that even though she was worried about the threat, she took consolation in the fact that she'd found love and that whatever happened no one could take that experience away from her.

"How long have we got?" asked Robert from the council, joining them together with Tommy Lee and Crockett, who dumped piles of papers on the ops map table.

"If they keep moving as they are and then deploy as they normally do, then it'll be tonight, maybe tomorrow morning," replied Jones.

"So the time's come. We either face our nemesis here or we leave and face it another day. It's just taken a little less time than we reckoned. What's the latest analysis say?" asked Tommy Lee.

"Same as all our sims before. Best chance is to adhere to our plan. We engage them here. If we take out this lot, then it should buy us enough time to grow even stronger. There will be more of them out there but, these being the first, I reckon they will be the biggest and toughest. Beat them and the next time will be easier," replied Jones.

"Great. Just great. How come we think they'll keep coming this way?" asked Olly.

"We think it's probably the comms beacon chain we've been using to communicate with Captain K and the others. Although it's on burst transmission, it's been running for a few weeks now, their mapping system must have detected it and they're following it to its source. It's the only logical explanation," replied Sanchez, wishing she could light a cigarette but adhering to her promise not to harm her baby.

"Unless they picked up Corporal Vinelli, or some Jute or other," said Olly, referring to Schaefer's section leader who had left them months before to search Sardinia for his and one of the Heidelberg student's relatives.

"No way Vinelli would have told them anything," said Sanchez vigorously.

*

An hour later, in the Hôtel de Ville, Alex assembled the town council, his HQ staff and all the combat team commanders. Sanchez looked around the room; most looked worried, some terrified.

"From the Musicians' recon, we now estimate that they're at least three companies strong, configured as a battle group. That's six-hundred plus. They have Stalkers, light artillery and AFVs. If they come – and there's no reason to think they won't – they'll come at us from every side except the sea."

"Major, what do you suggest?" asked the Countess.

357

"We do what we've prepared for. Our principal advantage is Saint C itself and the fact that they don't know our strength. Even though from the comms transmissions they probably know we're part military, they most likely think that we're just a few remnants from the allied forces," replied Alex.

Which we are, thought Sanchez.

"Any change in our strategy?" asked the Countess.

"No. Our strategy remains the same. In the open, we won't stand a chance. We draw them in, close-quarter fighting, so close they can't use their artillery. As Zhukov said at Stalingrad – 'I want every one of those bastards to feel they're under the muzzle of a gun'. Once we have them inside, we can then use Saint C to our advantage. It's a little like insurgency in reverse." Alex paused to allow Crockett to reinforce what he'd said.

"I'll repeat what the Major said; we keep drawing them in until all of them are inside the town. Timing will be everything; we must not show our hand too early. If we make too strong a showing, they'll simply withdraw and then flatten the town with HE and us with it. Understood?"

"We will need to get all non-combatants into the caves. I'll start the process," said the Countess.

Sanchez wondered whether the Major was feeling the same way she did. She knew he probably was but that he also cared deeply about Saint C and the whole ethos of what they were trying to achieve. Did she? She thought about it for a while before agreeing that she did as well.

"Now, we can do this. The odds sound bad but we've done it before. So have others. For those of you who don't know, there was once a little battle called Plataea which happened in 479 BC. Seventy thousand Greeks destroyed a quarter of a million Persians. All we need to do is do it again," said Alex.

Sanchez calculated the numbers as Crockett started the briefing.

"HQ will be here in the cellars. This will be manned by the Major, myself, Lieutenant Lee-Jones and the assigned HQ staff.

"Now, if everything goes wrong and it looks like we're going to lose, the chapel will be our Alamo. It will be at this point that we'll need to make the decision to evacuate and take our chances in the open. The decision will come from HQ, and if that ceases to exist it will be the Countess's call."

"There's no way. This time, Captain, we're going to finish them," interjected Olly.

"I heard that," echoed Jones.

"You've all heard this a dozen times before, and you've trained for it, but we'll go over it again. We're going to be organised into static, classical defence units that will engage then fall back before disbanding into small four-man insurgency style units.

"The first phase of the fighting will be the initial probing contacts; they'll come at us in some strength from all sides; they'll be looking for weak points to exploit. We'll give them what they want, drawing them in but staying in contact if at all possible. Remember, you will need to stay close to them and I mean close and mixed up. This way we deny them the effective use of their Stalker squadrons or artillery.

"Now for ORBAT... The north wall will be under the command of Lieutenant Claudia, call sign Bravo. Corporal Olly, call sign Alpha, will take the south wall and Corporals Galeago and Pavla, call signs Charlie and Delta, will take the eastern. It will be you guys who will need to judge when the tipping point has come and start to pull back into Saint C, and you'll have to do this in a way that encourages the bad guys to follow. You must keep them engaged and not break contact.

"During the initial contact we will hit them in the rear with everything we've got tucked away. The objective of this will be to destroy their command and control as well as weaken them as much as possible in terms of strength. Corporal Hodgetts and his team together with Jean-Jacques have already been deployed. Call sign will as usual be Shadow. They will locate and destroy the enemy's C4I2 and HQ staff. The timing of this is critical; we need to do this at the same time as we start to pull back into Saint C. After that, with no command and control, their natural thirst for our annihilation I hope will keep them coming.

"Air support will be provided by the Musicians under the command of Lieutenant Lee Jones and directed by Corporal Hodgetts in the field. Their mission is to destroy artillery, AFVs, and Stalker facilities. Additional air strikes will be provided by Lieutenant Lee Jones himself, who has volunteered to fly the Black Hole attack helicopter. He will only be released on a direct order from the Major.

"Corporal Sanchez and her team, call sign X-ray, will be a roving assault team based out of the abbey. Once released, she will effectively operate outside of the operational chain of command. Her remit is to weaken the enemy's forward command and control to an extent that local tactical situations dictate the enemy's disposition rather than any effective integrated strategy. Or to put it another way, she will kill anyone who is either an officer or NCO, and hit them hard in the back as many times as possible.

"Corporal Winston and his team, call sign as ever Sunray, will provide mortar and artillery support. He'll also command the minefields and other traps. We will only commit our artillery, or rather show anyone we have it, after their C4I2 is taken out.

"Sergeant Major Jones will command a strategic reserve of twenty volunteers, based here at HQ, call sign Romeo. They will be deployed as a blocking force to stop anyone getting back out, or if the Alamo itself is threatened. They will be released only under the Major's direct order.

"The close-quarter fighting within Saint C itself will be a mess. During this stage we'll most likely only have command and control within individual combat teams, possibly groups. Make no mistake, this phase will be chaos.

"Now, the last thing is target priority. Outside the walls, your killing priority will be the officers. We need to break up their chain of command. Once they're committed and inside the walls, it's the senior NCOs. They're the people who will know how to organise small squads in built-up areas. Don't bother about the officers at this stage. You will need to kill the NCOs and quickly. And I mean kill. If they're wounded they're still capable of communicating and organising. You need to pass this on to your teams and make sure people know what to look for.

"Rules of engagement are simple: we will continue fighting until they are all killed. If anyone ever doubts this, remember what we've seen."

"Sorry, sir? Are you saying that we should not take any prisoners?" asked Olly.

"Yes, Corporal. Now, any questions?"

"We've got six elderly volunteers for the smugglers' tunnel rear guard security. They're prepared to stay behind in the event we need to evacuate," added the Countess.

"I'd like to meet them," said Alex.

*

It was just after three o'clock the next morning when Sanchez was woken by Crockett.

"They're here. I've put us at Stand to," he said, referring to active defensive positions. "We've also lost contact with Captain K."

CHAPTER 32

WHO'S LEFT?

Have your soldiers adapt their movements according to your signals.

It was dawn when they finally declared the palace secure. Natasha felt drained. Alex had told her that her first real engagement as a combat commander would leave her questioning her own decisions, euphoric, guilty, but feeling a little taller. All of the emotions were there and she silently thanked him for making her aware that she was in the company of thousands of others who'd gone before her.

As the sun rose and warmed the wet ground, a light mist like that from a steam room hung over the gardens of Versailles. Natasha gathered them all together for a sit rep.

Tsang and Luc carried Stacey down onto the sun terrace using a chaise longue that had once belonged to the Dauphin of France.

"Well, Private, you're a lucky man. You need to thank Mr O'Reilly here. Without him you wouldn't be around to see the sun today," said Tsang. Stacey nodded, unable to speak.

Tired and still covered in plaster dust O'Reilly stood with the others, rubbing puffy red eyes and scratching his crotch.

"Fuck, I could swear I've got something living in my underwear," he said, changing the subject.

"Nah, don't worry, it's just the maggots feeding on dead flesh," said Frost.

"Oooh. That must have hurt," cajoled Hicks.

"Do you reckon we should clean up the mess we've made?" asked O'Reilly. "I mean the state of some of the rooms, especially the theatre. I feel embarrassed."

"You lying bastard. You've already stolen most of the stuff that wasn't broken," said Frost.

Natasha listened to the banter, happy to let it play itself out, before starting the briefing.

"All right, listen up. Captain Johnson's going to give us a little news. Last night during all the excitement we finished the analysis," she announced as Johnson handed out a sheet of paper to each of them.

RUN STATUS	
Total File Entries	636,237,389
Reviewed File Entries	636,237,389
Number of Deceased File Entries	104,616,948
Total Matched for Gene 169	615,041
Survivability Index	0.097%
Predicted Number of Survivors	513,909

Run Time to Date (days)	6.5
Remaining Run Time (days)	0.0

"As you can see, we've got ourselves more than half a million survivors here in Europe," said Johnson lighting a cigarette.

"And we know where every one of these people live?" asked O'Reilly.

"We do, at least as far as their latest recorded address. Mr Raven and Luc are working up a map."

"So the plan now is to go and contact everyone?" asked Cook.

"It is. Of course, the order we do this in is going to be the subject of some debate – do we go for the closest, the biggest population centre, the most useful, the youngest, the most helpless? More than one group at a time or singularly?" Johnson paused and inhaled on his cigarette before continuing. "We also reckon we can use what we've learnt here in other areas, certainly the US, Canada and parts of South America and Australia. Obviously, though, with the issue of the founder mutant gene, we don't think it'll be much use in Asia or Africa, although we'll try."

A spattering of "wows" came from the assembly.

"Excuse me, Captain. But how come the number of survivors is less than the number of matched files?" asked Frost.

"We've assumed that a number of gene 169 survivors would have taken their own lives, a little like the Lebihan family we came across," replied Tsang.

"Now, it doesn't take a lot to realise the value of this information, and that if lost or in the wrong hands it will spell the end of us. Last night we not only almost became permanent residents but also came close to losing what we're now fighting for. That's why we need to safeguard the data no matter what happens to us. Any ideas you have on this please let us know.

"That's the end of the good news. And now comes the bad…We've lost contact with Saint C. Our last sit rep wasn't delivered and we've got no return transmission. At first we thought we'd lost a beacon. It turned out we had but Lieutenant Byrnes says the problem is at beacon number two."

"Which is inside Saint C's outer perimeter," interjected O'Reilly.

"And no one has fixed it and five hours have passed," added Byrnes.

"And that means trouble. I want to move from here within a few hours."

"Ma'am, you reckon our little squabble last night is linked to the problem at Saint C?" asked Frost, clutching her bandaged hand.

"I think they must have mapped our transmissions and put two and two together. Do they understand what we've been doing? Almost definitely not. I think they're just hell-bent on eliminating all trace of us. It's that simple," replied Natasha.

"How come every time we get some good news it's always followed with shit?" asked O'Reilly rhetorically. "No, don't tell me… That's life."

"Either which way, we need to get back to Saint C. Captain Schaefer and myself are open to ideas."

"Well, if we charge straight down the main auto routes then we're highly likely to bump into some blocking force or other. If we detour to be safe we're going to lose time. It's a difficult decision to make without sufficient information. I could run some probabilistic simulations with O'Reilly to try and determine the best route," offered Byrnes.

"Guys, even if we go straight down the main auto routes, it'll take us sixteen hours. From everything we've learnt so far these bastards pop up all over the place," countered O'Reilly.

Stacey scribbled a note and passed it to Tsang. "Corporal Stacey has also raised an important point. The data. We need to protect it whatever we do," she said.

"I agree. But both Captain Schaefer and I are concerned that if Saint C is engaged they will have casualties, they'll need doctors, and the doctors are here."

There was a period of silence as they each considered the arguments.

"You know, there is another option," offered Dr Heymans; "we could just ignore Saint C. I know it's a painful thought, maybe heartless, but the data we have will change everything. Saint C could be sacrificed."

"What about splitting up?" offered O'Reilly. "Some of us could watch over the data, the rest charge ahead?"

"I agree," said Gyan. "We could switch to civilian vehicles. They'd be faster."

"There is another way," interjected Raven, who had been studying a map of their proposed routes.

"Go on," encouraged Schaefer.

"We go by air," he said.

"What?" asked a chorus of voices.

"Air. There's civilian airstrips all over the place round here; we've got one just over ten klicks away. I don't think we should try military bases. But a couple of civilian aircraft and we could be back in Saint C in a few hours."

"I like it. We've got pilots," added Natasha.

"The other good thing is that the airstrip is north of us, so if any of those bastards are waiting for us to head south and try and link up with Saint C, they'll not expect us to head the other way," added Raven.

"Any objections?" asked Schaefer.

There were none.

"Let's do it."

"Outstanding, Mr Raven. You ever thought of general staff college?" asked Tsang.

They buried Colins and Piper, making rough headstones for them using wooden stakes and their dog tags. They left their enemies where they'd fallen.

364

CHAPTER 33

AIR FLEET

The condition of a military force is that its essential factor is speed. Taking advantage of others' failure to catch up, going by routes they do not expect. Attacking where they are not on guard.

S hould come up on the perimeter of the airfield after the next bend," reported O'Reilly over the AFV's intercom.

"Threat boards are green," advised Frost.

As they cleared the bend, the airfield came into view. It was set behind a wire fence and peppered with the usual small, civilian, fixed and rotary wing aircraft, neatly lined up at intervals. They turned through the gate and sped out across a small concrete assembly area to where the administration buildings and several maintenance hangars were sited.

Natasha, Byrnes and Raven strolled along the lined-up aircraft. "Either of you two got any preferences?" she asked.

"I think we should take the helos. There's three of them, all jets. One trainer and a couple of passenger buses. They're Sikorsky 2100s, wire-guided, gyro-stabilised – should be a piece of cake to fly," said Byrnes.

"If we can find the manuals," added Raven.

Schaefer joined them. "I've got O'Reilly scratching around for fuel. Sergeant Gyan's sorting out weapons and air to ground comms… and I've been thinking."

"Go on," said Natasha, knowing what was coming.

"What would it take to turn these birds into something that could pack a punch?" he asked.

"I think we're going with the helos," replied Natasha smiling.

"I like it. Heli-borne assault. I haven't done one of those for years. That'll be a shock," added Byrnes, scratching his head in thought as he surveyed the aircraft.

"We could put the med team plus Luc and Stacey together in one of the buses. Raven and Lieutenant Byrnes can take the other, with you, the other grunts and a couple of door guns as an assault team," said Natasha picking up on theme.

"And you?"

"I'll fly the gunship with O'Reilly and Frost and as much firepower as we can pack in. It'll take us a few more hours to prepare but I think it might be worth it. We'll be able to provide air cover for you guys and then close support ground suppression."

"I like it. But are we sure we want to pack all the med team in one bird though?" asked Schaefer.

"It's a case of trading firepower for medical aid. With no news from Saint C, I reckon they're in trouble. We can drop off the data, Luc and Stacey a safe distance from Saint C then put the med team down on the beach at Saint C with another copy of the data."

*

Even though they took shortcuts on the pre-flight maintenance, such as not changing the lube oil and filters, it still took them the rest of the morning to prep the helicopters for flight, having to fuel, recharge batteries, synchronise instruments and the like.

"I hope you lot know how to fly these things," muttered O'Reilly as he disconnected the fuel lines from the aircraft.

"Don't worry," offered Byrnes, smiling from the cockpit. "I've read the instruction manual. It's in French but I understand most of it."

"Great," replied O'Reilly, shaking his head.

"Nah, in all seriousness, the control and avionics packages are just about standard for any civil aircraft. It's really only the performance envelopes that vary. Bit like driving a car."

*

366

Raven, Byrnes and Natasha each took turns experimenting with the machines over the airfield, taking off, hovering and landing. After a few practice sessions they felt confident that they had a feel for the machines. As Byrnes proudly explained to O'Reilly, "See, you've got auto take-off and landing. Then once you're up all you have to do is use the joystick and the throttle. Easy, eh?"

"Piece of cake," said Raven as he strolled past O'Reilly after his test flight.

Whilst they'd been test flying, Gyan and the others had stripped Natasha's aircraft of seats, body panels, air conditioning, insulation and any equipment that they felt they could to allow for the weapons payloads she would carry. The machine now looked more like an experimental submersible than a helicopter, thought Natasha looking it over.

"I know it looks a little odd but it'll do the job, Captain," said Frost as she wiped sweat from her forehead after finishing drilling yet another series of holes into the air frame to secure a mine dispenser.

"More than," added Raven who was running control cables back into the rear of the aircraft where O'Reilly would eventually command the various weapons.

"We've stolen a couple of fuel bladders and I reckon we've got the range we need and about sixty-odd minutes of combat time over Saint C without refuelling," said Byrnes who was looking over the performance envelopes of the aircraft.

"Great," replied Natasha, feeling tired but excited.

"Stacey's working on it already; he's directing the med team who are rigging a manifold."

"Jesus, I thought he was wounded."

"Yeah. But Captain Johnson couldn't keep him down, and Stacey convinced everyone that if anyone else tried to do what he wanted they'd more than likely blow themselves up in the process."

Across from them, Gyan heaved a gyro-stabilised Gatling up onto the air frame. They went across to look at how it was shaping up.

"You know, I'm wondering whether you need to take Frost. Then we could mount another Gatling on the starboard side. I know that all up it will be a little more weight but... twice the suppressive fire. What do you think?" asked Gyan.

Byrnes thought about it for a second before replying. "Yeah, I thought about it but the weight we're carrying already means this thing is going to lumber around like a log in a pond. We're pushing the envelope on the centre of gravity in the flight software; if we're not careful we'll just roll over at take-off and crash."

"It would also mean I'd lose my threat analyst. I'm going to be busy enough just keeping the thing in the air," added Natasha.

Raven joined them, dragging a small trolley loaded with sensor arrays from the AFV.

"Where are we gonna site these?" he asked.

"We'll do four sets, forward, aft, port and starboard, and I want look up and down as well. Hook the lot into the cockpit with a repeater for O'Reilly in the back."

"You got it. Jesus. This thing is going to have more holes than a cheese grater," he said as he picked up a drill and looked for a point to secure the sensors.

As the sun set over the airfield, both Raven's and Byrnes' aircraft were almost finished; only Natasha's still needed work, hooking up the threat sensors and systems they'd removed from the AFVs. She and Frost were sitting in the cockpit checking the interfaces between the sensors and the threat analysis processors, when Byrnes tapped on their window.

"I've done some calcs on the electrical power reqs," he said. "We're going to need another fuel cell off the AFV for the extras, and that's more weight."

Natasha sighed, and looked around inside her aircraft. "OK. Let's strip all the survival crap out of here. I'm sure we won't need life rafts and survival packs. And let's get rid of the fire extinguishers in both the cockpit and the engines. I'm sure that if we get hit with something we'll have more to worry about than a fire. That'll give us an extra hundred and fifty pounds or so, that enough?"

"Just."

When they finished just before midnight, Natasha's helicopter boasted mine, flare and chaff dispensers, a gyro-stabilised Gatling door gun, and two missile tubes mounted either side of the area where the sliding doors were once positioned. Byrnes and Raven finished hooking up the wiring and electronic systems and then walked Natasha, Frost and O'Reilly through the system displays.

"Great. Just like the AFV. I reckon we're good to go," announced Natasha, clambering out of the cockpit and narrowly avoiding getting entangled in loose wiring harnesses.

"I'll get Luc to tape those wires up for you," said Byrnes, wiping sweat from his eyes. From across the airfield they heard Sergeant Gyan scream at Johnson to stop "fucking smoking" whilst they finished fuelling.

"Assuming of course they don't blow each other up," she said, yawning and calling a halt to the work. "Right. All stop. Get yourselves a little sleep. We'll do a pre-flight briefing at 0330 hours. I want to be airborne by dawn."

As they settled down to sleep in the airfield's recreation room, O'Reilly noticed a sign on the wall proclaiming the airfield to be the site of a Roman battle from AD 64.

"Fuck. You noticed that wherever we go there's either been a fight or we end up in one? And you know we haven't even had the time to divvy up Piper's and Colins' stuff yet?"

Natasha smiled to herself when the only reply was from someone snoring.

CHAPTER 34

CONTACT AT SAINT CHRISTOBEL

When warriors are in great danger then they have no fear. When there is nowhere to go they are firm. When they are deeply involved they stick to it.

Facing them were nearly 600 elite airborne armoured infantry, forty light AFVs and two flights of six Stalkers.

The enemy had set up their camp just over 3 kilometres to the south of Saint C, as the day had passed they'd made no effort to either approach the town or conceal their presence, and in some way this had seemed to make them even more threatening.

2130 HRS: SANCHEZ – THE ABBEY

Sanchez and her team, covered by thermal blankets, lay prone in the derelict ruins of the abbey 200 meters from Saint C. She'd separated them into two groups, about 20 feet above ground level on either side of the cloisters that ran the whole length of the abbey.

She thought of the chapel service the Countess had conducted earlier. Although not religious, she'd decided to attend and lit a candle for Schaefer and their baby. She'd even said a little prayer.

After the heat of the day, the gentle early evening breeze that slid across the surrounding fields, up the hillside and into the ruins was almost refreshing, cooling the beads of sweat on her blackened face.

She thought about her combat team and the final briefing she'd given them: "Each one of us is going to have to kill six of the shitbags just to stay even. So I want you to be ruthless but calculating. Remember, those of you tagged to go after officers and NCOs do it. Don't get distracted. Those of you on free range – kill everything and everyone; if you injure don't bother wasting any time looking for the kill shot, just move on. Remember, six each and your loved ones will survive. Five and they won't. We beat these bastards and the next time the odds will be better for us."

The sun slipped beneath the horizon, slowly turning the sky a deep velvet blue streaked here and there with lighter blues and pinks. Venus appeared, shining brightly, and as night came the odd star started twinkling in the dark satin sky. As she checked her fields of fire for the hundredth time she reckoned it was one of the most beautiful evenings she'd ever seen.

2330 HRS: HODGETTS' – 3 KM EAST OF SAINT C

They'd built ten hidden FOPs around Saint C, each consisting of two tunnels in a T-shape. The tunnel with the observation and firing slit was the top of the T, whilst the sleeping and messing quarters occupied the other.

In FOP 'Golf', Wilcox and Jean-Jacques were on stag overlooking the fields to the south. Hodgetts and Strachan, who'd got back a couple of hours earlier from a recce, were sleeping. They'd located the enemy C4I2 and their secondary HQ.

Jean-Jacques tapped Wilcox on the shoulder and pointed to the centre of a cornfield, about 300 metres distant. Wilcox looked through the old binoculars at where the old man was pointing. For about twenty seconds he didn't see anything but the corn which was a deep gold under the night sky, gently waving in the breeze. Then for just an instant, a figure appeared, popping up above the corn to check his bearings before moving off again. Wilcox could now see all of them; there were six, moving from right to left in a slow, crouched run, weaving in a pattern that mimicked the wave-like motion of the corn. He went back to wake up Hodgetts and Strachan.

"Do you see them?" he asked.

"Well, fuck me. Nice trick. Running like a wave. I'll have to remember that one. There's more behind," commented Strachan.

"Here we go, then," said Hodgetts.

They counted the enemy, type of weapons and formations, assigned them a formation name, time, direction and sent a sit rep to Alex and Sanchez.

A reply arrived within seconds.

"The boss says leave them. Sanchez will deal with them. We've got the go to get eyes on our first targets. Let's move," Hodgetts told his colleagues, as he liked to call them.

2330 HRS: SANCHEZ – THE ABBEY

Sanchez marvelled again at the abbey's beauty. Its tall sandstone block arches reached upwards to where a roof would once have been but which was now open to the stars. The stonework was covered in a dark green ivy and moss that at night took on a hue of black velvet. Around the abbey were pine trees, their sentinel-like trunks were widely spaced and she reminded herself that the ground was covered with pine needles and soft grass. Good for silent approach, she thought. She scrutinised one of the trees, the pattern of the bark amplified in the moonlight. The sound of insects boomed out above the gentle rustling of dry leaves and swishing of corn as a gust of wind overtook the gentle breeze. She smiled as the thought of holding a christening party for her baby in the ruins popped into her head from nowhere.

Through an oval-shaped gap in the tree line, a bright, almost blinding moon slid in and out of the cloud formations. In response, the fields and copses of trees were draped in and then out of shadow, the texture of the land changing but always retaining a rich, dark, exquisite softness. The land seemed to be calling her to come and curl up and go to sleep.

Her comms set beeped and a female computerised voice spoke into her left earpiece: "Shadow sit rep 2331 hours. FOP Golf. Designate force as Foxtrot One. Eight pathfinders on foot, heading NNE at jog. Fifty plus infantry in five assault sections following. Marine recon – unit name unknown. Standard formations. Weapons standard. No mortar or heavy. DRP camouflage. Look well trained. Very fucking clever advance to contact – look for them 'snaking' through the fields. ETA your pos thirty mins.

Instructions from Six will follow. We are moving to C4I2. Good luck and fuck them up. H."

Sanchez appended a file that described the profile and gave some pictures and details of an enemy marine recon unit to the message then added a note from herself: "See attached. This is what we will face. We will not engage until advised. Luv and kisses, S." She then sent it to all of the team.

A branch snapped somewhere out in the distance. Sanchez moved her sights across the mid distance and stopped at a clump of trees that sat astride a hedgerow. She thought – but wasn't sure – that she could make out a figure. *Wait, she told herself. Be patient. It's the one who first gives himself away that loses.*

Two more messages came in; the first was from Hodgetts: "Shadow sit rep follows 2335: FOP Golf. Second wave designate Foxtrot Two. Heading due north at walk. Airborne. Arch Angel. One hundred plus. Combat engineer formations. Light mortar sections two. Sniper sections two. ETA three zero mins. H."

The second message was from Alex: "Maintain silence until advised. Sunray will engage Foxtrot Two."

She could picture the command and control centre located in the stone vaulted cellars 20 feet below the Hôtel de Ville in the main square. It was full of the usual paraphernalia of screens, power and data cables, tactical computers, comms systems and outputs from the 200 mini cams. In the middle of the room was the centrepiece of their tactical situation monitoring: a scale model of the town. A gift from the Countess to the children of the town several years before and used as a Christmas display, it was perfect in almost every respect and even included the surrounding trees and fields. Placed on the model were the blue markers indicating the positions and strengths of friendly forces. To these would now be added red markers, firstly outside the town walls and then inside showing who owned which building, or WOW as it was now referred to.

0005 HRS: HODGETTS – SW OF SAINT C

Hodgetts and Wilcox, and Jean-Jacques and Strachan, had formed two, two-man teams for their approach to the enemy C4I2. In addition to their LA-51 sniper and assault rifles, they each carried two anti-armour mines, silenced competition standard pistols and three FAE munitions.

Their plan was simple: they would get in close and destroy the AFVs with mines, then take out the igloos with the FAEs.

From Hodgetts' previous reconnaissance they knew that the enemy were relaxed and confident, and it was this over-confidence that they'd relied on to work their way past the perimeter security. Despite this, though, they'd almost been rumbled twice, the first time whilst they were crossing the river, when an AFV column had halted by the side of the riverbank and a trooper had dismounted and relieved himself barely a metre from where Hodgetts was lying. The second was when they had taken cover behind a cowshed only to find that minutes later the forecourt was being set up as a base of operations for a Stalker flight.

But Hodgetts now had eyes on the C4I2. It consisted of four AFVs and attached igloos; they were loosely spaced around the pond used for watering cattle. It was sheltered from direct view by trees on all sides interspersed with dense bush. A narrow farm track 200 metres long led from the main road to the area. Sentries had been posted in a loose inner perimeter and along the farm track.

Wearing their Zute suits, Hodgetts and Wilcox had approached the clearing around the pond using the wild boar runs that ran beneath the thorn bushes and allowed the animals unobserved access to the pond, which they too used as a watering hole.

Hodgetts tapped Wilcox on the shoulder and indicated that he should start mapping the sentry positions. From the way they were behaving, laughing, talking and smoking he didn't think it would take long. He checked for any new messages. There were none, just the previous "Get eyes on and hold". He didn't dare send out a message this close to the enemy, so he settled down and tried to while away the time by searching the area around the pond for any sign of Jean-Jacques or Strachan, mentally recording the positions and routes of the sentries, working out details of the insertion, the order he would take out the C4I2 assets, where he would place the explosives, and finally their exfil.

0015 HRS: SANCHEZ – THE ABBEY

The first firefight erupted from Saint C behind Sanchez. A few seconds later her ear piece announced a message from Alex. "All stations, this is Six. Insurgency phase. South teams on wall engaged. All comms functioning. Larger formations now working their way past X-ray and entering minefields."

Fifteen minutes later a message came in from Claudia: "Bravo withdrawing". This was followed by updates from Olly and Pavla on the south and west walls indicating they were under growing pressure.

The message board beeped again; "All stations. Shadow is weapons free. Sunray will go loud in five mins. Beethoven is weapons free to engage rear soft targets. X-ray is weapons free in ten minutes."

"We're live in ten," Sanchez let her team know.

0040 HRS: HODGETTS - SW OF SAINTC

Hodgetts smiled as the message came in from Alex telling him he was free to engage. He had 20 metres of open ground to cross to reach the first of the C4I2 AFVs from its left forward side. The approach was in deep shadow and the only way he could be spotted was by a sentry who was off to his left.

He made sure his muscles were ready and wouldn't cramp when he began to move, then slowly raised himself on to his elbows and toes ready to start a leopard crawl.

Halfway across the open space he heard Winston's minefield detonate in the distance, the series of explosions coming in rippling waves and drowning out the small arms firefight. The sentries guarding the C4I2 stopped talking, their curiosity peaked by the change in the sound of the battle. Hodgetts knew this was a dangerous moment; the sentries had been jolted out of their relaxed state of mind and were now alert and he was laying in full view of them with only the temperamental Zute suit as camouflage. But Wilcox, whose job it was to cover Hodgetts, understood the situation and reacted, dropping the nearest sentries with silenced rounds. Hodgetts now started counting the seconds. He rose and ran the remaining few metres to the side of the AFV. Six seconds. He taped an anti-armour mine and an FAE grenade to the front windscreen. Ten seconds. Next he set the fuse for ten seconds and checked it. Fifteen seconds. Not bad, he thought. He armed it and then ran 10 metres at right angles to the route he'd used to approach the AFV, sliding down the shallow bank to the pond for cover. He had barely hit the ground when the mine detonated, followed a split second later by the FAE grenade which exploded, accompanied by a heatwave that sucked the breath out of him and burnt his throat.

Just as he was getting his breath back, Jean-Jacques' FAE detonated, showering the area with white globules of sizzling material that seemed to hover just off the ground or whizzed around in small circles in the pond.

Hodgetts peeked over the bank and using his weapon sights searched for targets. A large crater was now where the AFV had once been. The area was covered in burning branches and debris. Two other AFVs were on fire, a third looked intact. A torso lay in the foreground with two legs missing. The surrounding trees had been stripped of their branches and were now just trunks. It looked like a scene out of World War One. Two figures ran towards one of the burning AFVs to help several of their comrades who were crawling down the stern ramp with their clothes on fire. He shot one of the rescuers, someone else got the second. He ducked back down behind the bank and rolled three times to his left, before starting a search again. Two more figures emerged from the intact AFV and ran in a crouch towards cover. He fired twice and missed, and again slid back down the bank and rolled again this time four times to his right. Again he searched the area; three more ran towards the farm track. He was about to fire when a round thudded into the earth bank just to his front followed by another that hit his weapon's sights. "Fuck it!" There was another explosion, probably from rounds cooking off in one of the AFVs, and more debris splashed into the pond nearby.

Strachan joined him. "You all right?"

"Yeah. Round went straight through the sights, look," said Hodgetts holding up the sights of his rifle.

"You seen Jean?"

"No. He'll be around. You get them all?"

"No probs. Wilcox took out the three trying to bug out down the farm track. I got two others," said Strachan.

"Bastards; those sights cost me a lot. Cover me. I'm going to check out that last AFV."

As Strachan provided cover, Hodgetts moved quickly towards the remaining AFV. Its stern and side ramps were open and the interior glowed with battle-red ambient lighting. He noticed a shadow and dropped to one knee, ready to fire. Jean-Jacques emerged and sat down on the stern ramp wiping his brow.

"Christ, you gave me a shock," he said.

"*Bien sûr*. They're all dead, there's a lot of blood but I figured we could use some transport."

Hodgetts looked inside the AFV. He counted five bodies. Three had been shot, one had had his throat slit and the last had what looked like a tomahawk stuck in his forehead.

"Jesus, you're an animal," he said, feeling his boots slip a little on a pool of blood.

They checked the AFV; all the tactical screens and sensors were still running with videofeed of the battle inside Saint C. Strachan clambered into the driver's seat and checked the drive systems. "All good. The systems are in warm standby," he reported.

"I think we should pay that Stalker site a visit. I'll send Six the good news," said Hodgetts.

They gave Wilcox the all clear to join them.

"Wicked," said Wilcox after finding out what they were going to do.

"We need to be quick. They'll lock down the data and command and control telemetry links as soon as they realise they've been compromised," said Hodgetts as he dragged one of the bodies by its feet down the stern ramp.

"What the fuck are you doing?" he asked Wilcox, who was spraying the outside of the AFV in red paint.

"Just a bit of advertising," he replied, pocketing his can of spray paint and standing back to admire his artwork that was scrawled along the side of the AFV and proclaimed *Fuck You! With love the 1st / 9th.*

0045 HRS: SANCHEZ – THE ABBEY

The enemy was moving in force through the trees to her left and in front of her. They were laughing and joking, smoking and behaving as if they were on their way to a party rather than a battle. Behind her the sound of the firefight that was raging along and around the town's walls continued.

The old silicon night vision camera she was using caught a moonbeam and flared in response to the overload. She cursed as her night vision decayed, then stifled a surge of adrenaline as Winston's minefields suspended in the trees erupted. The sound was like a prolonged series of shotgun blasts interspersed with the sound of timber splitting; it went on for about twenty seconds before dying away. For a few seconds thereafter, there was silence, and then came the screams of the wounded, followed by the shouts of anger, commands and small arms fire as the enemy fired blindly around them. It took them a minute to work out that they were in a minefield and should change their direction of advance. The only direction remaining to them was that which would bring them into the abbey and the cloisters below. An area she'd christened the killing room.

Two messages arrived; the first was from Hodgetts. "Shadow confirms C4I2 destroyed. Proceeding to Stalkers."

The second was from Alex: "Insurgency phase continues. Shadow confirms C4I2 destroyed – now moving to Stalker site. Alpha, Bravo and Charlie teams engaged. Beethoven is down. Stalkers inbound. Saint C going hot."

She relayed the news to her team. With the Stalkers inbound Alex was going to switch on every electrical field-generating piece of equipment in the town and light numerous flares and strobes. This would, it was hoped, overload or at least confuse the Stalker's tactical target acquisition systems for a while.

"Shit," muttered Sanchez to herself. They couldn't afford to lose their air power. They'd lose. She was getting frustrated just waiting as the battle raged around her. Then the cloisters below her started to fill up with the enemy force avoiding Winston's mines. She waited until the lead elements were two-thirds of the way through before she shouted, "Open fire!"

Her Cyclops registered the splinters and sparks flying off the ancient stonework as her team unleashed short controlled bursts of aimed fire. As she fired she found the activity almost comforting after the long wait. Ignoring the incoming fire from the enemy as they tried to find shelter and regroup, she worked her sights down the length of the cloisters. She fired two and three round bursts, targeting their leaders each time. A man rolled away from the opposite wall into middle ground as if this would put him beyond reach. Sanchez centred the sights on his back and fired twice.

One of her team on the opposite side of the gallery was firing almost continuously and, in the excitement and intensity of the firefight and mortar barrage, stood up. Sanchez willed him to get down but it was too late, he presented too easy a target; a round struck his left arm taking with it the lower half. He looked at where his arm had once been and then toppled off the gallery onto the floor below. For an instant there was a lull in the firefight before multiple weapons were turned on the wounded man and his body jerked as the enemy exacted their retribution.

Above the sound of the firefight she recognised the noise of mortar shells as Winston commenced a rolling mortar barrage in the surrounding fields. Below her the enemy had been reduced to dead and wounded; she tossed several anti-personnel grenades into the area then gave her team the order to move. "Time to play hide and seek. Put down smoke and AP."

Under cover of a rain of grenades and smoke, her team now withdrew along the gallery and down a recessed stone staircase that led to an underground tunnel that had been built by the monks centuries before. Sanchez was the last in and, before lowering the flagstone that concealed the entrance, she checked to make sure that the two climbing ropes at the back of the wall were still in place. Anyone now brave enough to investigate the gallery above would assume they had bugged out using the ropes and fled back towards the town.

She recovered her breathing. "Well done. Now let's settle down. No e-sig. We're cold tack now. We'll wait for a while before the bastards sort themselves out and move past us. Then we're going to pop back up again and kick their backsides."

She reckoned they'd left at least thirty dead or seriously wounded in the abbey for the loss of one of their own. *Not bad*, she thought. *We only need to repeat that another twenty or so times and we'll be home free.* She gave Williams, the trooper she'd been with at the bridge all those months before, a smile. The nervousness he normally exuded had gone and his eyes were now confident.

0055 HRS: STALKERS – OVER SAINT C

With the decoys inside Saint C, the Stalkers' sensors had detected so many sources compared to what they had become accustomed to over the past months that the onboard processors had twice dismissed and dumped the data as erroneous and instigated diagnostics checks on their own systems. Eventually, though, with each Stalker confirming one another's data, the processors allowed the data to be uploaded to the tactical analysis program. This promptly dismissed nearly 30% of the sources as militarily insignificant; however, the rest were classified as potential and mapped. This indicated that more than half of the targets were too close to friendly forces to engage. The situation was classified as fluidly confused with friendly and enemy forces interspersed over a wide area and their respective positions changing frequently.

It was Winston's mortar barrage that finally broke the Stalkers' software logic jam by providing a clear, high value target. By backtracking the trajectory of the old non-stealthy rounds, the Stalkers determined that the mortar battery was located on the north-west of Saint C on the beach. The Stalkers headed due west out to sea before reversing their course. On the inbound leg their sensors confirmed the battery location using a combination of image recognition, and the residual heat trace from the mortar tubes, which, when viewed against the ambient temperature of the wet beach sand, was easy to differentiate.

Leading away from the battery towards the steep cliffs were residual heat traces in the shape of footprints from Winston's mortar crew who had displaced as soon as they had fired. The Stalkers ignored the footprints and instead discharged a spread of aerial mines across the battery's position before continuing back into the battle area.

0115 HRS: SANCHEZ – THE ABBEY

In the tunnel and satisfied that enough time had elapsed, Sanchez pushed the heavy stone entrance cover away with care. Behind her, having finished their weapons and ammunition checks, her team were waiting, their legs slightly cramped from the narrow tunnel. Her adrenaline, already running, surged as the tunnel was filled with the noise of the continuing battle.

A message came in: "All stations Black Hole being readied". Sanchez imagined Lieutenant Tommy Lee being helped by some of the villagers in his wheelchair to the garage where they'd pre-positioned the Black Hole attack helicopter that O'Reilly had hauled back from the Reforger site.

"Let's go," she whispered, clambering back out onto the stone gallery in the abbey. The dead from the earlier exchange lay piled up in the cloisters below. Towards the town walls bright white and orange flashes lit up the night sky, replacing the stars and moon. She felt oddly detached from the raging battle, almost as if she was a voyeur.

"Williams, you watch our six."

They'd moved about 200 metres towards Saint C when she called a halt.

"Set Love and Marriage up here," she ordered, referring to two robot sentries they would use to bushwhack the enemy after they retreated again back to the abbey.

Satisfied that the sentries were ready, they continued their advance along the pathway to the south wall. She called another halt and sent them to ground before moving forward alone to reconnoitre the situation. Shadows from the bushes and trees danced on the ground from a mixture of moonlight and flares. As she looked around the last corner she had trouble assimilating the picture that presented itself. The fighting resembled something out of a medieval siege. Ladders and ropes were being used to scale the steep slope up to the town wall's ramparts, upon which hand-to-hand fighting was taking place lit up by flares which burst periodically above the combatants. Squads of enemy were clustered at the foot of the slope waiting their turn to join the assault. A grenade landed in one group, showering the area in phosphorous. A ladder toppled backwards and crashed into the trees as a 2-foot diameter concrete ball flew out of one of the cannonier in the walls, carrying a man with it.

She brought her team forward and prepped them for the assault.

"Jesus, all we need now are some archers," said someone.

"Shall we fix bayonets?" asked Williams.

"Not yet. Engage only those on the ground. Fire at will," she ordered.

0120 HRS: OLLY – SOUTH WALL

On the ramparts directly above Sanchez, Olly kicked a heavily black-bearded face that belonged to a hulk of a man who was lying on the stone-flagged floor. As Olly brought his short-barrelled assault shotgun to bear, someone smashed into his back knocking him over on top of Black Beard, who having quickly recovered from Olly's kick now took the opportunity to try and strangle him. Luckily, Black Beard's strangling efforts were hampered by Olly's neck armour and Olly let him get on with his attempts whilst unsheathing the diamond-tipped combat knife that was strapped to his right leg. As Black Beard adjusted his weight to get a better purchase on Olly's neck, Olly stabbed the giant in the neck, just between the helmet line and the body armour, severing the man's spinal cortex in the process. Black Beard went limp and collapsed onto Olly, who had to work hard to get him off.

He looked around to assess the situation; one of his team, a girl in her mid-twenties, hurled a knife at a small man who was charging towards her screaming. The knife hit the man's helmet and bounced off. The act only seemed to excite Little Man even more and his screams rose to banshee level as he closed the distance to the girl.

Well, the Major had wanted close contact and you couldn't get much closer than this, he thought. The problem was Olly's team were now in danger of being overrun; they needed to get off the wall and into the town where they could fight on better terms, but without disengaging. Olly groped for his throat mike only to discover that it had been torn loose, probably by Black Beard. The entrance door to the main gate tower was blown open and plumes of powdery white stone dust enveloped everyone. A Stalker appeared, hovering, watching the chaos. Two enemy had grabbed one of his team and hurled him over the ramparts. He felt the concussion of air as a round whizzed past him as he finally managed to locate his mike; "All stations, this is Alpha Six. Bug out now. I say again, fall back to green zone. I say again, fall back to green zone. Pop smoke and decoys."

0120 HRS: HODGETTS – STALKER SITE

Just over 5 Kilometers south of Saint C, in their captured AFV, Hodgetts and the others were driving in plain view across a cornfield and approaching the Stalker base, which they could now see consisted of three flat-bed and one HQ AFV sited in a small copse of trees.

"Nice night for a drive," announced Wilcox from the driver's seat.

"We'll drive up to them like we're their best pals. Jean-Jacques, you get up top with the Gatling and engage the furthest target. Strachan will take the near side one with HE mini missiles," ordered Hodgetts as he continued checking the threat boards and watching data feeds from the enemy Stalkers over Saint C.

"Jesus. You should see the state of Saint C, it looks like a mad house, but we should even things up a bit."

"Shit, the command screen is asking for a code. Must be on a timer or something. I guess we've only got a few minutes left before they shut us down," advised Wilcox.

"Just hit the acknowledge button or something. Unless of course you know the code," replied Hodgetts.

"Shame O'Reilly isn't here," replied Wilcox.

Hodgetts' messaging system beeped. "Jesus, this is never-ending. The Major's reporting they've got a column of six AFVs driving up the approach road to Saint C. I hope the pit works or the guys are going to be in real trouble."

0125 HRS: MOZART – BENEATH THE RIVER

The lead AFV of the enemy column had dropped straight into the vehicle trap they'd dug weeks earlier; in a state of confusion the following five AFVs were now bunched up on the narrow road behind it 500 meters east of the main gate.

Twenty metres away at the bottom of the river that ran alongside the road, Mozart, the squadron's last Musician, sat amongst the weeds, listening for commands from a thin antennae wire that floated on the surface. Alex's command arrived and the little machine activated its warm start routines, spinning up gyros and powering up its main processors. It then inflated its buoyancy bags and drifted up to the river surface, where it required just three seconds for its rotors to get up to speed and lift it a few feet into the air, covered in weeds and draining water. Its tactical software had been pre-programmed with what to expect and its sensors verified the situation within another third of a second.

The AFVs were starting to reverse back along the road but it was too late. A small panel in Mozart's matt black hull slid open and ten mini HE missiles sped out in a fan shape targeting the track assemblies. The little craft, still draining water, then rotated through 180 degrees and repeated the process. Satisfied that the column was immobilised, Mozart now climbed and swung through a wide left-angled arc that positioned it above the rearmost AFV. Here it paused momentarily as its mine dispenser deployed like a proboscis before flying almost lazily along the column showering the AFVs with anti-armour and personnel mines, some delayed action, some detonating on contact. As soldiers crawled or ran from the AFVs, its sensors tracked their progress against the discharge pattern of its mines, and its tactical processor occasionally instructed the mini Gatling to kill those it considered as having a chance of escape. The whole contact took less than two minutes.

0125 HRS: STALKERS – OVER THE TOWN

Above Saint C the Stalker flight was trying to establish mission profiles in the increasingly confused combat environment, when it received a compromised communications warning flag, indicating that their command and control centre had been overrun or destroyed.

What no one knew was that two of the Stalkers had the latest version of the AI tactical operating software that had a bug. Similar to the problem that Raven had explained had plagued the aircraft manufacturers years before, the Stalkers' software had a flag designated FLAG966(j,k,l) that was used in both the Indication – Friend or Foe and the Communications Compromised subroutines. The two Stalkers now had warning flags that indicated that both the IFF and their command and control systems were compromised. As a consequence the master control software instructed the machines to go to autonomous mode and disregard IFF; they would now engage targets irrespective of who was on which side.

0150 HRS: HODGETTS-SE OF SAINT C

"Strachan is dead," announced Wilcox as he tended a wounded Jean-Jacques, who was laying on the ground next to their wrecked AFV.

"Fuck it," said Hodgetts, looking at his message communicator. "The message relay is down. I'm going to have to use voice; we need to get through to Six."

They had pressed home their attack on the Stalker site and destroyed it, when they themselves had been shot up by what they thought was the Black Hole.

384

"Any station. Any station. This is Shadow. Requesting a VOX priority relay to Six. Over."

"Shadow, this is Delta. VOX relay now," responded Pavla.

"Six, this is Shadow. Call back."

"Shadow. This is Six. Go ahead," replied Alex.

Hodgetts could hear the fighting in the background; the Major's voice sounded out of breath. Not a good sign, he thought.

"Stalker site is history. Say again, Stalker site is history. Shadow has one KIA and one SWIA. We were in a bad boys' AFV and got hit by what we think was Bird One. How copy?"

"Copy Stalker site is down. But say again about Bird One. Over."

"Shadow, this is Bird One. Say your position," interjected a voice Hodgetts recognised as Tommy Lee's.

"Grid reference one zero five niner two three. How copy?" asked Hodgetts.

"Bird One copies that. En route your location. ETA six zero seconds. Will come in from east. IR strobe, three short three long. I have located AFV laager. Say again, I have located AFV laager. Can also confirm Bird One as attacker on your position," replied Tommy Lee in a sad voice.

"Standing by. Three short three long," said Hodgetts whilst setting up one of his IR strobes so that it flashed three short and three long flashes in series.

"Six copies. Be advised VOX comms is intermittent. Good luck. Out," replied Alex.

"Fuck it!" shouted Hodgetts. "We got shot up by Tommy Lee. Poor bastard."

A minute later the matt black helicopter, amiably known as the Black Hole because of its silent rotor system and stealth profile, landed next to them, the downwash blowing pieces of the destroyed AFV's composite armour into the air.

"I'm sorry," shouted Tommy Lee from the cockpit.

"Don't worry. Not your fault. Shit happens."

"I can't seem to communicate unless the VOX relay is set up by someone else. Anyway, I've found the bastards' nest. There must be twenty AFVs laagered there. Together we can take it out."

They laid Jean-Jacques out on the ground beneath an oak tree and set up a plasma bag.

"We need to insert a chest drain. Give me the kit," said Hodgetts, injecting adrenalin into the hunter's thigh to wake him up.

"Jean. Jean, listen to me. You've got to hang out here for a while. We're going to set a chest drain for you. You must stay awake and open it up every half hour or so. We'll leave you enough blood and pep-up pills for the next ten hours. You understand?"

"No problem. Where are my cigarettes?" mumbled Jean-Jacques.

0220 HRS: HODGETTS – SE OF SAINT C

They'd hit the jackpot, thought Hodgetts, as they completed their flyover in the Black Hole. He counted twenty-seven AFVs laagered in the large depression that was sheltered from any direct line of fire and surrounded on all sides by trees.

If they could take this lot out, the battle outside Saint C would be all but over. All they'd have to then do was kill the ones that were inside Saint C. He studied the laager pattern – it was in the shape of an open-ended triangle, each side of which contained ten, with the remaining in the centre.

"We'll do this the old way," explained Hodgetts. "Combined air and land. Lieutenant, you take out the western and eastern legs of the triangle. Wilcox and I'll wait for your run then go in by foot."

At the end of his run, Tommy Lee pulled the Black Hole through a tight turn and lined himself up for a touchdown in a depression.

"Ten seconds. Immediate dust-off. And remember to shut the doors after you leave otherwise I'll be lit up like a Christmas tree," he called out.

In the rear of the Black Hole, Hodgetts and Wilcox slid open the doors on either side of the helicopter, appreciative of the cool night air that rushed in as the Black Hole dropped to the ground. Hodgetts felt the bump as the machine touched down and marvelled at the silence of it; you could hear the wind it was so quiet.

"One out. Two out. Doors closed," said Tommy Lee to himself. He checked his instrument panel to make doubly sure the doors were closed and then lifted off back into the night sky to start his attack run.

It was said the only way you could tell if a Black Hole was nearby, was by watching the night stars vanish as it flew across them or by feeling the down draft of the rotors. Too true, thought Hodgetts, it was spooky; aircraft should at least make some noise.

In the cockpit, Tommy Lee waited until he had cleared the brow of the hill before he turned on his passive sensors and let the onboard computers eat up the data, map the situation, select the various weapons and then advise him; if he needed to initiate any active scanning. This took a millisecond. The system had everything it wanted; a line of ten AFVs stretched out before him; the sensors had even managed to identify stealthy vehicles and igloos by detecting the differences in texture compared to the ground and foliage. *Just goes to show*, he thought, *that even in these modern times, the old ways shouldn't be forgotten.* If they had chucked a few branches or plants on top of the AFVs he might have missed them. He switched to automatic and sat back to watch what happened.

The Black Hole's tactical AI system selected three out of the five available mine dispenser pods, each of which contained fifty anti-armour aerial mines. Of these, half were programmed to detonate on impact, whilst the remainder either switched to timers or activated proximity sensors.

Tommy Lee pulled hard back on the controls as a row of trees reared up to meet him. He hadn't reckoned on the pace of the slope and because he wasn't using active sensors he nearly grounded the aircraft. His heart raced as the top of a tree scraped against the bodywork and he breathed a sigh of relief as he gained height.

Back on the ground, Hodgetts and Wilcox took advantage of the diversion that the long series of explosions from the Black Hole's attack run created and moved inside the perimeter. There was pandemonium in the laager; personnel were running around shouting, as mines exploded and AFVs burned. Speed was the key as Hodgetts had told Wilcox. "We can't dick around with all that sneaky beaky stuff. In. Do it and out."

Thirty seconds later, Wilcox and Hodgetts rolled under an engineering AFV and caught their breath. Wilcox pointed out the AFV's service access panel, which was located just behind the forward right track assembly. Hodgetts released the simple quarter turn locking device and the panel dropped down. Inside he could see the gentle glow of the fibre-optic cable harness and junction box which was busy shuffling data to and from the various systems. He yanked it out and bent it backwards on itself, severing the delicate fibres, before crawling across to Wilcox who had released another panel and was busy cutting through a hydraulic line and the backup fibre-optic harness.

"I told you, their AFV data links are their weak links," whispered Wilcox.

"Piece of piss. I always knew engineers were simple bastards. Let's move," replied Hodgetts, showing Wilcox an FAE grenade, which he armed and set for five minutes' delay. "Just in case we need another little diversion."

0227 HRS: TOMMY LEE – 4 KM SE OF SAINT C

Tommy Lee was setting himself up for another attack run when the radar warning threat display lit up, faded and then lit up again. A lock-on tone announced that somehow he was being tracked. "Fuck it. They're full of surprises these bastards."

On the ground, a phased array radar mounted on one of the engineering AFVs had locked on to the tree branch that had got caught in an intake on the first attack run.

The AI software did not need to analyse anything, it already knew that several friendlies had been destroyed by some form of aircraft and this was the only target it had found. It fired two SA3 missiles, both of which detonated within 10 feet of the underside of the Black Hole. Inside, Tommy Lee knew the aircraft was finished, its controls were sluggish and the master alarm together with about fifty others had lit up. The only problem with the Black Hole was that the rotor blades were effectively joined to form a wing. This meant they could not be detached so the pilot could eject vertically. Escape therefore meant ejecting downwards. This needed height, and Tommy Lee did not have any.

Amongst the alarms, the target display beeped at him, showing a group of four AFVs parked in the centre of the laager. He overlaid a glide path and then punched the Shoot All button on his weapons panel, which released every available munition he had left. As his seat harness wound in automatically in preparation for the crash landing, Tommy Lee felt satisfaction.

CHAPTER 35

REINFORCEMENTS

Thus one advances without seeking glory, retreats without avoiding blame. Only protecting people to the benefit of the government as well. Thus rendering valuable service to the nation.

At about the same time as Tommy Lee was preparing to crash, Natasha crawled out of bed and was welcomed by Luc and Stacey who had cooked breakfast. Natasha accepted a coffee and glanced at the superman pill that was beside a glass of orange juice.

"We thought this might be the last time you guys get a good meal for a while, so we took the liberty of emptying the AFV," Luc told them.

As they gathered around the table to eat, Natasha called for their attention, and began the briefing.

"We've still had no contact with Saint C. So I think it fair to say that the game is on. Now for approach; I will be IC. Each bird will carry a copy of the Versailles data. We'll fly in along this route," she said, spreading out a map that she'd purloined from the flight school, on the table amidst the breakfast plates.

"Raven's uploaded the co-ords together with the aerial maps we found in the flight school and Luc's managed to patch in the magnetic field analogue nav system we took from our friends a while back. We're not sure it's going to work so we'll have to do this the old way – landmarks, compasses, time of flight and speed. The flying will be low level, ceiling is eighty feet, preference is fifty. We've done our best to mark all the obstacles, power lines, that sort of thing, but each bird will need a spotter on all the time in fifteen-minute rotations.

"We lift off at 0330, so just enough time to finish eating, study the map and grab a shower. At 0700 we will put down at this old watch tower," she said, indicating the position on the map, whilst taking the opportunity to scoop a fork of scrambled egg into her mouth.

"It's about twenty klicks east of Saint C. We'll set down and prep the birds for the final run in, leaving Stacey and Luc with a copy of the data.

"Radio silence is a must, no radar, no active sensors. The weather looks good here so it should be a lovely day for flying. Any questions?"

"What about formation profile?" asked Byrnes, referring to how close the helicopters should fly to minimise radar profile.

"Loosey goosey to start with. The route we've picked has the lowest threat profile: countryside, no roads, nature reserves, that sort of thing. We'll tighten up for the last hundred klicks but I hope they won't be expecting us to fly in to the town with gunships."

"Weapons tests?" asked Gyan.

"Definitely. We want everything warmed up by the time we put down at the tower, that's the last chance we'll have to fix anything. So fire away."

"Couldn't we transfer a Gatling and mini launcher to the med bird there? With Luc and Stacey off, we'd have spare payload?" asked Raven.

"Why not? I like it. It'll drop the weight on my machine and make it a little easier to handle, as well as give us two armed birds," she replied.

"What about ERV?" asked Tsang.

"We'll stay in visual contact. Any bird goes down between here and the watch tower we all stop and try to fix it. After that ERV, will be back at the tower."

"We'll get some tools and spares together. We've got a little payload capacity left in Captain Johnson's boat," said Raven.

"Now Captain Schaefer will give us the plan for insertion."

Schaefer stood up clutching a coffee. "For insertion and contact, we don't think that there will be comms and the situation will be confused with a lot of close-quarter fighting.

"So we've decided we'll fly a wide loop out over the sea and come into Saint C from the north. We'll stay together in close formation until we're ten klicks from the beach, then Captain Kavolsky will split off from us and head west.

"Raven's med bird will head straight for the beach, and drop off Captain Johnson and Dr Heymans as soon as they get painted with any sort of threat.

390

They might have to swim ashore but, as Captain Kavolsky said, it's a nice day.

"Their entrance to Saint C will be via the smugglers' cave. If still able, Raven will then fly escort for Lieutenant Byrnes and my team. We will fly directly over the town where we will assess the situation and deploy with Sergeant Gyan and the boys where we can do as much damage as possible.

"Meanwhile, Captain Kavolsky will continue looping around offshore and then come in from the south-west, which should put her right up the backside of who's causing this shit, and where she will also do as much damage as possible.

"We go hot as soon as we hit the ten-klick marker. Everything up, IFF squawking, the lot. We'll also try to establish voice contact on the UHF air to ground sets. Call signs will be Kavolsky, Johnson and Schaefer. That way they should know we are who we say we are. Any questions?"

"Should we paint some visual identifiers on the helos just in case?" asked Johnson.

"Why not? Let's use the inverted V. We can paint it on the birds," replied Natasha.

"Didn't the Spartans do that?" asked Luc.

"Yep. And they won," said Gyan.

"After they all got killed," added O'Reilly, "but I like it. We can also paint it on some of the white curtains they've got hanging up in the admin building."

"Insertion is going to be low and fast the whole way. No more than twenty feet," said Natasha looking at Byrnes and Raven and absently wondering how O'Reilly noticed things like curtains. "You guys comfortable with that?"

"No worries," came the response.

"Good. Now, I see no one's yet touched their pills. I suggest you leave them until we get to the watch tower. Most of you can sleep on the way or just enjoy the view. OK. Let's go. We can leave the washing-up until later," she said.

*

On the apron, they went through their final pre-flight checks and loaded their personal kit.

"Oy! Those are my bags!" shouted O'Reilly as Gyan tossed some heavy bags out of his helicopter.

"Well, whatever it is, it stays here. We didn't budget for all this crap; it's either your gear or we lose weapons and ammo. It's the same for the rest of us."

"But they're family heirlooms. They're priceless," bemoaned O'Reilly.

"Well get Cook to mark them as 'Fragile Heirlooms – Personal Property'. But they stay here," he responded in a tone intended to shut down any further debate.

Natasha, overhearing the banter, chuckled to herself in the cockpit. The emotional resilience of them amazed her. O'Reilly, who was seated in the rear with his weapons control console, muttered, "Oh what the hell. They were just a few trinkets. I guess they'll be safe here."

Ten minutes later they were airborne and flying in a triangular formation at 50 feet across fields and the occasional farmhouse. Natasha soon found herself struggling to stay awake as the noise of the rotors, coupled with the morning sunlight shining through the Plexiglass window, lulled her into a relaxed state of mind. She adjusted the air blowers mounted in the windows, opening them fully to capture as much fresh air as possible.

"Anyone got a mild upper?" she asked.

"Here, try this," offered Frost; "it's a cut-down version of the super pills."

"Thanks. Byrnes, close up a little," ordered Natasha noticing the gap between them widening too much.

"Roger that."

They entered the gorges around Avignon and sped across the still waters between the white cliffs.

"Fuck me, this is like something out of a sci-fi game," exclaimed O'Reilly as Natasha pulled them hard to the left and dipped lower beneath some power transmission lines that spanned the gorge.

In response Natasha took the helo lower; "I reckon I can see the fish we're so bloody close," as the water surface flashed in the sunlight beneath them.

"Thanks for that illuminating description," said Frost.

"How's our nav performing?" asked Natasha.

"Neat. It's amazing; the magnetic analogue system is working like a dream," said Frost looking at her repeater screen, overlaid on which was the threat analysis.

O'Reilly started his weapons tests and fired off a few short bursts from the Gatling.

"All good?" asked Natasha.

"Yeah, Captain. Not bad, considering. The gyro's working well; can you roll us a little? I want to try again."

In Byrnes' helicopter, Schaefer and the others had finished reminding and testing one another on the layout of the Saint C defences and were now just enjoying watching the scenery flash by.

"See those caves?" said Gyan, pointing to the cliffs about a hundred feet above the river surface that glittered in the sunshine. "They're world treasures; that's where the oldest paintings in the world are. Prehistoric. They're sealed up. If the air gets to them they deteriorate."

"I wonder if anyone will remember them soon," commented Zimbabwe as he finished assembling his weapon after cleaning it for the third time.

CHAPTER 36

THE ALAMO

When your form is concealed, the enemy is in doubt and so divides up his company to be on guard against you. This means that enemy groups are small and easy to hit.

0330 HRS: SANCHEZ – CELLAR - SAINT C

After bushwhacking the enemy twice more, Sanchez had brought her team back into Saint C and hooked up with Claudia, who was defending the perfumery building in the town square. Intense fighting was now raging, house to house and room to room. Sanchez and her team were occupying the cellar, getting themselves sorted out and reloading ready for the next engagement. She felt proud of them as she looked them over.

An explosion from upstairs rocked the building and dust floated down from the cellar ceiling, accompanied by pieces of stonework. She noticed a ham and cheese-filled French bread baguette on a nearby table, untouched and covered in dust, which made her realise how hungry she was. She wiped off as much dust as possible before taking a huge mouthful, washing it down with some water from her pack.

"Who controls the square will control the battle," Crockett had said. Sanchez was worried. At that moment nearly the whole of the south and east sides were in enemy hands; they were in danger of losing.

A message came in from the Major: "Estimate is three hundred plus bandits inside walls. Tactical analysis software showing high error rate on the recognition system but estimates two hundred and ten have moved within last fifteen minutes and more than four hundred as being recorded."

"Dominique, tell Claudia that she can blow C thirteen. The place must have a dozen of the bastards in there by now," she said referring to a building just behind them that Claudia had told her was filling up with enemy. "You guys ready to get back into it?" she asked.

Before anyone could reply a massive explosion from upstairs brought large pieces of masonry and rubble down into the cellar.

She looked at the dust-covered faces who all looked to her for leadership and some sign of confidence. She marvelled at the trust they had placed in her. All that stood between absolute panic and consequent certain death was a thin veneer of behaviour that people called different things: discipline, defiance, heroism. What she was seeing was all of these but something else as well; something she couldn't pin down. Another explosion brought more rubble down around them. She wondered whether they knew just how close they were to losing, and decided they probably did, which made her even more proud of them, and also humbled.

"I think we better go up and help out Claudia," advised Sanchez, pointing to a crack that had opened in the ceiling through which they could now see the rooms above.

The cellar was now heavy with the smell of perfume; that and the dust somehow seemed to be reacting, making her skin itch. The first person she saw as she crawled up into the shop was Claudia's comms officer who had a steel post from one of the shop's display cabinets embedded in his forehead. She felt someone tug on her arm; Pierre Mancon, the town's baker who had become a demolition expert, was laying on his back, his intestines on the floor beside him.

0333 HRS: OLLY – SAINT C - NORTH SIDE

Olly was experiencing one of those strange situations that could arise in battle. After getting separated from his own team in the fighting up on the town wall he had bumped into Winston and his mortar team and together they had moved to rejoin the fighting. The problem was that the fighting itself always seemed to have moved by the time they got there. He had heard of this before; soldiers could sometimes wander around a battlefield throughout an engagement without coming into contact. Hand-to-hand fighting could be going on in one area, whilst over a hedge others could be drinking coffee.

"This is becoming fucking ridiculous. Where the fuck's the action?" he muttered.

"Well, nasty business!" crowed Winston. Olly looked at Winston's team to see if they looked concerned but they seemed to be used to his behaviour.

As they made their way through the alleyways their route took them past areas where fierce fighting had recently taken place. Smoke poured from some of the buildings, others looked untouched. Some of Crockett's natural man traps had been tripped; a pile of rocks had been released from beneath an archway, burying one of the enemy and spilling thick, dark blood onto the stone-flagged street. Two more lay crushed under a wooden log that had swung down, trapping them against a wall. But their own people had also suffered, and the manner of some of the deaths confirmed the true feelings that the enemy harboured for them. Some had been bayoneted, and two brothers that they knew quite well had had their eyes removed and stomachs cut open.

"What do you reckon?" asked Winston.

"Shitbags," replied Olly. "Let's go up to the main square, near the gate. I want some payback for this. Don't bunch up. Watch the windows. Pace your distances so we arrive at each simultaneously."

Olly conducted a quick mental evaluation of himself. He was concerned that the environment and his own reactive behaviours might send the others over the edge. He mulled the thought over a little more, before deciding that he, as well as them, probably had several more notches of sanity to click through before trouble. But it was getting close. He thought about it a little longer then said, "You know, what we're seeing is insanity. But we need to stay sane. This was not our doing."

"Apart from the fact that I'm insane and most people would therefore not normally want to speak to me, I still can't get anything on the comms; maybe we should take five and try and hook into the hardwire system again?" said Winston, obviously choosing to ignore him.

"All right, we'll give it another shot," replied Olly, checking the colour codes on the surrounding buildings to make sure the building was rigged with a comms connection.

Sanchez felt like she'd been fighting for weeks; in her years of front-line service she'd never experienced such sustained intensity. They'd left the perfume shop to Claudia and were in the process of repositioning at another strong point when she and Williams had come across a young girl who'd celebrated her nineteenth birthday only days before and who now lay in an alleyway having lost her left leg below the knee.

"Williams. Give me a hand with her. Let's get her to cover."

Together they dragged the unconscious girl by her webbing harness along the alleyway to a doorway.

"I'll cover. You get her inside."

Williams had her halfway through the door when a grenade detonated nearby knocking Sanchez onto her back.

Before Sanchez could recover she realised that two figures were standing over her. Her weapon was 6 feet away and she knew she wouldn't have time to get to her sidearm. A smile of satisfaction was on their faces, and stayed even as both disappeared in a cloud of red mist and body parts.

"Don't fucking move! Stay down. You've got a Stalker overhead at your six," came a shout from above.

Sanchez stayed where she was.

"You're clear. We're on the second floor three doors up to your left. We'll put down covering fire. Go."

As the covering fire erupted she crawled into the doorway, finding Williams who was holding a bandage to his mouth. He'd lost two of his front teeth but otherwise appeared all right.

"She's still alive," he announced, chucking his blood-soaked bandage to one side.

Pavla came down the narrow flight of stairs into the hallway and took in the scene.

"Fuck me! Williams, have you seen the state of your teeth? Like fucking Bugs Bunny but in reverse."

"Fuck off," said Williams spitting blood out and checking to see how many other teeth were wobbly. "We need to get her sorted out. You got a med kit?"

"Phillipe, take care of Charlene here. Two minutes then we displace," said Pavla, calling over one of his medics to tend to the girl.

Sanchez used a small endoscope that was taped to the side of her weapon to check the alleyway. As she rotated it she caught a glimpse of a Stalker as it flew past almost lethargically. She rotated the little camera, tracking the Stalker as it took up position and started to engage a nearby house.

"I thought that place was full of bad guys?" she asked Pavla.

"It is."

"Bloody hell. Have they changed sides?"

"No. Any armed target, them or us, and they go after it."

"The new peacemakers," said Williams.

"Jesus. Did you hear that?" asked Pavla. Someone was shouting at them from across the street.

"The bastards are calling us names," said Williams.

"We can use the tunnels. How's she doing?" Pavla asked Phillipe who was busy stemming the blood loss from Charlene.

"I've stopped the blood loss. She'll make it."

"Good. Let's go."

0645 HRS: OLLY – SW SIDE TOWN SQUARE

Olly had placed Winston and his squad in an extended line along one side of the town square with the objective of bringing as much fire to bear as possible whilst presenting a spread-out target. He reckoned the fighting had entered its final phase.

"Displace! Next door!" he shouted as incoming fire started tracking its way along the front of the building he'd occupied.

As he and two others crawled over timber and masonry, carrying the squad automatic weapon, showers of glass rained down on them from a skylight.

"We'll set up here," he ordered, finding a recess that gave them cover but offered an unrestricted view of the town square. Outside, an RPG sped across the square and detonated on the fountain. An explosion behind them shook the roof beams, sending plaster down on top of them. Somewhere nearby he could hear Winston singing.

As they set up the squad weapon Olly noticed a small box of chocolates dressed in blue satin wrapping paper with a gold bow. He picked it up, wiped the dust off and offered them around.

"I'm going upstairs. You two stay here and shoot anything that looks bad until I get back… Got it?"

"Yes sir," replied the two villagers.

"And stop calling me sir, I hate fucking officers. Corporal will do fine."

"Yes sir."

"Fuck off."

0650 HRS: ALEX – THE CHAPEL

Alex and his headquarters had abandoned their primary HQ and were now in the smugglers' tunnel behind the chapel, trying to re-establish communications with the various combat teams. From his perspective the situation looked grim. There was fighting inside the chapel itself. The only good news was that there was still intensive fighting in the town square and the surrounding area. The Alamo, as he'd described it, had still not lived up to its name. As long as the fighting continued outside, there was some hope. But he needed to prepare for the worst.

"Captain Crockett, let's get the Countess up here for a moment."

A few minutes later the Countess arrived. She was wearing a medical smock stained with blood.

"The boats are ready. Shall I start getting the wounded loaded?"

"Yes. Do it. We can hold out for another thirty minutes, maybe a little more, but unless something major changes we'll need to issue the evac order." As he finished, the noise of the firefight increased in the chapel.

"I'll tell them. The older gentlemen who are going to stay behind are waiting further down the tunnel. You mentioned earlier you wanted to say a word or two," she continued.

"Definitely. Let's do this together."

Together they went further into the tunnel, past the remains of the long-dead and down some steps. At the base of them stood the ten men who would stay and act as a rear guard. Their squad leader was in his early sixties and shouted attention as Alex approached. Alex responded with a salute and asked them to stand easy.

"It's going about as well as we could have expected but their numbers are just too big. I think we can hold them for another thirty or so minutes. If nothing changes in that time I'm going to have to issue the evacuation order. The Countess has started loading the wounded.

"I wanted to thank you for what you've offered to do, but also try and give you some hope that your families and loved ones will stand a better chance if we can get them out. If I don't see you again, good luck," he finished.

"Thank you, Major," said each of them.

0705 HRS: NATASHA - OFFSHORE SAINT C

Natasha could see the dark smoke plumes rising above Saint C into the blue sky, casting grey shadows onto the otherwise sparkling Atlantic as she lined up for their attack run.

"Jesus. Look at this," said O'Reilly whilst adjusting his Cyclops.

"Back to civilisation, eh?" added Frost.

"Saint C. Saint C. This is Natasha. How copy?" radioed Natasha.

After three more attempts she got a response.

"Natasha. Natasha. This is Saint C. Sit rep?" came Crockett's voice.

"ETA three minutes. Approaching from offshore north. Assets as follows: three helos. One medivac, one grunt, one ground attack. How copy?"

"We copy that. Wait out."

Alex's voice came up over the net and Natasha felt the helo wobble a little as she involuntarily tensed. All she wanted to do was hug him.

"Welcome back. We've got regimental plus bandits. Stalker and AFV support. Estimate two zero zero plus bandits remaining in Saint C. Close-quarter fighting. No safe LZ. Suggest you drop grunts on east side. It's bandit country. Be advised we have Hodgetts and company in the rear. I say again, we have friendlies in the rear."

"Holy shit," said O'Reilly.

"You got that right," echoed Frost checking her threat display and hooking her safety line to the airframe.

"Saint C, be advised; we have the data. I say again, we have the data. Spare copy at separate location. It's good, Alex; very good. Medic bird will drop doctors' feet wet at beach tunnel. Copy?" she wanted to tell him she loved him. Was that allowed in these situations?

"Copy that. We'll send everyone the good news and arrange a meet and greet for the wet doctors."

"Love you," she ventured.

After a brief pause there was a reply. "Love you too. Good luck."

Natasha could imagine the conversation in the C4I2 as the HQ team tried to patch their new-found assets into the ops plan. She pulled the aircraft into a hard right turn and dropped down to within 6 feet of the sea.

"O'Reilly, Frost, you guys do what you do. I'll just fly. How's the finger?" she asked.

"Not bad," replied Frost as O'Reilly fired off a quick burst from the Gatling.

"I'm in heaven! Two beautiful girls and my own private helicopter," shouted O'Reilly.

Frost's threat boards lit up, warning her of just about every threat known. "Christ, any more and we'll overload the system. Prioritising now. Wooah. I've got a SAM, phased array. Must be coming from an air defence battery. They're not after us, they're lighting up Raven. Designate Tango One."

"Great news. They're mine. The radars must be feeding the Stalkers. I'm going with two missiles," O'Reilly advised. "I've got tone. Got lock. Missiles ready. Standing by."

"Good news? Can I ask what would be bad?" asked Frost.

"Well, it's rare that a man can really show two women what he's capable of," came the retort.

Natasha couldn't help but admire the banter as she slowed her speed to just ten knots, hovering at sea level. The missiles from the AFV they had were ground to ground so it was important that they be fired within their launch envelopes, and this invariably meant speed and initial altitude.

"Inside launch envelope. Missiles away! Next target."

The two missiles left their rails with a slight time delay between them, and sped away across the sea before going vertical up into the morning sky, leaving a white vapour trail behind.

"We've got two airborne telem links and imaging radars. Stalker class. Designate Tango Two and Tango Three. Looks like they're scanning for ground targets. I don't think they know we're here yet," said Frost.

"Missiles encore! Uploading. Missiles away," announced O'Reilly.

Frost's display refreshed as the red dots indicating the status of the enemy radio jamming and air search radar went green. The missiles had done their work.

"Search radars offline. Confirm Tango One, Two and Three are history. Resetting priorities. Advising HQ."

"Let's get in there," said Natasha, accelerating towards the land again.

0715 HRS: GALEAGO – EAST SIDE OF SQUARE

Through the remains of the second-floor apartment wall, dust and smoke, Galeago could see that it would be a fine day. Blue sky, sun and a beach. If it wasn't for the fighting he could be on holiday.

Of the twenty people he had started with under his command, he had lost six killed and two wounded. Now, together with three of the remaining, he sat covered in white dust doing an ammo check. The rest of his team were camped out on the floors above and below. A strange lull had settled over the fighting in their area; it was as if both sides were taking a deep breath.

He had no real idea how the other groups were doing, although by the intensity of the other firefights some were obviously alive and fighting. He plugged his comms unit into the socket in the wall. As he sipped water from his draw straw to clean off the dust that had caked the back of throat, his ear piece crackled and whined, then died. It did it again, this time beeping, signalling that a message was waiting. He punched in his three-digit code and hit receive and relay.

"VOX data priority relay," announced a voice. "All stations. This is Six. Be advised we have friendly birds from Paris in the area. They have good news – they got what they went for.

"Romeo team under Sergeant Major Jones is being released. They will move towards south wall. Captain Schaefer is deploying to east wall. All we have to do then is what we've been doing. Bandits have got nowhere to go but the sea. Out."

A few cheers went up from his team and someone threw down a hunk of bread with some cheese in it through a gaping hole in the ceiling from the floor above. He nodded a thanks, unable to recognise the face beneath the dust. Jesus, he was hungry.

"Charlie stations, listen up. This is Charlie Six. We need to get the bad guys into yellow three or six. Then we'll detonate the fuck out of them. It's like the Major said it would be. A bloody shambles. Now we're tired and beat and that's when we need to start getting very nasty, very aggressive. Every one of these bastards we nail is now more important than ever. Alpha will advance into yellow sector with Bravo in support. We'll go through the walls. Echo, you will remain here as reserve. Confirm over," he ordered before taking a huge bite of cheese and bread.

0725 HRS: NATASHA – EAST SIDE OF SQUARE

As Natasha flew over Saint C she could hardly comprehend what was happening. The Hôtel de Ville was on fire, grenade explosions were going off everywhere, and tracer arced back and forth between the buildings. Glass, wood and lumps of masonry littered the streets. Someone jumped out of a window, with his or her clothes on fire, smacking into the cobbled street. Bodies lay strewn across the square with burning embers and ash eddying around them. Someone wearing an allied uniform was being bayoneted by three enemy by the side of the fountain. There didn't appear to be any clear demarcation between the combatants; every part of the town was being fought over in small separate engagements. Ahead of them was more chaos; plumes of black smoke arched up into the sky, a burning column of AFVs lay by the river.

Suddenly her Plexiglas windshield shattered, blowing pieces into the cockpit. "Fuck it, I can't see," said Natasha as she squinted through a hole. Frost, sitting in the co-pilot's seat, knocked the shattered windshield out with a couple of hard kicks.

The noise of O'Reilly's Gatling, the helicopter blades and the remains of the windshield magnified the mayhem below.

Across from her she could see Byrnes moving into position to put down Schaefer and the others on top of the roof of the burning Hôtel de Ville. Rappelling ropes dropped down from Byrnes' heli onto the roof.

"Jesus," commented Frost in admiration.

"No one in their right minds would expect anyone to clamber around on top of that," said O'Reilly, continuing to fire.

With Schaefer and the others near the end of the ropes, Byrnes' heli suddenly lifted in response to incoming fire. Schaefer and the others let go of the ropes and dropped the 10 feet onto the sloping slate roof just before Byrnes was forced to bank steeply.

Schaefer hit the roof and punched straight through, ending up waist-deep in the roof with smoke billowing out from around him. Gyan and Zimbabwe made perfect cat-like landings but Cook fell awkwardly, lost his balance and rolled down the sloping roof, falling three storeys into the town square.

0726 HRS: GALEAGO – EAST OF SQUARE

Cossack and Smelly hadn't rated Galeago's chances when he'd charged into the square by himself in a fit of rage having seen someone being bayoneted to death by three of the enemy. But somehow he'd survived, running the culprits to ground before shooting them.

"Shit, I never saw..." was all Smelly could say before a single round blew the back of his head out, showering Cossack in his best friend's brains and skull fragments.

0728 HRS: SMUGGLERS' TUNNEL

Medic Nancy Strong was finding it increasingly difficult to cope as more wounded arrived in the hospital at the bottom of the smugglers' tunnel.

She cursed Johnson, Tsang and Heymans for not being there. "Fucking bastards. Should never have all gone off like that. Jesus, they're trooping around Paris and we're left to deal with this," she said, wiping her brow whilst plunging a syringe full of morphine into what remained of the young girl called Charlene, who'd lost half of her leg. "Where's her blood group tag?" she asked.

"Here. It's O pos," replied medic Rider, mixing up a survivor's cocktail of anti-shock serum, plasma and blood crystals.

"Will someone please get these children out of here?" shouted Strong, noticing some of the children peering into the room from behind the surgical curtains. "And, Jesus Christ, get that lamb out of here!" she shouted again, this time noticing O'Reilly's pet lamb that was in the middle of the operating area licking from a pool of blood that was slowly congealing.

Medic Rider put an arm around her. "We're all they've got. Come on."

"Yeah I know, but I'm still pissed. You wait till I see that Captain again."

"Well, I'm here," announced Johnson, striding into the room still dripping from his swim. "Right. Where are the priorities? And how many?" he asked, referring to the seriously wounded who would die if not treated immediately.

"Captain. Good to see you back. We've ten priorities. They're lined up in the next corridor," replied Strong, wondering why Johnson's clothes were soaking wet.

"Well done. Dr Heymans, you take the head wounds. Lieutenant Tsang, stomach. I'll do vital organs. Medic Rider, can you tag them accordingly?"

0730 HRS: JONES – SEWERS

Behind Jones the twenty villagers that made up the Saint C strategic reserve combat group were strung out along either side of the sewer beneath the south gate. Alex had dispatched him to reinforce Sanchez, who was under enormous pressure. Above them they could feel as well as hear the dull thumps of explosions.

Jones called a halt at a bend and gingerly manoeuvred his camera around it. No more than 20 metres away and moving towards him were ten enemy. He held up a hand to cover his face, signifying that imminent contact was going to occur, then opened fire using his bendy weapon as he called it. An assault rifle designed to shoot around corners. With a muzzle velocity of 7,000 feet per second the energy from his rounds at so close a distance caused carnage, severing limbs as well as penetrating body armour. As his dual magazines clicked dry, two of his team tossed fragmentation grenades. Jones used his camera again to check the tunnel was clear as a severed arm followed by a body floated past him on their way to the ocean.

"Marie Louise is going to be pissed. She runs the discharge treatment plant," said someone.

0740 HRS: ALEX - CHAPEL

After clearing the chapel once, the enemy were back inside. There were six of them using the stone columns as cover. Without Jones, it was left to Alex, his headquarters staff and the rear guard to clear the chapel once more. They were positioned behind the stone tombs of the knight and his lady, exchanging small arms fire. The inside of the chapel was littered with smashed wooden pews, pieces of timber and masonry, although miraculously the stained glass windows were still intact, casting colours across the interior.

"Grenades!" screamed Lefevre as three grenades were tossed into the centre of the chapel and bounced along the stone floor towards them. Stone splinters and chips pinged off the walls and a stone statue crashed to the floor.

"Up and fire!" ordered Alex as stone splinters flew off the stone sarcophagus, cutting his face in several places.

As Lefevre and the old guard returned fire, the intensity of the firefight picked up, both sides now seeming to realise this was the turning point. Through his Cyclops, Alex could see the numerous aiming lasers moving around the chapel as well as tracer.

"Lefevre jammed!" shouted Lefevre, letting the others know he was in trouble.

Alex's headset crackled, as Crockett gave him an update on the situation outside.

0740 HRS: SANCHEZ - MAIN GATE

In the eastern guard room off the main gate tower, the iron-reinforced oak door, blackened by the years, bowed and then split from the overpressure of an explosion in the adjacent room.

A second explosion blew the door off its hinges, whereupon it collapsed onto the floor sending a billowing cloud of dust into the room enveloping Sanchez and Williams.

"Grenade!" Sanchez screamed as a grenade bounced into the room detonating almost immediately. She felt several stings on her legs and arms. Ignoring the pain and the urge to check out how badly she'd been wounded, she flicked the select mode on her weapon to auto-sight-dual bore and instead of waiting to see who came through the entrance, rose and charged into the dust cloud, firing on full automatic and working the weapon from side to side and up and down. Her weapon sights counted four enemy and three of her own team amidst the dust and rubble.

She moved towards the opposite doorway which led onto a long corridor inside the south wall. Aiming lasers penetrated the dust cloud setting off an alarm in her Cyclops. Dropping to a kneeling position she fired single shots back down the tracks of the lasers, satisfied to see the lasers either go off or drop to the floor. More lasers appeared, six, seven, then more. Fuck it. She needed Williams.

"Williams, call back," she tried on her radio. There was no response.

"Williams! Watch my back! You got that?" she shouted back to where she'd last seen him.

Several shots slammed into the stonework next to her. Fuck it, where was he? "Williams!" she shouted again but still got no response. She retreated back into the room, firing as she withdrew.

"Yoh, Williams…" She didn't finish the sentence as there was no need. Williams' upper torso lay against the far wall, the lower half of his body was missing.

0740 HRS: JONES – SE SIDE OF SAINT C

After finding the entrance from the sewers up to the main gate blocked by a mini Gatling with a six-man gun crew, Jones left a team to occupy the Gatling while he led the rest up a tributary that came out next to the town wall in the south-east corner.

"We need to work our way along the wall to the main gate. Shoot and scoot. In your teams. Let's go," he ordered.

As he led his team in a dash, he felt a hot stinging sensation in his right leg. "Get to cover! I'm fine," he ordered in his best Sergeant Major's voice.

As his team moved on he was hit again, this time in his left leg, and he had no choice but to crawl across to a low parapet wall where he positioned himself with his back against a wall, looking diagonally back towards the main square. He watched as two enemy ran into a doorway. Bringing his weapon up he fired a grenade at the doorway but watched angrily as it bounced off the surrounding wall and exploded uselessly in the open. He was hit twice more, this time in the right side of his chest.

"Fuck it!" He could feel his right lung filling up with blood.

"All Romeo stations, this is Romeo Six. Advance to main gate. I say again, all Romeo units to advance on main gate."

0741 HRS: NATASHA – EAST SIDE OF SQUARE

Natasha regained consciousness as O'Reilly pulled her out through the shattered canopy and into cover underneath the wrecked heli. She tried to recall what had happened.

"You OK, Captain?" asked O'Reilly.

"Yeah, thanks. What about Frost?"

"I can't get her out, her arm's caught under the wreckage. I've shot her up with some morphine and set up a drip. She'll have to wait," he said whilst checking his sidearm.

"Did you get the Stalkers?" she asked.

"Abso fucking lutely!"

"What happened?"

"We got taken out with two SAMs; the whole bird rolled over onto its side and we ended up in the café. Miracle we survived. Raven's down somewhere as well."

Natasha could feel her adrenaline levels falling.

"Anyway, I'm going to get one of our AFVs out of the garage. What do you think?" asked O'Reilly.

0745 HRS: SANCHEZ – MAIN GATE

Sanchez felt dazed and she could taste blood. She groped for her weapon in the dust-filled room. Fuck it! All she could feel was the stone floor and rubble. There were unfriendly figures clambering over their dead comrades in the corridor that led to the doorway of the room she was in. Where was her weapon? She drew her pistol. The first of them rushed through the doorway into the room, noticing her immediately. She fired twice directly into his face, he dropped, but others had replaced him. She rolled across the floor, firing as she did so. A huge hulk of a man fell on top of her, his warm blood spurting over her own face. She tried to get him off but before she could she felt a sharp pain in her stomach. One of the other bastards had bayoneted her! She pointed her weapon at the nearest figure and pulled the trigger. There was no recoil. She had a feed jam; must be all the stone dust, she thought. She pulled the slide back to clear the jam and as she did someone kicked her in the head. She saw a white light and stars, then felt two more sharp pains in her neck and right arm that forced her to release the grip on her pistol; she could hear someone laughing! She felt alone and angry.

As she detonated the fuel air grenade, her last thoughts were of Schaefer and their unborn baby.

0746 HRS: JONES – MAIN GATE

Where the main gate had been was now a heap of rubble. Half a dozen enemy staggered from the wrecked gate buildings only to be cut down by members of Jones's squad. A stretcher team, making use of the lull in fighting, made a dash for an injured trooper who lay unmoving next to a burning piece of timber. Jones could feel himself losing consciousness; a mist was descending across his eyes.

0746 HRS: PAVLA – SE SIDE OF SQUARE

"Fuck me!" exclaimed Pavla, picking himself up after the FAE had detonated. As he shook the rubble off his weapon he looked around for Winston and the others.

One of their own AFVs crashed through a set of wooden doors and stopped in the square. Winston walked out to meet it and gave it the thumbs-up sign, before pointing out a building. The AFV's Gatling traversed towards it, spun up and then discharged a prolonged burst.

"Jesus, what the hell does he think this is, the Wild West or something?" said Pavla, noticing that Winston only had a sidearm that was hung in a holster like a gunslinger.

Natasha opened the stern ramp of the AFV to a scene of desolation; the sound of burning timber and the occasional rumble of the collapse of a part of a building echoed around the square. Oddly, the fountain was still flowing, although several of the statues of dancing children had disappeared and bodies and debris lay around it. Her helicopter lay half buried in the café; it looked surreal amongst the tables, chairs and sun umbrellas.

A group of old-looking men whom she guessed were the rear guard for the Alamo emerged from the chapel; they were covered in dust. She recognised Crockett with his limp.

There were a few sporadic shots fired from one of the alleyways and for an instant the old men paid attention before the firing stopped again.

Her headset burst into life; "All stations. This is Six One. Sit rep, by station," called Crockett over the radio.

As the various stations called in, Crockett walked slowly across to Natasha. For a moment she denied the reality but, as he hugged her in consolation, she started to weep, gently at first but then uncontrollably.

SEVEN MONTHS LATER

Good warriors make others come to them.

I t was one of those early winter evenings when a bright sun gently smothered by low clouds changes the colour of lakes to pure gold. *Louis Armstrong's Summertime* played in the background. It was the type of weather that Natasha thought made you want to be outdoors but at the same time remain inside your home watching from the warmth. She paused from her work for a moment realising that the scene was reminiscent of the home she grew up in on the shores of Lake Michigan. She wondered how it was faring. There was a knock at the door.

"Come in."

"Good evening, ma'am. Brought you some coffee and biscuits," said Stacey.

"Thanks. Just put them on the table."

They had not taken long to collectively make the decision to remain at Saint C and rebuild it. The easy thing to do would have been to relocate, simply occupy another nearby village. But each of them felt this was their home, a place they'd fought and died in and one that they would never give up. So they'd set to work, buried their dead, and now partially rebuilt the town.

They'd had several more contacts with small enemy formations, although nothing of the scale they had faced a year earlier. Rogue Stalkers still ranged, and they'd encountered the odd group of renegades resembling the Jutes, but they now had a confidence born of battle and one that made them feel empowered.

411

Johnson had set about establishing contact with an increasing population of survivors, that now numbered more than 5,000 people across France, Germany and Scandinavia. They were now planning the campaign for the following spring, when they would mount contact missions into other countries.

In August, Corporal Vinelli had returned from Sardinia with the Heidelberg student, Isabella Ronaldi's brother and his own cousin. Vinelli had stayed for a week before Johnson had dispatched him with two escorts and the last-known names and addresses of nearly 200 potential survivors on Sardinia and neighbouring Corsica.

In early September, a British Royal Navy deep submersible frigate had surfaced and anchored just offshore, and contact was established with another 200 souls who in turn spoke of contact with others. With all of this came hope that some of the remaining squadrons' loved ones may have survived, and to this end the frigate had departed together with Luc and Lieutenants Byrnes and Tsang for the United States in an attempt to access the North American genetic archives.

In October, they'd unveiled a memorial to the men and women who had fallen defending their town and families. The new memorial stood in the town square next to the Great and the Second World War memorials.

Johnson had chosen the inscription which read: To the Men and Women of The Last War.

Natasha had told him it could be construed as having a number of meanings. In reply, he told her that he was beginning to wonder if all the pain and brutality that humanity showed to its own kind was perhaps genetic.

Natasha looked out of her window; the abbey looked like it was sitting on a carpet of red and gold leaves. As she took a sip of coffee, she felt a little kick from inside her and smiled.

There was another knock at the door and Schaefer let himself in.

"Sorry to bother you but I wanted to let you know before the rumour mill got going. The Countess and I are going to get married."

Natasha looked at him and wondered why he looked so sad.

"You don't look very happy about it?"

"It's strange, I've tried to make sense of my emotions a million times. Sometimes I feel guilt, then happiness."

"Here, look at this," said Natasha showing him a dried flower that Alex had given her during their picnic.

"You loved him like I loved her, didn't you?" replied Schaefer.

"I did. We both loved, and that makes us pretty special. Don't feel guilty."

Schaefer left her alone; and through her tears she signed off the logbook for the day: *Officer commanding 1ˢᵗ of the 9ᵗʰ Mountain Squadron and Saint Christobel allied militia.*

GENE 169

There is evidence that a gene mutation referred to as CCR5 Delta 32 results in immunity to the Black Death or Plague which began in China in 1334 and spread rapidly along the trade routes into Europe killing more than a third of the population.

The evidence for this first surfaced when researchers investigated the descendants of a village in England called Eyam from which half of the residents survived the Plague that swept across England in the 1660s.

Delta 32 is a gene that codes for a protein on the surface of white blood cells which acts as a receptor for other molecules involved in inflammation. Essentially, since the CCR5 Delta 32's receptors are 'turned off', it makes a person resistant or immune to certain viruses because they cannot latch onto the receptors. People who have two copies of the Delta 32 mutation are considered virtually immune to the Black Death and HIV, whilst those with one are considered resistant.

The mutation occurs predominantly in Euro-Caucasian people.

QUOTES UNDER EACH CHAPTER TITLE

The quotes beneath the chapter titles are attributed to *Sun Tzu*.

GLOSSARY OF TERMS

2IC – Second in command

APM – Anti personnel mine

AVM – Anti vehicle mine

AFV – Armoured fighting vehicle

AI – Artificial intelligence

APC – Armoured personnel carrier

AWACS – Airborne warning and control system

Bergen – Standard military issue backpack

BIBs – Built in breathing system: apparatus designed to allow crew of AFVs to breath in a polluted atmosphere (similar to aircraft oxygen supply)

CBRN – Chemical, biological, radiological and nuclear warfare

CM – Cargo module; there are four within the Stratocruiser

C4I2 – Command, control, communication, coordination, information and interoperability

Det Cord – Detonation cord – rope of HE (commonly used for destruction of structures e.g. antennae, trees)

DTM – Digital terrain map (3D image of terrain)

ECM – Electronic counter measures

EMP – Electromagnetic pulse (energy pulse that can, if focused and of sufficient energy, destroy electronics); this is generally a million to ten million times the voltage of a normal radio signal and has a pulse time that is typically a hundred times faster than lightning

ERV – Emergency rendezvous

E-sig – Electronic signature given off by any electronic device that is powered up

ETA – Estimated time of arrival

EWO – Electronic warfare officer

FOP – Forward observation post

GPMG – General purpose machine gun (normally half inch calibre)

HD – High definition

HE – High explosive
HF – High frequency
KIA – Killed in action
ICU – Intensive care unit
IFF – Indication friend or foe (an electronic signalling device used widely to determine if assets were friendly)
IR – Infra red
LR-51 – Snipers' rifle, range up to 4,000 metres with intelligent scope and sensor arrays.
LUP – Lay-up point (defended area for preparing further ops)
MBT – Main battle tank
MIA – Missing in action
MLRS – Multiple Launch Rocket System
MP – Mission profile
MRE – Meal ready to eat: standard rations for field operations
NCO – Non-commissioned officer
OIC – Officer in charge
OP – Observation post
PFC – Private first class
Polymer Paper – Electronic paper – currently under development
PLD – Personal location device
PULK – A wooden sled used for carrying large loads, pulled by humans
ROE – Rules of engagement
RTB – Return to base
RV – Rendezvous
SAM – Surface to air missile
SAR – Search and rescue
Stag – On watch
SMG – Sub machine gun, used for close- quarter combat in built -up areas
Stood to – Ready for contact with enemy
Stand to – Contact with enemy
SWIA – Seriously wounded in action
UHF – Ultra high frequency
UPS – Uninterruptible power supply (array of chemical or metal based batteries, designed to support critical systems in the event of a main electrical power supply failure)
US – Slang term meaning useless or broken

UV – Ultraviolet.

VCP – Vehicle check point

VTOL – Vertical take off & landing

VX – Nerve agent

X-ray – Term to identify enemy

CPSIA information can be obtained
at www.ICGtesting.com
Printed in the USA
BVHW071921070121
597268BV00006B/507